Of
Diamonds
and
Vengeance

by

Rachel Fallon

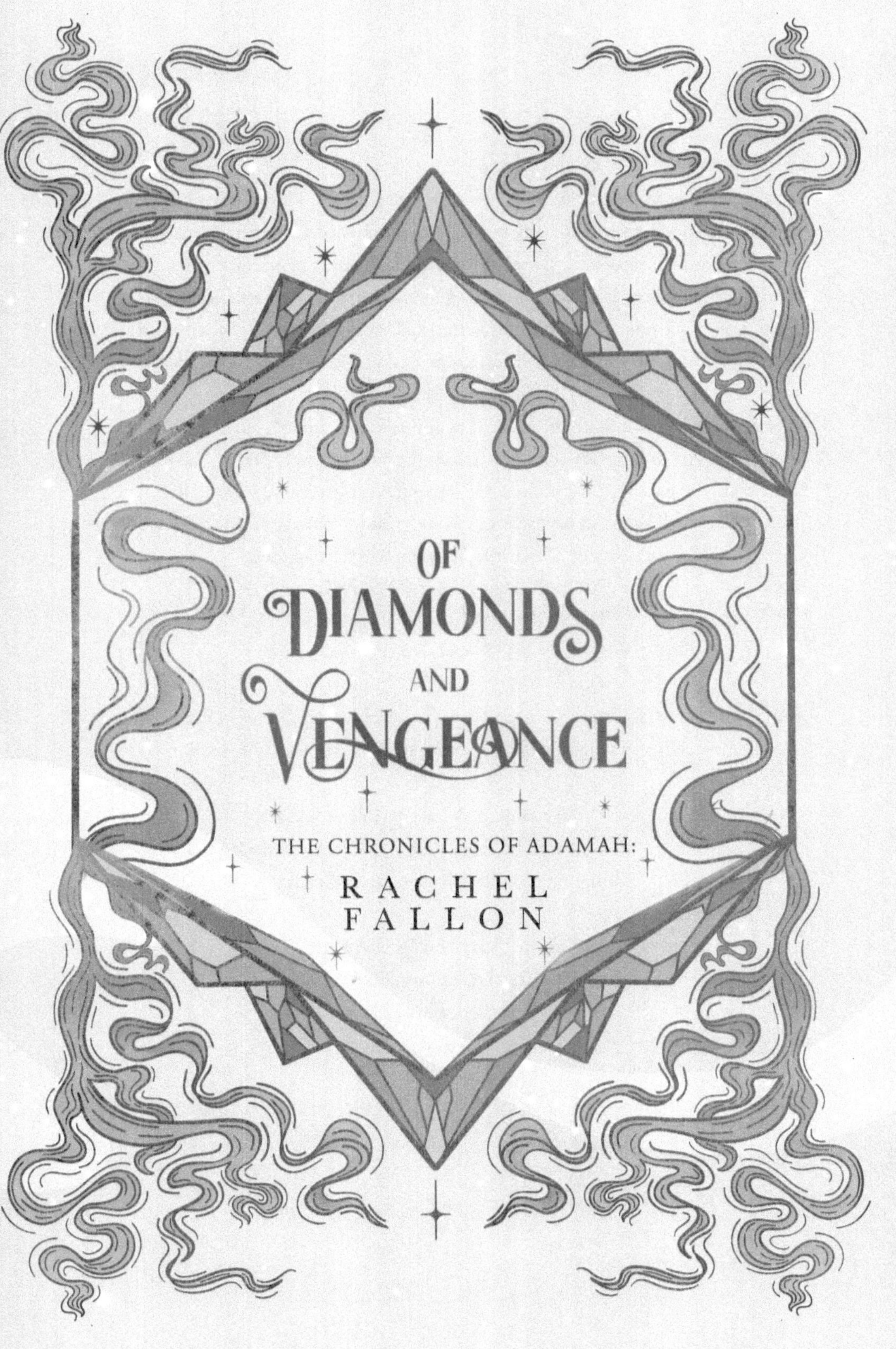

OF
DIAMONDS
AND
VENGEANCE
THE CHRONICLES OF ADAMAH:
RACHEL
FALLON

ISBN: 979-8-9894637-6-3 (Digital Online)
ISBN: 979-8-9894637-8-7 (Paperback)
ISBN: 979-8-9894637-7-0 (Hardcover)

Any references to historical events, real people, or real places are used fictitiously. Names, characters, and places are products of the author's imagination.

Front cover image by Rena Violet @violet.book.design.
Book design by Rena Violet @violet.book.design.
Editing by Heather Creeden @creedreads

Printed in the United States of America.
First printing edition 2026.
Rachel Fallon
Billerica, MA 01821

To those lost in the past, may you find your way to a future that shines as bright as a diamond.

"The pearl is the queen of gems and the gem of queens."
— Grace Kelly

GEMARIA
AMETHYST
OPAL
SAPPHIRE
ONYX

RUBY
DIAMOND
EMERALD
PEARL

Contents

Scan the QR Code to be brought directly to the official Spotify playlist for Of Diamonds and Vengeance!

Guide

Jacinth Marit: Ja-sin-th Mar-it

Ula: You-lah

Juvela: Ju-vel-ah

Zav: Z-av

Diamond Court:

High King Azurill Kyanite Alankar: Az-ur-ill Kai-uh-nite Uh-lun-kar
Prince Ruri Kyanite Alankar: Rur-ee Kai-uh-nite Uh-lun-kar
Prince Gardevoir Kyanite Alankar: Gaar-duh-vor Kai-uh-nite Uh-lun-kar
Queen Mother Elestren Alankar: El-es-tren Uh-lun-kar
Balthazar Cyprian: Bal-thuh-zaar Si-pree-uhn
Emrys Upalos: Em-riss Up-ahl-os
Arianell Upalos: Ah-ree-a-nell Up-ahl-os
Brokk Vermilia: Buh-rock Ver-mill-ia
Alwyn Corunne: Al-win Kuh-rune
Alfrikr Helithine: Ahl-frikyr Huh-lith-ine
Faiza Nabhas: Fye-za Nah-bhas
Ikelos the Gemholder: Ih-keh-los

Ruby Court:

Lord Carnelian Rousseau: Kaar-neel-yn Roo-sow
Lady Sienna Rousseau: See-eh-nuh Roo-sow
Casaan Rousseau: Kah-sa-ahn Roo-sow
Karmir Rousseau: Kar-mir Roo-sow

Emerald Court:

Lord Khader Giada: Kah-der Jah-dah
Lady Umina Giada: You-my-na Jah-dah

Zumra Giada: Zoom-rah Jah-dah

Opal Court:

Lord Eirian Beryl: Air-ee-an Beh-ruhl
Lady Arianell Beryl: Ah-ree-a-nell Beh-ruhl
Laxus Beryl: Lacks-us Beh-ruhl
Elouan Beryl: Eh-loo-ahn Beh-ruhl
Allirea Beryl: Ah-lee-ree-ah Beh-ruhl

Pearl Court:

Lord Darcel Helmi: Dar-sell Hel-mee
Lady Grethyn Helmi: Gret-hin Hel-mee
Sania Helmi: Sa-nee-ya Hel-mee
Lord Elros Marit (deceased): Ell-ross Mar-it
Lady Lulit Marit (deceased): Loo-leet Mar-it

Onyx Court:

Lord Emzar Nephrite: Em-zar Neh-frite
Lady Zariza Nephrite: Zah-ree-zah Neh-frite
Ophira Nephrite: Oh-fee-ra Neh-frite
Zahavi Nephrite: Zuh-haa-vee Neh-frite
Finbar Nephrite: Fin-bar Neh-frite

Sapphire Court:

Lord Neel Mazarine: Neel Maz-uh-reen
Lady Azura Mazarine: Ah-zur-ah Maz-uh-reen
Kai Mazarine: Kye Maz-uh-reen
Safira Mazarine: Suh-fear-uh Maz-uh-reen
Celestine Mazarine: Sell-uh-stine Maz-uh-reen

Amethyst Court:

Lord Tyrian Iolanthe: Tee-ree-uhn Eye-oh-lan-thee
Lady Galena Iolanthe: Guh-lee-nuh Eye-oh-lan-thee
Amatista Iolanthe: Ah-mah-tee-stah Eye-oh-lan-thee
Viorel Iolanthe: Vee-oh-rel Eye-oh-lan-thee

Pantheon of the Gods

Veritx: God of Diamond; truth, power, courage

Ceridwen: Goddess of Amethyst; intelligence, clarity, wit

Delphira: Goddess of Sapphire; wisdom, prophecy, judgements

Erodite: Goddess of Pearl; love, affection, sex

Fortuna: Goddess of Ruby; wealth, safety, passion

Osseus: God of Onyx; manipulating the body, chakras

Soteria: Goddess of Emerald; protection, ability to see past and future

Sirona: Goddess of Opal; healing, disease protection/causation

Other Places:

The Otherworld: The afterlife where all beings go when they die; split into **Elysium** (paradise) and **Tartarus** (hell); there is a separate section inaccessible to fae and humans where the gods live.

Adamah: The world in which Celesterra, Gemaria, Weathrian, and Chromatos are continents on.

Celesterra: Continent ruled by the fae and blessed by the higher gods with celestial magic; kingdoms are balanced amongst each other.

Gemaria: Continent ruled by the elves and lesser gods are prayed to; magic is accessed via use of gems and mixed into potions.

Weathrian: Continent ruled by nature spirits who command magic related to their seasons.

Chromatos: Continent ruled by pixies whose magic is based in color.

CHAPTER 1

Jacinth

Darkness was the best friend of many a thief, but as I gazed out over the castle before me, waiting for the sun to set, I couldn't help but curse it anyway.

Darkness meant another moment closer to losing Ula. Every minute spent not getting her a cure did, and I couldn't lose another damn person.

Never again.

It felt like it took hours for the sun to finally sink behind the horizon and for the castle to wind down for the night. If I hit it too early, the guards would still all be present and accounted for. If I hit it during the shift change, however, there would be fewer men on the doors and perimeter.

Especially the door to the kitchens. *That* door led to a hall that contained a hidden trap door, one that would lead down into the bowels of the castle. Overlooked and forgotten for the most part, but a vital shortcut to the interior maze. I pulled out the map I'd traded for, hoping it would pay off. Checking it over, my finger traced along the path I needed, burning it into my brain.

When the time came, I watched the guards disappear inside, and moved to finally scale the perimeter wall. My hands and feet found holds to boost me up before I dropped softly onto the grass inside the grounds. Looking in each direction, I ensured the new guards weren't yet approaching, and no one had seen me. Some good news for once.

I sprinted as quickly as I could across the lawn to the castle, putting myself flush against the stone. Ruby Court still had a proper castle instead of a palace. While most courts had grand palaces instead of ancient stone castles like this one, the ruling family here seemed to like the traditional aspect of it, at least from what I understood.

I paid close attention to politics in the realm, eagerly gathering every bit of knowledge I could. Unfortunately, Gemaria was expansive, making it difficult to get as much information as I liked, especially for someone in my position in society.

Even with that difficulty, I was still fully aware that Lord Carnelian, the Lord of Ruby Court, didn't like new policies, new palaces, new *anything*. He was a creature of old traditions, and his castle reflected that.

I slunk along the side, sticking close to the stone wall of the castle, and noticed the red flecks shining from within them, rolling my eyes at the realization. Of course, they didn't use regular stone; obviously, that would be too *common* for the lords of Ruby. At least it gave a glint of color to all the drab grey. A branch snapped to my right, and I instantly froze, quickly looking to see where it had come from. I couldn't see anything within the darkness of the surrounding wood, and when no guards appeared, I figured it must have been an animal. Still, I waited for a beat more to be safe before I continued.

I thankfully made my way around the side with little issue, finding the door that led into the corner of the castle that held the kitchen. Only servants came to this section, and at this time of night, there should only be a couple of people preparing for tomorrow, if anyone at all.

Peering in the closest window, I saw one lone servant remaining, her back to the door as she stood within the kitchen, rolling some kind of dough. I opened the door and shut it quietly, not letting it make a sound, before I quickly turned down the hall with silent footsteps that ghosted along the floor.

Sure enough, the small hall was all but deserted, and I was able to locate the painting that concealed the level to the trap door with ease. I swiftly triggered it and lowered myself in with no issue. That was the easy part. Now, I had to find the crumbling hole that would lead me to the heavily locked and guarded area that contained the vault itself.

It was only thanks to a servant discovering this hole and blabbing drunkenly at the right person that I had this chance. I hoped his instructions were correct, or I was going to kill him for this. Getting caught here would be a death sentence, but I had to do this now. The servant had already informed his lord about the issue, and it was due to be fixed within a few days.

I had only the tiniest window of time to get my hands on the coin of the wealthiest lord in Gemaria.

I made my way down the hall, keeping my footsteps silent and my pointed ears perked for any noises. As I hit a four-way intersection of halls, I reached up and ran my hand along the seam where the ceiling met the stone wall. The feeling of the mortar changed about halfway through, and I ran my hand down from there to find the loose stone. I nearly cheered when I discovered it before catching myself and merely pressing on the stone to trigger the mechanism.

Slowly, a section of the wall peeled open, revealing the hidden door in its entirety. Darting through it carefully, I found another hall, but it was one that only led in one direction. I wasn't a fan of not having multiple exits, but I knew going in that this would be a tight fit. I just needed to breathe through it.

As long as I was mindful of my breathing and gave myself a focus to keep my mind out of the past, I shouldn't panic while stuck in the enclosed space.

The crumbling hole I needed to find next was about halfway down the hall, and I smiled in victory as I spotted it. Contorting myself through it, I put one leg in before ducking and swinging my head through, pulling my remaining leg deftly through the air and out of the hole, putting me in the new space fully. I stood up, looking at a nearly identical hall.

A maze, indeed. At least I had the damn map, or I'd never find my way through.

Creeping through the tiny stone hall, however, my instincts began screaming at me that something wasn't right. Something beyond my aversion to being closed in. I'd stolen into enough places to know to listen when my intuition flared, so I paused on silent feet and cast my eyes up and down the hall.

Nothing.

Only a faint wind whistling through the cracks in the old stonework, the dust floating in the air, and my own breathing.

It was times like this that I wished we Elves had the same magic the Fae or Pixies did. If I could summon shadows or fire, or even red destruction magic, I would feel a lot better. *But no.* Instead, Elves got the short end of the stick.

While our magic might be more varied, it was much more complicated and had to be prepared in advance. Not to mention, you had to be able to afford the materials for it.

Or steal them.

But I hadn't stolen enough recently to afford the gems I required. I desperately needed to reup my supply, especially with Ula sick. Living on the streets didn't exactly lead to the healthiest of conditions, and Ula only got more ill as time went on. We needed to get our hands on some opal and onyx to fix whatever ailed her before it was too late.

Which was what had brought me to Ruby Court in the first place. Finding the servant was a stroke of luck, admittedly. I'd been hanging around trying to find anything I could use, which was the only reason I was in the right place at the right time to hear about the weakness in the castle's vault.

Rubies were the gem of wealth, thanks to the magic of the patron goddess of Ruby, Fortuna. Ruby Court itself was responsible for all the banking in the realm for this very reason. I knew if I was guaranteed to get a good score anywhere, it was here. Lord Carnelian was said to be the richest lord in the land, with only the High King of Gemaria able to boast of a vaster fortune.

And I was staying as far away from that bastard of a king as Elvenly possible.

Without any magic at my fingertips, I was left with only my dagger to defend myself. I pulled it from my thigh sheath and palmed it, fingers tightening at the ominous feeling that was rising in my gut.

Breaking into manors and mansions to steal wasn't exactly the safest gig. I'd almost been caught before, but had thankfully managed to escape every time. I preferred easier scores, when possible, of course, but I also preferred to target the ultra-rich among us when I could. They could handle the loss, after all.

It wasn't like I *enjoyed* stealing from people, but living on the streets left me with little in the way of options. I couldn't even try to lift myself into a better position where I didn't have to steal to eat, as some of my fellow street rats attempted from time to time.

Not when being found would likely result in my death.

No, anonymity was key. And staying anonymous meant staying below the realm's radar. Only those of us living on the streets truly went unnoticed and unrecorded. While everyone else might consider it the most dangerous way to live, for me, it provided *safety*.

I crept forward once more, my eyes roving around the tight hall for anything amiss. As I made my way to an old wooden door at the end of the hall, I took a deep breath. I let it rattle through me, and then slowly reached a hand down to grab the latched handle. Using my thumb to press down on it, I listened for the click and then slowly pulled it open a crack.

Only for it to fly the rest of the way open and right into my face.

"Argh!" I screamed as it smashed into my nose. But I couldn't focus on that or my now fucked vision, as several blurry figures that seemed vaguely man-shaped grabbed me. I tried to fight them off, but with my nose bleeding and my vision drastically reduced, I only succeeded in landing a single punch before my hands were yanked behind my back, and a punch sent in return sent me into complete, punishing darkness.

I GROANED, PAIN radiating through my head as I slowly tried to lift it. The pounding that occurred when I did had me cease that motion quickly. Instead, I tried to pry open my eyes and see where I was. The sight of cold stone flooring greeted me, and, raising my head a bit, the bars of what appeared to be a dungeon cell appeared. I groaned louder.

Great. Just great.

After years of stealing, I should have known this would happen eventually, but I'd foolishly believed I'd gotten this down pat and didn't have to worry.

Arrogance before the fall and all.

I slowly pushed myself up from my inelegant sprawl, checking myself over to ensure nothing else had been damaged. My black leather pants were scuffed and dirty, but otherwise had been left undisturbed, thank Erodite.

At least my captors weren't creeps.

Similarly, my tight black jacket was as expected, and my favorite black leather gloves had been left in place. I'd heard about this style used overseas by female warriors, and copied it myself by cutting the tips off the fingers of each of my gloves. They were ideal for stealing into places and maintaining full range of movement.

Wisps of pink invaded my vision, and I huffed, pulling my braid forward. It was a complete mess now, having gotten rucked up in the scuffle. Looking around the dungeon, no one seemed to be waiting for me to wake up, so I shrugged and set to the task of rebraiding the mound of voluminous, bright pink hair that tumbled free. Said hair made it difficult to remain unseen, hence the braid I wore on jobs like this. I could usually tuck and hide it under my hood, leaving only a few stray pink hairs to hang around my face, which was better than nothing, at least.

My hair, of course, matched my eyes perfectly, as was the case for all Elves. Sometimes, I found myself wishing I had a black-on-black or a white-on-white combination that would be easier to hide with. While bright colors were extremely common, no one had the same shade of bright pink as I did. Lighter pink shades weren't exactly *un*common, but even the lord and lady of Pearl Court were lacking the vibrant pink I had, by all accounts.

Which made staying under the radar a real bitch at times.

The sound of metal creaking slowly over stone had me falling still just as I finished my braid. I arranged myself cross-legged, a tactic to show my captors I wouldn't be hiding or cowering. I would sit calmly and accept whatever fate had in store for me.

Some would say I'd already lived past my time, and I would have to agree with them. Normally, I would say I wasn't sure why I still lived, or what the point was.

But right now, Ula was counting on me. Without the right gems to heal her, I feared she wasn't long for this plane. She had been the one to take me on and show me the ropes when I first found myself scavenging on the streets, desperate and starving. Without her, I would certainly have been long dead by now.

I needed to find a way out of this for her at least. Even if I didn't much care about my own pointless existence.

An Elven man came into view, boots first. I could tell he was a guard immediately. His militant black and red style was more than enough to go on, so I didn't even bother looking up until the baton he was holding hit the bars with a loud smash that reverberated through the cell.

I sighed, looking up reluctantly. My eyes widened as I realized he was unlocking the cell door.

"Get up. Lord Carnelian wishes to see you," the guard spat, his pale red eyes looking me up and down derisively.

Clearly, he thought his lord had no business dealing with me himself. That I was too far below his notice. I had to begrudgingly agree. I thought one of his underlings would likely sentence me, and the unusual demand put me on edge immediately.

I stood smoothly from the floor, my past having given me, if nothing else, the ability to gracefully move and twist. It helped more than anything else since that fateful day I was forced to run. All those dance lessons gave me the flexibility that usually made my work as a thief much easier, at least.

The guard grabbed me by the arm, jerking me forward to a sudden stop before slamming a set of manacles on me. I tried twisting my wrist to test them as he turned to lead me out of the dungeon, gripping the chain as he pulled me forward with it, but I could already tell that there was no weakness in these to take advantage of.

They'd been magically enhanced, and the only weakness present was the one rapidly taking me over.

My strength and will were sapped from me with each step I took, until my feet were dragging and the Elf in front of me, yanking on the chain, was doing most of the work to get me moving forward. I inspected the manacles sluggishly, and sure enough…

Fucking onyx.

Onyx was used to manipulate the body in different ways. Some bad, some good. The Onyx Court itself specialized in all things related to the body, from anatomy to massage. While onyx could be used in healing, they weren't actually healers; that was Opal Court's specialty, since opals were used for healing and preventing disease.

Of course, opal could also be used to *cause* diseases, because there was never a reaction without an equal and opposite.

Even Pearl Court, which specialized in all things love and sex, whose residents preferred matchmaking and brothels, which used the pink pearls the court was named after for love and affection, could also use them to cause hate and disgust.

Nothing good in Gemaria came without a bad side. That was true about everything and everyone.

But the onyx in use here meant there was no point in trying to pick the locks on the damn cuffs. I was stuck, and being half-dragged toward the fucking *Lord* of Ruby Court himself.

Well, I couldn't say it had been a good life, but it was certainly a longer one than I'd been meant to have.

Even walking toward certain death, however, the thief in me couldn't help looking through drowsy eyes at all that was on offer as I was led through the halls. The interior walls were a dark stone and ornamented with gold and ruby at every possible juncture. A golden orb sitting out on display seemed all too easy to grab, and I would have if my hands weren't fucking stuck together.

There was so much lining the halls, I wondered why I even bothered going for the vault. Well, I knew that answer. The treasure I would find in that vault would put all this wealth to shame. It could have saved Ula. It could have changed my entire life.

I suppose it *was* still changing my life, just not in the way I expected.

CHAPTER 2

Azurill

IT took everything I had in me not to slump down on my diamond throne. Only years of lessons ingrained in me from my father and all my other teachers about how a king *doesn't slouch* kept me upright.

But I was more exhausted than I could ever remember being. After a long day of funeral rites and a long night of mourning, followed by what seemed to be the entire population of Gemaria coming out to give their condolences today, I wanted nothing more than to sleep. Anything to avoid facing the reality of what had happened.

My little brother was dead.

I looked at my youngest brother, Ruri. The red-rimmed frosty blue-green color of his eyes showed just how difficult being here was for him. I knew both of us would rather be mourning Gardevoir alone, but instead, we were forced to put on a show of our grief for the entire court.

Gardevoir had been my advisor, my friend, and my brother. He'd always been the dutiful middle son, trying to show he could be just as good as the heir or as lovable as the baby of the family to our parents. Even after Father passed to the Otherworld and I took the throne, he struggled to let go of that mindset. Never mind that none of us *ever* saw him as anything less; he felt a need to prove himself that couldn't be shaken.

And now he was gone.

It was just Ruri and me now. The royal family had never been so vulnerable, not in hundreds, maybe even thousands, of years. I'd already seen the *looks*. The vultures preparing to descend. A few had even mentioned how lovely their daughter or their niece was, and how I just *had* to meet them.

I was surprised I hadn't broken a tooth, clenching my teeth so hard.

Thankfully, Balthazar was there to steer me away on "urgent business". While he was the head of my royal guard, having taken over the position from his father a few years ago, he was also my best friend and could easily tell when I was about to lose it.

I caught myself just before reaching up to run a hand through my dark blue-green hair. Well, dark in comparison to my brother's frosty blue. Mine was a richer hue, more teal, while Gardevoir's had been a shade in between the two of ours. I took more after our father, Ruri took after our mother, and Gardevoir had been a perfect mix between them.

Veritx, just thinking his name hurt.

Balthazar, of course, seemed to realize that I was at the end of my rope, while Ruri's eyes were looking deader by the moment. He gestured to my Gemholder, Ikelos, who was responsible for overseeing the protection of the Sacred Gems on my behalf, along with my scepter with the Royal Diamond sitting atop it. But his role also included acting as something of an elevated herald, which meant clearing rooms, thankfully.

Ikelos stepped up and banged my scepter once on the ground, bringing all conversations to a halt.

"King Azurill Kyanite Alankar, the High King of Gemaria, Lord of Diamond Court, Sovereign of Theiapolis, and Protector of the Sacred Gems," Ikelos began, voice loud and resonating around the room, "Calls court to a close for tonight. He thanks you all for being with the royal family during its time of mourning and welcomes you all to avail yourselves of the accommodations made available."

With a last deep nod to the room at large, I stood from the throne, and everyone bowed as Balthazar and Ruri fell in behind me. We walked down the halls strewn with diamonds and kyanite, the silver and blue representing our court and family history. The palace had been updated many times over the years. While it had initially been made with just the two gems so precious to us, renovations had added in all of the gems of the other courts in some way or another. All in an effort to reflect the fact that the palace was the seat of the high king of *all* Gemaria.

The family wing still maintained the pure blue and silver, however, and it was a welcome relief to just be surrounded by the reminder of our family. It was just down to us now, and I could already anticipate what was coming when we entered the shared living area and crashed down onto the sofa and chairs.

I closed my eyes, tipping my head back, hoping to prevent, or at least delay, the inevitable conversation.

"Az," Ruri called, his voice still hoarse from crying. I sighed heavily, wrenching my eyes open and forcing my head up to meet his eyes.

"You know this wasn't an accident," he declared, raising a brow mulishly, his jaw jutting out like he expected a fight.

"We can't prove that." Balthazar reminded him, his own voice weary from the strain of the last few days. He sat in the chair beside me, his elbows on his knees and his hands in his hair, the green tone with just the slightest hint of blue making him look so much like his father.

"Maybe not, but we also can't take any chances now," Ruri argued back, and he wasn't wrong there. "Gardevoir was healthy. There was no reason for his heart to just *stop*. It had to be magic. And since he was your heir, it means your number of remaining heirs has been halved overnight."

"Looking to be high king?" I teased him, despite the mood in the room.

"Fuck no." He snorted, making Balthazar and me laugh lightly. "You couldn't pay me enough. I enjoy being a prince with little responsibility."

I shook my head fondly, rolling my eyes at him. "You have responsibilities."

"Yes, but nothing like what you deal with." He conceded cheekily, though I knew he truly relished the responsibilities he *did* have. He may not want anything to do with politics, but his interest in academia had already improved our potion stores. "You cannot fucking die on me, Az."

His tone was teasing, the way my brothers always teased me about remaining alive, so they didn't have to sit the throne and deal with all the political fuckery of the courts. But despite the teasing, the knowledge hit all of us at the same time. *Gardevoir was dead.* And if it had been magic, there was every chance this was a targeted attack, one aimed directly at the throne. At my line. At *me*.

"I'm not convinced Gardevoir was the intended target either," Ruri added, looking hesitant as he spoke. His fingernails dug into his knees as he looked down, his mind already working through possibilities.

"We don't even know if this was an attack. We have no proof," I reminded him, but he simply brushed me off with a roll of his eyes, cocking his head at me in a gesture my brothers and I had all shared many times. Simply translated, it meant "you're an idiot".

"You think they were aiming for Az?" Balthazar asked as he sat up straight, looking at Ruri intently. I could practically see him vibrating in impatience as Ruri deliberated with himself for a moment.

"Either that, or they're trying to take us out first before targeting Az," Ruri confirmed softly, and I had to shake my head at them both.

"I'll up the protection around you for the foreseeable future, just in case," Balthazar murmured to me. I sighed miserably but nodded in acquiescence.

"You're just guessing, though, Ruri," I told him firmly. "We have no way of knowing this wasn't natural."

"Call it a hunch," Ruri responded grimly. "Remember that carnival we had several months back? I had a reading done by one of the prophets there."

I rolled my eyes at him incredulously. "At the carnival?"

"This was one of the real ones!" He protested, his frosty blue-green eyes wide, making him look even younger. I almost wanted to send him off to our mother for reassurance. She couldn't bring herself to attend court today, still too heartbroken over the loss of her son. Perhaps sending Ruri to her would help them both.

"They told me there would be those who went after my brothers. And then this happens?" He shook his head, slumping down and looking like a pouting child, his court jacket wrinkling as the collar slid up his neck.

"So what do you suggest?" I nearly winced as the question left my mouth. I already knew what was coming. Mother had already hinted earlier that it might be time, and I was sure she'd mentioned as much to Ruri.

But I wasn't going down without a fight, either.

"We're too vulnerable. You need heirs, brother," he said quietly, at least managing to appear apologetic through his worry. "And, if you host the traditional Diamond Queen Competition to find a wife, we can use the presence of all the nobility who attend to investigate this further."

From my peripheral, I noticed Balthazar trying to hide his smile in his hands. I narrowed my eyes, shifting a heated glare between them.

"The two of you were already conspiring about this, weren't you?" I grumped, crossing my arms, even as it pulled at my jacket, the stiff, dark teal fabric encrusted heavily in diamonds, giving it little flexibility.

"Not just them." Another voice called, and I swung my head to see Emrys enter the living room. I rolled my eyes as he sat down beside me and threw an arm around my shoulder, his long white hair brushing across it. I preferred keeping my own hair short with only enough on top to style it, the edges both shaved down entirely. Meanwhile, Emrys kept his well past his shoulders.

Emrys's hair was certainly the longest of us all, with waves hanging down his back. Balthazar's, while short, was much shaggier than mine, and Ruri liked to wear his long enough for the waves to cascade down and frame his face. He claimed the ladies loved it. I was sure they were humoring him.

"As the head of inter-court relations, I can tell you that literally everyone is talking about the fact that you only have one brother left as your heir." He told me plainly, ignoring my wince. It's what I paid him for, and as a friend, he also knew skirting around the issue would get him nowhere with me.

"They're nervous about the stability of the crown," Emrys told me, his voice gentler as his opal-colored eyes softened. "They need you to find a queen and start popping out some heirs."

"And I need to investigate what's going on," Balthazar added, his eyes darkening at the thought of this being a larger plot against the throne. I was positive he would have his guards sweeping the palace for clues in no time. The poor courtiers weren't going to know what hit them.

I groaned, tossing my head back again and looking up at the ceiling. There was no other way forward. I knew I needed a queen. *I did.* But…I had hoped I might meet someone who was worthy of it, one day. It was one thing to fuck a woman who wants nothing more than to crawl onto my throne and who accepts that my bed comes along with it, but it's another to actually *marry* one.

"The tradition is bullshit," I argued hopelessly, looking back up and turning my eyes to each one of them in turn. "It's an excuse for the ladies of the realm to squabble and fight, then crown one of themselves queen over the others. It has nothing to actually do with me. Or wanting to marry me."

"Maybe." Ruri shrugged sadly, but a spark of hope brightened his eyes. "But who knows, you might actually meet someone you like. Someone you could see being your wife and the mother of your children."

I scoffed, shaking my head at his naivety. "You actually expect me to find someone worthy of Mother's crown in that bunch of harpies?"

Ruri winced, but it was Emrys who laughed loudly. We all turned to look at him, my eyes clearly communicating that I didn't see the humor in what I'd just said. He shook his head at me, snickering.

"Your own mother was one of said harpies, if you remember," he said smugly, making me glare back at him.

"That was different," I argued. She may have gone through the competition, but my parents were already hoping to marry. Tradition had merely stated that she had to win the competition to be able to marry him. So she did.

"Was it?" Balthazar asked quietly, his eyes meeting mine.

I groaned, my hands reaching up to rub my face in aggravation. "If I do this, I'll never be able to find a woman who is worthy enough to sit the throne, one who can be a partner to me and actually help me rule. I'll be stuck with some vapid lady who just wants the crown on her head."

"You have no way of knowing that," Emrys argued passionately, hands flailing around. "You're assuming because you don't want to do this. Though I don't see why, I'd love to have all of the most eligible ladies of the realm fighting over me." He shrugged, and I reached up to slap the back of his head.

"I'm sorry, brother," Ruri said, leaning forward. "But I truly don't see another way. We're too vulnerable right now. And you know some courts will pounce on that immediately, if they haven't started already." He finished darkly.

We were surely all thinking it. Any one of my troublesome lords could already be plotting. Like Lord Carnelian of Ruby Court, who had been a pain in my ass since I took the throne. From talking down to me to ignoring orders, he had made it more than clear that he thought my whole family had a position we didn't deserve. Before he died, my father had warned me to keep an eye on him. While he'd never acted before, Father believed he would take the chance if one ever appeared.

Was this that chance? Could *I* take the chance that it wasn't?

I knew Carnelian wasn't the only one, either. Neither Lord Neel of Sapphire nor Lord Khader of Emerald could truly be trusted, not when their ambitions were all too clear. I was only thankful that there were lords I *could* trust among the courts. Maybe one of their candidates would work.

"Fuck." I groaned loudly, the slightest whine making it into my voice. The sympathetic looks, and one gleeful one trying to feign sympathy, which surrounded me only cemented my misery.

"Fine," I ground out between clenched teeth. A bleak future began rapidly stretching out in front of me as I agreed, cementing my fate. "We'll announce the damn Diamond Queen Competition."

"Perfect!" Emrys's sister, Arianell, called as she swooped into the room. Like her brother, her white hair and eyes had a distinct sheen to them that made it immediately clear that she was from Opal Court. While not directly in the noble family, they were cousins of the lord and had been in Diamond for years now. They'd each made a place for themselves among my court, and I was truly thankful for their presence…most days.

"We'll send out the announcements to the courts tomorrow," she cheerfully continued, already brimming with excitement. Arianell was in charge of all royal functions, and she loved nothing more than planning a party. The traditional marriage competition was a new challenge for her, and one I knew she was more than ready to embrace.

"We'll need to arrange each challenge carefully. It will need to exceed the last one held on all counts, of course, but we also need to ensure the challenges weed out any ladies who won't be a good fit for Az," Emrys told her, making her roll her eyes in response. "For example, she shouldn't be a dolt when it comes to politics and all that entails if she's going to navigate court."

"Of course." She sniffed, clearly insulted that her brother believed she even needed to be reminded.

"We need to ensure she can protect herself, along with our king and people," Balthazar spoke up, his mind on my protection, as always.

"And she should be able to use magic well enough not to embarrass our family," Ruri added, a small smile pulling at his lips as he looked to me. His love of magic was always endearing, and his studies at the academy had proven to be helpful many times over. There was so much the gems were capable of when mixed, and the experimentation of their alchemy proved to be the thing to truly gain his attention. He'd already come up with new potions that had proven had valuable his knowledge could be.

"She needs to be compassionate to our people." I sighed heavily, adding my own request to the list. "I don't want a queen who looks down at the common people."

There was a moment of silence, everyone looking at each other as they surely all realized what a stretch it would be to find someone like that. Arianell was biting her lip, her finger tapping against her chin.

"I think I have an idea that could work for that." She nodded decisively before smiling slyly at me. "We also need to ensure you two can get along on a personal level."

We spent the next hour debating different challenges and coming up with a list of trials that Arianell would have to organize quickly. We needed to get this moving before any enemies could begin enacting their own plans. We were vulnerable enough that one lucky attack could potentially wipe out our entire line. By the end, I was at least more or less happy with what we'd come up with, but still less than impressed with the fact that I had to do this.

Hopefully, the challenges will succeed at weeding out any vapid crown chasers. Leaving a winner who was actually worthy of the honor of being my queen.

CHAPTER 3

Jacinth

T H E guard came to a stop outside of a large, ornate wooden door that had rubies lining the edges and carvings I could barely make out in my weakened state covering it. He knocked sharply twice, and I could just make out a muffled voice answering. The guard opened the door, yanking the chain and forcing me to stumble in after him.

He came to an abrupt stop, and I all but collapsed to the ground behind him. The lethargy was taking its toll on me, and I struggled to take in the details around me. Dark walls lined with bookcases surrounded the space, and a large wooden desk that was surely twice the size it probably needed to be sat upon a large red and gold rug. There were what I knew had to be high-value items sitting on display throughout the room, just out of my grasp.

But it was the man who stood behind the desk and slowly walked around it who caught my attention. Long, vibrant red hair and matching red eyes were set in a long, severe face. Everything about it was sharp, from his nose to his cheekbones to his chin. He was beautiful, of course, as most Elves were, but the red of his eyes was too intense, practically glowing, giving him an intimidating aura.

I hadn't allowed myself to be intimidated in years, and I wasn't going to cave to it now. I refused to go to my death cowering before someone who thought themselves better than me.

And I knew immediately that was indeed what he thought. His sneer down at me was quite the clue, after all.

"*This* is the one?" he asked, sounding disgruntled for some reason, besides the obvious.

"This is her." The guard nodded once, but I could just make out the tremble in the hands clasped behind his back.

Huh, not so tough now, was he?

"You're dismissed." The man, who could only be Lord Carnelian, told the guard. The Elf faltered for a moment, clearly surprised. He looked like he wanted to argue, his mouth falling open, but the lord narrowed his eyes a bit, and the guard immediately nodded, dropping the chain and handing the key to his lord before darting out of the room as fast as possible.

I wanted to laugh, but my own predicament certainly wouldn't be helped by that.

"So, you're the one who thought it a good idea to try to rob me." Carnelian's slitted red eyes took me in carefully. The ruby pools flared before he reached out, fingering a lock of hair that had escaped my braid. "Tell me, what were you hoping to get?"

I struggled to open my mouth, wanting nothing more than to fall asleep where I kneeled. The lord rolled his eyes, stepping back and leaning down toward my chained hands. He stuck the key into the lock, and I watched as the manacles fell to the ground. I hesitantly reached up and rubbed my wrists, feeling my strength come back to me in a dizzying rush.

"There, that's better, isn't it?" He smirked, straightening up. Before I could get my bearings, he grabbed my chin, forcing me to look up at him. I glared back at him, but he seemed more amused than anything. At least if the smile tilting the corner of his lips was anything to go by.

"Now, what were you after that you deemed important enough to do such a foolish thing?" He crooned, but I stubbornly kept my eyes narrowed on him and my lips firmly shut.

"Come now." He tutted, shaking his head as he leaned down to meet my eyes. "You don't actually want to die, do you?"

"I wasn't aware there was another option." I spat, making him chuckle.

"Death is so permanent. What use could you possibly be to me if you're dead?" he responded, his voice carefully blasé. I looked him over as he straightened, trying to figure out what his angle was. But if there was a chance I wasn't about to die if I talked…

"I needed money," I admitted, slowly, *carefully*. "My friend is sick, and I can't afford the gems to help her."

"So altruistic," he scoffed, shaking his head again and looking almost disappointed as he began to turn around.

"I owe her," I said, voice carefully emotionless. His head tilted to the side as he stopped mid-turn, before shifting back to inspect me again.

"And where are you from, girl?" he asked, making my heartbeat speed up. I didn't think I'd ever seen him before, but I could very well be wrong. I was so young back then… If he recognized me, I was truly fucked.

"I'm not really *from* anywhere," I told him, making eye contact and forcing a veil of truth over myself. As long as I believed what came out of my mouth in that moment, no courtier would be able to read a lie on my face. It was a tactic that Ula had taught me to survive, but it worked just as well for uppity lords. "I live on the streets, and we tend to move around. I've been everywhere from Sapphire to Amethyst to Emerald."

"Hmm." He hummed, rocking back on his feet, his eyes still way too intense as they examined my features. "And what would you give to escape death today? To help this friend of yours?"

I considered his words, tilting my head to the side. I didn't know what game he was playing here, and that put me on the back foot. But at least it meant there *was* a game to be played. One I could learn the rules of if I played along. So I told him what he clearly wanted to hear.

"Anything." It wasn't far from the truth, after all. Maybe *a bit* of a stretch.

Lord Carnelian slowly smirked, satisfaction rolling off him. "Then you'll do just fine."

He moved to sit behind his overly large desk, waving a hand at me to sit opposite him. I carefully lowered myself into the tufted leather wingback chair, watching him as he watched me.

"How do you feel about our High King?" he finally asked, after an extended silence. I raised an unimpressed brow, but couldn't help thinking back to blood pooling on the floor and dead eyes staring back at me. I couldn't stop my nose from wrinkling in disgust at the very thought of the king who oversaw the deaths of everyone I loved.

It was enough to make Lord Carnelian smile truly. "Good. You see, I'm also not a big fan of our High King."

"You don't say," I responded dryly. He narrowed his eyes, but his smile never left his face.

"His brother has just died, leaving him with only one younger brother to serve as his heir. One who has no true skill and wouldn't last a day as king." He explained, folding his hands together as those creepy red eyes watched me, trying to pick me apart.

"Which means," he continued, "that should something terrible befall our king, it would be quite easy for another to take over. Especially with the right people in strategic spots."

"And let me guess?" I asked sarcastically, raising an eyebrow at him, "You happen to have just the right people?"

Instead of snapping at me, his inspection only sharpened, and I knew I'd done something I shouldn't. Men like him weren't used to being spoken to in such a way. Hopefully, he chalked up my impertinence to my being unfamiliar with how to behave in front of my "*betters*". Most street rats wouldn't know the first thing about how to act in court.

"I hope to. Thanks to you." My eyebrows flew upwards, but I quickly rearranged my face into something more neutral, making him smile slightly.

"Me?" I asked incredulously, my bad feeling about this somehow getting worse. I had no qualms about getting rid of the king; I'd relish it, in fact. But I didn't really like the idea of *High King Carnelian* either.

What was I thinking? That wasn't my problem. Courtly issues were so far down my list of worries. I only kept track of the gossip to ensure I was safe at the end of the day, not so I could play this game with them.

But...an opportunity for vengeance? *That* I could get behind.

That was worth *everything*.

"Yes, you." The lord nodded once in confirmation. "You're a beautiful young woman, who—with a little polish," he sneered slightly, looking me up and down as I grit my teeth in irritation. "Would catch the eye of any man. Even a king. As it so happens, due to their vulnerable position, High King Azurill has called for the traditional Diamond Queen Competition."

I stifled my gasp, preventing myself from showing a reaction at all. It shouldn't have been so surprising; it was bound to happen sometime after all. But the king had seemed reticent about marrying by all reports, so I hadn't been expecting that to change any time soon. He clearly realized that the sharks were circling.

One of said sharks stared back at me from across the dark, stately wooden desk. The other stared right back at him.

"Each court is required to present a lady to compete for the chance to be the next Diamond Queen." Carnelian smiled fully and truly then, and the image of a shark with its prey suddenly felt very apt. I wasn't sure I'd ever seen such an unsettling sight. "You will go as Ruby Court's competitor."

I nearly sputtered from shock at his declaration. That was *not* where I was expecting him to take that plan.

"Me?" I managed to choke out.

"Yes, it will be quite perfect. It will get you close enough to him to carry out the true plan," he told me proudly, sitting back in his chair and tapping his fingers along the edge of its arm for a moment before he continued. "You will win this competition, you understand. You *must*." His voice took on a threatening undertone now, but I was too shocked still to feel any fear.

"*How* am I supposed to do that? *Why* am I supposed to do that?" I asked, completely confused. How could he begin to think someone like me could beat the noble ladies of the realm? It was absolutely preposterous.

Carnelian sighed long sufferingly. "You will be my assassin. When you win, you'll take him out that very night, and I'll have someone nearby to discover the body and give you time to get away. The timing is crucial; you must not kill him until you have been announced as the winner. I will be providing the king council along with all the other lords, helping him decide who to eliminate at each trial. I will ensure you stay in the running, don't worry about that. But you must do your part. We will go over everything you need to know to play the part of a distant family member of mine, one with *my* noble blood in their veins, and ensure you do not embarrass me in the process."

His voice hardened as he watched my reaction, my pink eyes wide as I tried not to panic at the thought of entering the competition. "You carry yourself with more dignity, more grace, than any street urchin I've ever seen. We'll be able to polish you up enough to pull this off. Do you understand?"

I understood perfectly. If I didn't play the part correctly, the high king wasn't the only one who'd wind up dead. I swallowed hard. Entering back into the world of courts and nobles wasn't something I ever expected to happen. It was too dangerous. There were too many opportunities for the king to realize who I was. And I wasn't sure how to play the part of a delicate noble lady anymore, not really. I'd been roughed up around the edges since my childhood, to say the least.

Hence the thievery I was sure had my mother rolling over in her grave.

"How do you expect me to kill him?" I asked, knowing it was all that truly mattered in the end. This chance might be the only one I ever had.

The slow smirk he answered with was a frightening sight. He stood up from his chair and strode over to one of the bookshelves on the wall, pulling out a book for some reason. Or, I thought he was, but the book stopped partway, and the shelf began to move. A hidden door. This castle was just full of them, apparently.

He waved me over, and I reluctantly stood up, following him into the secret room. My jaw nearly dropped as I cleared the doorway. I hadn't seen a room quite like this since I was little, when I would play at my father's feet, pretending I was doing magic. The ones at market couldn't begin to compete with the sight before me.

It was a full Gemlab, with potions bubbling away and bottles full of all sorts of swirling potions in numerous colors sitting on shelves around the large room. Against the far wall was an entire shelving unit containing piles of raw gems, enough to make me incredibly aggravated that I hadn't known about this room. I would have definitely raided this instead, had I known.

Though I probably would have gotten caught anyway. It seemed like he kept this room quite private. It was odd, considering every lord had their own Gemlab. Why would he hide his?

He walked toward the table in the middle of the room, containing a smoking beaker full of a shimmering white opal, dark black onyx, sparkling green emerald, and a light sheen of purple amethyst. I'd seen similar combinations before, of course, but none that looked quite like this. Depending on how much you use of each gem, and the method of brewing, you could use them to very different effects.

The alchemy of Gemwork was quite a fascinating subject, really, but not one I ever had the opportunity to explore the way I wished.

I slowly followed Carnelian over to the wooden table the potion was set on, and his red eyes took on a sheen I couldn't quite decipher. His small smirk was no less discomforting, but I locked down my own face to ensure I didn't let a single emotion flicker across it.

"This," he announced proudly as he gestured to the potion, "will be what takes down the king."

I eyed the swirling mixture, the smoke slowly dissipating as it neared completion. I couldn't help the hard swallow I took as I contemplated what it meant. I was really going to do this. I would kill King Azurill. Maybe then, my family would be able to rest in peace.

Maybe then, I could find some peace, too.

As much as I hated the bastard, however, I'd never actually killed anyone before. Injured a few guards here and there, sure, but now I was being forced to become an assassin, all because I was foolishly overconfident in my ability to steal without being caught. Even if ending the king served my own ends, it was a thought that lived only in dreams until now.

But I'd done this to myself, and now I had to face the consequences. I just couldn't live with myself if others were forced to face them too.

"And what about my friend?" I dared to ask, raising my chin as I stared the lord down. "She's dying, if I don't get her help—"

"Yes, yes." He waved me off, irritation lacing every word, "I will send my men to pick her up."

"Pick her up?" I asked, my pitch rising as I stiffened in alarm.

"Of course!" He smirked, relishing in reaction. "My people will watch over her and ensure she remains alive. Once you've succeeded, I will have her healed fully. That should give you proper incentive, should it not?"

I ground my teeth together, jaw working back and forth as my hands fisted tightly to prevent myself from reaching out and punching the pompous prick. I should have known it wouldn't be so simple; nothing was ever straightforward with nobles.

I knew Carnelian would dangle Ula over my head until this was finished. Clearly, he didn't believe my own life was inventive enough, but I would never forgive myself if I didn't try to save her from this.

"I have just as much reason as you to want him dead," I argued fiercely, and his eyebrow spiked, curiosity written all over his face. "You don't need her."

"Do you now?" he murmured, ignoring my last words as he continued to watch me. It took everything I had in me not to shift on my feet under the intensity of his gaze, my nerves rising at what he might see. Anonymity had been my only defense for so long; being *seen* was a nightmare beyond comprehension.

"Yes," I stressed, shaking my head slightly. "If you heal her, I'll do whatever you want. You don't need to keep her captive."

"Who said anything about captive?" He gasped as if offended, pressing a hand over his chest. "I'm merely carrying out our agreement. A favor between…business partners, even. I believe you care more about the safety of your friend than you do your own. So I will keep her safe and well while you do your job. I can't just trust a thief such as yourself, after all. That would be incredibly foolish of me, and I'm not in the habit of being foolish."

I bristled at his pointed tone, opening my mouth to argue once more, but he spoke again before I could. "Tell me, though, why do *you* want Azurill dead?"

His palms hit the table as he leaned over it, all but towering over me, and I had to suppress my flinch. I cursed the day I bought that damn map to his vault, and I was sure I would be cursing it and myself many times over before this was through.

Whatever he saw in me, it was too much. My nameless, invisible existence was key to my survival. If he knew who I actually was…

"I live on the streets and have nothing to my name. Is that not enough? He runs this system that sees so many with nothing left to rot, while he lords over us all in his damned diamond palace." I obfuscated, hoping he wouldn't press the issue.

"Hmm." He narrowed his eyes, while I prayed to Erodite to obscure his sight and not let him see the truth of me.

Something I knew would be ever more challenging to hide in the heart of Diamond's court.

CHAPTER 4

Jacinth

"Chin up." The cursed stick struck underneath my chin again, forcing my head up. I glared at the ruby-haired woman, biting back a mouthful of insults I wouldn't dare speak, but she merely sneered at me like I was a bug to be crushed under her shoe.

"We have extremely limited time to make a proper lady of you," she snapped, crimson eyes flaring with impatience. "If you embarrass Ruby Court, you *will* feel my wrath, do you understand me?"

I tried not to roll my eyes. I'd heard this refrain several times already from Lady Sienna. As the lady of Ruby Court, she was counting on her husband's plan to work just as much as he was, but she was less than impressed with his choice of competitor.

"I understand," I ground out, keeping my chin up as I glanced at the clock hanging on the far wall. The party Carnelian sent out was due back today, and we'd received word that they weren't far out nearly an hour ago. I was practically shaking with the need to go see Ula.

And possibly beg for forgiveness.

I was forced through another excruciating half an hour of lessons in being a lady, however. Sienna had been drilling me nonstop since the day I was caught, and nearly a week later, I wanted nothing more than to scream. I hadn't had to worry about appearances in this way since I was a child. And what child honestly cared about abiding by the boring adult rules?

Now, I was getting the crash course I thought I'd never have reason to catch up on. Within another week, we'd be setting out for Diamond Court, and the competition would begin shortly thereafter.

They had no idea what kind of challenges I'd be thrown into, so Carnelian and Sienna decided to cover their bases as best they could. They were using the last competition as a template, but we all knew it was likely there would be some surprises. Apparently, the nature of the trials was kept under tight security, with no one outside of the high king's inner circle allowed to know of them.

All I wanted was for Ula to be safe and the king to get what he deserved, but I knew both depended upon the outcome of this competition. I was determined to find a way to win, even if I had to lie, cheat, and steal my way to it. Which is what I knew Carnelian was banking on.

"Ugh, will you pay attention!" Sienna snapped, making me wince. She shook her head at me derisively, "Fine, go see your little friend."

I practically ran for the door, but unfortunately, I wasn't quite fast enough.

"Jacinth!" she called, and I froze in place at the name, my hand mid-twist on the doorknob. "Remember, her life depends on this. Go see her and clear your mind, but tomorrow, I expect you to be here bright and early, ready to absorb every single thing I teach you. Understand?"

The threats never stopped with these two. They were truly a match made by Erodite.

How could my goddess do such a thing to me as to pit these two against me?

"Perfectly." I reluctantly answered with absolutely zero venom in my voice. The emotionless courtly tone that wouldn't give anything away wasn't far from what I'd used as a thief. I could go toe-to-toe with the best of the nobles when it came to hiding what I truly thought. A skill I'd had to use more in the last week than I'd had to since I first found myself living on the streets.

I ducked out the door and hurried along the corridor, hoping Ula didn't kill me the moment I walked in. I wouldn't blame her if she did. She'd lived by her own merits for years, and now she was finding herself a "guest" of the Lord of Ruby.

A knife was all but hanging over her head, thanks to me.

I'd set out to help her and somehow only managed to make things worse. She'd told me the job was too risky, with Carnelian overly paranoid and the castle too protected, but I'd been desperate to find a way to help her. I knew she wasn't going to last much longer, no matter what she claimed.

"Ah, Jacinth." I winced, coming to a stop as the heir to Ruby Court sauntered down the hall from the other direction. "On your way to see that street urchin friend of yours?" He sneered, red eyes flaring as they looked me up and down.

I bowed my head placidly, biting my lip hard before I answered, "Lord Casaan."

He sniffed, probably insulted that I wasn't clamoring for his attention. "You know, there's no need to play coy. If you'd like a step up from your pauper's quarters, my bed is always open."

I struggled to keep my face blank this time. Since I'd arrived, he'd vacillated between disgust and lust every time he looked at me, seemingly unable to make up his mind.

I knew that, objectively, I was attractive, but my circumstances meant that I never much thought about it, at least outside of using it to charm people out of their coin and gems. But dropped into the world of courts and nobles, my looks suddenly became a focus in a whole new way. How attractive the high king would find me. How attractive the heir of Ruby found me. I felt like livestock being weighed and measured.

"I'll be sure to keep that in mind, my Lord," I replied, keeping my eyes firmly on the ornate rug lining the halls. On the gold embroidery over the deep ruby red color. On the slight texture that helped shape the patterns within it. Anything but looking up and catching his eye.

Casaan scoffed, leaning into my space as I willed every muscle in my body not to twitch away. "I know my father is a punishing taskmaster, and my mother puts him even him to shame."

He laughed like he'd made a grand joke, while I stood silently, letting him carry on a conversation by himself.

"I'm sure you could use a release after all that," he purred into my ear. "And I could certainly use some careless fun before I'm yoked into a marriage. Despite your low status, you are quite beautiful. I've never seen hair such a vibrant pink before." He reached up to play with a lock of my hair, twirling it around his finger.

Interesting. I hadn't heard anything in the grapevine about a prospective marriage for the Ruby heir.

"You're too kind, my Lord," I replied blandly, wishing I could rip my hair out of his hand. "But I'm afraid your mother wears me out entirely. I just crash into bed at the end of the day. Besides, I'm certainly too lowly a beggar for you to bother yourself with."

Casaan's lip curled as he pulled back, finally releasing my hair before straightening his jacket. It was a shame he was such a horrendous dick, because he had all his father's good looks and none of the terrifying intensity. His short red hair was slicked back, just a few pieces falling onto his forehead strategically, leaving his long, pointed ears fully exposed. It was a surprisingly boyish hairstyle, but it was offset by his regal attire.

The collar of his black and red jacket flared out high on his neck, and the chain connecting the two flaps of the jacket at the top of his chest was crested with a giant ruby. The shoulders of the jacket had a red quilted pattern that continued down the sleeves, while below that was a vertical pattern that blended nicely. The primarily black fabric was accented with rows of gold embroidery and numerous red rubies—an outfit fit for a prince, let alone the heir to a lordship.

One that I could probably sell for enough coin to feed us for a year.

"That is true," he mused aloud, and I'd never wanted to roll my eyes so badly. "Well, you know where I am should you change your mind. We can keep it just between us." He winked before resuming his walk down the hall.

I shook my head the moment he was out of sight. Even if I wasn't technically his father's captive, his personality was off-putting enough that I would be staying well away. I suppose I should count myself lucky that I would never be forced to marry one of these pompous lords.

But I would have put up with literally any marriage if it meant my parents were here to arrange it. Had the gods given me the chance to fix what happened, I would even marry Carnelian himself in trade.

I brushed the encounter off and continued my rush down the hall until I reached the room Ula was to be staying in. I paused outside of it, taking a deep breath and preparing myself for the worst. I knocked once and then slowly opened the door.

My heart kicked hard in my chest, and a fear I rarely felt made my hands shake slightly as I took in the sickly pallor of Ula's normally bronze skin. Her light, mint-green hair was matted with sweat and stuck to her neck. It was so much worse than I expected.

I rushed to her bed, kneeling beside it, and taking her hand. "Ula?"

She cracked a mint eye partially open, taking a moment before she truly saw me, and then forced them both open fully. "Jac?"

"It's me, I nodded, trying not to let any moisture reach my eyes.

"What the fuck have you gotten me into?" she croaked hoarsely, making me laugh tearfully.

"I think I've got us both into a world of shit," I admitted with a frown. "But at least it gives us the chance to get you some help."

"Hmm," she hummed in a weak rasp, "They've already given me something. I can feel it working. It's easier to talk already." I let out a sigh of relief at the news, though I couldn't imagine how much worse she must have been for this to be an improvement. I was more right than I knew about there not being much time for her.

Maybe Carnelian's deal had a silver lining, after all. If he could get her strength up and keep her going until I did what he wanted, that would be blessing enough compared to what we'd been facing. The fact that he'd heal her once I was done was all I wanted.

Well, that, and a couple of other things. I didn't exactly wish for death myself, but I did wish it upon High King Azurill quite fiercely.

"That's good. Did they explain what's going on?" I asked, apprehensively.

Her eyes narrowed at me, "They mentioned I was being kidnapped by the Lord of Ruby to have my life held over you while you compete to become the damned *Diamond Queen* of all things. I thought—they must be either out of their minds or lying through their teeth. Only for the lord himself to greet me upon my arrival and explain a few things."

I winced hard, and she squeezed my hand that was holding hers to the point of pain.

"What *the fuck* were you thinking?" she demanded as steam practically came out of her ears. I wilted a bit at her anger, an instinctual response to disapproval from the one woman I hated to disappoint. At least she seemed to be feeling better already.

"I was thinking you were sick," I admitted, shrugging lightly and avoiding her eyes. "We didn't have a way to heal you without magic."

"And now you've landed yourself in the most dangerous situation I could imagine for you." She grumbled angrily, shaking her head as much as she could manage. Her glare was reproachful, but I could only sigh deeply.

"I'm sorry you're stuck here, truly, but I'm not sorry they'll heal you," I told her, and the raised eyebrow I got in response was somehow full of her usual sass. It made the corner of my mouth lift in an almost smile to see it.

"*If* they heal me. It seems that depends on you winning this competition somehow," she argued, looking at me critically through narrowing eyes. "You aren't nearly as worried about that as you should be."

"This gives me a chance I never would have gotten otherwise," I said quietly, trying to avoid her knowing gaze.

"All this is worth it?" Ula questioned, her mint green orbs flaring as she stared me down. "All for a chance at the damn high king?"

"Of course it's worth it!" I snapped, angry that she couldn't understand this after so many years. "I will finally be able to avenge my family."

"He wasn't there," Ula responded quietly, squeezing my hand lightly this time and forcing me to look at her.

"But we both know he was responsible." I ground out, just thinking of the man made me want to hit something. It was a good thing I had still been in such shock when faced with Carnelian, or I might have spiraled the moment he brought him up.

Ula said nothing for a moment, just watching me quietly. She carefully lay back against the bed, fluffier than either of us was used to after years of sleeping on the ground or beat-up mattresses we'd found left on the floor of abandoned homes. We moved around a lot, but nowhere we'd ever stayed had beds like this. I hadn't slept in a proper bed like these ones since the night I'd been torn out of my own and thrown to the wolves.

"Do you truly think vengeance will bring you peace?" she finally asked, and I felt my heart give a painful thud.

"It's better than nothing," I responded, forcing down any emotion that tried to rise in my eyes. "I can't get my family back. I can't get my home back. I can't get my life ba—"

I cut off, swallowing painfully as I squeezed my eyes shut. I refused to cry about this. I'd spent my tears on it long ago.

"But I *can* get vengeance for them." I continued once I'd gathered myself, my voice hard with resolve. "That's all that's left now."

"No," she said quietly after several minutes of silence had passed between us. "There's still so much left, Jac. You just need to open your heart to the possibility."

"You're the one who taught me that survival was all that mattered." I scoffed, shaking my head. "That chasing the idea of a life beyond what we had was nothing more than a fantasy."

"Maybe for people like me, that's true." She admitted ruefully, a heavy sigh escaping her lips. "But you're different. You always have been. And now, you have the opportunity to step back into the life that was stolen from you."

I shook my head immediately, the wrenching in my gut a physical ache that spread through me. "That life isn't for me. And there's no place left for me in it. House Marit is dead. Pearl Court now belongs to House Helmi. I'm not a lady, I'm just another street urchin the nobles would sooner pretend doesn't exist."

"Saying the words doesn't make them true." She argued back. As I should have known she would. The woman was as stubborn as a mule.

"No, them being true makes them true." I cocked my brow at her, making her scoff.

"If you get rid of the king, the danger may be gone." She suggested softly despite the hard look in her eyes. "You've had to spend your life hiding, but think of the good you could do if you could take back what rightfully belongs to you."

I nearly laughed at the thought.

"You think the new High King Carnelian will give one single shit about my sob story?" I shook my head at her. She wasn't usually so naive. She'd taught *me* better, for fuck's sake.

"I think you can use this opportunity," She stressed, grabbing my chin forcefully and pulling my face toward hers so I was incapable of looking away. "Be smart, like I taught you. These nobles aren't the only ones who can be devious. Don't let this fancy Ruby lord walk all over you. He needs you. Find the power within that."

Find the power, she says. Like I hadn't had all power ripped away from me, along with everything else.

"But you can't live for only vengeance, Jacinth." She added tiredly, eyes beginning to slip closed once more. "Just as diamond is ground into dust to become something new, vengeance will break you just the same."

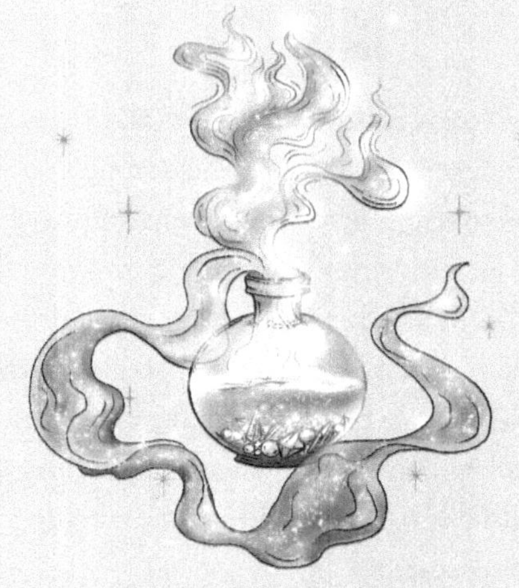

CHAPTER 5

Jacinth

NIGHTMARES always found me when I slept. It was an inevitable part of my life, making me dread every night when I closed my eyes and went to sleep. Outside the typical danger that came with lying your head down on a street in some dodgy neighborhood, the nightmares were what I always feared most.

It was always the same thing. Always the same guard shaking me awake and shushing my questions before pulling me up and into his arms. A dead little girl with a head of hair only a shade lighter than mine dropped by his hand into my bed. A little girl I instantly recognized as my cousin, Peony.

The horrified cry that left my mouth was insanely smothered by his hand, as he raced out of the door and through the halls, passing into the main room where my family usually gathered. By the light of the moon, I could tell it was only an hour or so since I'd gone to bed, and my parents, along with my aunt and uncle, should still have been there.

And they were, in a fashion. I'd twisted my head and thrown up when I realized what I was seeing. The blood splattered over the walls. The dead eyes of everyone who loved me looking back. I felt like I'd been ripped in half. I had never known pain before, not really. A stubbed toe, a hairbrush pulled too harshly through my hair. *But this?*

This was pain that ripped through you and incinerated the person you once were in its wake.

I'd fought my way out of the guard's arms and raced to my father, his usually vibrant pink eyes lifeless and staring at where my mother's body was slumped against the wall. I ran a shaking hand over his hair as I struggled to

31

catch a breath, afraid to touch him and make all of it real. Like the nightmare might end and let me wake if I didn't prove it true.

I'd tried to crawl to my mother then, reaching my hand to her with tears streaming down my face in torrents I didn't even know my body was capable of producing—that it hadn't before or since that day. My mother's usually shining eyes were so blank, her expression so slack, and her curly hair was matted with blood where her head must have been bashed with something.

I ached to grasp her hand, her own still extending out toward my father even in death. I could almost pretend she was reaching for me, ready to pull me into her arms one last time.

But then voices echoed from the hall, and the guard grabbed me back up, despite all of my kicking and flailing as he tore me away. I tried to scream for my family, grief and pain like I'd never known making a home in my heart, but a hand over my mouth stopped any noise before it could escape. The guard raced with me in his arms to a nearby closet door, sticking me inside and telling me to hide—and then once the opportunity came, to run as fast and as far as I could.

I only realized then that I knew this guard. In my shock, I hadn't registered who it was, but now I recognized it was Cor, the guard who usually watched over me and who had been for as long as I could remember. He'd play with me when I demanded a tea party, and help me sneak around the castle to steal sweets or play outside when I was supposed to be at lessons.

He'd shut the closet door, and I wanted nothing more than to pull him back in with me, to keep someone familiar by my side. But I knew Cor was a loyal guard, and his actions only proved that tenfold. He would never hide when he could defend.

I'd watched through a small hole in the wall while a man wearing a black mask entered the room. Cor drew his sword, and the ensuing fight was hard to follow. All I could remember was watching in horror as his body was cut down and added to the piles around the room. Yet not before he took the man down with him.

He'd given his life to save mine. And now *everyone* was truly gone.

I'd smothered my own screams, forcibly keeping my lips pressed together and holding both hands over my mouth. When more masked men came, I'd made myself listen, even while shaking in the small, dark space. Somehow knowing, despite being all of ten years old, that it would be important.

Their words stuck with me even fifteen years later.

"The girl's dead, looks like Aron got her before he got cut down." One of them chuckled, and I realized with a cold pit in my stomach that he was talking about me.

"Good, we can't have any of Marit blood left to claim Pearl." Another spoke in a gravelly voice. "He'll be pleased, at least. The first step to getting lords he can truly trust in place."

One of the others chuckled, "All hail the High King."

Later, I heard the gossip about what had happened. A robbery gone wrong, they all said. Only I knew the truth. That High King Azurill had killed my entire family, all to clear the way for another lord he could trust in their place. I didn't know why he thought my family couldn't be trusted, but I knew that they were *good*. And the king had proven with this act of cold-blooded murder that he was decidedly *not*.

Waking up, the nightmare felt especially vivid. The knowledge that today was the day was clearly affecting me. I would finally come face to face with the monster responsible for the destruction of my entire family, of my entire *life*, today.

I reached for my wrist, lightly touching the silver bracelet dotted with pink pearls and accented by diamonds. My parents had given it to me for my birthday only a few weeks before they'd been killed. It had been passed down in my family for generations, and they thought I was now old enough to respect its history and take care of it.

I'd luckily fallen asleep that night with the bracelet still on, having passed out fully dressed on my father's lap at the party. They must have just stuck me in bed once I drifted off, not bothering to have the maids wake me up to change.

Thank Erodite they did, as it was now the only thing left from my life as the noble daughter of Pearl Court.

I only cursed the presence of the diamonds on it. A reminder of the man responsible for their deaths. Diamond and Pearl forever, horribly, intertwined.

I could never bring myself to sell it, even at my lowest. Maybe if I had, Ula would be safe now. But I couldn't let go of this last piece of my parents. Despite the diamonds on it, it still made me feel like I had a piece of them with me every time I looked at it.

Plus, not selling the bracelet had inadvertently led me to this once-in-a-lifetime opportunity to kill the High King, which was a gift I'd never expected.

I sighed, forcing myself from the bed and shaking off the nightmares. I had to be strong today. I would face the king and remain resolute. I wouldn't cry. I wouldn't scream. I would be the *perfect* lady. One who would gain his attention.

I couldn't let myself do anything different.

I closed my eyes for a moment, sending a prayer to Erodite, goddess of Pearl, to make my work easier. She oversaw love and affection, and if she could inspire such in the king, it would certainly make my life easier. I knew it was futile even as I prayed, however.

She inspired matches between Elves, sure, but only fated ones. They were few and far between, and she only inspired them; she did not force them together. She couldn't make the king love me any more than she could make me love him. Something so impossible would mean erasing free will, and the gods refused to do that to their disciples.

But I could ask for her help, and I begged for it today. I needed any help I could get to ensure I got the vengeance my family deserved.

I'D AVOIDED GOING to Diamond Court since the night I fled my home. I hadn't been there since I was very young, and could barely remember it in truth. Thus, today would be my first real sight of the court ruled by the monster I'd always feared.

The carriage rolled along the road, winding through the city of Theiapolis. It was a hive of activity, with a sprawling market that I itched to explore. We passed restaurants and shops, houses and townhouses, a park and a large arena. There was so much to see, and despite myself, I found I was actually excited to do so. It was a beautiful city, with bright colors, gorgeous plants and flowers dotting the area, and gems sparkling from everywhere I looked.

A large silver and blue gate was wide open before the palace itself. And the palace…my mouth actually dropped open. I remembered my palace perfectly to this day. The pink pearl and white marble had been uniquely stunning, but the diamond and kyanite that Diamond's palace was made from was certainly impressive.

It sparked under the sun, the gems reflecting the light. The bones of the palace were silver and then studded with diamonds, while the blue kyanite covered twisting domes that crested the top of each tower. Ornate scrollwork and arches ornamented every window and door, adding elegant touches to an already gorgeous building.

The front entrance was covered with a dome as well and had a scalloped-patterned roof that was covered in rows of gems representing all of the other courts. It was a nice touch, especially at the entrance, welcoming everyone equally.

Scenic gardens surrounded the palace, and I eyed them as we made our wat through the gates. There were clusters of naturally growing gems shooting out of the vibrantly green grass, with manicured trees and flowers sprouting around them and making the place look like something out of a dream.

I knew it was anything but, however.

The carriage came to a stop in the drive, and a footman appeared, opening the door and helping everyone out. I was the last to exit, and I took his hand as it was offered, a deep breath leaving me as I reckoned with what was to come. I couldn't let a beautiful outside blind me to the rotten inside.

I stepped down and smoothed my dress carefully. It was a teal velvet, chosen to appeal to the high king specifically. It was studded with pink pearls to match my hair, diamonds to honor the king and capital, as well as rubies to represent the court I was competing for. It was gorgeous, I had to admit, and fit me perfectly.

It was designed to have what looked almost like a cape over it, but was instead built into the dress. It had straps a few inches wide that sat on my shoulders and were part of the main piece of the dress. It scooped down before splitting to plunge deep, leaving plenty of cleavage on offer to entice the king, and similar dramatic splits went up each side of the skirt, letting my legs peek out all the way to my upper thighs.

The fabric of the cape left a gap between the straps of the dress and where it connected further down my arm, leaving the curves of each shoulder fully exposed. It then flowed down around me and created a train. While the dress was embroidered and studded with gems nearly over the entire front, the cape was mostly bejeweled around the bottom, with some added where it was split to allow my arms free range of movement.

A ruby and diamond necklace was added, taking up my entire collarbone and dipping low to my breasts. Matching earrings dangled from my pointy ears, at least where they peeked through the curtain of my hair. The bright pink mass was left down, but had been styled with half of it swept up into a braided crown halfway back on my head. Diamonds were inserted into the braid, making even the top of my head shine. Two shorter pieces of hair were left down in front to frame my face, which I was informed quite strictly was important for some reason.

I felt like a fraud.

Or at least, like a version of myself from another life. One where the high king of Diamond had never sent his assassins after my family, and I'd grown up as I was supposed to. A noble lady, the daughter of the Pearl Lord, living in the lap of luxury, even though I couldn't be my father's heir as a woman. Which was certainly some bullshit, and I remembered thinking so even as a child, as my parents tried for a boy.

They never got the chance, however, leaving only...*me*.

In another world, I would be the rightful heir to Pearl. What Ula didn't understand was that because I was a woman, Pearl Court likely would have gone to our cousins regardless. There was a chance I could have gotten it, if the king had agreed to my petition, but I knew how small a chance that was even without his extermination of my blood. So despite how distant, House Helmi now had full right to it, because they had the closest male of blood relation to my father.

Walking through the doors of the palace in Theiapolis on the arm of Lord Casaan now, a part of me wondered what would become of me if anyone found out the truth. Would I be forced to marry some lord's heir, like Casaan, to brush it all under the rug? Or would I be taken out before the public could find out I was even alive?

I shuddered, though whether that was because of my thoughts or my escort, even I wasn't sure.

We were greeted by a man with opalescent white hair and eyes, his smile large and welcoming, but it looked forced as he greeted Lord Carnelian. His long black jacket was trimmed with opals and diamonds, a nod to his original court and where he now served.

"And this is Lady Jacinth," Carnelian said, motioning to me with his hand. Casaan stepped forward, bringing me with him, and my eyes met the opal ones of the Elf before me. I could see his surprise, his wide eyes taking in my coloring, before his own shot to Carnelian, but he'd locked his face down after his initial surprise, leaving me to only guess at what he might be thinking.

"She's a somewhat distant cousin, but of my blood," Carnelian told him with a disdainful sniff. "She's the only option Ruby Court has for an unattached female of noble blood, Emrys. If his majesty has a problem with that—"

"No, no." The man, Emrys, shook his head quickly. "Of course not. I was merely surprised we hadn't heard of Lady Jacinth before." He raised an eyebrow at Carnelian before turning to me with a smirk, leaning in like we were sharing a secret. "Treasures such as yourself rarely stay hidden for long, my Lady."

I smiled demurely at his put-on show of flirting. "You'd be surprised, my Lord."

He chuckled at my response, "Well then, let's ensure such hiding is long in the past now, and get you situated here at court, shall we?"

If only he knew how much I wished to go back to hiding from it.

I caught sight of Carnelian's stern warning glare and managed to nod graciously, "Of course, my Lord."

"I'll take her from here, Lord Casaan," Emrys told the heir of Ruby with a little wave of his fingers that had him narrowing his eyes, but he reluctantly passed my arm to him, nonetheless.

Emrys quickly snaked my arm through his and set off down the hall, forcing me to keep pace with him as I tried to take in the palace around me. It was much grander than anything I'd seen before, as befitting the seat of the high king, I supposed. But my fingers itched to snatch the trinkets we passed, knowing it was unlikely they'd even notice or care they were missing with so many people converging on the palace today.

"Now that we've gotten you away from such bores, Lady Jacinth, why don't you tell me about yourself?" Emrys suggested with a twinkle in his eye.

I remembered from Sienna's lessons that this man was responsible for inter-court relations. He was a ruthless politician according to her, one able to sniff out lies and able to finagle nearly any situation to the king's benefit. I'd have to be very, very careful with my words.

"I'm afraid there's not much to really say, my Lord." I tried, hoping against hope he'd think me boring and leave it alone.

"Oh, come now." He snorted inelegantly, surprising me. "We all thought Carnelian had no female relatives, yet here you are, crawling out of thin air. A stunning creature such as yourself does not just go unnoticed for years. Not in this court."

"Maybe that's precisely why I stayed out of this court." I countered, raising a brow at him. I nearly cursed myself for my combative attitude, as it certainly wasn't very ladylike of me. But Emrys, even more surprisingly, seemed to enjoy it, laughing at my response before tipping his head toward me.

"Touché, my Lady." He watched me for a moment before shaking his head slightly, and I prayed he was only amused and not seeing anything deeper. "A Ruby Court competitor who tried to stay out of court. There's one for the books."

I snorted in response before my eyes widened and I brought a hand up to cover my mouth. "Forgive me, my Lord."

"Nothing to forgive." He waved it away with a smile. "Let's say we keep what we discuss between us," he whispered, leaning closer again. "What Carnelian doesn't know won't hurt him. Secrets are best kept between friends anyway, and I think we'll be great friends indeed."

His large smile had me shaking my head in amusement, but I knew I had to be careful. That affable smile and shining personality were exactly what made him so skilled in his position, and that's all this nice act was. He was trying to find information, and I refused to let any slip.

"You'll be staying in a separate wing with all of the other competitors," he explained as we turned down a new hallway, but this one was very different from the others. It led to a large dead-end circle, with eight doors surrounding the space, and nothing else. Inspecting the area, I realized each door represented a different court, and it didn't stop at the door either, with the entire section of wall surrounding it decorated in the colors and gems of that particular court.

I glanced longingly at the door for Pearl Court. The pink door was arched, just like the others, with beautiful white filigree encrusted with pink pearls outlining it. A mosaic of pearls in various shades of pink reached up to the ceiling. Each court had a similar one, but Pearl's depicted an image of our patron goddess, Erodite. She was said to be the most beautiful of them all, as one would expect from the goddess of love, and they certainly did her justice here. Her form was almost entirely made of pink pearls, but they had used white and grey ones to outline and enhance her features. The only outliers were the two bright sparkling diamonds used for her eyes.

As I admired the other depictions of the gods and goddesses of our Pantheon that were created for the entrances to each competitor's rooms, I noticed diamonds had been worked into each of them in some small way. While Emrys led me straight to the door for Ruby Court, I examined the red door outlined in black filigree, with the goddess Fortuna being of course, made up of bright red rubies, with black to outline her form and diamonds once again used for her eyes. The biggest difference was that they had placed diamonds along the arched outline of the door, subtly included between the rubies, and across the dark filigree.

It was clear that a lot of work had gone into creating these rooms, all for a competition held once every few hundred years, if that. I couldn't imagine having enough space to be able to dedicate this much to such a rarely held event.

Emrys turned the knob, and I was brought into what was, shockingly, a much more tastefully decorated room than I'd been expecting based on the exterior. I'd been thinking it would be like rubies had been thrown up across the room, but instead I was brought into a small entrance hall done in black with a large crystal chandelier hanging above us. Walking further in, we came to the large living area.

The space looked nothing like I expected. The ceilings were high enough to include large arches, connecting each area within the suite of rooms. Ornate silver designs spiraled out across the ceilings from the center point of the chandeliers. While the walls were a subtly sparkling white flecked with red. It made it feel open and airy, not consumed and overbearing with the ruby red of the court it was meant for.

Columns flanked the large windows, with rubies and diamonds added into the designs, while long, velvet drapes in a deep burgundy color were pulled to each side of the windows. The view looked out on the gardens, and I found myself wishing I could explore them instead of facing what came next.

"I hope your accommodations are to your satisfaction, Lady Jacinth." Emrys's voice stole my attention, having nearly forgotten about his presence as I took in the space I'd be residing. I turned to face him with a fake smile, nodding pleasantly.

"Of course, my Lord." I agreed, "More than."

"Good, good. Then let me introduce you to your guard for the remainder of the event," he said, spiking my alarm instantly.

"Guard?" I asked, trying to maintain my composure. The last thing I needed was one of the king's guards up my ass while I carried out my mission. "Is that really necessary?"

"Unfortunately, at this time, it is," Emrys informed me apologetically, but more seriously than he'd said anything thus far. "It's for your own safety, as well as to maintain the sanctity of the event."

I tried not to grind my teeth in annoyance, dipping my head deferentially. "Of course."

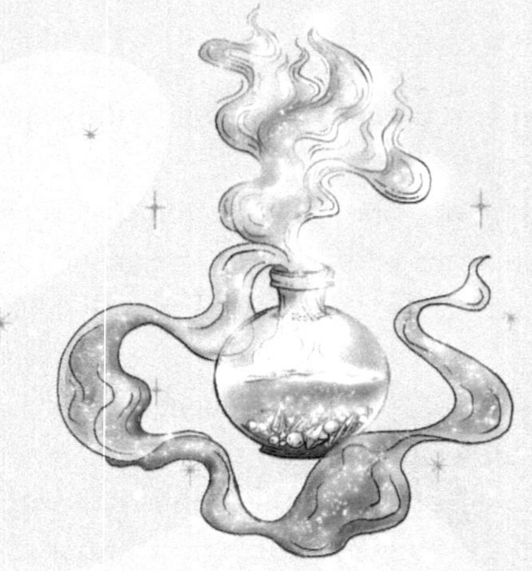

CHAPTER 6

Jacinth

"Ah, and here he is now!" Emrys smiled widely, his arm waving toward the door, where a tall Elven man walked through.

His hair and eyes were lavender in color, with his long strands pulled back at the edges and worked into two braids running down each side of his head, while the rest remained long in the back. A couple of smaller braids on top pulled any shorter sections of hair out of his eyes. His face was thin, but with a strong jawline and facial structure. He looked quite roguish, with charms hanging from his braids and tattoos covering every inch of skin I could spot below his chin.

I'd met men like him before. He looked more like a pirate than a royal guard, only his uniform showing him to be so. I raised an eyebrow at him, looking to Emrys for an explanation.

"This is Alfrikr, formerly of Amythest Court, clearly." Emrys introduced him. "We tried to switch up which guards served which competitors, to keep things fair and inspire the spirit of collaboration between the courts."

Or more likely to ensure said guard would spy on their charge, instead of being loyal to their original court.

"So Brokk, our Ruby Court guard for this event, will be serving Sapphire, while Wyn, our Sapphire Court guard, will serve Emerald, and so on, so forth. But only our very best guards were selected for this task, I assure you," he finished explaining.

Alfrikr and I stared at one another, weighing and examining what we were each working with. I watched a small smirk kick up his lips before he nodded deferentially.

"My Lady," he greeted me.

That would never stop being strange.

"Alfrikr, a pleasure, I'm sure." I returned politely. I wondered if I'd be able to find out more when Emrys left. He'd mentioned he was *formerly* of Amethyst Court, meaning he very well could have been a pirate. I'd traded with some before, since they usually had no use for gems beyond their value, while I had none for relics. They made for good trading partners in that regard.

While pirates were usually human, I'd seen a couple of other races who'd turned pirate. A Fae once, down by the docks in Sapphire Court, and an Elf among the ship's crew in Onyx. It seemed the one thing we all had in common was the desire to get away from our lives. The only reason I hadn't turned pirate myself was that I had no wish to live at sea.

"You'll be called for the formal introduction to High King Azurill in a bit," Emrys informed me, smiling widely. "All the competitors will be joining you, and you'll have a chance to meet everyone before we begin."

Oh joy. A bunch of pompous noble ladies fighting over a crown. How could I possibly wait?

"Of course. I can't wait to finally meet the High King in person." I smiled widely, as if excited, hiding my desire to meet him for much more murderous reasons.

WHEN THE TIME came, I found myself actually nervous to be in the presence of so many nobles. I was diving straight into the heart of Diamond Court, with all the nobles of Gemaria present, and all of them would be watching me. All *seeing* me.

Would they think anything of my eyes and hair? Was it reasonable to assume a cousin of the red-haired Ruby lord could have coloring that lightened to pink? Or would they see the truth through my lies?

Alfrikr opened the door to a circular room that contained a long white couch that curved to the shape of the room. Purplish blue walls were highlighted by hanging lights, and there were smaller seating arrangements with chairs and tables set all over the room. The far wall held a champagne fountain surrounded by glasses that a few of the ladies already present had clearly made use of, gripping their drinks as they glanced around.

I looked once more at Alfrikr, who nodded once as if urging me on before he took a spot along the wall where other guards were stationed. I made my way to the champagne, quickly taking a glass for myself and welcoming the fizzling silvery-pink drink's bubbles as they calmed me.

I subtly looked around at the other ladies to see who I was up against. A woman with turquoise hair in long, voluminous waves falling down her back, topped with a diamond hairpiece set with turquoise feathers, was the first I noticed. Equally stunning turquoise eyes were set in a delicate face that turned to face me and inspect her own competition. Her brown skin was nearly glittering in the light, and her dress was off the shoulder, a silver and blue ballgown encrusted with what had to be thousands of diamonds more than my own.

My heart sank. I had no idea how I was going to win this competition. It was ludicrous to assume I could ever earn the coveted spot as the Diamond Queen, even before I saw the other ladies fighting for the right to the title.

But said woman seemed to set her shoulders, highlighted by the diamond and kyanite necklace adorning her collarbone, and made her way to me, much to my surprise.

"Hello," She smiled nervously, smoothing a hand down her dress. "I'm Lady Faiza Nabhas, daughter of Earl Gohar Nabhas of Heer County, of Diamond Court."

Ah. Diamond must have struggled to find a lady to compete, since they couldn't have anyone even tangentially related to the king himself. The daughter of a minor lord who oversaw a province of Diamond Court must have been the best they could get.

Explaining why she was so nervous. She was technically the lowest ranked of us all—and wasn't that a dizzying thought.

It wasn't even a lie, technically. I was as much a full-blooded noble lady as any of them.

"I'm Lady Jacinth Tawny." I introduced myself with the last name Carnelian had assigned me. One belonging to a distant cousin with no children, but who had agreed to the ruse. "Cousin of Lord Carnelian of Ruby Court."

"Oh, thank Veritx." She laughed lightly, her relief instant. "I thought it'd be the only one who wasn't the daughter of the lord."

I couldn't help smiling back. She seemed entirely too genuine to be here.

"Do you spend much time here at court?" I asked her with a friendly grin, and she relaxed even further, her eyes sparkling.

"Oh no, I try to stay far away," she said, her happiness dimming slightly. Before I could ask her what in Tartarus she was doing here then, another voice interrupted.

"Oh, would you look at that." I turned to see a woman with long, curly emerald-green hair and bright eyes set beautifully against her tan skin. Another woman with pale white skin perfectly complemented by her cobalt-blue hair and eyes had her arm linked with the first woman.

"I didn't realize the Diamond Queen Competition was open to everyone now. It's so kind of High King Azurill to be charitable to the less fortunate." The woman dressed in the matching emerald-green of her court said, her sweet tone so fake that it set my teeth on edge.

The cobalt-haired woman tittered beside her, covering her mouth with her hand. "I'm sure you'll both make a valiant effort."

My eyes narrowed as Lady Faiza seemed to wilt where she stood, like a flower falling to the freeze, and I set my sights on the two before me.

"As I'm sure you will, my ladies," I told them in the same sickly-sweet tone. Faiza's eyes widened, while the cobalt-haired woman, Safira, if I remembered correctly, blinked rapidly. But the emerald-haired one narrowed her eyes at me, a viciousness behind her own I recognized from years on the streets. The look of someone who'd do anything to keep what they viewed as *theirs*.

"I'm Lady Zumra Giada, daughter of Lord Khader Giada of Emerald Court." She smiled that fake smile at me. "And who might *you* be?" She looked down her nose at me, sniffing in disdain.

I smiled slowly, "I'm Lady Jacinth Tawny, cousin of Lord Carnelian of Ruby Court, and the winner of this competition."

Lady Zumra's head reared back a bit, before she started laughing and shaking her head. Safira looked between us, seemingly uncertain, before laughing weakly.

"Oh, are you now?" Zumra asked, her laughter finally trailing off. I barely noticed some other ladies had joined us in the room while I was stuck dealing with the brat before me. "And I suppose I'm the next High King!"

Safira laughed dutifully at her joke, but looked distinctly uneasy, while Faiza looked almost scared on my behalf, shaking her head at me discreetly. Another woman with amethyst hair watched on with a critical eye.

"Let me make one thing clear, right now for you, *Lady Jacinth*." Zumra smiled before leaning in, that smile disappearing to show her true face.

Narrowed eyes and a sneer met my completely blank expression. "I will be the next Diamond Queen, no matter what it takes."

Safira frowned at her side, clearly not agreeing. We were all here for the same reason—to compete *against* one another. Whatever friendship the two had, I had a feeling Safira was rapidly discovering that it didn't extend to such high stakes as a queenship.

"We'll see." I shrugged casually, enraging Lady Zumra further.

"Yes, we will," she said heavily, exposing all her teeth like a feral wolf snarling. "I'd be careful in the challenges. You never know what can happen." She tutted before walking briskly away to another side of the room, talking quickly but quietly to Safira.

"Veritx, do you have a death wish?" Faiza asked me with wide eyes. I laughed, shaking my head.

"One thing I've learned is that you can never give in to those who think to demean you. If you allow it once, they'll just continue. Standing up to them is the only way," I told her, leaning in conspiratorially.

She shook her head. "I don't think I could dare. My position doesn't allow it."

She looked down, as if ashamed, and I suddenly found that despite her being my competition and all that was riding on me winning, I could not in good conscience allow her to continue believing such bullshit.

"Your position does not define you," I told her quietly, and she looked back up at me curiously. Surely, she'd been hearing the opposite her entire life. "You're already more privileged than many out there, who would kill for the luxury of being an Earl's daughter. You have more power than you think."

The irony struck me, having disputed the same argument to Ula only a few days prior.

"But even despite that, what position you hold in society doesn't define who you are as a person. Only you can do that. You can step outside the role you think you're meant to play, and instead play the one *you* choose." I finished, happy to see the small smile she now wore.

"You make it sound so easy," she said ruefully, reaching up to twirl a turquoise curl around her finger as she ruminated on what I'd said.

"It's not." I admitted, smiling wryly. "Just remember that you're more than you think." I looked her over for a moment, considering.

"Do you *want* to be the Diamond Queen?" I asked her curiously.

Faiza looked around wildly, and upon seeing that everyone was a good distance away, she shook her head slightly in the negative.

"Then why are you here?" I couldn't help asking, raising a brow at her.

She sighed heavily, her misery peeking through for the briefest moment. "They needed a woman with noble blood from Diamond, and I was the only one available who's not related to Az—" Her eyes widened in fright. "Uh, High King Azurill."

Hmm. Close enough to be on not only a first name, but a nickname basis, with the king?

"How about when it's just us, we dispense with all the cumbersome titles." I smiled, leaning in and bumping her shoulder with my own. "If you don't want to win, we're not really competition anyway, right?"

Faiza sighed gratefully, smiling with a hope that made me feel like the absolute worst. Here I was thinking of how to use her connections, while she was excited to find a friend among the vicious sharks they called ladies.

Despite all her time at court, she couldn't even recognize the predator circling around her.

Yet somehow, that fact made me want to fend off the others more than take a bite myself.

"Right. So, do you really think you can win?" she asked, her eyes sparkling with mischief.

I laughed lightly, "I certainly hope so! But I suppose we'll see. It would be quite the improvement from Ruby." I improvised, not wanting to seem like another one of these women only chasing a crown. "My Lord is…"

I trailed off, shuddering slightly, and her eyes instantly softened with compassion.

"I understand. Az and father have both always said he was quite *intense*," she said, putting a hand on my shoulder. I smiled at her softly, nodding my head.

"Ladies of Gemaria!" Emrys all but bellowed as he swept into the room, taking everyone's attention. He seemed to revel in it, smiling brightly at us all as the lights sparkled over his opal curls.

"You're all here today for the same thing, the Diamond Queen Competition! In a few moments, you'll be introduced to High King Azurill and the court formally as the competitors for this year's competition. During this, you'll learn the next steps and what the first challenge will be," Emrys explained, his opalescent-white hair shining under the hanging lights.

"Will we have time with High King Azurill?" Zumra asked, and I couldn't help rolling my eyes at Faiza. She snickered, covering her mouth with her hand.

Emrys seemed to be having trouble not rolling his own. He tilted his head at the emerald-haired lady and very patiently said, "You'll learn everything in a few moments, Lady Zumra. From High King Azurill himself, even."

With that, we were quickly shuffled into a line and arranged according to our courts. Thankfully, I found myself right behind Faiza, Ruby Court being shown in second after Diamond. Nerves clanged through me, and I bit down hard on my lower lip, trying to chase them away.

Faiza reached out a hand behind where she stood, and I grasped onto it, truly grateful for some solidarity in this cesspit.

"Aww," Zumra crooned from right behind me. "They've put the two lesser contestants up first, before getting to the real competitors. How sweet."

"Or they've put us in order according to the map." I snapped back, rolling my eyes as I ignored her huff.

Before I knew it, Faiza was called forward, and I instantly missed her. Zumra and Safira were spitting venom behind me. Everything from picking apart each lady present to how they'll win the challenges to how they'll change the palace once they're queen. It was ridiculous and everything I hated about this life.

I just had to remind myself of the goal.

A dead High King.

Vengeance for my family.

The ability to sleep without nightmares.

Peace.

CHAPTER 7

Jacinth

WHEN my name was called, I walked forward with my head held high, my dress flowing behind me as I prepared myself for what was about to happen. I walked from the antechamber into the throne room, finding Faiza standing to the side as I stepped toward the diamond throne.

The room itself was large and circular, crafted in a white, silver, and blue color palette, with diamonds sparkling along all the edges. I hated to admit it, but it was very tastefully done. Not too much, but just enough to show their station and wealth properly. Paintings depicting past kings and queens, battles, and moments in history were hung on the walls, while chandeliers dangled from the ceiling, and each column surrounding the space was crafted to mimic one of the gods, with gems adorning their visages and creating beautiful works of art from them.

And then my eyes turned toward the spot I'd been avoiding.

The throne.

And the Elf sitting on it.

The throne itself was cut from a giant diamond, and the piece was one smooth jewel that shimmered in the light. The diamond had a blue core that matched the kyanite shade used in throughout the room, while a matching blue was upholstered and affixed to the seat to make it comfortable to sit on.

My pink eyes connected with the teal blue ones of the Elf sitting upon the throne, and it felt like the entire world stopped.

High King Azurill.

He was, without a doubt, the most attractive man I'd ever seen. I stopped myself before I could cringe at the thought, and instead, bowed before the king I would never truly yield to.

I peeked up at him through my eyelashes as I rose. His hair was as teal as his eyes, and it had been shaved on the sides, with only some left on top so he could style it to the side in an unfairly handsome swoop that left some hair curling toward his left eye. He had a strong jawline, with pouty lips and, surprisingly, a nose that looked like it had been broken before. It didn't look bad at all, but the middle of the bridge was definitely a bit off.

He was wearing a teal jacket that was covered in diamonds and accented with kyanite, while silver embroidery matched the undershirt I could see underneath. A tattoo on his neck grabbed my attention, and I followed the design down to his shoulder, disturbed as I found myself wanting to chase the ink to see what lay beneath.

"Lady Jacinth Tawny," The High King greeted me with a nod of his head, his eyes roving over me. His stare was too intense, leaving me feeling stripped bare for a moment. As my fake name left his lips, a pang rang through me, and I found myself wishing I could scream my true name to the world. The name I left behind when I ran from my home because of this man.

"Your Majesty," I replied, dipping my head in deference, my skin crawling all the while.

It was always worse when monsters didn't look like the beast beneath.

And he looked more like a god than a monster; it was truly unfair.

"Welcome to Theiapolis," he rumbled, almost quietly despite the show he was putting on. He eyed my hair and eyes speculatively, setting me on edge. The need to derail his examination had me blurting out the first thing I could think of.

"Thank you, Your Majesty. The city is even more beautiful than I imagined. Not unlike its king." I simpered appropriately, wanting to puke when I looked briefly to the right and saw the approval shining in Lord Carnelian's eyes.

"It's certainly made even more beautiful with your presence, my Lady," he replied dutifully. I was sure he meant his words just as much as I did—that being, not at all.

Or perhaps I meant them too much. But I brushed that thought off quickly as the nonsense it was. I had to remember *who* this was.

I looked up, meeting his eyes, and he looked briefly surprised. But I looked deep into those teal orbs, imagining my family's blood soaking his hands, staining his clothes…and then I imagined stabbing him through the heart. The way he'd stabbed through mine.

"I thank you, Your Majesty." I forced my tongue to form the words.

"I look forward to getting to know you, Lady Jacinth." The way his mouth shaped my name was curious. Those pouty lips should be illegal on a man. I silently swore to Erodite. I knew she had to be responsible for this travesty.

"And I you, Your Majesty." The dull back and forth required of us was finally over, and Alfrikr stepped forward, nodding to the king once before taking me by the elbow and leading me to stand beside Faiza. She reached down and gripped my hand, and I squeezed it in return.

Zumra was announced next, and the king waved her off quickly to my amusement. She still seemed much too proud of herself, like she'd managed to accomplish something spectacular.

My breath caught as the next competitor was announced.

"Lady Sania Helmi, daughter of Lord Darcel Helmi of Pearl Court." The herald introduced her as she walked in.

My distant cousin, whose family currently ruled Pearl Court for lack of anyone else with Marit blood. It seemed the rumors were true, which I was somewhat pleased about. Her hair wasn't the same pink as mine *at all*, but instead a bright yet muted orange. A pink rose was set within it, with pink pearls dangling from it as if they could fool people into thinking her hair was any kind of pink.

It was styled similarly to mine, but her hair fell in long waves past her hips, while mine stopped right at them when unbraided. Her skin was as pale as mine, but with a golden flush from the sun. Her face was topped with delicate features, her nose surprisingly the same upturned shape as my own, but her lips were doll-like, small and shapely, while her eyes were wide and outlined in black.

Her dress was a pretty coral color that didn't clash with her hair and eyes the way bright pink might have. The tight corset was outlined with pearls, as was the line where it met the voluptuous skirt as it poofed out. Her necklace matched, with layers of pink pearls falling toward the center of her chest.

Her orange eyes met my pink ones briefly, flaring slightly and making me very nervous.

No, I was being silly. It was easy enough to imagine she would be threatened by a girl with pink hair, since she didn't have the historic coloring of Pearl Court's nobles. Everyone thought I was dead. A random girl with vibrant pink hair wasn't going to be mistaken for a child killed long ago.

My heart ached at the thought of my cousin Peony. She was so sweet, and we were the best of friends. The sight of her limp body being laid out on my bed, faking my death so Cor could protect me, was ingrained in my mind. Cor had played with us both often, and I knew how much he loved my family. It must have ripped him apart to have to do that.

I wondered if Sania could be a true cousin to me, like Peony was, or were she to ever realize the truth, would she tell the High King immediately?

Would I be family, in her eyes, or a threat?

Said king paid her just as much attention as the former lady, leaving me confused. She was, by all accounts, better behaved than Zumra, and I'd yet to see her act in the same entitled way Emerald's lady did.

When the competitor from Onyx was announced, I realized the king was only briefly greeting them before they took their place beside us.

I was the outlier.

I shivered, dreading what that might mean, but forced myself to focus. These women were my competition, and I needed to know them to beat them.

Lady Ophira Nephrite of Onyx Court was beautiful, as they all were. With dark black skin topped with shining golden hair and eyes. The deep black hair that Onyx was once famous for had been bred out long ago, with gold being the dominant color for many years now. She wore a golden dress that was studded with onyx across it, and it was quite a striking look, I had to admit.

Lady Safira Mazarine was next, followed by Lady Amatista Iolanthe of Amethyst Court. Her amethyst-colored hair and eyes were set in a beautiful, sharp face. Her dress was so deep a purple, it was practically black, with small beads in the same dark hue covering the cloth. It had amethysts set into the design, including trailing along her sweetheart neckline, which plunged just a bit deeper than normal. Her sleeves were off the shoulder, with beads at the top that hung delicately, before a transparent tulle billowed out, before being brought back together and gathered at her wrist, where delicate lace circled them.

Her gaze was as sharp as her face, and she took everything in with the kind of calculation that told me she was playing to win.

"Lady Allirea Beryl, daughter of Lord Eirian Beryl of Opal Court." The Gemholder called next, and I watched as a woman just as gorgeous as the rest walked out. Couldn't one of them have been unattractive? It was truly unfair to have to compete against these women when I was nowhere near their caliber. What was Lord Carnelian thinking?

Allirea's deep black skin was topped with opalescent white hair and eyes that, in the light, seemed to shine with all sorts of colors, just like Emrys. Only the color was even more interesting on Lady Allirea. The contrast against her skin was stunningly beautiful, and I felt my heart sink as my chances of winning seemed to drop ever lower.

But I had no choice, I had to find a way.

It wasn't just my life that depended on this, Ula's did too. And it was the only chance I'd have to avenge my family. The memory of my parents' dead eyes haunted me, and this could be just the thing to make the vision disappear forever.

Allirea gave her customary greeting to the High King, her oval face tilted down slightly and her tone soft, before taking her place among us. We were now in a semicircle before the Diamond throne, with the rest of the court arranged behind us, leaving about ten feet of space between us.

Azurill stood then, looking regal in a way that made me want to gouge his stupidly pretty eyes out. "Welcome, everyone, to the Diamond Queen Competition!"

A rush of cheers rang out, and Azurill smiled at the crowd, but it looked just the slightest bit forced.

"Each of your noble courts has done me a great honor, putting forth a lady from your lands to compete for the chance to become my wife and the next Diamond Queen. This tradition is one of our oldest and most noble, dating back to before the courts were brought together by the first High King," he explained, his tone dropping and becoming more serious. "I hope to find among these competitors a wife and queen who will be everything both I and this kingdom need. Our challenges were designed to find just such an individual among those gathered here."

"So, I thank you, my Lords, for bringing such lovely ladies before me." He continued, looking down at us from his throne before turning his eyes back to the crowd behind us. "But I'm sure you're all eager to find out which lady will win the coveted crown and be my bride?"

The crowd cheered once more, while I bit the inside of my lip to stop myself from sneering. He was *charming*, and that was a problem. Seeing the truth through that charm would be a challenge. Men like him put on airs all the time, hiding beneath a façade. But I was determined to rip it open and claw out the truth of him.

Revealing the monster that I knew lived beneath his stupidly perfect tanned skin.

"Then let us not delay!" Azurill smiled widely, "The first competition will take place in three days. Tonight, we will start by hosting a ball where I will begin getting to know each competitor. That will give them two full days to prepare for the challenge afterwards."

He smirked slightly, but his pointed ear twitched as if irritated. He watched the crowd, who were eating all this up, excitedly tittering to one another about what the first challenge would be and the excitement of a ball. He seemed to relish making them all metaphorically scoot to the edge of their seats.

"There will be eight challenges in total." He finally announced, his teal eyes gleaming. "Meaning at the first challenge, no one will be eliminated, ensuring we have two competitors for the final bout. We will begin with a show of talent! Each competitor will showcase a talent for us, allowing us to learn a bit about each of the ladies competing!"

A show of talent? That was certainly not the cutthroat activity I expected out of this farce.

My mind began running through possibilities for my talent, and I nearly missed the moment Azurill concluded his speech. The Gemholder banged a scepter on the ground, and everyone dropped to their knees. Thankfully, I was only a split second behind everyone else, and I didn't think anyone noticed my blunder.

The king made his way down the dais and out of the room, his curious eyes meeting mine briefly before turning his head and leaving. A shiver made its way down my back, the ghost of his stare not leaving me until I made it all the way back to my room.

The ball was to take place in a few hours, and I was surprised to find a bevy of maids and stylists bustling into my room to get me ready as soon as I walked in. I was quickly taken out of the dress I'd arrived in, and wrapped in a soft and stupidly plush light grey velvet robe as my hair was undone, only to be brushed and wrapped up onto my head, with the shorter front layers left flying free.

They cleaned my face, only to darken my eyes and pinken my cheeks, painting a stunning rouge color across my lips, while a light dusting of shimmering powder was pressed on what seemed to be every inch of my skin. Once they were finished, I was brought over to a dressing area that contained a tall threefold mirror, and a low oval stand I stepped up onto. It seemed like a mere blink of an eye, and they had me transformed with whatever magic they were clearly working.

I was never a fan of red before. The color was much too similar to blood for my liking, and it always stirred thoughts I felt best left suppressed. But this was…I mentally sighed, begrudgingly forced to admit that it was absolutely stunning.

Across my forehead dangled a ruby, attached to a diamond piece that connected to a cluster of rubies and diamonds that sat within my hair itself. The dress was a ruby red to represent the court, but it was packed with actual rubies and diamonds, and even a bit of kyanite. There was a high collar that swept behind my neck, tilted away from me, and did not constrict at all. A red tulle cape fell from beneath it to the floor.

The dress sat off my shoulders, the neckline contouring to my chest. The bodice was ornate, with diamonds creating a crisscrossing pattern across the cups that covered my breasts, with rubies sitting between each space they created within the design, and a giant one sitting right between my breasts. Under the cups, the diamonds and rubies created a swirling pattern, with a few kyanite gems added into the design for a pop of color—and a nod to the High King.

The skirt was large, larger than anything I'd ever worn, at least. I could already imagine it twirling across the floor, the diamonds and rubies stretching out across the top of it, like rays of the sun coming off the end of the bodice. Small diamonds fell the rest of the way to the floor, like small stars dotting the bottom that shone in the light as I twisted the skirt back and forth.

The skirt would surely lift and twirl in the way I used to imagine when I was a little girl, dreaming of attending my first ball after entering society. I might even have dreamed of dancing with the High King himself, not that I'd ever admit to that now, even under pain of death.

I remembered one particular day when my mother discussed the responsibilities of a lady with me. How, as the eldest daughter of House Marit, I'd be married to a lord of high standing, with a palace of his own for me to live in one day.

"What could be grander than the palace of the High King?" I'd asked, and she'd laughed merrily, brushing my hair back from my face.

"You're right, my pearl." My father had spoken from the doorway, making my mother huff fondly. "Only the best will do for my daughter. We'll ensure you wear the diamond crown, ruling as queen beside the High King, hmm?"

I'd seen the genuine promise in his eyes. He surely saw the benefit of his daughter marrying the king; what lord wouldn't? But it was his softer promise that night as he tucked me in that shone as brightly as a diamond in my memory.

"While I'd be quite pleased to see you crowned queen, little love, I want you to know that's not what's most important to me. I want you to find love and happiness in your marriage, like I've found with your mother. So if the day comes and you change your mind, I will always support your choice."

Knowing that even as lord, he still valued my happiness over his political power, I knew I had been immeasurably lucky to have him as a father. If Azurill hadn't taken him from me, I would have had a future of love and happiness, instead of one full of strife and fear.

CHAPTER 8

Jacinth

"So, what should I expect tonight?" I asked, making my way to the ballroom.

"Dancing," my shadow replied gruffly. His purple braids had small diamonds placed within them now, and he'd switched from armor to more courtly attire that would blend in as he followed me around. The blue suit jacket was trimmed in silver and had a large diamond on the back, delineating the guards even as they blended in.

I sighed heavily, rolling my eyes back at him.

"Thank you, Alfrikr, I would never have figured that out," I replied sarcastically, giving him an overly bright smile I knew he'd see the truth of.

He huffed, but I noticed a small smile curling up before he caught himself. We continued walking for a moment before he heaved a put-upon sigh. "The High King will use tonight to dance and speak with each of the competitors. He can't really get a good first impression just from you all being introduced to the court."

"So he's trying to get an idea of what we're actually like?" I asked, my eyebrow rising.

"Basically." He nodded once in confirmation. "He can still only get so much from a limited interaction, of course, but this is your opportunity to catch his attention."

He eyed me speculatively, and I couldn't help feeling that same self-conscious need to hide.

"What?" I eventually snapped, and he actually laughed a bit. I hadn't been sure he even knew how to do that until now.

"That," he said, as his smile widened. "You put on a good show of courtly grace in the throne room earlier, but alone, you seem much more…"

He trailed off for a moment, tilting his head to the side as he thought it over.

"Authentic." He concluded with a satisfied smirk, even as my stomach dropped. "If you want a piece of advice?"

I nodded eagerly. If he knew the king well and knew what he was looking for, I definitely needed that information. Knowing how to play this to ensure I got his attention would be a definite boon.

"Az will like that. Show him there's more to you to than a title and a pretty face." Alfrikr informed me, making me frown slightly.

Him wanting someone *authentic*, versus a pretty but empty-headed wife on his arm, didn't quite fit with the pompous asshole I always imagined him to be. Maybe he just didn't want to be bored.

I certainly couldn't show him the *real* me. That would end with me quite dead, after all. But I could show him a facsimile of my authentic self. It couldn't hurt to show him *some* of the truth of me, if it would entice him, just not *all* of it.

Alfrikr shadowed my steps as the noise coming from the ballroom grew louder the closer we got to its doors. My heart was beating twice as fast as the steps that brought me to it. My breath caught in my throat as I walked through the open doors and got my first glimpse of the room inside.

I'd heard plenty of legends about the Sacred Gems, of course, but never in my life did I think I would ever see them.

The circular, domed room was at least ten stories high, making those of us on the ground look like ants in comparison. But the height was necessary to fit the large centerpiece. The palace had supposedly been built around this very spot, and the high kings became the sworn protectors of the stones that now dominated the middle of the room.

Gigantic gems, of a size I didn't even know were possible, stood before me. Diamonds dominated the arrangement, but every other gem that we drew magic from was also present. The kaleidoscope of colors in varying sizes was all pointing toward the sky, growing straight out of the ground and coming up through the floor. The most massive piece was a diamond larger than many buildings, and bigger by far than any of the others, in the dead middle of the bouquet of oversized jewels.

Some, like the shining pink pearl that caught my eye, was a rounded, not quite full circle, growing from the ground like a giant mushroom cap.

Above them, the ceiling had a circular window in place, allowing the moon to shine down and illuminate the gems. It allowed different colors to shine within the facets of each side of the jewels and project around the room, casting a variety of shades on the walls and floor. The domed shape of the ceiling meant it appeared like the arches surrounding the room were swaying towards the gems, drawing every eye in the room to that one point no matter where you tried to look.

Legend said that the gems were a gift from the gods, the tool by which the Elves had been granted magic, and looking at the magnificence before me, I could very well believe it. These were not normal gems in any way, shape, or form. There was something otherworldly about them, besides their abnormal size.

Alfrikr subtly nudged my arm, and I started, not realizing I'd been caught up in staring at them from the entrance. I forced my feet to move, and a waiter quickly rushed up to me with a glass of some sparkling, light blue drink.

I thanked them with a nod, and they shot me a surprised, but grateful look in return. I realized my misstep immediately; nobles didn't thank servants for doing their jobs. I felt eyes on me, but held my chin up high and began to make a slow circle of the room.

"Lady Jacinth." I turned, finding, to my relief, Faiza was striding towards me. Her turquoise hair was pulled back into a complex updo, with a few strands left in the back to hang in long curls. Her dress was a beautiful light blue, like spun candy, with a lace overlay dotted with diamonds throughout.

"Lady Faiza." I greeted her with a smile, and she linked her arm with mine, falling into step with me immediately.

"I was a bit worried about traversing the court on my own," she admitted, biting her lip slightly. "Father told me we were encouraged to mingle. He said even if I don't win, I could meet someone who'd suit."

"And are you keeping your eyes peeled for someone in particular?" I eyed her, and she flushed lightly.

"Maybe," she whispered, eyes looking anywhere but at me.

I laughed lightly, finally getting her to meet my eye. I shook my head at her, "You have nothing to worry about with me, I promise."

She relaxed a bit at the reminder, and she smiled shyly before it slowly shifted into a sad frown. "Father would never allow me to marry someone like him, unfortunately."

"Who?" I asked, my brow rising. "And why not?"

"Brokk," she admitted, brown cheeks blushing prettily. "He's the son of an Earl, like myself, but he's from Ruby and father—"

She cut off immediately, looking mortified as her other hand came up to cover her mouth. "Oh, Veritx. I'm so sorry, Jacinth, I truly meant no offense! I just—"

"Faiza!" I snapped, cutting off her babble before she went any further. She looked so embarrassed, and a bit scared, like she'd ruined any potential friendship between us already. *If she only knew.*

"I promise I'm not upset." I chuckled, unable to contain my amusement. "Your father is probably being cautious, and I can't blame him when it comes to his daughter's future."

She relaxed instantly, seeming satisfied. After a moment, she added, "Brokk isn't like his father. That's why he came here to serve as a guard. His older brother is just like him, sadly, and they both made Brokk miserable."

"So you two know each other well then?" I teased, making her skin darken further.

"I spent a summer here at court a few years ago," she confessed, trying to hide a fond smile. "Az and I have been friends for much of our lives, but Brokk had been new to Diamond then. We spent time together, exploring the city and palace, or sitting out in the gardens."

She trailed off dreamily, and I wondered if there was anything I could do— *No.*

What I should be doing is seeing how this could help *me*. Faiza seemed determined for us to be friends, and Brokk was from Ruby, for all he had left years ago. Maybe the two could help me with my own plans.

I wasn't here to make friends or play matchmaker. I didn't have the luxury of it, much as I may have wished it were different. But *Erodite*, those long-forgotten childish wishes seemed determined to rise once more. *This* is what I had once expected my life to be, and the loss of it choked me for a moment as the grief overwhelmed me.

"Oh, there he is," she whispered, clutching at my arm. Turquoise eyes found mine, and her nerves made that deep-seated instinct rise again.

"Go talk to him." I urged her, a smile growing.

"I can't." She shook her head. "It wouldn't be right for me to approach him while supposedly competing for the king's affections," she muttered lowly, and I tried to stifle my laugh.

"Let's see if we can get the king's attention then," I told her mischievously, and her eyes widened. I began to steer us toward where he stood, and Faiza shook her head frantically.

"Lord Brokk," I called as we approached, and fiery, orange-red eyes met mine before quickly skipping over to Faiza and widening briefly.

He turned to us fully, and I took him in. His short orange-red hair was swept to the side, similar to the king's, except Brokk's hair was merely cropped short on the sides instead. He wore a black jacket over his doublet, with gold sewn into the large lapels, making it shine under the many lights bobbing through the air. Golden chains crossed down the middle, and the chain at his neck held a single ruby within it, the one and only nod to his actual court, outside the sword on his belt, which contained a large ruby on the pommel.

"Lady Jacinth, Lady Faiza." He nodded to us both, an amused smile quirking his lips. His eyes skipped back to his charge, the back of Lady Safira's cobalt hair all I could see of her, before turning back to us.

"Lady Faiza was just telling me about the summer she spent here, and when we spied you, I figured it was only polite to say hello. Especially with us being from the same court."

"Of course," he said, lips turning down briefly as if the mere mention of Ruby Court soured his mood. Good to know, certainly, but not why I was here.

"How have you been?" Faiza finally spoke up quietly, and he zeroed in on her immediately, as if he'd just been waiting for the excuse. I was forced to hide my smile before they noticed.

"I've been fine," he replied with a slight smile, before tilting his head to the side, "Though the city is much less interesting without your presence." His brow quirked upwards while a smirk grew on his lips.

Faiza blushed again, looking down and biting her lip, before looking back up, a new bravery on her face. But as she opened her mouth, another voice sounded from behind us.

"Ah, I see your guard duties have seemingly been extended to the other ladies as well now, Brokk." The king stepped up beside his guard, and I caught myself before I could glower at him.

High King Azurill was dressed in his colors, with a dark blue jacket embroidered in silver and bedazzled with diamonds across the high collar. Diamonds had also been used in the design of the jacket, accenting the embroidery, and covering the shoulder caps in rows that hung off the side and shook as he turned to look at us directly. The white shirt he wore underneath was unbuttoned unfairly low, exposing part of his chest, along with a bit of the mysterious tattoo that slithered down from his neck. A silver vest with blue ties rested atop it, pulling the outfit together.

Faiza and I both curtseyed, though I grit my teeth through it. When we rose, the king was smirking slightly, eyeing us both.

"Have the ladies of the realm forsaken their own guards now?" He joked, making Brokk roll his eyes, while I gave an overdramatic gasp, putting a hand over my heart.

"I would never hurt poor Alfrikr in such a way!" I played into his joke, hoping this was the kind of *authenticity* my poor guard had meant. I turned my head back to Alfrikr, "You mustn't listen to such lies, darling. I think the High King is merely the jealous sort."

I turned back to face the king with my brows raised and a smirk on my own face. "I think having two of his *eight* dates tonight, paying attention to another man, has hurt his feelings."

Faiza giggled hysterically beside me, trying to choke the sounds back as she covered her mouth. Brokk's mouth had dropped open while he blinked quickly. Azurill, however, had an unexpectedly delighted look upon his face. Those blue-green eyes positively lit up as he stepped closer to me, and his smirk grew exponentially.

"Would you not be hurt, Lady Jacinth?" He rumbled, his voice lowered so only I could hear him clearly. "To see such lovely women here to see you have shifted their attentions?"

I leaned closer, fluttering my eyelashes at him coquettishly, as I whispered, "Perhaps, if my ego was so delicate as yours."

His head tipped back on a full laugh, and I noticed another man with icy blue hair, containing only the slightest tinge of green, blinking even more rapidly than Brokk at the sight. He shifted closer, as if curious, but kept his distance. It took me a few seconds to place him as the younger prince, Ruri.

When Azurill finished laughing, he smiled at me and bowed his head, "Well, since my ego is so clearly delicate, you must make it up to me with a dance, my Lady."

"Oh." It was my turn to blink now. There was a lot of that going around, apparently. "I…"

I swallowed hard. I had, of course, practiced dancing with Sienna before coming here, and despite the fact that I had yet to actually dance in front of people, I was looking forward to the act itself. Dancing had always been my favorite as a child, and I'd kept the gracefulness gained from my countless lessons and hours of practice.

But to dance with *this* man?

It would taint everything I loved about the freedom dance offered. My eye caught on Lord Carnelian, who was hovering around the edge of the room, watching me with calculating eyes.

I hardened myself. Ula's life was on the line, after all. There was more to this than just my own vengeance. I would need to get close to him to enact that anyway, so I needed to get used to his presence sometime.

There. Perfectly acceptable reasoning.

"Of course, Your Majesty." I nodded, taking his hand. "I would hate to have you absent your own competition to recover from such a blow."

He chuckled deeply, leading me to the dance floor with a large hand on my lower back that warmed my skin even through layers of fabric. He leaned his head down to whisper in my ear, and the chills that spread over me from the disgust of having the mastermind of my family's murder so close could at least pass as being affected by him in a more sensual manner.

Which I *wasn't.*

"I can't say many ladies have dared to speak to me in such a way. At least not ones who actually want to win. Only ones like Faiza who couldn't care less," he said, his question quite implicit.

"Hmm. Is that so?" I asked, not giving an answer to an effect to see where I could lead the conversation.

Give little, take a lot. Sienna's instruction rang in my ear.

"Yes," he countered, sweeping me into his arms as we began to dance. Our hands clasped together, with one of his resting on my waist, while my other lay on his shoulder. I relished the movements, enjoying the feel of my slippers brushing the dance floor, but I couldn't lose myself in the dance, not when I had other things to focus on. But it unfortunately seemed like he wasn't going to say more.

Otherworld damn him. I had to get him talking.

"Well, fret not, Your Majesty." I smiled winningly. "I'm certainly not here for no purpose."

His eyes met mine as we twirled around the other couples dancing. Teal clashing against pink as we stared at one another, neither looking away. His lips tilted up, and he huffed softly, even as we moved in sync across the floor.

It was too easy to dance with him. Some partners just clicked better than others, and I was furious at how naturally we moved together.

"Well then, what is this purpose?" he asked, and I barely caught it, in my peripheral, but as he glanced over at Lord Carnelian, a suspicious glint appeared in his gaze.

Uh oh.

I forced myself to giggle merrily as I turned in his arms, directing his attention back to me.

"I would think that quite obvious." I made a show of looking him up and down when he spun me out, and hated that I couldn't ignore how fucking gorgeous he was, even with the blood staining his hands.

"Most ladies here would look more to the crown on my head than at me directly," he stated bleakly, though he grinned wolfishly a moment later. "Though none have ever complained either."

"I don't doubt it." The words slipped from my lips before I realized it. But his eyes lit up in response, looking like lapis lazuli in this light, and he pulled me flush against him.

"A charmer, aren't you?" he whispered, before releasing my waist to tug lightly on a strand of pink hair. "And a sight for sore eyes, at that. Like Erodite, come again. We haven't seen anyone with this shade in far too long."

I forced my muscles to stay loose and relaxed, to not go stiff all at once like they desperately wanted. I chuckled, proud that I had managed to get the sound out of my mouth, and shook my head at him.

"Ah, if I knew I'd be compared to a goddess, I'd have forced my father to let me tag along with Lord Carnelian sooner." I gave him a sultry smile, "If I'm Erodite, does that make you Veritx come again? You have the inflated ego to believe yourself godlike, I think."

I winked, even as his crown of diamonds winked back at me in the light, as if taunting me.

His sudden laughter was shocking and bright. Not dissimilar to his first laugh when I caught him off guard. A true, full laugh.

"Perhaps it's vain to claim such godliness; we wouldn't want to upset them after all." He smirked. "Perhaps you are like a mini Erodite. A Mini-Dite." He chuckled, looking quite pleased with himself, while I rolled my eyes at his ridiculousness.

"Then you certainly can't claim Veritx. Perhaps you should be Veri, as in very self-important." I countered, and he stilled for a moment, blinking owlishly before that same laugh rang out again, and I couldn't help joining him.

"I can't say I've laughed so much at one of these things before," he said when he calmed, a warm look in his eyes. But as Lord Carnelian circled, he seemed to remember himself…as did I. We both straightened a bit, and as the song came to a close, we slowed to a stop. He took my hand, lifting it to his mouth and pressing his lips to my skin in a soft kiss.

My heart beat in my chest became very noticeable, the sound ringing in my ears. I only hoped my family forgave me for the sins I'd have to commit to win this.

"I shall look forward to seeing your talent at the first competition, Mini-Dite," he murmured, his lips a searing heat on my skin.

"As I look forward to astonishing you with it, Veri." I returned with a curtsy, my brow rising.

He chuckled, leaning close to whisper in my ear, "You could just call me Az."

"As you could call me Jac." His own brow rose at that, and he nodded deeply before a woman with long opalescent hair and eyes appeared beside him.

"You need to make the rounds. Dance with Zumra before she explodes, please. Her pointed hints are getting on my last nerve." She directed him in a whisper, surely expecting me not to be paying such close attention. She gave me a smile when she noticed me watching them.

"Lady Arianell," She introduced herself, "I'm in charge of event organization here in Diamond. It's lovely to meet you, Lady Jacinth."

"And you, Lady Arianell." I nodded and noticed Emrys making his way over.

"Ah, sister!" he called, and she rolled her eyes at me before muttering *"Brothers"* under her breath and walking to meet him.

I was glad for the moment alone, however, and quickly found a waiter who carried a red drink with rose-gold flames on top, tasting of cherry and lime. The alchemy of drink mixtures in Gemaria was just as convoluted as its magic.

I somehow managed to find a quiet spot along one of the walls, set back from the arches that made up the dome above us. The alcoves sat just past each arch, creating a more intimate sitting area, and most were already occupied. This one had a sapphire-blue sofa with diamonds running along the edges, and I swiftly relaxed into it, arranging my skirts as I did so. I closed my eyes, breathing deeply before taking another sip.

I wanted to beat myself up for getting lost in the game for a moment, because that's exactly what it all was—*a game*. To survive this court, this competition, and Lord Carnelian, I needed to don that veil of truth and believe the lies I spewed.

I just didn't expect it to be so easy.

The high king, or *Az*, as he said, was not what I had been expecting. I'd expected a cold and pompous king who was excited to have women fighting over him. A man not unlike Lord Carnelian, really. But instead I found a charming and seductive man who was almost too easy to spend time with.

I needed to get my head back in the game. A few minutes of conversation wouldn't erase the past, and I was determined to make him pay for what he did.

CHAPTER 9

Azurill

SHAKING my head, I made my way over to where Zumra was eyeing me, as indiscreet as Elvenly possible. I needed to get the encounter with Lady Jacinth out of my head, and the superficial conversation this particular lady would provide would undoubtedly not help much.

The moment she'd walked into the throne room earlier was like flashing back to the past. Her hair and eye color were so alike those of the prior ruling family of Pearl that it was uncanny. It felt like the past was haunting me for a moment before reason finally caught up with me.

Those from Ruby Court had ended up with pink eyes and hair before, after all. Red wasn't so far from pink, and all it took was one pairing of red and white for it to happen. The variation had shown up in other courts before. *That was totally normal*, I reminded myself.

What was more concerning was that she was here on behalf of Lord Carnelian, whose snakelike eyes were glued to our every step on the dance floor. Ruri's warnings echoed in my head, despite trying to tell myself there was no reason to believe them yet.

But my heart ached for my lost brother, and I couldn't rule out that Carnelian might have done *something*.

Even if he hadn't, it was clear he wanted to. Either this girl was a spy, or she was a lure, trying to win a crown and get a member of Carnelian's bloodline on the throne. Whichever it was, I had to resist. I wouldn't allow Carnelian's machinations to ruin what my forefathers had built.

But those pink eyes…there was something haunted about them that drew me in, wanting to know more. And her personality was indeed as charming as

I'd expect of Erodite herself. Perhaps I should have compared her to Fortuna, since she was from Ruby Court, but the pink hair screamed Pearl, and I found it an apt comparison.

A beautiful lure was a distinct possibility. She was undeniably gorgeous, with wide eyes, delicate features, and a body that sculptors would ache to replicate. But her conversation hadn't seemed contrived at all, and I had to admit that she was much less proper than I'd expected of a lady from Ruby. Faiza had even seemed to enjoy being in her company. Perhaps I could get her to tell me more, and figure out what exactly Lady Jacinth's plans were, and how worried I should be.

Emerald-green banished my thoughts of cotton candy-pink as I approached a practically vibrating Lady Zumra. She didn't speak, honoring the court custom of the king having to make the first move. I nearly rolled my eyes at the ancient rules, appreciating more when those little ones were ignored. The newer generations were more apt to do so, but some nobles refused to advance with the times.

"Lady Zumra," I greeted her, holding out a hand reluctantly, and putting on a facade that would make me seem less displeased as I did so. "Would you honor me with a dance?"

"Your Majesty," She curtsied, emerald-green eyes glittering with satisfaction as she took my hand, "I would be honored."

I walked her onto the dance floor and placed my hand around her waist while hers found my shoulder, our other hands clasping together. We began to move, and she, of course, perfectly danced each step, but yet I couldn't help thinking she lacked the natural grace in her movements that my last dance partner had possessed.

"I'm so thrilled to be representing Emerald Court in this competition, Your Majesty." She smiled up at me, some cross of sultry and polite courtliness that didn't quite achieve either. "I confess I have long wished to be able to get to know you on more…familiar terms."

"It's an honor to have you among the competitors." I smiled blandly. "I'm looking forward to getting to know all of you better."

"I know you'll find me a most adept choice of Diamond Queen, Your Majesty." She squared her shoulders, looking determined. "I have been trained to be a perfect wife since I was a child. I have the looks to stand beside you and create a child that would carry on the traditional look of the high kings. Not unlike your own mother. Your father chose well, ensuring his wife's coloring would not taint his own."

Her words left me speechless. While women had often tried listing off their many characteristics to me in the hope of being chosen as my queen, none had ever brought my parents into it, claiming my father chose my mother for such a ridiculous reason. Unfortunately, my silence only allowed her to continue.

"Her sapphire hue certainly darkened your own, but it maintained the blue-green coloring perfectly." She smiled, looking pleased with herself. "My own emerald coloring will balance that sapphire with green and ensure another generation."

"I appreciate your perspective, Lady Zumra." I finally forced myself to say politely, despite wanting to walk away without another word. "Though, I will consider all competitors equally, regardless of coloring."

"Of course, Your Majesty." She smiled, but her bearing screamed her insincerity. Her shoulders were stiff as we danced, but she forced herself to relax after a few moments. "I know you will choose the correct wife. After all, you will have to spend the rest of your life with them, and trust them to run your household."

I nearly sighed miserably. I had hoped to trust them with more than that. To have a partner who could help me with everything. Someone who could be an equal. My only hope now was finding someone in this competition who could be that. Sadly, with only eight competitors, one of whom wasn't a real option, I didn't have much hope to work with.

I knew Faiza and I would never work. She was more like a little sister to me than anything else. Not to mention that she had no desire to be queen. She'd only agreed to this for lack of any other options from Diamond, but I'd never force her into something that would make her miserable.

Listening to Zumra go on and on now, I was surer than ever that my own misery was guaranteed.

When the song ended, I had to hide my gleeful smile that it was over, "Lady Zumra, I thank you for the dance."

"It was an honor, Your Majesty." She smiled, but it dipped as I kissed her hand as quickly as possible, moving back and nodding at her. Arianell found me right away, leaning in to whisper in my ear.

"After your dance with Lady Jacinth, you need to put a bit more effort into not looking miserable, I'm afraid." She sounded amused, her expression showing that even more clearly as I pulled back to look at her, my eyebrows creased in confusion.

"What do you mean?" I asked, tilting my head to the side slightly.

"You seemed to enjoy the dance with her. Laughing, smiling, and whispering into her ear." She raised her brows with a growing smirk. "Your interaction with Lady Zumra by comparison was quite obviously cold."

I groaned, tipping my head back in aggravation. "It wasn't like that. I'm trying to figure her out."

"Oh, I bet you are," she replied sarcastically, opal eyes shimmering with mirth.

"Not like that," I snapped back, tasting the partial lie like ash on my tongue, "She could be a spy, for Veritx's sake. We need to know if Lord Carnelian is up to something. Ruri can't investigate her in the same way I can. I'll leave him to handle the lords, and I'll handle her."

"Mhm." Arianell hummed, looking entirely unconvinced. "Well, for now, you need to *investigate* elsewhere, Lady Safira in particular. You can *handle* Lady Jacinth again later."

I just barely managed to prevent myself from letting my eyes roll, both at Arianell and her suggestion. Safira was just as bad as Zumra, only without the same level of overconfidence. But I dutifully made my way over to her, asking her to dance. Sweeping onto the floor, she smiled brightly at me.

"This must all be quite tiring for you, Your Majesty. Especially with all that's gone on." She looked sympathetic, her brows creasing and lips turning down, but her words came out unnaturally, making me think they hadn't been hers at all.

"Dancing with eight beautiful ladies of the realm?" I raised my brows, and her mouth opened and closed for a moment before she finally settled on an answer.

"Dancing with us all while grieving," she replied softly, looking down at her feet as she followed the steps of the dance to avoid my gaze.

I knew she'd lost her mother five years ago, and her father had been wrecked ever since. I felt for her, truly. Despite many of the ladies' actions at court, no doubt spurred on by their father's, they were Elves with hearts that bled just the same.

"I thank you for the concern, Lady Safira," I told her earnestly. "Grief has a way of dulling the edges of everything in your life."

"Yes, it does," she agreed softly, her hand beginning to play with the diamonds hanging from my shoulder. "I think we could truly comfort one another in our grief, Your Majesty. As your wife, I would always be there to support you."

An uncomfortable feeling crawled along my skin. It always came back to this. Even a genuine moment of warmth was stolen away by the games of court.

"I suppose we will see how the challenges go, my Lady," I told her, since it seemed to be the only response I could muster with any sincerity.

After several more dances with the ladies competing for my hand—who was I kidding, competing for the crown—I finally managed to steal away for a break. I grabbed a glass of champagne and drank it all down in one go before grabbing another and escaping into one of the alcoves.

"Your Majesty." A musical voice greeted me, and I nearly swore, *so much for escaping.* Looking up, I found Lady Sania sitting on an emerald-green sofa, her orange hair done in long curls that framed a delicate face with wide eyes, watching me with an amused smile quirking her pouty lips.

Taking her in, her hair and eye color slowly shifted in my mind's eye to candy pink, the color of the court her father ruled over. I shook myself quickly out of it, but the way everything pearl-related reminded me of Jacinth couldn't continue.

Dammit, I shouldn't even be calling her that. *Lady* Jacinth was the proper address. Flirting with her to find out her secrets was fine, but the genuine amusement and delight she stirred was a problem I needed to get a hold of quickly. Especially when I knew her coloring would give me nightmares, bringing back memories of a time in my life I wanted to forget. What I'd done might have been able to be hushed up among the other courts, but it never left my mind.

Besides, she was here for her lord, who wouldn't hesitate to stab me in the back if I turned for a moment. She was likely the same. Every single person at court was only working for their own advancement.

"Lady Sania, forgive me, I thought I was alone." I gave her a tight smile, which made her own broaden.

"Clearly." She patted the sofa cushion beside her, and I slowly moved to sit beside her, leaving enough room for propriety's sake.

"I promise I won't bite, Your Majesty." She giggled, and the sound warmed something within me. I had always been a sucker for a pretty face, I could readily admit. My attention on them may not last long, but the women never complained when they got it.

"What a shame." I teased her as I sank back into the sofa, my arm resting along the back of it as I tilted my body toward her.

She blushed prettily, the red on her cheeks making me smirk, and I lowered my eyes to survey her. She was wearing a pale pink ball gown with lines of actual pearls running down the skirt and a velvet bodice that hugged her breasts and lifted them.

"You looked as if you needed to hide," she said once she gathered herself, shifting in her seat. She alternated between looking down at her hands in her lap and up at me. The shift in conversation left me curious.

"Are you hiding here, my Lady?" I asked, raising a brow at her.

She bit her lip for a moment, and my eyes were drawn to the movement. "Perhaps. Or maybe I was just waiting for the right moment."

I chuckled, cocking my head to the side, "And is this the right moment?"

"It certainly seems to be, Your Majesty," she countered, an impish little smile on her face. Unlike Lady Zumra or Lady Safira, her flirting was more subtle. More like Jac's—*Jacinth's*—than the others. Though I had yet to dance with them all. Perhaps there were more ladies who knew how to properly flirt rather than shove their expectations in my face.

"And what does the right moment mean to you?" I asked her, leaning a bit closer, just to watch her blush again. This was a candidate I could flirt with without any of the complexities Ruby Court brought with it.

She cocked her head to the side, making the orange hair piled on top of her head shift slightly, while the curls hanging below it fell to the side, exposing her lily-white neck.

"I suppose it means having a chance to be alone with you. When there are so many of us all competing for your attention, it's quite a challenge," she explained, keeping her eyes lowered coquettishly.

"Well, you have me alone." I waved my arm, indicating the space around us was empty. "What now?"

She turned fully to face me then, her skirts ruffling with the movement and giving me a glimpse of matching pale pink heels. As pretty as the color was, I found myself wishing for a more vibrant shade.

"Why don't you tell me what you're looking for, Your Majesty?" She smiled slightly, fluttering her lashes over keen orange eyes.

I observed her quietly for a moment, debating whether to answer. The last thing I wanted was for these ladies to try to turn themselves into someone they thought I'd choose. I wanted to know their true selves, not a persona they'd don to win.

"Where would the fun of the challenge be if I told you, my Lady?" I smirked at her. "You'll just have to figure that out yourself."

Her lips twisted in what seemed to be an uncharacteristically sharp movement, but it disappeared as quickly as it came. The fierce look was so at odds with her demure attitude, I was sure I had to have imagined it.

Still, I knew no one in this game could be trusted. I would be keeping a wary eye on all of them until we found the truth of what had happened to my brother.

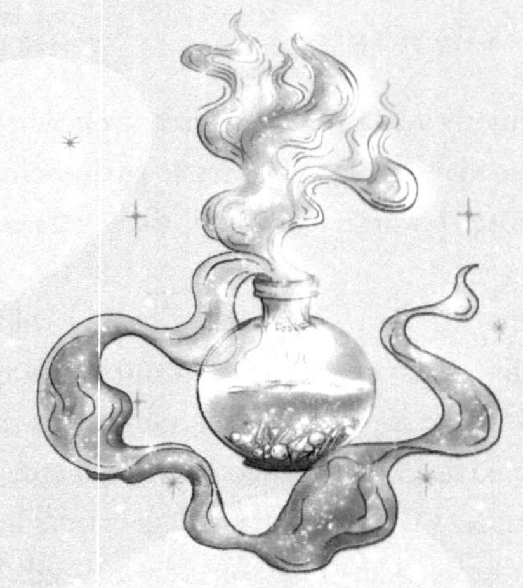

CHAPTER 10

Jacinth

THE ball last night had been tiring, but I knew we only had two days to prepare for the talent competition. Despite the fact that no one would be eliminated quite yet, I knew each challenge would be counted when determining who would win.

These challenges were not abstract. They were pointed. Az—*the High King,* I corrected myself mentally—and his council had created them specifically. They were all more than challenges. They were concocted to bring parts of us to the surface. Alfrikr said Az—*the High King! Ugh*—wanted someone authentic. These challenges would expose different parts of who we were at our core. He was trying to crack us all open, so he could see who the best wife and queen would be, for him and the realm.

That meant each trial would be a chance to prove myself to him. To show him parts of myself that were real. I laughed at the very thought of any genuine part of me being anywhere close to good enough to be queen, but it was the only strategy I thought might work. Carnelian said he'd ensure I won, but having now met Azurill, and seeing how untrusting he was of Carnelian, I couldn't count on that.

Not when my vengeance depended upon this. Not when Ula's life depended upon it.

First, I had to stop thinking of him as Az. I grimaced at the thought, knowing it would be too easy to begin separating the charming king from the ruthless murderer in my mind. I needed to remember who he truly was.

Today, I was determined to get to work. Faiza joined me, bringing me down hallways in all sorts of colors that reflected the different gems of all the courts, and finally into one that made my breath catch in my throat.

This hall was partly exposed, with rounded ceilings stretching high and curving upwards, and circular open sections where the daylight streamed through in pools of light. The pearlescent walls were trimmed with gold, and vibrant pink flowers stretched up the walls and grew across the ceiling, ringing each opening within it.

The floor was marble, with white, pink, and a bit of black swirling around it. Gold lined the marble, leading visitors down the path. The hallway was long, but there were doors on each side, with gold-lined pink marble steps leading up to each one.

Tears came to my eyes so quickly that I had to shut them before Faiza caught a glimpse. It just looked so much like a piece of Pearl Court—*of home*—that I was thrown into the past for a moment. My heart ached more than it had in years.

But I pulled myself together and opened my eyes to Faiza's concerned look, worry filling her turquoise orbs as her hand landed on my arm.

"Jacinth, are you okay?" she asked, her eyebrows creasing.

"I'm fine," I told her, forcing a smile. "It's just so beautiful, it's nearly overwhelming!"

Faiza's face cleared, her shoulders dropping as she relaxed. "It is, isn't it? Az's family updated the palace many times. Each time, they added more to represent the other courts. This is for Pearl Court."

She eyed me for a moment, "You know, with your coloring, you almost look like you belong here."

My eyes widened, but her impish smile broke out after a moment, making me force a laugh. I pushed her shoulder, like we were two friends joking around.

"Well, lucky me." I joked, "Now I'm here."

"Yes, you are," she chuckled, waving a hand toward the door to the left. "Here it is."

I looked at her to double-check she wasn't kidding, but she looked serious despite the faint smile still tilting her lips upwards.

I stepped up the stairs, following Alfrikr as he opened the double doors covered in pink flowers too close to the same shade as my own hair. I truly hoped no one thought twice about that coincidence.

As the doors opened fully, the room inside was revealed. Mirrors surrounded the space, with plenty of light coming in through the round opening in the ceiling, just like the hall outside. It filled the room with a sunny, floral scent, making it feel more like home than anywhere had felt in years.

I stepped in, heading for the back, where a music player sat on a small but ornate golden table. My steps bounced as I crossed the floor, the excitement running wildly through my veins. I set the music to play, ignoring Faiza watching curiously from the corner. It was only fair to let her watch after she'd set this up for me and even procured the music.

I let myself get lost in said music now. When I was a child, I was enthralled by the pixie carnivals that would come and entertain us with marvelous feats. While I'd always enjoyed the acrobats and lion tamers, it was the dancers who truly stole my focus. The way their bodies moved was mesmerizing, and I'd wanted to be just like them.

My parents had easily agreed to more dance lessons, since I'd needed to learn the proper dances as a lady anyway. But whenever I was good and performed a *proper* dance perfectly, I was able to practice the less *courtly* routines as well.

These days, I only ever danced through halls as I stole into and out of places. Being able to dance at the ball wasn't even the same as *this*. The dances were dramatic and acrobatic, with all sorts of flourishes I'd only ever seen the pixies bring to life. I'd lived for these dances as a child, and returning to them once more left me nearly overwhelmed.

I let my feet carry me across the floor, twisting and twirling in movements my muscles remembered like an echo through time. Just like my heart, they ached, but they remembered.

I spent hours practicing, getting the hang of the turns and twirls again, making sure my hands and feet were in the correct places, refamiliarizing myself with every flip and split, and starting over every time I made a minor mistake. But I couldn't have cared less, it was time well spent as far as I was concerned. I didn't even notice when Faiza eventually left.

Here, I could close my eyes and escape into the dance. The music washed over me like the ocean lapping the black sands of Jet Beach, bringing me up and down as the emotion rose and fell. The violin wailed and softened as if it felt the joy and pain consuming me, while the movements of the routine brought me into another world. A tragic one, perhaps, but I was used to that.

The magic of it all consumed me, until before I realized it, the glow of sunset was taking over the sky above me, washing the room from pink to orange.

It was enough to pull me out of the whirlwind. Panting and exhausted, my muscles screamed for rest, yet I felt wholly satisfied. Only that orange glow creeping along the pink left me frowning, thinking of the state of Pearl Court.

I didn't *want* to think about that, however. It was no longer my business, so I quickly left the room, finding poor Alfrikr slumped on the ground outside.

"Were you out here the whole time?" I asked, blinking in surprise.

"Of course I was," he grunted, standing back up. "I'm your guard. The last thing we want is one of the other competitors trying to off you while you're distracted."

My head reared back in shock. "Has that happened before?" His expression was grimly serious, adding more discomfort on top of my aching limbs.

"Not for a very long time," he answered reluctantly, the words seeming to be dragged from his lips. "Now, let's go. You'll be late for dinner."

"How long is a long time?" I pressed him as we began the walk back.

He groaned, shaking his head, "I shouldn't have even mentioned that."

"Well, too bad. You did." I smirked at him, and Alfrikr rolled his eyes, his head tipping side to side like he was debating with himself. Until finally, he released a sigh of resignation, watching my eager expression.

"You're not going to let this go, are you?" He asked, trying to look gruff and angry, but his twitching lips gave him away.

"Nope." I popped the 'p', making it very clear that, *no*, I would never just *let something go.*

His exaggerated sigh was certainly impressive, though.

"It was several competitions ago," He began as we walked the halls back to my room. His armor clanged softly with every step as my dance slippers whispered over the marble floors.

"The competition can get dangerous, that's not a secret. But it used to be much more perilous than it is now. The ladies were brutal and bloodthirsty in their quest for power." Alfrikr shook his head solemnly, his purple braids swaying with the movement. "Az's great-grandfather's competition was particularly bad, and one of the competitors decided to take out her competition."

I gasped, my hand flying to cover my mouth. I knew the prior competitions had been more treacherous, but I had no idea threats of that magnitude were at risk.

"For all her effort," he smirked slightly, "High King Alberich chose some-one else. But the memory is not forgotten." He eyed me pointedly, and my eyebrows scrunched in confusion.

"What does that mean?" I asked warily.

"The competitor who killed the other ladies was from Ruby Court," he revealed, looking surprised at my ignorance. "It's well known that those from Ruby will do whatever it takes to get the throne."

"But I don't—" I cut myself off before I could say anything incriminating. My eyes shot to Alfrikr, whose head was tilted to the side as he inspected me too closely. Panic clawed up my throat.

"But I don't have any intention of hurting anyone," I finished lamely, the lie tasting like poison on my tongue. I couldn't very well tell him that the oth-er ladies were safe from me because I only wished to hurt one specific person.

Not when he'd strike me down where I stood if he realized who my target was.

CHAPTER 11

Jacinth

"THIS seems a bit over the top," I whispered, my arm threaded through Faiza's as my wide eyes took in the craziness surrounding us.

Faiza giggled lightly. "It's the official start of the Diamond Queen Competition, of course, it's over the top."

Right. For all Faiza didn't enjoy the politics and underhandedness that came with being at court, she was still part of this world in a way I would never be. This was normal for her.

It was just more proof that I didn't belong here.

In another life, I thought wistfully, before forcing my mind onto more important matters.

The talent competition would be taking place in the city's arena rather than inside the palace, allowing all its citizens to come and watch as we made fools of ourselves for a man. Or a crown. Or an assassination, in my case.

It wasn't just the competition, however, as the entire city had been overtaken by this madness. Vendors were set up along the streets, with sweet confections and gorgeous accessories, bubbling drinks and fun toys for the children. A group of women was even handing out magical fancies to any who passed by. Some got a stick that sparked and sparkled at its end, while others got flowers that rapidly changed color, and I even saw funnels of fluffy clouds that children could shape to their heart's desire.

It was all a bit overwhelming, with loud noises and people running about, not to mention the explosion of colors that kept the eye darting every which way. Faiza led me through the vendor-lined street, each of us looking around to see if anything grabbed our attention. We had a bit of time before we had to arrive at the competition, and with our ever-alert and very stiff guards following closely behind us and refusing to let us out of their sight, they would undoubtedly ensure we didn't run late.

I may have been here on a mission of a different sort than anyone else, but there was no harm in having some fun while I did it, was there? If anything, it would make me more convincing in my role.

So I allowed myself to smile, wide-eyed with a magic I hadn't experienced since my childhood when the carnival would come to Pearl. We floated along, and I watched as the blue and pink pennants representing Diamond and Pearl Courts that were hanging off the roofs of the buildings we passed changed to the green of Emerald and the purple of Amythest as we made our way down the road.

"For you, my ladies," one of the women handing out treats said as we neared her.

"Oh, thank you." I smiled as she handed Faiza and me each something. Faiza quickly downed the mini cake she received, the bright gold frosting decorated with sapphire swirls and covered in a shimmering dust. She popped off the candy diamond that topped it, only to eat it as soon as the cake was gone. I switched focus to see what I'd received, only to find a clamshell in my hand, making my heart pound too loudly as my blood whooshed in my ears.

"That's a very lucky one you got." Another woman spoke, her face creasing with a soft smile. Elves aged so slowly that I knew humans considered us near-immortal. We could live many, *many* years before the signs of age found us. This woman must have been one of the oldest Elves I'd ever seen to have wrinkles lining her eyes like little scratches denoting her years on Adamah.

"Why is it lucky?" I managed to ask, my tongue trying to tie itself in knots as my palms began to sweat.

"It's said the goddess Erodite blesses one out of a hundred clams with her pearls. They're the rarest type of pearl, the ones found in those clams, very unlike the ones that grow from the land. Each god and goddess has their own rare types, of course. But—" She nodded slightly toward the shell in my hand, "It seems like it's Erodite who has a gift for you, child. Whatever it may be that's inside, don't let it be lost."

I laughed uneasily, but the woman's face remained earnest. Beside me, Faiza had stiffened uncomfortably, and she looked to the woman with a slight frown. I told myself I was being ridiculous, that Erodite had nothing to do with this, but my hand shook as I slowly opened the clamshell.

A gasp ripped its way out of my mouth before I could stop it. Inside was something that most certainly shouldn't have been there. Visions of the past flashed through my head as my chest hollowed out and I—I couldn't breathe—blood soaked the walls and dead eyes stared back at me and—

"Jacinth!" I didn't recognize my name as belonging to me. That wasn't what I was called, but it was *now*, and I came back to myself in a rush to find Faiza's worried turquoise eyes staring at me, her body nearly radiating alarm as her hands shook my shoulders.

I gulped in a breath of air, looking for the woman to ask her how—but she was gone.

Uneasy suspicion crawled through me. It felt like every eye in the kingdom was on me as I looked around, positive someone would call me out at any moment.

"Jacinth?" Faiza called once more. "What's wrong? What was it?"

"Nothing." I nearly yelped. "It's nothing." I shifted on my feet, my silver slippers crinkling with the movement.

"Uh huh," Faiza replied skeptically, but her concern was very real, and I wished for a moment I could tell her the truth, just for the opportunity to discuss this with someone.

But how could I ever explain it? My dead mother's necklace was in my *hand*. I recognized it immediately. It was made of the rarest pearls, bright pink like my hair with an opalescent sheen. Pearls that had originally been harvested from the rare clams, the woman had explained. The necklace had a large teardrop pearl at the bottom that would dangle from the end, and smaller pearls were placed between the diamonds on each side, all strung on a shining silverium chain; a very rare commodity to find in Gemaria.

My father had commissioned it for my mother to match the bracelet I now wear on my wrist. He'd had a particularly successful trade with Day Kingdom, and he'd celebrated with this gift for my mother.

I'd never found out what had happened to all of our things after the High King I was about to go perform for had everyone killed. I figured the new lord would have taken everything. I knew my mother had been wearing this necklace the night she died. I'd seen it still around her neck when I'd last glimpsed her body lying across the floor. Had someone stolen it? They apparently hadn't sent her to the Otherworld with it, which made me irrationally angry when compared to the other sins committed that night.

My fingers closed tightly around the necklace, brushing against the brace-let on my wrist that it paired with in the process. I took another deep breath, trying to find my equilibrium again, and then hid the priceless piece within the pocket of my cape.

"It just took me by surprise. I'm fine." I tried to reassure Faiza, but she didn't seem to buy it. "Come on, let's see what else there is!" I tried to sound excited as I dragged her along to see the different items on offer, but dread continued to weigh me down inside.

I tried to shake it off the entire rest of our trip through the marketplace that had popped up overnight. As we approached the large entrance of the arena, lined with flowing teal fabric embroidered with shining silver, I forced that veil of truth over myself once more.

I got a quick look at the section of the arena we'd be performing in, seeing the stage at the far end and the tall columns of seats surrounding it that would allow everyone to get a good look. Banners and pennants were hung along the walls, and flowers accented them at every turn. Gems sparkled in the light from where they decorated the edge of the stage. Gems from every court were sticking up along the sides, representing all the competitors.

We were whisked away to the back end of the arena to a spot behind the stage. Since the arena was circular and fully enclosed, the section of seating behind the stage was closed, but there was a staging area of sorts set under-neath that section, which we were brought to. The other ladies were almost all there already, except for the Opal and Amythest contestants, who were ushered in not long after us.

The sound of the crowd filling in the many seats created a cacophony of noise that nearly made my ears weep. While we waited for his Majesty to make an appearance, I shed the white cloak I was wearing. The cloak had arrived with the other items I'd requested. Since we'd been told that Azurill would ensure we were provided with whatever we required, I took full advantage of the situation, requesting an outfit that was fit for a combination of a queen and a pixie dancer.

The white cloak was embroidered with red and set with rubies along the trim from the neck to the floor. The red fox fur along the collar was especially lovely, and while it was a bit over the top just to use as a cover-up until we got here, I wasn't going to complain. The fabric was soft and supple, and it created a striking look, so I fully planned to nick it before fleeing. It would help keep me warm when I was forced back into sleeping on street corners and abandoned houses.

Erodite, I'd really miss the luxurious beds you could sink into.

The bedroom designed for the Ruby competitor was obviously designed for someone *from* Ruby, with red being the dominant color. But it was so easily ignored when I sank into that bed. It felt like sleeping on a cloud.

Removing the cloak, my outfit for the challenge was revealed in its entirety. My slippers matched the shimmering silver tutu that surrounded my waist, offsetting the ruby bodysuit that was dotted with diamonds along the front. My hair had been braided to create a crown atop my head, while my makeup had darkened the rims of my eyes and brightened the pout of my lips.

But it was the diamond dust across my lids and the tiny diamonds added to the edges of my eyes, creating a swirl on each side, that really brought the look together. It was attention-grabbing, which was exactly what I needed here.

All the clamor from up front finally came to a stop as the crowd hushed, and I knew *he* must have appeared.

"Welcome, my dear citizens of Theiapolis, to the first event of the Diamond Queen Competition!" Azurill's voice boomed around the arena, magic amplifying his voice. Loud cheers, whistles, and claps met his announcement.

Once they finally quieted down a bit, he continued, "Today's challenge is simple, but it will allow us all to learn a bit more about the ladies vying to be the next Diamond Queen: a talent contest! While no one will be eliminated this round, we still need a winner, one who will receive the chance to spend some extra one-on-one time with me!"

While the crowd went wild, I eyed the other ladies around me. Most of them kept to themselves, all narrowed eyes and pursed lips as they looked around at the other ladies in turn. Faiza and I stuck together, but the glares of Lady Zumra and Safira were intensely focused on us.

Then there was Lady Sania, whom I ached to approach, but whose face might as well have been carved from diamond itself. It was a completely blank slate and not exactly welcoming. Lady Ophira's nose was firmly in the air, which was about what I'd expect from a woman with hair of liquid gold, while Lady Amatista was watching everyone with too much calculation in her amethyst eyes to ignore. Meanwhile, Lady Allirea was fiddling with the ends of her opal hair, avoiding looking at anyone else entirely.

Faiza's name was called first, and I wished I'd been able to watch her performance. She was an artist and planned to create a magnificent painting right on stage. Unfortunately, I didn't have much time to think about what she might have created, as I was called up for my own turn next.

Walking onto the large stage, I noticed the throne set dead center before it, slightly elevated to ensure the high king had the best view. This throne was a plush silver and blue, with tufted velvet inset with diamonds instead of buttons, and the gems of all the courts lined the sides, completely covering the arms and legs, as well as around the backrest. His council surrounded him on either side, and I forced myself to smile and curtsy to them all when I arrived in the middle of the platform.

The smirk on Azurill's face as he watched me with those intense teal eyes was infuriating, but it only pushed my desire to prove exactly what I was capable of higher. To him. To the court. To *everyone*.

The music began, and Azurill shifted forward slightly on his throne before setting himself back into it, as if he didn't want to be caught in the act of actually being interested in the happenings on stage.

I let a smile grace my full lips as I launched into my routine. My arms swept up before I twirled in a tight circle, bringing my leg up as I bent backward before snapping back and jumping into a spin to the other side of the stage. I spun, tucked, flipped, and rolled. It was quite an acrobatic dance, with a lot of exaggerated, dramatic movements, but it also told a story—and a tragic one at that.

The tale of the Wolf Princess was well known and mostly used for children's bedtime stories these days. It told of a princess who rejected a cocky prince and fell in love with a common man, marrying him instead. Sadly, her love story didn't last long, as the common man merely wanted her for her money and title. He cursed her into the form of a wolf, enabling him to take over everything and steal her entire life from her.

She was unable to change back, except for one night a year, when the moon was full and bright, the closest to Adamah it ever got, where she would be allowed to regain her Elven form. Only a kiss from her true love on that night, given to her at exactly the moment the moon's light kissed her true form, would break the curse.

The irony of the story was that she'd already rejected her true love. He'd been too afraid to show her the truth of himself, so he'd played the role of the cocky prince instead, only succeeding in making her interest in him turn to ashes in her mouth.

The story ended with the she-wolf constantly roaming the lands, always looking for the true love she didn't know she'd already turned away.

I thought it a fitting story for a high king who showed everyone a false persona.

My pointed toe hit the ground, my leg bent at an angle while my other remained straight, my arms out to my sides, as the music came to a slow stop. A beat of silence, only broken by my panting, terrified me while it hung over us, but it was quickly eclipsed by the rush of screaming cheers that followed. I looked up to see an array of expressions staring back at me. Smiles or stunned looks on some, envy or respect on others, but there was only one expression I cared about.

And it wasn't the satisfied smile on Lord Carnelian's face as he nodded to me slightly from the front row.

Azurill's mouth was slightly open, his eyes widened, but he clapped wholeheartedly along with everyone else. It was enough.

Erodite, I hoped it was enough.

Faiza met me with a broad smile as I stepped off the stage, pulling me into a hug. I stiffened, feeling distinctly like the alley cat I'd grabbed when I'd been a child, all alone and scared in the world. I'd just wanted to cuddle into its soft fur, but the thing had bristled and clawed as it snapped at me with its tiny fangs.

The damn things were adorable yet vicious, and they did not know how to handle any kind of affection.

I made a valiant attempt, however, remembering I was supposed to be Lady Jacinth, not Jac…not even Lady L—*no*.

No.

We quickly settled in to watch the rest of the competitors, and I couldn't help the amusement I felt observing the ladies who truly cared about getting the king's attention, for reasons other than murder anyway.

Lady Zumra showcased her singing voice. She performed a famous wedding song, *of course*. The presumption was about what I expected from her.

Lady Safira read the future. She foretold that Azurill would find great love in this competition, and then proceeded to flutter her eyelashes at him. So clearly, *that* reading could be trusted.

Lady Allirea read a poem that she'd written. It was surprisingly good and had nothing to do with love, which served as a pleasant break.

Lady Sania showed her skill at reading body language like a born matchmaker. She pulled volunteers onstage to pick apart their thoughts and feelings with astonishing accuracy.

Lady Ophira did a chakra cleansing. There were eight chakras in an Elven body, each corresponding to one of the Sacred Gems. She brought her brother on stage, and we all watched as mist, black as onyx, poured from his ears.

Lady Amatista recited obscure facts. I wouldn't have thought that a talent, but she had people from the audience shout out different questions they wanted answers to—and she *always* had an answer. I had no idea if they were correct, but she *was* from the court of scholars.

When the last competitor finished and left the stage, Azurill stepped up to announce the winner. We were all on the edge of our metaphorical seats as we waited for the result. Faiza's hand found mine, and instead of finding an excuse to let go, I squeezed it tighter.

"Thank you all for attending this wonderful event, setting off a month's worth of festivities for the city!" Azurill smiled widely, showing off a perfect smile. The crowd ate up every word he said. *They loved him*, I realized as I watched them respond eagerly to their king. The knowledge burned, scorching through me like a lava flow. But they didn't know what kind of monster was hiding beneath that charming veneer.

"All of the ladies have showcased magnificent talents today, haven't they?" he asked, and the crowd answered with a roaring cheer. "Unfortunately, only one may win. It's a hard decision, given how brilliantly they all performed. Any ideas for who deserves to win?"

He cupped a hand to his ear dramatically, welcoming the crowd to call out answers back to him. My hand started to sweat as I ground my teeth back and forth in irritation. Was he really going to let the crowd choose?

Listening to the many names being called out, my mind started to change as I realized what was happening. I heard everyone's names, of course, but my own rose above the din. My heart pounded, and as Azurill glanced over and flashed a smirk at me, I was sure the sound of it must have been audible to everyone present.

"It sounds like we have a winner!" Azurill cheered, his arm flying out to the side toward me. "Lady Jacinth Tawny!"

The crowd never seemed to actually stop making noise, but I suddenly couldn't hear it. Faiza's hand squeezed mine before letting go and practically pushing me forward. The movement brought me back to reality with a jarring thud. Just in time to see Azurill's amused smile as his eyebrow quirked upward.

I set my shoulders back and marched up the stage toward him. He reached out a hand for me, and I reluctantly placed mine into it. My skin sizzled from the contact, and his eyes heated in a way I wanted to run far, far away from.

He lifted our joined hands in the air, and this time I heard the crowd as their whoops and cheers rang out, my name being cried out in excited clamors. I was busy enough during my dance that I didn't have time to appreciate how overwhelming it was to have so many eyes focused on me. It felt inherently wrong. Staying out of sight had been my primary defense for years, leaving me with no idea how to handle this much attention.

"The next ball we attend, I'm expecting to see some of those moves, my Lady," Azurill whispered, his voice laced with amusement as he leaned towards me.

"Play your cards right, Your Majesty," I replied, raising my eyebrows pointedly as I played into my role.

His surprised expression made me laugh, lifting my hand to hide my smile behind it. Azurill shook his head, a defeated smirk rising on his lips.

"Something tells me that things are about to get interesting," he crooned in my ear, pushing a lock of candy colored hair back behind my ear from where it had once again escaped its hold. Goosebumps broke out along the back of my neck, right where his fingers had grazed as he slowly pulled away.

I had the terrible feeling that he was absolutely right.

CHAPTER 12

Jacinth

I SIGHED deeply as I woke, snuggling into luxurious blankets and a cloud-soft mattress I couldn't have dreamed up a few months ago.

Of all the things I'd run from as a child, this might not have been the most heartbreaking, but it was certainly the most backbreaking. I'd *missed* this. Fiercely. Passionately. I was a person who loved sleeping comfortably, but who ended up sleeping on the ground more often than not. It was the cruelest of ironies.

I'd probably agree to assassinate anyone for a chance to sleep in one of these beds forever. Well, maybe not anyone—but close.

A knock sounded on my door, making me groan as I forced myself out of the warm and inviting cocoon of soft red sheets. I threw on the grey and red velvet robe that came with the room to make my way to the door. They'd really thought of everything. Every luxury I could think of was in this suite; enough that I'd never have to leave, outside the competitions, if I didn't want to.

Someone obviously did want me to, however, as the knocking continued. I threw open my bedroom door to find Alfrikr, looking grumpier than usual with a scowl marring his uniquely handsome features.

"What's wrong?" I asked wearily, leaning against the doorframe as a yawn overtook me.

"What's wrong is I've been turned into a delivery service," he groaned, stepping back and waving a hand toward the table in the living room. My eyes went wide as I took in the giant basket sitting on the black marble dining table.

"What is this?" I questioned him hesitantly.

"A gift from the High King," he sighed, shaking his head. "There are two envelopes inside the basket, one with instructions for today, and the other with instructions for the next trial."

"Okay." I drew the word out as I stepped closer to the mysterious basket.

"Gift and message officially delivered." Alfrikr rolled his eyes before stepping back out to his post at my door, probably anxious to be back among his fellow guards so they could complain about all of the uppity ladies they were being forced to protect.

I rolled my own eyes, even though he couldn't see me any longer, but the basket quickly grabbed my attention again. I unwrapped the fabric surrounding it and blinked in surprise as it revealed two very different outfits inside. My fingers itched to inspect them, but I figured it was probably better to read the letters from the king first, since they'd likely answer any questions I had.

Taking the first envelope with *Lady Jacinth Tawny* inscribed on the outside, I unfolded the heavy diamond-dusted silver paper to read what he'd written in an elegant, looping script.

Dear Lady Jacinth (Mini-Dite),

Congratulations on winning the favor of both the crowd and me with your impressive show of talent. It is difficult to get to know someone in the short bursts this competition has us interacting in, but I do believe that discovering what it is someone enjoys doing with their time allows one to gain a bit more insight into them.

Since this first competition had no elimination, I thought the additional time with me as a reward was a good trade-off. Though I'm sure you'd say that was merely my ego talking. I would like to get to know everyone better as we head into elimination rounds, and this will give me a chance to know more of you before that time comes.

I thought we could visit one of my favorite spots together for a picnic. A bit cliché, I know, however, I wanted an activity that would allow us to actually speak with one another.

I've included an outfit for you that will be appropriate for where we're going. I look forward to the opportunity for us to speak again.

Yours (for today),

His Royal Majesty

High King Azurill Kyanite Alankar

aka Veri Full of Himself

I tried to stop the smile that lifted my lips at his farewell address, but it was somewhat impossible. *Murderer*, I reminded myself. A murderer I plan to *kill*. I sighed heavily, closing my eyes for a moment. At times, this utterly overwhelming experience could almost lull one into thinking this a fairytale, but in reality, it was a tale of cold, hard revenge.

I picked up the second letter, which merely read *Ruby Court Competitor* on it, and was considerably less personal.

"Dear Diamond Queen Competitor,

The first trial was a mere practice run, but now we're getting to the good stuff. Tomorrow, the first *real* challenge will begin. You're to wear the outfit enclosed, with only the accessories provided. No additional weapons or magic are allowed and are grounds for disqualification.

Your guards will take you to the location of the competition at ten sharp, so be ready to go by then. I'm anxious to see how you all fare tomorrow. May the gods shine upon you.

His Royal Majesty

High King Azurill Kyanite Alankar"

I dove into the outfits immediately to see what hints I could get. Thankfully, they'd been helpfully labeled. The first garment bag had "Today" written on the tag attached to it. Opening it up, I found a beautiful day dress with pearly-pink skirts and a cream bodice with pink embroidery on it. The sweetheart neckline and cap sleeves were perfect for a picnic. Azurill, or one of his staff, had helpfully included accessories as well.

There were sturdy slippers in the same pink as the skirts, along with a simple diamond lariat necklace, a matching pair of earrings, and a bracelet. I noticed he hadn't included any red, which made me more than a bit anxious.

I had to hope the colors were chosen because of my hair and not that he had any suspicions about the truth. I shook my head at the silly thought, I wouldn't have survived this long if Azurill had figured me out.

But just in case, I needed to be incredibly careful.

Opening the second garment bag, my eyes widened to find an outfit remarkably similar to the one I usually wore. There were black leather pants, a black top with a leather corset that buckled over it, black knee-high boots, and a matching fitted jacket. They'd even included accessories with this outfit, but instead of jewelry, there were shoulder pauldrons and a jeweled dagger. It had a ruby set into the pommel, but diamond and kyanite had been worked in a swirling pattern down the hilt.

Interesting.

Were we going to be stealing or fighting, or some combination perhaps? I was too curious and would certainly be questioning Azurill about it today. If he were smart, he wouldn't have given any hints about the upcoming trial before our little date.

Blech. Just thinking that word in association with him made me want to throw up.

Checking the time, I decided I'd better head to breakfast and worry about this later. I made my way back to my bedroom, and knowing it was likely to be a full hall, I changed into a red and white off-the-shoulder gown. It dipped down from the shoulders to between my breasts in a gentle slope, where the fabric then twisted together, merging the white on top with the red below. Diaphanous bell sleeves paired wonderfully with the high-low skirt that looked like it had been dipped in diamonds around its edges.

I made my way out of the suite and raised my eyebrows expectantly at Alfrikr. He grunted and began following me after offering a nod to the few guards remaining in the hall. Most of the ladies seemed to already be up and out for the day.

We made our way down to the room where meals were served. It was a massive, domed hall with silver walls and a blue ceiling, with twisting columns made of amethyst, emerald, opal, onyx, pearl, ruby, and sapphire. The gems had clearly been added later, as blue and silver remained the dominant colors, a holdover from when House Alankar were merely the kings of Diamond as opposed to high kings of Gemaria.

Most of the ladies had already arrived, but Faiza waved me down to an empty seat near her own. Unfortunately, that put me directly across from

Zumra, who at least seemed to be busy glaring at Sania and Ophira, since they were sitting next to Azurill this morning. Faiza was seated beside a man I recognized but didn't know the name of on one side, with Prince Ruri on her other, leaving me to take a seat next to him.

"Jac, have you met Ruri and Balthazar?" Faiza asked, her voice weirdly high-pitched, as if she was slightly nervous. I narrowed my eyes at her, tilting my head slightly.

"I can't say I've had the pleasure yet," I murmured in response, watching her carefully to try to figure out what was going on.

"This is Prince Ruri, of course, and Balthazar is Az's best friend as well as the head of his guard," she explained with a smile.

"Lady Jacinth." Balthazar nodded stiffly, but Prince Ruri turned a charming smile my way and lifted his hand in expectation. I placed mine in it and allowed him to kiss it softly.

"Lady Jacinth," he murmured, but I caught Balthazar watching the interaction, his eyes cutting back to us constantly.

"Prince Ruri, it's wonderful to finally meet you," I told him, wondering if he could scent the lie, as his smile turned sharp.

"Oh, I've been waiting for the opportunity," he said, as his sharp smile turned into a charming smirk. "We were all surprised to hear of you. I don't think your name has been uttered a single time at court before now, and for a lady related to the lord of Ruby himself?" He whistled softly, but my anxiety spiked as I realized why Faiza was nervous. The prince and the head of the guard catching me at breakfast was far from unintentional.

"Oh." I looked down, letting my hair become a curtain to hide my face, as if I was bashful. "I suppose I'm too minor a figure in Ruby Court to matter much."

"Nonsense!" Prince Ruri replied, his frosty blue eyes peering through my hair to see my own. "Come, tell me about yourself."

"There's not much to say, my Prince." I sighed, as if disappointed I didn't have much gossip for him. "I spend most of my time at home."

"Is that where you learned to dance?" he asked, lightning quick.

I swallowed hard, trying to think of the best way to answer. I knew Azurill was suspicious of Lord Carnelian, and with good reason, but I couldn't understand why he'd sick his younger brother on me when he was going to meet with me today.

"I had wonderful instructors, yes." I smiled placidly at the prince, but his mouth pinched together like he was frustrated.

"Brother." Azurill suddenly appeared, clamping a hand down on his shoulder, "Stop harassing the ladies here to see me and go find your own."

Ruri laughed, shaking his head at his older brother, but his eyes were tight as the two traded a loaded look.

I needed to charm the fuck out of Azurill today.

Anything to make him trust me enough to get through to the end of this. Where I could finally bring my family peace, and a vengeance that I'd long thought out of my grasp, but was now so tantalizingly close.

"Oh, he's no bother, Your Majesty." I smiled at them both. "I'd love to get to know your family better as well."

"We'll have to make time for that later, unfortunately. Ruri is needed elsewhere," Azurill said, eyeing his brother sternly before pulling him up. Something told me that Ruri had stepped over a line somewhere.

"Lady Jacinth." Prince Ruri nodded in farewell, a light in his eyes I couldn't quite make sense of.

"Don't mind them." Faiza leaned in, trying to reassure me in a whisper, but we were unfortunately too close to the others for them not to overhear.

"Prince Ruri does have a point." Zumra sniffed in disdain. "How exactly have you hidden yourself away before now?" she questioned, leaning across the table toward me, her emerald eyes blazing with ill intent.

I glared back at her. "I wasn't hiding."

I kept the veil of truth over myself, especially when telling such a blatant, bold-faced lie. It was too important that no one here glean anything that indicated I wasn't telling the full truth. Carnelian was already distrusted, and my sudden appearance had clearly stirred suspicion. I needed to diffuse it if I had any chance at succeeding.

"You could have fooled me." She laughed, a nasty thing that set my teeth on edge.

"Some people don't feel the need to make themselves the center of attention to validate their own existence," I told her with a bright smile, cutting into my food and plopping a piece in my mouth, keeping my smile around the fork.

Zumra's face instantly dropped, and I heard several people beside us trying to smother their laughter, only to fall totally silent as she speared each with a look in turn.

"I will figure out the truth," she hissed at me, throwing her napkin on the table as she stood, her chair making a racket as she flung it back. "And when I do, well—"

She smiled widely, exposing all her teeth, even as she trembled slightly from the sheer force of her rage, her emerald-green eyes burning with hatred. "You can kiss any far-fetched dreams of being the Diamond Queen goodbye."

If I had any dreams of such to begin with, maybe I would be worried, but as it stood, my only concern was this damn woman getting in the way of me gaining the trust I *needed* to win to achieve my real goal.

CHAPTER 13

Azurill

"What was that?" I asked angrily, dragging my brother by the arm into the workroom of his Gemlab.

I'd set aside this space for Ruri the first time he came home on break and expressed his interest in specializing in the alchemy of gem magic. Now in his third year of study at Ceridwen Academy, he always managed to disappear into this room for hours at a time whenever he was home. The Gemlab had everything he could possibly need, from overflowing piles of gems to extra potion bottles for brewing up his concoctions.

"What was what?" he asked innocently, making me scowl at him until he rolled his eyes and cracked. "We know we can't trust Carnelian, right?"

"Right," I drew out slowly, raising an expectant brow.

"Then we can't trust this Lady Jacinth either," he stated, like he was explaining something to a child.

I crossed my arms and glared at him slightly, "I'm more than aware of this, but we also don't want to tip her off that we're suspicious of her."

"Are you sure about that?" he asked in return, folding his arms across his chest as he leaned against his workbench.

"What is that supposed to mean?" I asked irritably. I was already holding this stupid competition against my wishes, and being quizzed about my interactions with our suspicious competitor wasn't helping my mood, to say the least.

"I mean that you seemed awfully taken with her at the ball." Ruri countered, and I rolled my eyes.

"Appreciating her attitude doesn't mean I'm *taken* with her, Ruri," I told him tiredly, sinking into a chair and putting my elbows on my knees as I leaned over, narrowing my eyes at him.

"We both know if there is anything afoot, Carnelian is a likely culprit. Getting to know her will help me determine if she's in on it or an unwilling accomplice to his plans," I explained, looking up at him.

"So you're telling me you're not attracted to her at all?" He pressed, clearly skeptical, and I found myself wishing we were still kids who could get away with smacking each other around in the halls. Finding the high king wrestling with his brother over a girl probably wouldn't end well.

"She's obviously attractive, okay?" I snapped, shaking my head. "But that doesn't matter, they're all attractive!"

Ruri snorted, tipping his head in acknowledgment that I was right, but then let out a deep sigh, sinking into the chair at his workstation. "I'm just worried. I've been watching Carnelian, but he makes it hard to have an actual conversation with him. And every other lord I try to talk to just wants to talk themselves up."

I laughed, shaking my head at his naivety, remembering how young he truly was. It was my responsibility to take care of him. Even with mother here to help…our father was gone, and I was king—I knew it was on me. Not to mention that Mother wouldn't even leave her room at this point, too grief-stricken over the loss of her son.

"Go talk to Mother." I smiled slightly, my tone warmer now that the argument had died down. "She's been working this court long before any of us were born. Plus, women tend to talk among their own circles; she might be able to help."

Ruri's head fell forward, his hair obscuring his face as he admitted, "I just can't lose you, too, Az."

His voice broke, and my heart broke along with it. I slung my arm around his shoulder, pulling him into my side so I could reassure him. "You won't, okay? I've got Balthazar watching my every move, and guards watching the ladies all day, every day. With you getting in amongst the lords and heirs, we'll find something before long. If there is indeed anything to be found."

"Do you really doubt there is?" he asked, slow and unsure. For all that he was technically an adult, he was still extremely young compared to my one hundred and twenty-six years. I didn't even become king until I was over one hundred, our father having passed when I was a decade in.

"I have a feeling there's more to this than we know," I admitted with a deliberately casual shrug. "There are always plots circulating among the court," I told him ruefully, but my voice deepened with raw anger as I continued. "I promise you this, though. If I find out that any of that plotting led to our brother's death, I will bring the fury of the gods down on whoever's responsible."

I raised a hand to my neck, reassuring myself as I traced the lines of my tattoo. I would be ready to wield whatever was necessary when the time came. And despite what I said to Ruri, I had a feeling it wouldn't it long before it did.

GETTING READY TO meet Lady Jacinth, I found myself deliberating between two outfits. I needed to get close to her to see if she was involved in any of Carnelian's plots or if she was entirely innocent. The tone I set for this would either help or hurt that goal, but I didn't know if the proper court attire or the more casual outfit would help in this case.

I'd given her a day dress that would work for an outdoor picnic. I didn't want her to look *too* good, and for me to forget why I was there. For all I'd brushed off my brother's questions, there *was* something different about her that pulled me in every time I was in her vicinity.

But equal to the strange magnetism she radiated was the haunted feeling that rose up and repelled me. Her coloring was a constant reminder of sins of the past I wanted to forget. *Needed* to forget, especially if I were to face Lady Sania, as well. My guilt over House Marit meant facing her was a challenge, but at least she was a distant relation. Her orange hair didn't summon the same images as Jacinth's candy-pink locks. I could almost imagine the daughter of House Marit when I looked in her eyes, the image a terrible vision of what could have been.

With that thought in mind, I went for the more casual outfit. The teal button-down was embroidered slightly with silver along the collar, and I decided to leave it open down to the top of my chest. With the buttons undone my tattoo was more visible, starting with the diamond on my neck and swirling down to each gem in turn. All the court's gems were represented across my neck, shoulder, chest—a reminder of my commitment to the realm, a fact repeated to anyone who asked, and ensuring no other questions arose.

A knock on the door heralded the basket containing our lunch, and left me with no choice but to get on with it. Resentment for this entire fiasco rose within me once more. A picnic with a beautiful woman should have been an appealing idea, but knowing it was fraught with potential treason and definite gold-digging made it hard to see the bright side.

I waited for Jacinth near the entrance to the palace, nodding absently to courtiers who passed by. When she appeared from around the corner, my breath caught for a slight moment; even in casual day clothes, she was gorgeous. I had hoped it was just the elaborate gowns making her seem more alluring, but I should have known better. She'd managed to pull off the outfit she wore during the first challenge after all, despite being dressed like a carnival dancer. And the way her body had moved…*fuck*, I was definitely looking forward to seeing her in the tight leathers tomorrow.

Dammit, this is exactly what my brother was worried about.

I needed to keep a clear head and figure out any plots she may be involved in, not lose my head in daydreams of what she was like in the bedroom.

"Lady Jacinth." I bowed to her, kissing her hand in greeting. "Thank you for joining me today."

"Your Majesty." She curtseyed flawlessly, her hair half pulled back on top with a cream-colored pearl barrette that matched the dress I'd left for her. As she bent down, her breasts strained against the corset, giving me a mouthwatering view that I had to ignore for my own sanity.

"Thank you so much for inviting me," she continued with a wide smile. "It's wonderful to have the chance to spend some time with you." I offered her my free arm, and she looped her own through it.

"I'm looking forward to it as well," I told her, a polite smile firmly in place as we began walking out of the palace. "Have you ever been to Diamond Court before?" I asked her curiously.

"When I was a child, yes." Her smile stiffened for a moment before turning down into a slight frown. "But it's been so long, I barely remember it." Her smile reappeared, but the ease in it was gone.

"Well, today you'll get to see one of my favorite spots," I told her, watching her eyebrow peak in interest.

"Is that so?" She hummed, looking at me thoughtfully. While I'd tried to avoid gazing into her eyes, not wanting to be dragged into the past, I found I couldn't ignore them either. Her stare was somehow weightier than any of the ladies I'd met before. "And what is this spot?"

I managed to smirk, shaking my head, "It wouldn't be much of a surprise if I told you, would it?"

She pouted, and I found my eyes drawn to her lips against my will, nearly tripping as my distraction made me almost miss a step. She giggled, and I shook my head at myself, knowing I couldn't allow such distractions when this much was at stake.

This woman was a hazard to my health.

I brought her through a few winding city streets before we reached the hidden entrance to the woods. This one was completely safe, whereas the forest on the other side of the city was its polar opposite. I looked at Jacinth, wondering how she would handle it. Would she be able to make it through the next competition?

Watching her navigate through these woods with zero issues, I found myself believing she might. I knew many of the ladies rarely left their cities to venture into nature in this way, but Jacinth seemed entirely capable of traversing the terrain.

As we approached the area I intended to bring her, I watched for her reaction as we crested the hill. I wasn't disappointed, and I couldn't help my slight smile as her breath caught and her eyes went wide with wonder as she took in the majesty below.

This field was all the proof I needed that broken things could be made even more beautiful in the aftermath of their destruction.

The space had been completely destroyed once upon a time, with jagged cracks running across the ground like a spider's web. The fissures hadn't been left to scar the land for long however, as flowing water filled the gaps, leading to a pool in the middle that constantly spouted the sparkling water high into the sky. Colorful flowers dotted the landscape, surrounding where giant diamonds had shot up out of the shattered land. The diamonds varied in height, with some as tall as the tress and others only as tall as an Elf. It was a magical sight that never failed to capture my attention.

I frequently found myself here when I needed to be alone to think, and seeing the awe and wonder on Jacinth's face brought a soft smile to my own. My suspicions of her aside, it was nice to be able to share this place with someone and have them appreciate it the way I do.

"You like it?" I asked her quietly, and her head swung to me, looking indignant.

"Like it?" She breathed, shaking her head. "It's incredible. I've never seen anything like this before."

My smile widened at her answer, and I slowly led her down the hill onto the field itself, watching as her free hand brushed the flowers and gems we passed. I went to help her over one of the wider cracks in the ground so that she wouldn't fall into the water flowing through it, but she jumped so easily over it that I found myself shaking my head at my own folly. I should have known after seeing her dance that she'd have no issue with it.

"How did it get like this?" she asked as we made our way to the spot I'd chosen for our picnic. I began to lay everything out once we did and took the time to answer her question.

"No one's really sure," I admitted, sparing a glance around. "My father used to say the ground cracked open when the gods gifted this land with their magic. The force of the diamonds rising just ripped the land apart."

She began helping me sort everything from the picnic basket, shocking me that she had no issue serving herself. She easily pulled out plates and cups and poured a drink for each of us. I'd seen noble ladies scandalized at the idea of pouring their own drink. It was refreshing to see she didn't hold to such proper etiquette, despite coming from the most traditional of all the courts.

"Is that what you think happened?" She asked curiously after a moment, and I gave the question due consideration. Over the years, I'd spent time thinking through several theories, but never really landed on a definitive one.

"I don't know," I smiled ruefully. "I've come here so many times, and each time I do, I consider a different reason this could have happened. There are stories of the earth shaking and opening, of the gods throwing down thunder that was so strong it cracked the earth." I shook my head. "But I honestly enjoy not knowing for sure. It allows us to make up our own story."

She smiled slowly, almost like she didn't mean to do it. This smile was different from her others, and I found myself thinking this was a *true* smile. Not a court smile, not a masked smile—this was the kind of smile she should always have, and I mourned that it disappeared just as quickly as it arrived.

This woman was an enigma.

"Tell me about yourself." I found myself demanding, and winced a bit at my delivery. Thankfully, she seemed amused, but her eyes dimmed after a moment, and I nearly cursed myself for causing it. But I needed to know the truth of her. Beyond my need to protect my family and my own life, as the lord of Diamond Court, that *need* for truth thrummed deep in my soul.

"There's honestly not much to tell, Your Majesty," She said, pushing a strand of candy-pink hair behind her ear.

"That can't be true. And please, call me Az." I sighed tiredly, leaning back on my elbows on the blanket. "Titles get old quickly, and I'm looking to find someone I can be myself with, as well as the king." It was probably more honest than I should have been—especially to this particular lady.

She looked down for a moment, and I wished I knew what she was thinking, but when she looked back up, her pink orbs locked me in place. She rearranged herself so she was lying on her stomach beside me, her chin on her fist as her eyes twinkled up at me.

"Tell me about yourself first, then." She all but demanded in return, her eyebrow rising in challenge. I huffed a small laugh, reaching over for my glass and quickly downing a gulp of champagne.

"I've always known this day would come," I told her, my eyes scanning the horizon as I considered what I'd gotten myself into with this competition. "But I had wanted to put it off for as long as possible. I had no interest in being fought over like dogs over a bone."

"What changed your mind then?" she asked quietly, her posture shifting until she was on her side, and I found myself rolling to face her head-on. We were closer now than propriety allowed, but neither of us seemed to mind. I knew I shouldn't, but something about her made me want to get closer, like a whisper at the back of my mind urging me on even when the rest of it told me to stop.

"I'm sure you're aware that my brother, Gardevoir, recently died?" I asked mournfully, and she nodded silently. Her eyes spoke of an understanding of grief that was deeper than anything I'd gotten out of her yet. I couldn't help but wonder who she'd lost to affect her so strongly.

I let myself feel that grief, stew in the loss and the pain, before I forced it down once more. My responsibilities didn't allow me the time I wished to mourn, not when Ruri might be at risk too. Losing one brother was unacceptable, but losing both would be catastrophic.

"It left us too vulnerable. Ruri is my only heir now, and everyone wants to ensure the royal family is secure." I scoffed, shaking my head. I was surprised to feel her hand close around mine, where I gripped the glass's stem to the point of cracking. She loosened my fingers around it and then replaced it with her own hand, twining our fingers together.

"I'm sorry," she said quietly, *earnestly*. "No one should be made to endure this circus while in mourning. Everyone deserves the space to grieve properly."

I took a heavy breath, appreciating the words more than any of the other banal platitudes or fake understanding I'd received thus far. "But as the high king, I can't afford to."

"Well, maybe here you can." She suggested, her free arm swinging wide to indicate the empty space around us. "I've lost much in my life." Her voice wavered, and her hand tightened almost to the point of pain around my own. "And I feel their loss every day. It's what gets me up in the morning and what puts me to sleep at night. I live and breathe that grief."

"Ah," I said, a slight smirk growing as I teased her lightly, that shared understanding giving me the confidence that it would be accepted. "So, I bury my grief, and you revel in yours? What a healthy pair we are, huh?" She scoffed, rolling her eyes at me, and I couldn't help laughing softly.

"How can you stand to feel that grief so often?" I asked her after a moment, honestly baffled. I had to ignore it, or it would consume me, and I didn't have the luxury of losing myself in my position. She looked out at the geyser going off beside us, avoiding my eyes for a moment. When they met mine again, there was a fire in them that made me much too intrigued.

"I refuse to forget. To let their memory fade into the winds of time like they meant nothing." Her voice was tense, weighed with something I couldn't quite understand. "But one day..." she sighed, trailing off for a moment, and her eyes skittered away from mine. "One day, I will be able to lay those ghosts to rest."

"And when will that be?" I encouraged her to speak more, wanting to know what drove this woman, but she smirked slowly, shaking her head at me.

"I'll know it when I see it." Was all she said. Her enigmatic answer made me want to push for more answers, but I could tell she was finished speaking on it.

We both drank and ate for a few moments, enjoying a comfortable silence, before she looked up at me with a curious expression.

"So, what do you do when you're not attending to your kingly duties?" Her voice was slightly teasing. "Surely it's not all proclamations and parties with women fighting over you."

I laughed in response, my head falling forward before I got myself together. "I spend time with my friends: Balthazar, Emrys, Alfrikr, Arianell, Brokk, and Alwyn. My brother Ruri, when he's home from the academy. I take care of my mother as best I can since my father passed. I spend a good deal of time with my friends in the training yard, and when I can, I try to attend the games put on in the arena. But most of my time is unfortunately taken up with my kingly duties."

She hummed, bringing my attention to her lips as she sipped her champagne delicately. Her tongue swooped over her bottom lip to catch a rouge drop, making me lick my own unconsciously.

"And plenty of women, I imagine." She stated, raising a brow at me playfully.

"Well, I have been quite single." I lifted my own eyebrow back at her. "Have you been waiting for marriage?" I asked her, knowing some of the ladies had been forced to, but thankfully, and especially for me, not all of them kept to the practice anymore. Another antiquated tradition of court that was thankfully fading away.

Jacinth snorted, looking amused, "That would be a travesty." I couldn't help my firm nod of agreement as my eyes ran over her. She had a body that was meant to be enjoyed and appreciated. To prevent her from reaping those rewards would be a crime. If I didn't have the intrigues of court to consider, I would have already been doing my best to divest her from that horribly tantalizing corset.

"I'm surprised Lord Carnelian let you get away with it, to be honest. He's quite the traditionalist," I confessed to her, hoping to get some insight into her thoughts regarding her cousin. I'd been too distracted by her pouty lips and large doe eyes. I couldn't prove Ruri right; I had to keep on task and work on getting some real information.

"That's one way to put it." She laughed musically. "But there are plenty of ways to get what one wants beneath his notice. He doesn't really bother himself with me."

"No?" I asked, hoping a leading question would get her to spill more. So far, the relationship between her and Carnelian was confounding, and I needed to unravel the truth of it. That urge to scrape and claw until the truth revealed itself was pumping inside me like it was on overdrive. "I would think, as the only female of his blood, you would have been cloistered away."

She sighed, looking down at her drink as she swirled it. "In a way, yes, but Lord Carnelian only cares about himself. His heir is much the same in that regard. It's easy enough to get away with murder without them noticing a thing."

"And how many murders have you hidden that I should be aware of, Mini-Dite?" I laughed as her cheeks turned as pink as her eyes.

"Probably less than you, Veri," She countered, sticking her tongue out at me, shocking me. I couldn't remember the last time someone had done that to me. *Many* years ago, certainly.

But Jacinth didn't seem to care at all, merrily teasing me like I was anyone else.

I liked it *too* much.

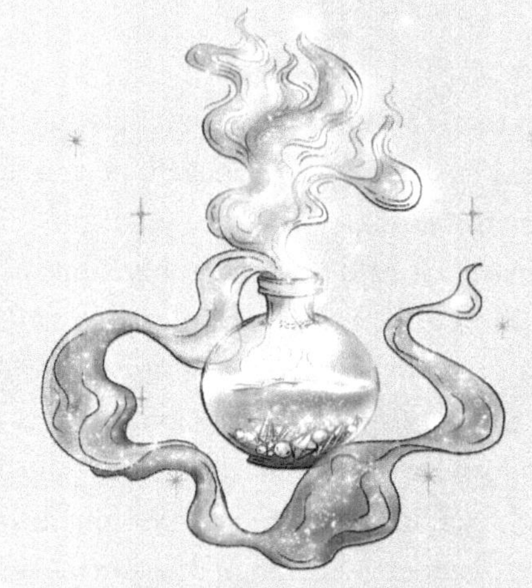

CHAPTER 14

Jacinth

I zipped up my jacket, sheathing my weapons as the morning dawned. Unlike the others since I'd arrived at the Diamond Palace, this time I couldn't lounge around in bed, soaking up the luxury for all it was worth—*and it was worth a lot*. But this time, I had a timetable to keep, and a competition to get to.

After my picnic with Azurill yesterday, I found myself spending the night reminding myself of every reason he needed to die. The horrors he committed couldn't be excused because he flashed his sad teal eyes my way. I understood the way grief shrouded a person, and I wouldn't wish it on anyone. But he was the one who caused *my* grief, so he didn't deserve the sympathy that welled up within me.

I couldn't blame him for wanting to push this ridiculous competition off, either. Who *would* want to find a wife this way?

But none of those things were my problem, and before long, he wouldn't have to worry about them either. He'd never live long enough to actually take a wife, and he could rejoin the brother he missed so much.

I rubbed at my chest, hoping to banish the throb that struck through it. Maybe I ate something that didn't agree with me, because it certainly wasn't regret pulsing in my heart.

Opening my door, I found Alfrikr waiting. His eyes trailed over my outfit before tugging at a strap and correcting the position. He nodded sharply before turning, his boots hammering on the marble floor as he led me down the hall.

"Any hints as to what today's event is?" I asked flippantly, not expecting him to reveal anything. Alfrikr missed half a step, but didn't react otherwise. It was only as we began to pick up the sounds of the other competitors up ahead that he turned to me. His amethyst eyes locked on mine as he leaned over and grabbed me firmly by the shoulders.

"Be quick. Be smart," he told me sternly, his expression far too intense for my liking. I nodded in return, assuring him he had nothing to worry about. We then joined the other ladies who were already milling around as they waited for everyone to arrive, and I quickly joined Faiza.

"Any guesses as to what today's trial will be?" she asked nervously, her turquoise hair pulled back into a high ponytail, much like mine, only I had braided it to keep my wavy mane contained, where hers was left to spill like a waterfall from the tie. Her unease was clear, from the wavering expression on her face to the way she picked at the leather straps of her outfit. She seemed to regard her leathers as if they were foreign, forcing me to hide a snort of bitter amusement. Despite the fact that I was the one born of a higher station between the two of us, I was also the one who all but lived in such attire.

"Something active, certainly," I murmured, looking at the other women present as I answered. Safira was fluttering around Zumra, assuring her of their imminent success. Sania was watching everyone with eagle eyes that I quickly evaded, feeling distinctly uncomfortable. I couldn't let any hint of the relation between us manifest. No matter how much I might have wished to reach out to any blood of mine still walking Adamah.

It was better I stayed dead and buried.

Lady Amatista was the last to arrive, her amethyst hair braided back like my own, and looking more comfortable in her leathers than perhaps any of the others but myself. With all of us now present, we were finally led through the city by our guards, leaving us to talk quietly among ourselves until we reached the large coliseum on the outskirts of the city.

Perhaps we were going to fight?

We were guided through a side door and into the arena, where the sound hit me like a wave. The stands were certainly packed; it seemed like the entire kingdom had come out to witness the spectacle of the trial today. When the interior of the arena finally came into sight, my breath caught in my throat.

The coliseum's rounded walls were tall and wide, leaving a giant space in the middle completely open for what appeared to be an obstacle course of some kind. The royal box was seated in the middle of the stands, providing a perfect view, and was open like the rest of the seating to allow the royals to see everything at a wide angle. And there was certainly plenty to see, as the entire place was filled with all sorts of different contraptions, some even clouded in a tell-tale mist and obscured from sight.

We came to stand below the royal box, bowing to the High King, before he stood up himself and called out to the arena at large.

"Ladies and gentlemen, today we are here for the first true challenge of the Diamond Queen Competition!" Azurill proclaimed, his voice projecting clearly through what was surely an amplification potion. "Each lady must complete the obstacle course before us, but the trial does not end there."

The crowd murmured excitedly amongst themselves, and I eyed Faiza beside me with some trepidation as we waited anxiously to find out what we were about to face.

"Should they make it to the end of this course, they will find themselves somewhere that doesn't wish them to linger. They must survive this place and make it back to the palace before sundown! We will be holding a party at the palace following the first half of this trial, so you may see which ladies return, and which, if any, fail to meet the challenge!"

His eyes scanned each one of us, and when his eyes landed on me, I met his in turn. I lifted my chin, determination pulsing through me. I had to make it through, there was no other option. Once Azurill broke our stare, I found Lord Carnelian glaring at me intensely from his spot in the royal box beside the other lords. With everything going on since we'd arrived, I'd been able to avoid him, but I knew he would want an update before long. And I needed to make sure he was keeping his word about Ula.

I found myself feeling a bit guilty that I hadn't been focused on her, but I had to believe she was okay. I couldn't afford the distraction of worrying about her, she had taught me that. I needed to live and breathe this lie, and thoughts of her would bog me down into the past.

I'd had quite enough of that already.

"Ladies, may Veritx smile upon you and grant you the courage needed to complete the trial before you today!" Azurill said, his charming smile firmly in place. Meanwhile, I forced my eyes to remain still, preventing them from rolling back into my head.

We were quickly ushered into order, lining up by court to determine who would go first. To my surprise, our guards quickly brought blindfolds for each of us. Alfrikr smiled smugly as he tied it around my head.

"Azurill wants this to be fair," he explained, whispering into my ear. "The first lady through won't know what's coming, and this way none of you will have an advantage from seeing what the others do to get through."

I grunted in acknowledgment, knowing it made sense, but…

"Can you at least tell me if Faiza gets through okay?" I whispered back to him. He paused in tying the blindfold for a moment, possibly from surprise. I hated not being able to see him to see why he stilled. Reading people's expressions and body language was a helpful skill in both thievery and court. My mother had started my education, with help from my nanny, Juvela, who'd been like a second mother to me, but Ula had finished it. I had been so determined to do both Juvela and my mother proud that I'd been an apt student. It wasn't foolproof by any means, but my own veil of truth was created bit by bit through those lessons, refusing to allow anyone to read me.

Not being able to read someone in turn made me irrationally uncomfortable, however.

"Fine, but only because you'll know once you take the blindfold off anyway," he sighed with an air of long-suffering annoyance, and I could practically *feel* his eyes roll.

Even without my sight, I could still hear the crowd's reactions as Faiza began. I bounced on the balls of my feet, anxious despite myself. I shouldn't care. It didn't make any sense for me to worry. And yet, I found I actually liked Faiza. She was a truly *good* person; a rarity in this world.

One who would hate me as soon as I accomplished my goal.

Azurill was her friend, a close friend at that, and one she'd known for many years. She would never forgive me for killing him. Which shouldn't even matter, considering that I would disappear once I got my vengeance. I'd be back to skulking through the streets and ensuring no one found me—except even more paranoid after assassinating the High King.

My life would never be like Faiza's. It wasn't fair, but life never was. I ached for the future I had imagined for myself as a child, the one that had been so cruelly ripped away from me. This wasn't that life, despite the similarities they shared. This was all make-believe, and allowing myself to believe anything different, as if I were really Lady Jacinth Tawny, would only lead to heartbreak.

So I listened to the crowd's *oohs* and *awws*, focusing on bringing my mind back to the void I always found inside myself before breaking into targeted places. That was what I needed now—the agility and grace of a dancer paired with the cunning and skill of a thief.

I sank into that mindset and stilled my anxious movements, breathing calmly as I waited. Time passed, but I couldn't even tell how much as it all blurred together in the darkness, until finally Alfrikr leaned in to whisper in my ear.

"Faiza's gotten through. She had some trouble with a few obstacles, but you'll see her on the other side." He chuckled, his words good-natured but laced with the ominousness of whatever lay on the other side of the course.

The moment the blind fold came off, and I finished blinking into the sun as my vision adjusted, my eyes unerringly found Azurill in his box. He was leaning forward, watching intently, and I sent him a smirk, letting my cockier side come out to play. I may have gotten myself captured by Carnelian, but I'd escaped ridiculous odds until that point. I knew I was good, and now it was time to prove it, even if this uppity ass believed it had something to do with him. Azurill raised a brow at me, his lips twitching like they wanted to match it, but too many eyes were on him.

"Lady Jacinth," Alfrikr stepped in front of me, taking up my vision and successfully blocking the king. "You will be ranked according to both how fast you get through the course and how quickly you make it back to the palace. Those points will continue through each challenge, being weighed when discussions of eliminations come about, and should the need arise, those final points will be used to break any ties."

He eyed me intently. "Do you understand?"

"Crystal clear," I responded, knowing that each moment that eclipsed was vitally important, and I wouldn't take that knowledge for granted.

"In three…" He raised his hand, and I spotted Azurill watching me from above as I adjusted my stance, preparing to run. "Two…one…go!"

I took off immediately, letting Azurill and the crowd fade into the background completely. This was just like when I broke into an Earl's home in Sapphire; they had put in all sorts of traps that I'd had to navigate. It still stung that I managed all that, and yet got caught in Ruby Court's ancient castle of all places.

The first obstacle lay in front of me, with a dangling rope leading up to a high wooden platform with low walls on each side. I grabbed the rope firmly and pulled myself hand over fist up to the top. *Easy.* Looking around after I landed, I realized nothing but empty space stretched in front of me, the next tower some distance away. Much too far for me to jump, even with a running start.

Looking down, there was no rope, no ladder, just a too-high distance clearly not meant to be traversed, and what seemed to be a number of wooden planks lying across the ground, like a bridge had been ripped down. Checking over the platform I stood on, I noticed the small tiles scattered across the floor, and on one wall, there it was: a puzzle set into the wall. I groaned, but knelt down and turned my attention to it.

I ruminated on it for a moment, eyeing the row of blocks that each had a word or two written across them. Underneath each block, there were differing numbers of empty spaces where the tiles would go. Each tile depicted a gem, and I figured we must need to find the right combinations used in the alchemy of gem magic.

The first block read "future love", and there were two empty spaces beneath it. I merely needed to fill them in with the gems necessary to fuel the magic of a potion that would reveal a future love. I grabbed the pearl and sapphire tiles, fitting them into the puzzle. Sure enough, a piece of the bridge below popped up to the platform's height.

The next word was 'honesty', and I grabbed the diamond, filling it in. 'Self-protection' followed, and I put in the emerald and onyx. The combinations got more and more complex, but I quickly matched them all up until the bridge was whole and I sprinted across it.

Upon reaching the tower, I found a series of bars leading out over a large pool of water. I jumped up to grab the first bar and then swung myself over to the next. I nearly squealed when I felt a splash hit me, more water circling and wrapping itself around my legs like a pair of boots. I looked down to see the pool below had risen like a giant tidal wave, making me swallow slightly as it loomed below me, threatening more than I could handle. When it began to yank on my legs, weightier than water should've been, I let out a stream of all the vicious swears I'd learned on the streets.

I fought against its hold, kicking and flailing my legs until I finally broke free. The moment I did, I acted quickly, using all of my core muscles, and I lifted my body until it was flat against the bars. I watched the wave below to see what it would do, even as my muscles burned from my position. To my surprise, the water lowered back down until it dispersed into the pool. I took the opportunity presented and resumed swinging across the bars.

Unfortunately, the water must have hit the bars when it rose, leaving it wetter than I'd expected, and my grip began to slip. I tried to tighten my fingers around the bar, but I couldn't get them to stick, and despite my struggle, the fingers of my left hand slid off, causing me to nearly lose my hold on the bar entirely. I was hanging by one hand, my body heavy as I fought to keep my right hand wrapped firmly around the bar.

A spark of fear rushed through me. I couldn't lose this, not when *everything* was at stake. I took a deep breath, calming myself as I ignored the crowd. They were all sitting forward in excitement, the anticipation of watching me fall into the water below nothing but a thrilling show to them.

As the wave began to reform and rise again, I thought through the options available to me. Try to grab another handhold and hope it worked, or…

I moved my free hand back to the last bar I'd left behind and swung myself up above the bar itself, the wave crashing against it just as I lay myself flat on top of it, the bar digging into my waist. The wave seemed to hover for a moment, as if looking for its target, but I seemed to be out of its reach now. Thank Erodite, it was just as I suspected. They'd rigged it to pull us down, but didn't think of setting it up to reach *above* the bars.

As soon as the water fell again, I quickly maneuvered over the bars and began to make my way across them. I took a moment to congratulate myself on outsmarting the damn water and the king as I hit the last bar and began lowering myself down the ladder that led to the ground below.

Except once I'd lowered myself fully, the ground I had seen on my way down was nowhere to be seen. Instead, I was in some sort of dark corridor, enclosed on all sides. Dread filled my throat, nearly choking me, but I managed to take a step forward.

And let out a scream as I was attacked.

CHAPTER 15

Jacinth

IMMEDIATELY dodged the attack, retaliating with a punch sent towards them, only for my hand to sail through right through thin air. I staggered for a second, off balance from the attempted hit, before I straightened in shock as what just happened registered fully.

How was there no one there? I'd felt the attack, the air moving as a hit sailed towards me, my intuition screaming at me that it was heading right towards me.

I dodged its attack, but ended up crashing into the wall. I huffed angrily as I looked around critically, trying to figure out what in Adamah was going on. I finally caught the barest glimpse as it approached once more; a dark shadow, barely noticeable in the darkness surrounding me. All I could make out was that it was shaped vaguely like an Elf, only with no features or true form to it. As I dodged another hit and tried to counter with my own once more, I still couldn't land a single hit, my fists meeting nothing but air.

That told me one thing: *It wasn't real.*

It had to be an illusion of some sort, one that kept coming at me, likely trying to force me off course like the water. I wasn't sure if it could actually touch me, it would depend on what kind of magic was used in its creation, but I wasn't taking any chances. Examining the tunnel, I could see it wasn't strictly a tunnel, as other paths split off from it, making it all too easy to get lost in the darkness. I could only guess that I had to make it to the other end without getting sidetracked.

More shadows appeared, but I forced myself to ignore the projections chasing after me, barreling onward so I wouldn't lose the path forward.

A new illusion popped up, trying to wave me over to a tea party that was taking place at the entrance to one of branching paths. All the ladies around the table invited me to join them with loud shouts of welcome. Fortunately, I had absolutely zero desire to spend time with most noble ladies, so the temptation failed to take hold. I merely shook my head and continued.

More illusions popped up as I went, and I ignored each and every one, unwaveringly set on my course. As I neared the end of the visible path, I expected it to continue or open or *something*, but instead I hit a wall, nearly smashing my face off where the tunnel apparently came to an abrupt end. I immediately began running my hands along the wall, looking for a lever or a rock to push, anything that would trigger an exit. A spike of panic shot through me as I realized there was no way out.

No way, except doubling back.

Fuck.

One of these illusions had to lead me to the right exit. My very incorrect assumption of how this worked had already cost me precious time. I hadn't paid any attention to the illusions after passing the tea party, but I would need to evaluate them and see if there was any way to determine which was the right one. The wrong choice would only cost me further. I slowly retraced my steps, ever mindful of how much time it was taking me. Every second counted when it came to my chances of winning.

My vengeance counted on those seconds.

"*Linnea.*"

Every muscle in my body froze, and my heart contracted like someone had reached into my chest and squeezed. That name had no place here. There was no way for anyone to *know* that name—not in connection to me, at least.

"*Linnea. Come here, my little pearl.*"

My breath caught in my throat alongside the sob I tried to strangle down. This was too cruel.

I hadn't heard my father's voice in years, but I remembered its resonance easily enough, and there was no mistaking it now. My feet led my trembling body forward without my mind's command, aching to be closer to the voice calling out.

"*This way.*" he whispered, and I sped up, his voice a lighthouse in the suffocating darkness, a shining beacon to save me from the storm of my existence.

Except...he wasn't there.

I tried to see through the gloom, but even Elven eyesight was useless in this. I put my hands up to feel for anything that may be around me. I found a rock wall on my right, and slowly started to walk along it, my fingertips never leaving the anchoring stones.

My father's voice echoed from a different direction, and I spun around, only to realize it was the same illusion as before. I stood still, gathering myself mentally and trying to regulate my breathing, all to prevent my body from moving toward the mirage it desperately ached for. The pieces of my pulverized heart slowly released the agonizing pressure on my chest, until—

"*Mommy!*" A little voice called, "*Mommy!*"

Fuck. These illusions weren't some preset image, which at least meant that no one had figured out who I really was, but they had to be using magic to divine our innermost fears and desires. I couldn't think of anything else this could be. Not when it somehow knew the things I kept closest to my heart.

My fear of attack. My desire to fit in. My parents.

They started out small and got worse the more we ignored them, digging the knife deeper each time.

My horrible, stupid, *useless* desire for family was now manifesting into the impossible. A future once promised to me, its potential torn cruelly away. I blinked, trying to rid myself of the moisture gathering in my eyes; tears were worthless here.

I instead focused on the rock wall under my hands. Feeling my way along it, I realized the wall bent to the left, except, no illusions were in that direction. Tilting my head to the side curiously, I followed the wall instead. The illusions began popping up then, getting stronger the further I went. So maybe my supposition about them was wrong, and this game was something else entirely. I forced myself to ignore them and continue along the contours of the wall.

When illusion approached with a flickering candle in hand, I took the opportunity to look around in the light. I gasped to find my arm halfway through a wall, everything past my elbow missing. I wiggled my fingers, feeling them brush the rock, and realized immediately what was going on here.

None of this was real. Not even the tunnel before my eyes. I didn't have to find the right illusion; I had to find the real exit under the illusion itself.

I saw a slight shimmer ahead, a tiny bit of magic breaking through, and made for it straight away. As I barreled through the shimmer, light assailed my eyes, making me blink quickly as my vision adjusted to the sunlight.

The crowd was cheering, and the noise was nearly grating after hearing only whispers in the darkness.

I looked up into the crowd, my eyes narrowing on the royal box. Azurill was smirking at me from where he was sprawled on his throne, but Lord Carnelian was sitting back, a satisfied look on his face. I set my shoulders back under their watching eyes and continued on, trying to shake off what had just happened. I had buried that desire for a family for years, and now was definitely *not* the right time for it to rear its ugly head.

I focused instead on the thin rope connecting the tower across the way from the one I'd found myself on upon escaping the tunnel. This course was seriously messing with my equilibrium, magic thrumming through every installation, explaining the strange topsy-turvy nature of its entrances and exits.

At least this next one seemed pretty straightforward. The rope made it very clear what I needed to do, but the beams hanging in disparate intervals on either side of it the entire way across made my success a little less certain. I swallowed hard; I had zero desire to be crushed to death today.

I centered my balance and stepped a toe onto the rope. I slowly put one foot in front of the other, ignoring the jeers from the crowd right along with the cheers of encouragement. When the first beam to my right started to swing toward me, I jumped forward on the rope, heart pounding as it *just* missed hitting me.

Of *course*, why wouldn't they put us physically off balance after doing it emotionally?

I took another step, and a beam on my left began to swing, moving even faster than the first, forcing me to back up a step to avoid taking a hit. I tried to move more quickly from there, but as I took another step, I heard the almost collective inhale of the crowd. It didn't take a genius to realize they were waiting for something to happen. I almost paused, but I forced myself forward, and as the beams began flying at me, faster and faster, I was thankful for my father's lessons about not hesitating when it mattered.

I wobbled when I stopped abruptly to avoid a sudden spinning beam, throwing my arms out to stabilize myself. I let out a low breath as the rope finally stopped jumping under my toes, and lifted my right foot to continue, but my eyes widened as I realized the beam on the other side was already coming at me. There was no way it wouldn't hit me, and the crowd clearly knew that too, as their collective gasps rang deafeningly in my ears.

I took a deep breath for all of half a second before I called on every dance lesson I'd ever been through and, with one wobbling, risky-as-Tartarus bounce, I threw myself up into the air. The wind rushed in my eyes as I flipped mid-air, timed to fall when the beam swung back—-*perfect.*

The crowd went wild as my toe landed back on the rope, but I made myself finish the last half of the tightrope before I allowed myself to celebrate. A quick glance at the royal box showed me that Azurill had collapsed back into his seat, a look of relief painted across his chiseled face. He ran a hand over the top of his hair, raking through the teal hair there as he rubbed his sharp jaw, speaking to the sapphire-haired man sitting beside him. I refocused my eyes forward, not wanting to lose because I was too busy watching the stupid king, and sighed deeply when my foot hit the wood of the tower's platform.

And yet, still, I was far from done.

I scurried down the side of the tower and found there was a small circular tunnel on the ground before me. It was so tiny that I had to contort my limbs just to get into it. I crawled through the dirty ground as my braid rubbed along the walls, pieces of pink hair coming loose and irritating me by falling into my eyes. My breathing sounded like the sharp whizzes of firing arrows, high pitched and frantic, the darkness somehow worse than the previous tunnel when combined with the enclosed space. I shut my eyes, blocking out the sight as I reminded myself that I wasn't in that small, dark closet.

I'd dealt with this kind of panic many times, and Ula's advice came back to me in a rush…

Ten…nine…eight…I wasn't there…seven…six…five…I was no longer small and helpless…four…three…two…I was going to kill the bastard who caused this…one…

When my breathing finally evened out, only slight hitches remaining, I forced myself into action, because yes—if I could just get through this, I could make the man responsible pay, but if I failed to win, then all of this was for nothing., Zumra would have to do this too, ruining her hair as she crawled through the dirt, which at least brought a smile to my face.

It didn't last long, though, as despite the fact that I was beginning to see light emanating from the end of the tunnel as I shuffle-crawled my way through it, the memories kept trying to drag me back. But with the monster who orchestrated that tragedy watching on, I couldn't afford to crumble.

When my head finally cleared the tunnel after what felt like years, I was able to breathe in the fresh air as the sun hit my face, allowing those memories to fade into the back of my mind once more. I crept all the way out and stood to face the next challenge, refusing to let it show that such a simple obstacle had affected me so powerfully.

I could see a rock wall waiting in the distance, but getting to it was obviously going to be another challenge. What had been the dirty, slightly sandy ground of the arena was now…broken. Vast voids instead yawned into an endless nothing, with only a map of platforms interspersed throughout providing a way across. I'd have to cross this wasteland before making it to the wall, and it was clear to me that I'd need to jump to each platform to even have a chance of making it with the large gaps between each one. They weren't all spaced apart evenly, either, with some smaller apertures and some much larger and riskier.

My years of planning heists came in handy now, with my brain automatically jumping to different tactics and mapping out the different routes I could take to reach the other side. After judging each platform's distance and which jumps would be easiest, I found the perfect path forward and jumped onto the first platform.

Once I'd landed, I couldn't help looking over, straight down into the void. Chills broke out along my skin, and I shivered, redirecting my focus forward. I had no idea what might be waiting below or if it was just some kind of illusion, but the idea of falling endlessly through that nothingness was a nightmare I had no desire to experience.

I hopped to the second platform, but as a bellowing roar echoed out into the arena, and the noise from the crowd picked up once more in tandem, I jumped in a rare burst of absolute fright. My head flew in the direction the roar came from, and I found a fucking *lion* bounding toward me.

My eyes widened in shock as I processed what I was seeing. It wasn't even just that there was a damned *lion* headed right toward me, but this was definitely not an ordinary lion. This was a beast made entirely of magic. The shimmering fur of silver, sapphire, emerald, and onyx made it crystal clear that it had been created with a specific purpose in mind. Each gem had its own properties, and each had been added to make a creature that would work to the exact goal they had in mind when creating it.

I eyed the rock wall I was heading toward and hurriedly jumped across to the next platform. Before I could get to the next one in my planned path, however, the lion had already caught up to me. I swore under my breath as, with a large leap, it skidded onto the platform, its claws digging in. It let out a bellowing roar, its multicolored mane shaking as it shook its head.

A shiver went down my spine as its multi-faceted diamond eyes watched me with the kind of intelligence that could only have come from the magic powering it. I tried to shuffle slowly right, and it followed me step for step, one large paw after the other shifting to the side. My perfect route across was definitely blown now, but I needed to get to that rock wall regardless.

They'd definitely put their all into this damned course. No wonder it felt like forever waiting for Faiza to finish; I was having issues, and I was already used to the obstacles that came with being a thief, activities that most noble ladies would faint at. I could only imagine how much longer it would take someone not used to it like I was.

But I'd been chased more than once to avoid capture, and a magical lion wasn't going to get the best of me now.

I kept moving to the right like I was going to continue in that direction, before abruptly turning on my heel and sprinting to the left, the roar of the lion's anger chasing me as I readied to jump the distance to the next platform. I sprang upward, flying through the air before landing on the next one, my breath coming hard and fast as I tried to get to the next best platform.

Except I felt the wind shift as it was displaced…the godsdamned lion had caught up again, landing solidly in front of me and blocking my way forward.

I looked up to where Azurill sat watching, narrowing my eyes at him in irritation. His lips twitched, like he was about to smile, but he managed to get his expression under control before I was forced to accelerate my plans for murder.

Smart man.

Considering my next move, I was forced to admit that the lion was much too fast for me to get across the easier platforms I'd planned on using without getting mauled in the process. I also wasn't about to attempt the ones spaced so far apart that I would need giant running leaps to make it across, if it was even possible at all. I had no wish to fall into whatever pit was waiting below.

Ula had taught me that it was always better to conserve your energy and use your brain to defeat your opponent when you could. Which left me with only one option.

Outsmarting the beast.

I shifted from foot to foot, like I might take off at any moment, and the lion bristled, its fur standing on end as it slunk low into a position that would easily allow it to pounce at the slightest wrong move. Massive teeth were exposed as it snarled at me, its tail flicking menacingly back and forth from high up in the air.

What I really needed was to get to the platform positioned directly behind the lion, but it was determined to block me from it, guarding its territory fiercely. It watched me closely, its whiskers twitching with the snarling movement of its upper lip, looking much too satisfied as I shivered in instinctual fear at the predator before me.

"Here, kitty kitty," I cooed at it, and its tail stilled for a moment before starting to swish faster, drawing my eye to it. It had a tuft at the end that was tipped in emerald with sapphire at its base, the colors bleeding into one another. The rest of its long rope of a tail was made up of a shimmery silver and black swirl.

Those colors were a representation of its magic. Emerald for protection, sapphire for wisdom, diamond for power, and onyx to manipulate the body, creating its form. It had plenty of power, surely, and the wisdom in its eyes gave it enough insight to be a problem, but more than anything, it was built to protect this spot, and it wouldn't be swayed. It would prevent me from reaching that rock wall, or it would die trying.

Which meant if I went in the opposite direction, I might stand a chance of confusing it, making it think I'd given up on trying to get to the wall. It was worth a shot, at least. I needed to do *something* to get this moving when every second counted towards my standing in the competition.

Bouncing on the balls of my feet, I looked into the lion's eyes and then spun around, running in the opposite direction. A confused rumble came from behind me, and I looked back to see its head tilted to the side like a bewildered puppy before it huffed and lay its head down on its paws.

Satisfied that it had scared me off.

A slow smirk grew on my face at the thought.

CHAPTER 16

Azurill

THE obstacle course was one of the more physically demanding tasks we had planned for the ladies over the course of the competition, but it would also tell me a lot about each of them. I wanted to ensure it was done early on, so I could see what each of them could potentially bring to the role of queen.

Each obstacle within the challenge would reveal much, not only about their problem-solving capabilities and their physical endurance, but also their cunning and willpower. All qualities that would be needed in the role.

This trial had been a bit of a team effort, with the original idea coming from Balthazar initially before being expanded upon by Arianell. They had first recommended this course as a way to test that the ladies were both intelligent and physically capable, but we'd adapted it to include challenges that would tell us much more. I was quite fond of Emrys's addition; he'd had the idea for the illusions. If the ladies could face their fears and resist their desires to find the right way out, it would prove their fortitude and willpower to fight through base emotions and focus on finding the correct path forward.

That was *essential* when it came to ruling…and to me. I wanted more than anything to find someone who could be more than a piece of eye candy or a womb to breed heirs. I wanted a *partner*. Like my mother had been to my father.

When Faiza began running the course, I was curious to see if she would throw the whole thing right away. I'd had to practically beg her to join this farce to begin with, since it required having someone from Diamond included. Thankfully, however, she made a convincing show of trying, and I let out a sigh of relief as she made it through the obstacle course.

Though it was not without issues. We knew some would struggle mightily, had intended for it even, which is why we'd insisted on blindfolds so that none of the ladies could watch the others go through the course. Faiza had gotten especially tripped up on the illusion tunnel. She'd followed the illusions out of the wrong exit twice before she figured out that she needed to look past them, forcing her to have to redo the course from the beginning each time she got the wrong one.

I had no idea what fear or desire had led her in there, since we couldn't see what illusions the ladies experienced. We thought that was only fair since the magic was pulling out such deeply personal information. We didn't have the right to see their deepest fears or desires, nor did the crowd of thousands.

Faiza wasn't a very active person in her day-to-day, so she'd struggled through much of the course. She did find a workaround for the tightrope, using her hands to swing through it like the bars on the prior obstacle, which also meant that she managed to avoid the swinging beams entirely.

But it was with the lion Ruri had masterfully created to guard the path to the rock wall that she'd surprised me the most. Faiza had always been the sweetest of the noble ladies at court, which is why I viewed her as something like a surrogate sister, and her actions today not only proved that but were also incredibly amusing. She somehow managed to charm the lion, sitting down and letting it sniff her, getting it acclimated to her until she had its giant head in her lap.

When she had the fierce supposed protector as docile as a kitten, she merely waited for it to drift off and then snuck out from under it, crossing the rest of the platforms to the rock wall.

I knew from the start that Jacinth would be very different. I tried my hardest not to show any special interest in her, not as a potential spy or as a potential *anything else*. Yet somehow, my eagerness to see her run the course must have been more obvious than I'd thought.

"My cousin will prove herself most adept with this task, I assure you, Your Majesty." Lord Carnelian announced boldly, smirking from where he sat a few chairs down.

"I suppose we'll see," I replied, giving him a nod and keeping my face as controlled as possible. His smug superiority was grating, and I preferred to deal with him as little as possible. On the other hand, Ruri's suspicions were clearly at the forefront of his mind, making him more than willing to jump in.

"And what makes you so sure, my Lord?" Ruri asked, raising a dubious eyebrow at Carnelian as he leaned around me to face him.

"Jacinth is, as you've seen, quite lithe and agile," he responded without hesitation, condescension dripping from every word. "I have no doubt she will manage the physical aspects with aplomb."

"And what about the mental aspects?" Ruri pressed, staring him down. "What kind of mental fortitude have you instilled the girl with?"

I closed my eyes momentarily, wishing I could shake my brother. He was doing everything he could to try to get information from the lords, testing their loyalties and looking for lies, all in the hopes of solving the mystery of our brother's death. While I wanted to know just as badly, I couldn't help but be concerned about the way he was chasing this.

"Well, I unfortunately can't take the credit." Carnelian sniffed, almost as if in distaste. It certainly wouldn't surprise me. "I had little to do with her until recently, since she wasn't raised in my court. But her cunning is without question, despite the lack of influence I've had over the girl. It must be something in the blood."

Ruri snorted softly, shaking his head in disbelief as he turned to me, raising a brow. Carnelian's deflection was expected, but his wording took me aback. While Ruri may doubt the truth of it, I knew Carnelian better than that.

The man preferred his lies to be told with nothing but the honest truth. He'd twist and turn his words until the meaning was unclear, sure enough, but he rarely outright lied.

This could be one of those rare times, but it could also be the absolute truth that he had ignored the girl until she was useful to him in some way. Say when the High King needed a lady from Ruby to compete to be his wife.

Lady Jacinth had been something different from the first moment I saw her. Every interaction with her left me more intrigued by her, needing to find out more about her. I couldn't tell whether it was from suspicion or attraction half the time, which was definitely concerning.

As king, I needed to maintain control over my desires as well as my actions, but…especially after the picnic, when I got to spend some one-on-one time with her for longer than the span of a single dance, I found myself lost on what I was feeling or what to do about it.

Watching Jacinth as her blindfold was removed, allowing her to take in the obstacle course set before her, I could see the fire scorching through her eyes as they narrowed. Her body straightened as she set her shoulders back, bouncing on the balls of her feet, preparing to take the course on with a determination I'd rarely seen in other ladies at court.

I was anxious to see how she would do. There were some ladies that I knew would have a terribly difficult time, Zumra and Safira coming to mind immediately, and I was already amused imagining them taking it on. Some I wasn't sure about, as I didn't know Sania, Amatista, Allirea, or Ophira well enough to guess, but I was positive that Jacinth would demolish this trial.

Thinking of Sania, remorse grew in my heart. Looking from her to Jacinth, it was too easy to imagine Jacinth as someone else. Sania wouldn't be the daughter of Pearl standing here today; instead, Lady Linnea herself would be here to represent Pearl Court. Her vivid pink hair and eyes would have been so similar to Jacinth's.

It was on me that she wasn't alive today, and that was something I had to live with forever. It was never easy when children got caught up in the political games played in court, but little Linnea's death had always weighed on me the most. Perhaps it was her father's fondly amused comments to me about her wish to marry me one day, or the brutality dealt out on a child who never should have gotten in the middle of that mess—either way, her blood stained my hands and refused to wash off.

Watching Jacinth now, her long mane of candy-pink hair braided back behind her head as she ran forward, I pushed all thoughts of the past away, focusing instead on the future.

Watching Jacinth contort her body over the bars and balance across the rope, I was wholly impressed. Maybe I shouldn't be surprised that a dancer had such skill, since she'd shown off her flexibility and agility quite clearly during her routine, but this was on another level. While I'd never admit Carnelian was right, she showed her cunning plainly as she found a way to work around the water attempting to drag her down or the beams trying to knock her off.

She didn't even take one of the false exits the illusions would try to lead her to, meaning she was able to master herself when it came to fear and desire without much hardship. A remarkable feat, surely, but as she approached the lion, I found myself leaning forward, intensely curious as to how she would handle the challenge.

I could practically see her mind spinning as she looked over the platforms she had to navigate, like she was mapping out the best course to take in her mind. When the lion appeared, my eyes eagerly awaited her reaction, and the narrow-eyed glare she sent me made me want to smirk back at her, but the eyes on me from everyone nearby kept me from letting my lips do more than twitch.

I was thankful Ruri thought of this just for her reaction alone. Something about the way she had no hesitation in challenging me was thrilling. It was so rare that anyone dared these days. It had been years since I'd had interactions with anyone outside my friends and family that felt so *normal.* Even the ladies I took to bed treated me as the king, not as a man.

With Jacinth, things were very different. I found myself wanting to earn the pleasure of her smile or the disapproval of her upturned nose. Every reaction had me wanting to push for the next.

It was ridiculous, and Ruri would certainly kill me if he found out. Only his avid desire to avoid kingship might save me.

Jacinth tried to run quickly around the lion, but that had no hope of working, and once she seemed to realize that she…turned and ran in the opposite direction she needed to be going, leaving both the lion and me utterly confused. Mutters rose around me as the nobles in the box continued their incessant chatter about every little thing that happened.

"What is that foolish girl doing?" I heard Carnelian mutter to himself, a scowl firmly set on his face.

I leaned further forward, trying hopelessly to get a better view of her. I watched as the perplexed lion looked back toward the wall, then huffed and sat down, which is when Jacinth turned her head to look back with a smirk. She somehow spun on her feet faster than I'd ever seen, and raced back toward the wall. She jumped from platform to platform more swiftly than I'd thought she was capable of.

And the lion hadn't noticed what she was doing at all. My breath caught as I realized the beast had assumed she'd given up—and thus let its guard down. It was only as Jacinth sped past him that he finally realized what had happened.

The crowd roared just as the beast did. Its ground-shaking anger was nearly silenced by the people standing up and cheering as Jacinth raced forward, outpacing the lion now running swiftly after her. My hands curled around the bar in front of me as my heart picked up speed in tandem with her.

Jacinth's head whipped backward to check on the lion, and seeing it was beginning to catch up, she faced forward once more, flat out sprinting across the platforms now. She neared the last one she needed to cross, but the lion was gaining on her, so close that when he swiped out a huge paw, her braid flew with the wind generated by the motion—

Until she pushed off her feet and sailed upwards in the air and over the chasm, clearing the last platform and landing nimbly, now standing before the wall she'd needed to reach.

My hands relaxed their tight grip as the crowd went wild, the lion dissipating into thin air with its role fulfilled for now.

I sat back in my seat, a small smile on my face as I looked forward to watching her complete this last challenge, which *we* would get to see at least. Almost as much as I looked forward to her comments about this later.

Only Ruri's watchful eyes kept me from truly feeling relief at that moment.

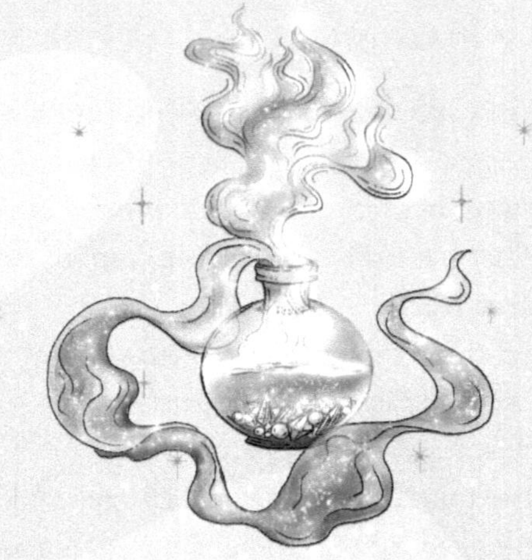

CHAPTER 17

Jacinth

Landing on the other side of the platform, my lungs screaming for breath and my muscles aching, I turned back just in time to witness the lion dissipating into smoke. I shook my head, taking a deep breath as I turned my head back to face the new challenge before me.

I was so close. I just had to push myself a little further, but dammit if that run hadn't taken a lot out of me. I haven't run so fast in years. Not since the time I had to outrun the guards in Emerald after Ula's contact betrayed us.

The rock wall before me looked mostly normal, but I'd learned not to take anything for granted in this course. I chanced a look toward the royal box but brought my eyes back to the wall the second they met the amused ruby-red ones of Casaan. The man made my skin crawl, not like the blue-green gaze I could also feel raking over my form as I lifted my hand to the first hold and gripped it to pull myself up the wall.

I found a hold for my legs, and lifted my hand for the next hand hold, only for the rocks to start shaking under me. I sighed in exasperation and watched as the rocks began to shift, moving left and right, up and down. I was forced to move quickly to accommodate the shifting rocks as the ones I was standing on began to shift, too.

It was all I could do to keep finding new handholds and footholds, not making any progress up the wall, but in fact barely managing to prevent myself from ending up further down. I rolled my eyes, huffing and just so done with this—I didn't even *want* to marry this damn man!

Maybe if I stopped thinking of it as winning the coveted title of wife to that monster, and more as a chance at winning the opportunity to kill him, it'd be better.

More accurate, at least.

Even if a distinctly uneasy feeling brewed in my gut now at the thought.

I brushed that feeling aside immediately. It was nothing but weakness, and weakness was to be mastered; any thief worth their salt knew that. I was getting caught up in comfy beds and noble friends, a dream life lost long ago, and that would be my downfall if I didn't get ahold of myself.

Reaching a hand up to grasp another rock, I quickly swung my feet as the rocks moved out from under me, grappling for another foothold higher up until one finally presented itself. I had to move fast, my hands and feet shuffling forward and backward as the rocks moved constantly. I felt like I'd barely made any progress in getting up the wall at all.

So instead, I examined the rocks, finding imperfections that would help identify them quickly. I moved when necessary, but kept my eyes on them, trying to find a pattern in their movements. It took two full rotations for me to see the way they were shifting and begin to anticipate them.

Right, down, down, left, up, up, left, up, up, left, right, down, down—on and on they went.

Knowing the pattern, I was able to figure out where the hand and footholds would appear, and was able to finally start making my way up the wall. As I neared the top, I heard the crowd behind me going wild, screaming my name and cheering.

A small smile took over my face, proud, despite myself, at what I had achieved today. As I reached the very top and pulled my body all the way up, I found what looked like an enclosed slide, something I would have to throw myself down into, facing the dark unknown.

They'd said this course was only the first half of this trial, and whatever was waiting on the other side wasn't going to be conquered any faster by waiting around.

I turned back to the cheering crowd and lifted my arms in celebration, which they seemed to love, and took the time to blow a sarcastic kiss to Azurill. I could still make him out from here, but not his expression. I enjoyed imagining it anyway, the eyebrow raising, the smirk growing, and took the image with me as I slid myself down into the slide before me.

I shot through the darkness, sliding down and down and across what felt like the entire city until I eventually was spat out—literally, as I tumbled out of the blasted thing, my knees hitting the dirt with an echoing thud.

"Oh thank Veritx!" Faiza's relieved exclamation had me blinking in confusion, and I looked up to find her rushing over to me. Her leathers were dirtier than when I saw her last, but she thankfully looked fine otherwise.

"Are you alright?" she asked worriedly, looking me up and down as she helped me stand.

"I'm fine, how about you?" I asked her, somewhat distracted as I took in the forest around me. The gloomy wood's treetops prevented any but the barest hint of light from shining in. The shadows seemed to dance around every tree, and a foreboding feeling was heavy in the air, causing chills to break out across my skin.

"I'd be better if we were anywhere else," she admitted, crossing her arms and holding her elbows as she shivered, looking around the area we'd been dumped in.

"Where are we, exactly?" I asked, unsure what was so bad about it despite the weird feeling it gave me. While my instincts said something was up, it seemed innocuous on the surface. A little darkness was fine, sometimes even preferred, as long as the space was wide open.

"The Forest of Discontent," Faiza answered, her face set in a frown. Her turquoise eyes were frightened, and even her brown skin had paled to a lighter shade as her eyes jumped around.

Fuck.

The Forest of Discontent, of course. I should have considered it, but I'd largely forgotten about the place. I hadn't heard much of anything about it since I was a child, when my parents had taken me with them to the capital.

The forest was shrouded in mist, but this wasn't normal mist. Whoever was unlucky enough to get caught in the mists, the forest would make its prey, hunting those who roamed it. The forest was a cranky bastard, for sure. Getting caught in its mists put a target on your back, as if the forest could see you once you were enshrouded in its mists, and it would reach out its spindly wooden branches and shrubby roots to attack.

"Okay, so we just need to avoid the mists and get back to the palace as fast as possible." I rationalized, looking around to see if any path seemed more likely than another to lead back to civilization. "We need—"

"No," Faiza said suddenly, stopping me mid-sentence. I looked back at her, my mouth still hanging open until I closed it with an abrupt clack of teeth.

"No? What do you mean by 'no'?" I asked her, confused at what else she expected us to do. I was surprised when she grabbed onto my arms, looking me in the eye quite seriously.

"Jacinth, you know I'm only here because they needed a candidate from Diamond." She began, her voice shaking the slightest bit. "I have no desire to marry Az and become queen."

"I know that," I assured her quietly, "but we still need to get out of here."

She shook her head, stumping me completely. "This is my shot to get out, Jac. You heard what they said. Any lady not back by sundown will be up for elimination."

"Faiza—" I tried, but she continued.

"Still, only one of us will actually be eliminated," she stressed heavily. "*One*. Which means if more than one of us doesn't make it back, Az could keep either of them. This is my chance to be so damn late, I'm guaranteed to be eliminated!"

"And what are you going to do?" I asked her incredulously. "Hide in the forest? Where the mist will get you?"

"I know a spot." She smiled, satisfaction written all over her face. "Az showed us when we were kids. It's the only spot in the forest where the mist won't go. I'll hide there. Don't worry about me, you need to make it back."

"Faiza," I said helplessly, wanting to convince her otherwise, but knowing I stood little chance. I hated to think of her being out of the competition. She was the only one who seemed at all tolerable. More than that, she was almost like a friend. I knew I would miss her once this was over, and I already mourned the relationship that would be broken with the end of this competition.

"It'll be okay, Jac," she reassured me, pulling me into a hug that made me stiffen uneasily. "And I'll still be here at court, so you're not getting rid of me as easily as Az is."

I couldn't help the laugh that came out of me at that, relaxing into her arms until I finally hugged her back, wishing for a moment that this was all real. That we were merely two noble ladies fighting for our lives to win a crown and a king to call husband…but it wasn't to be, and I knew I couldn't live in that fantasy.

Our friendship might be a fantasy as well, but it was one I could at least hold onto until Azurill was gone. I knew Faiza would never forgive me, not when she couldn't see the same monster I did. He had fooled everyone, and it only made the rage I felt burn that much higher.

As I pulled back, she nodded at me with a smile, "Now get out of here! You have a competition to win!"

"Any idea how to get back to the city?" I asked dubiously, looking around the forest with a wary eye. She giggled, shaking her head at me.

"Not a clue, they dumped us pretty far in, and nothing looks familiar," she admitted with a shrug.

"Then how are you going to find this supposed safe place?" I countered with a raised brow. She looked a bit sheepish, eyes trailing down to where her toe kicked into the dirt.

"Magic is weird sometimes," she told me in halting pauses. "I can find this spot because I've been invited to it by Az, but I couldn't take anyone else there, or it won't show up."

Her explanation left much to be desired, but it was clear her loyalty to Azurill was the reason for it, and not that she was putting herself in danger unnecessarily, so I was begrudgingly fine with it for now.

"You need to get going, though." She hurried me along, "The forest is vast, and you don't want to lose the lead you've gotten." She smiled nervously at me, hugging me once more, before taking off into the gloom.

I sighed, looking around and trying to decide where to go. Everything looked the same in all directions. The grey tree trunks led to deep blue leaves that looked black without any light to illuminate them.

Fuck.

CHAPTER 18

Jacinth

Hours spent wandering the Forest of Discontent left me just as damn discontent as it was.

I couldn't make heads or tails of a direction, and having to run to dodge the mist anytime it came near left me wildly off course whenever I thought I was making some progress.

The creaking of branches in the wind, the snaps as they cracked, the animals scurrying around the forest floor, making bushes and dropped leaves sound about ten times more intimidating than they should be, all of it left me desperate to get out of this place and back to the palace.

I was clearly getting soft. Ula would kill me if she could see me now. A few weeks in a nice palace and suddenly I couldn't rough it anymore.

It was a good reminder, at least. All of this was temporary, and once it was over, I would go back to living far away from the palaces and politics I was once meant for.

I arrived at an intersection with four different paths converging into a little clearing. I looked around, knowing that anything could be coming from the other directions, but I couldn't see anything that stood out. I stepped a foot forward when the sudden sound of shuffling feet made me pause.

I slunk back behind a tree, watching to see who would emerge. I wasn't sure how much time had passed; the lack of sun breaching the treetops made it impossible to track. It could have been any number of the ladies who went through the course after me.

I doubted anyone else was stupid enough to come in here. It wasn't exactly a place people went for fun.

The footsteps slowed as they approached the clearing, and I was just able to make out the purple hair from where I was hiding. Amatista, then. She wasn't the worst person to come across, at least. Had it been Zumra, I'd have run in the other direction.

Amatista came to a full stop, looking around the clearing. I hid further behind the tree since my hair was so brightly colored, and I didn't exactly have a hood to cover it up. A sharp crack rang out, and I cursed silently, picking my foot up off the stick I'd broken.

Amatista's head whipped toward me, and I sighed in defeat, slinking out from my hiding place. She looked me over with narrow eyes and a sharp eyebrow pitching upwards.

"Why were you hiding?" she asked suspiciously, and I appreciated that she wasn't concealing it.

"I didn't know who it was at first." I defended, putting my hands on my hips. Alfrikr's warnings about the cutthroat nature of this competition still rang in my ears, and this way, my hand was close enough to unsheathe my dagger if I needed to.

I was sure Zumra wanted to be queen desperately enough that she'd try to take me out at the first opportunity, but I had no idea about Amethyst's competitor. She remained frustratingly elusive.

"Plus, I don't exactly trust any of the ladies here," I explained, watching her closely enough to see her lips twitch upwards before she straightened them.

"You *do* seem smarter than the others," she said evenly, leaving me feeling vaguely insulted despite the seeming compliment.

"I certainly like to think so," I responded, and got another almost-smile from her.

"We should go together." She nodded, her tone decisive, as if she'd decided for both of us.

"And why would I go with you?" I asked her skeptically, internally weighing my options.

"Because two heads are better than one when it comes to getting out of here," she argued, blinking as if shocked that I would argue. "We're both smart, and you're different from the other ladies. Take Zumra, for instance. We both know she'd step over us to get to the palace first. I've been watching everyone closely, and you don't have the same entitlement the others do. You befriended Faiza right away, despite many seeing her as the weak link due to her position. So, I trust you to have my back should the need arise, and I'll have yours in return."

"Why would you bother having my back when we're supposed to be competing against one another?" I asked her more for clarification than for argument's sake. I didn't see why she would trust me when logic said the opposite should be true.

She sighed, frustrated, as she ran a hand through her voluminous amethyst hair. Her tie had come loose at some point, leaving the purple waves to fall around her face and down past her shoulders.

"My father insisted I enter this stupid thing," she admitted, looking down at the ground and avoiding my eyes. "I couldn't tell him the truth."

"The truth?" I questioned, my eyebrow raising.

"That I'm in love with someone else," she said quietly, as if her father might hear her from here. "He wants to marry me off for the biggest advantage he can get." She scoffed, shaking her head. "But I have no desire to win and be forced to marry High King Azurill."

She smiled, her hands coming out and flipping to show me her palms. "So, you see? We have no real reason to have any enmity between us. We might as well help one another out of this damn forest. Despite my lack of desire to win, I do want to live."

I couldn't help cracking a smile at that and sighed in defeat, nodding my head in agreement. "Alright, any ideas then, Lady Amatista?"

"Please, call me Tista." She smiled proudly, "And as a matter of fact, I do."

"Okay, Tista," I said, feeling a bit off balance to be seemingly making more friends among the nobles. More people who'd be hurt when this was all over. "What are you thinking?"

"I've been heading East for at least an hour, and this is the first intersection of its kind I've found," she explained, grabbing a stick to begin sketching in the dirt. "I know the palace is Northeast, so I think if we veer North, we might have the best luck at finding a way out."

My eyebrows flew upward, impressed by her navigational skills. I had no idea what direction the palace was from here. She was from Amethyst Court, though, known for its scholars, and she'd already proven at the talent competition that she had followed that pursuit avidly.

We began to turn Northeast when the hair on my arms stood on end. I paused, grabbing Amatista's arm and bringing her to a halt.

"What?" she asked, looking around with alarm. "What's wrong?"

I wasn't sure *what*, but something was definitely *wrong*.

It was then I spotted it, spitting out a curse as the mist flooded through the trees, heading straight toward us. The mist looked like regular fog, but I had no desire to find out exactly how it differed once you were inside of it. So we immediately began running Northeast, hoping to outrun the swirling haze that seemed to be chasing us.

Amatista kept up with my fast pace admirably, only panting a bit and lagging a step or two behind. Our heads were both constantly swiveling behind us to track the mist as we ran, branches and leaves swatting us in the face as we tried to keep heading in the right direction despite the mist trying to force us off the path as much as possible.

"Fuck," I swore, watching the way the mist determinedly kept after us, sweeping over the forest in the exact direction we needed to continue in. It seemed to be speeding up too, and I knew with a certainty that I felt in my bones that we wouldn't be able to avoid it swallowing us into its depths.

"It's coming straight for us!" Amatista practically yelled, the sound of the mist surprisingly loud as it loomed closer. As if an unnatural tempest existed within it.

"We're going to be swallowed in it!" I shouted back to her, a branch slapping against my thigh as I veered to the right. I swore as I stumbled, but kept on, not letting it slow me down further.

We both took deep breaths as the mist nipped at our heels, readying for whatever was about to come. With an almighty roar, the mist rolled over us, shrouding my vision in white and grey.

"Tista!" I yelled, my panic increasing with the lack of visibility.

"Still here!" she replied, her voice shaking a bit. I reached over to where her voice came from, finding her hand and interlocking our fingers.

"Hold on, and don't let go," I instructed her. Something about the fear in her voice made me determined to get her out of here.

The noise seemed to still for a moment, leaving us in a disturbing silence, like the eye of a storm. And then in a rush, the sound came back. Not just rushing wind, but a screeching sound that had me covering an ear with my free hand, hoping to dim the noise even the slightest bit.

"Jacinth!" Amatista called, her voice and hand both shaking equally.

"Keep running! We just need to outrun this and we'll be fine!" I replied firmly, but not unkindly.

Only it was then it began, like it saw my determination as a dare. The Forest of Discontent had earned its name, I thought ruefully, as branches and vines began snaking up from the ground, hitting my limbs with loud thwaps, digging into my skin with their thorns, and leaving trails of blood running down from the punctures.

I tried to keep running, but was yanked back by Amatista as she stopped moving. I turned to yell at her, only for her scream to ring out instead.

"Jacinth! It has me!" she cried, and dread pulsed through me.

"What do you mean?" I asked frantically, unable to see what was happening through the heavy fog.

"The vines wrapped around my ankles and won't let go." she replied shakily, and the tears breaking through her usually composed demeanor were all too obvious.

Before I could do anything, she was yanked away, my hand slipping from hers with the force of it. Her cry of fear told me everything I needed to know: the forest was trying to take her. I moved to help when a vine caught around *my* ankle. I unsheathed my dagger quickly and sliced the damn thing. It let out an unnatural screech but backed off, and I shivered in repulsion.

What the fuck kind of forest was this?

I rushed to catch up to Amatista, closing my eyes and focusing so I could listen closely. I could hear the telltale sound of her being slowly dragged across the forest floor. I ran forward, but I couldn't see more than the slightest impression of her shape through the heavy mist that blanketed the ground like thick morning fog. I brought my dagger down hard on the vines and branches digging into her, ripping them away from her. After a few minutes of working away at them, she was finally released from the forest's claws.

Her blood soaked my hands by the time I was done. While it wouldn't kill her, I'd feel much better if we got her to a healer sooner rather than later. I knew potions weren't permitted in the competition to prevent anyone from having an unfair advantage, but I resented that it now meant limping our way out with bloody wounds riddling our bodies.

Blood now coated my face, my legs, my arms, and even my back. Amatista had it even worse. We needed to get out of here before the damn forest nicked something important and we bled out, capturing us permanently. Erodite knows I refused to die at the whims of a damn insubstantial mist or a rogue branch.

CHAPTER 19

Jacinth

WE forced ourselves to start running once more despite the pain of our wounds. We were nearly completely blind within the thick swirling mist, but I noticed the constant sound of Amatista's panting was beginning to lag further and further behind me.

I slowed a bit, searching vainly through the fog for any hope of seeing her and checking she was okay, but it was in vain.

"Tista," I called into the void, noticing the breathless quality to my own voice, the strain clear after hours of activity.

"Yes?" she responded, her own weariness obvious as she struggled to respond.

"Are you alright?" I asked, before realizing how silly that question actually was. "Are you going to be able to make it?" I corrected myself.

She sighed heavily, her side brushing against mine as she fell slightly to the side. I propped her up, and I could practically feel the relief pouring off her as it took the pressure off her injured ankle.

"I have to," she replied belatedly. "This would be a pathetic way to go."

I barked a laugh in agreement, and we hobbled forward. It thankfully wasn't long before the mist began to slowly dissipate, beams of light penetrating it from a sun that we both knew didn't shine in this forest.

It gave us the motivation to keep going. We had to be close if light was breaking through. As we tumbled forward, tripping over tree roots, my vision finally cleared and revealed a dirt path lined with tall trees, with the bright, beautiful sun shining directly in from the end of the path. Completely visible, along with the buildings just beyond the forest.

I didn't care that it was the poorer side of the city we'd arrived in. I was used to living in much worse areas. I hated to admit it, but Azurill actually managed Diamond quite well, ensuring the residents of Theiapolis, in particular, were well taken care of—no matter their status.

Something told me that Carnelian wouldn't bother to continue that practice. What would happen to these people when he took over?

I shook my head, banishing the thought. It wasn't my problem.

Amatista and I looked to one another, a giddy laugh escaping us as we turned back to see the mist retreating deeper into the forest.

"We made it," I breathed out, elated. I was exhausted after the combined exertion of the obstacle course and the forest. My muscles screamed at me, aching fiercely. I could only imagine how much worse off the other ladies were.

"Not yet." Amatista reminded me with a wry smile, arching an amethyst eyebrow. "We still need to get back to the palace."

I sighed, allowing myself a moment to moan petulantly. Amatista laughed, falling into me as her ankle gave way. I shook my head, bringing her arm over my shoulder to help steady her.

"Alright, we just need to get across the city." I nodded resolutely. "We can manage that just fine."

"Speak for yourself." She laughed slightly before sobering. "Thank you, Jac. I wouldn't have been able to do this without you."

"You would have figured out a way," I assured her, but she shook her head.

"I can tell you don't trust easily, which is wise for a member of court," she replied seriously, her eyes searching. "But I'm glad you trusted me today. I promise I will not betray that trust. Not through this competition, and not after."

I was left slightly speechless and could only cover with a weak quip.

"Well, you don't want to win anyway, so…" I teased, and she huffed, rolling her eyes, but a smile appeared on her face regardless.

"We'd better get moving. I may not care about the rankings, but if you're going to win, you need to make good time," she said firmly, her hand flapping as she directed me onward.

I stepped forward, taking us toward the exit, but I couldn't help but ask, "You want me to win?"

"There are precious few ladies in this competition who would be competent consorts to his Majesty. You're one of them, and since we're now friends, obviously I want you to win," she said it so plainly that I was left blinking in surprise.

Friends were a dangerous thing to be gathering, but I couldn't seem to help myself. So many years hiding from my past had left me with only the other street rats for company. Even then, none of us trusted one another, always aware that we'd turn on each other in a heartbeat to survive. Ula was the only exception, having taken me on as something of a protege.

Oblivious to my thoughts, Amatista continued, "Plus, you two clearly have chemistry. It makes sense."

"Wait, what?" I asked, tilting my head in confusion.

"You and High King Azurill, obviously." She rolled her purple eyes at me.

"We have *chemistry?*" I didn't know what to think about the insinuation. I could admit to myself alone that I struggled to remember who and what he was with him. Something about him was magnetic, and I found myself flirting even beyond what was expected of me for my mission. Dangerous ground to tread, but one my feet kept walking me down, nonetheless.

"Of course you do!" She laughed incredulously, drawing eyes from the few people lingering by the buildings nearby as we exited the forest. We were officially free of that demonic wood and back in the city.

Dragging our tired bodies through the streets of Theiapolis garnered a lot of stares and whispers. Everyone knew who we were and what we were doing there. The gossip about the Diamond Queen Competition had to be all over the city. With all the events going on, there was no way to ignore it.

Thankfully, that meant no one really bothered us. A few smiled or cheered us on, and we thanked them with bobbed heads and exhausted smiles, but that was it. I was instead left to think over the idea of having *chemistry*, of all things, with the man responsible for my family's end.

That was a thought I wanted nothing to do with, but the city offered a number of distractions, thank Erodite. We passed bars and shops, houses and apartments, but more importantly, our path took us by the main Gem Market, and I looked around wildly for any glimpse I could get.

It was said to be the best market in the realm, with gems and potions of all kinds, plus any and all materials you could need to brew your own. And other assorted goods, of course, but everyone knew the real draw. Elves from all over Gemaria came here to shop for a reason.

Which is why spotting a human slinking inside the entrance had me blinking in shock. Their rounded ears gave them away immediately, despite the way he tried to use his dark, wavy, shoulder-length hair to cover them up. He was clearly trying not to stand out, but unfortunately for him, even among the beautiful Elves of the city, one couldn't help but notice the handsome man.

I'd heard rumors from a few people that a couple of the stalls here sold relics under the table to humans. It was incredibly illegal, and if they were caught, they would pay with their lives. Apparently, the risk was worth it to them for the amount of coin a human would pay to be able to access magic.

I couldn't even blame them. If I were able to access gems or potions more easily, my life would be infinitely better. But poor as I was, there was little chance of me getting my hands on the magic I supposedly had full right to access.

It was men like Azurill who kept magic so inaccessible to women like me. Stealing was my only option, so I wasn't about to throw stones at the humans for doing what they could to get by. They couldn't wield gems or any element, nor could they access the forces of nature or the bounty of colors.

They were magicless. A result of them being transplants to our world. They didn't belong here, and yet, magic had found a way to correct that imbalance. The humans in Adamah, at least the ones who were free, could wield those relics with just as devastating an effect as any Fae or Elf.

With the way the Fae hunted the humans, it was necessary if they wanted to maintain that freedom.

This man's clothing, from his long, black leather duster to his tall, scuffed leather boots screamed *pirate*. Many humans who found ways to escape the Fae joined those pirate communities shrouded in secrecy, where they could plunder the riches of others to get by as they pirated the seas.

I'd never been able to find out where the Hidden Isles they supposedly lived on were, and everyone I talked to had shut the subject down quickly. I couldn't help my curiosity as I watched the pirate, with two other human men dutifully following him, as they slunk into the market.

There was no time to stop and wonder; we had to keep moving. We dragged ourselves through the streets until we crested a hill, and the palace blessedly came into full view. I breathed a sigh of relief that Amatista mirrored.

We made our way inside to the cheers of the courtiers and guests who'd assembled for the trial. The party was in full swing, and Zumra and Safira were already present, making me grind my teeth as I watched them laughing over drinks. However, I took great pleasure in how bedraggled they both appeared. Their hair was a mess, their clothing ripped in spots, but they still tried to preen and present themselves as they watched Azurill with hawk eyes from across the courtyard.

With all the commotion of our entrance, Azurill smiled and made his way to us, all the while Zumra and Safira narrowed their eyes menacingly at us for taking his attention.

"I think Zumra is trying to kill you with her eyes," Amatista snickered, elbowing me.

I rolled my own eyes, shaking my head at how petty these noble ladies could really be.

"She'll have to try a lot harder than that," I told her with a slight smile.

Her face grew serious, and her amethyst gaze met mine. "Be careful, Jac, she may very well try. She knows you're *real* competition, even if she won't admit it."

I opened my mouth but failed to answer before we were swarmed.

"Healers!" Azurill called as he approached us, cataloguing our various injuries. "Ladies, congratulations, you've managed to be the second group to arrive back."

His wide, charming smile fell a bit flat, and I could read the concern on his face as the healers came over. Amatista gave me a knowing smile before dragging her healer to the side. I glared at her as she left me to the mercy of Azurill and the other healer.

"Come sit, Lady Jacinth," Azurill said, his hand finding my elbow and leading me over to one of the nearby benches.

"I'm fine," I argued, and the opal-haired healer gasped before I realized my mistake. "Your Majesty."

Azurill chuckled, dipping his head down to hide his smile from the offended healer. "Here, let me assist her."

He reached for the potion the healer was mixing, her eyes going wide. "Your Majesty, I can help Lady Jacinth without issue—"

"I'm sure you can, Healer Takara, but you'll be quite busy as the other ladies start arriving. I can handle this one," he promised, gently taking the potion ingredients from her.

"She'll need more of the opal than the onyx—" she directed in a rush, but Azurill shook his head.

"We'll be fine. I can mix a healing potion." He laughed softly, surprisingly gentle with her.

"Right, of course, Your Majesty." She smiled slightly, reaching up to pat his cheek. "You were always my best student."

To my surprise, a blush bloomed across his cheeks, and I had to bite my lip to hide the smile rising at his obvious embarrassment.

"Thank you, Healer Takara." He nodded, and she finally left, leaving me alone with the high king himself.

He cleared his throat, his eyes skittering away from my amused ones. "Forgive her. She was my teacher for all my health-related classes growing up and has always been protective."

"She's adorable," I admitted, shaking my head. His surprise flashed over his face quickly, and I was the one to look away this time.

Azurill began to fiddle with the two bottles of gem dust as he mixed the right amounts together for the healing potion I needed. I found myself watching his actions carefully, following the movements of his hands as they gracefully poured each ingredient in. The harsh shake of the potion bottle that followed jolted me out of the near trance I'd fallen into while observing him. He uncorked the bottle again, and it quickly began to smoke, indicating its readiness, thanks to there being such small amounts of each gem.

"Here, drink this," he said gently, putting the potion bottle to my mouth. I parted my lips, and he tipped it back, our eyes meeting as I swallowed the potion down. It felt uncomfortably intimate, and it was a good thing I was forced to swallow the liquid, or my very obvious need to swallow would have been as obvious as Azurill's, whose throat bobbed in tandem as he watched me.

He pulled the bottle away when I finished the potion, before looking down, taking in the rips to my clothing as he fruitlessly tried to evaluate the skin under them a surface look alone.

"May I?" he murmured in a husky voice, and I dipped my head in a slight nod. His long fingers circled my wrist, lifting my arm up toward him. His other hand reached for the torn leather and pulled it back, his finger tracing down the now-healing skin with a feather-light touch and leaving chills in his wake.

"Perfect," he whispered, and my breathing seemed to become heavier. I began repeating the name of every person lost because of him in my head until it finally regulated. He slowly dropped my arm, but our eyes didn't leave one another's.

"You did an amazing job today, Mini-Dite." He smirked slightly, but the honesty in his eyes, not to mention his voice, threw me completely.

I cleared my throat uncomfortably, looking down. "Zumra and Safira still beat me here."

He scoffed, shaking his head. "I'm certain their families would have assumed the Forest of Discontent would be included in some way and trained them on how to get out."

"Isn't that cheating?" I asked, my brows scrunching together.

"Technically—no." He smiled ruefully, a sad look in his eyes. "It would certainly make my life easier if I could eliminate them for cheating, though." I couldn't help the chuckle I let out, a smile creeping up on my face.

"Why, Veri," I gasped dramatically, putting a hand over my heart as if in shock. "Are you telling me you aren't enjoying the attentions of two such noble ladies?"

His laugh was bright and loud enough that I could feel Zumra's glare like a concentrated beam of light focused directly on my head, trying to burn its way through.

I couldn't begin to reconcile the man before me with the image I'd had of him my whole life. How could this warm and charming man be the same one who ruthlessly ordered the murder of my family?

"I find that the longer I'm forced to endure their presence, the shorter my patience grows, if you can believe it," he leaned in to whisper in my ear.

My smile grew as he pulled back, and I opened my mouth to respond when Prince Ruri appeared by his side. I stiffened, sobering immediately with the knowledge that the prince was the one I needed to be careful of. His testing was too pointed for comfort.

I didn't know what would be worse: him finding out who I really am or finding out why I was actually here.

"Lady Jacinth, congratulations on overcoming the second trial." Prince Ruri smiled brightly as he handed me a glass of sparkling blue champagne. I took it carefully and tipped it against his glass as he congratulated me. "You must be very proud."

"I'm certainly pleased to have gotten out with my life intact anyway," I told him with a wry smile. Azurill chuckled, laying an arm across his brother's shoulders.

"I was very impressed with your control in the obstacle course. How did you learn such resilience?" Prince Ruri asked me, his eyes boring into mine.

I forced myself to smile despite wanting to throw my glass of champagne in both of their faces.

"Unfortunately, the world is an unkind place, full of unkind people, Prince Ruri." I stood, meeting his eyes. "I hope you never have to learn in the same way."

Something told me it was a slim chance.

CHAPTER 20

Jacinth

THE long wait for everyone to arrive back from the trial was agonizing. Faiza clearly kept to her wish to be dead last, and it was nearing time to retire without her having returned.

"Everyone, thank you all for coming to today's trial!" Azurill said, getting the crowd's attention from where they were all split up into small groups across the large, colorful courtyard.

The wall of the courtyard itself was made of solid diamond, and inside were benches made of every type of gem one could think of. Flowers were planted throughout or hung down in bunches, while vines crawled across one of the diamond walls.

"We are still waiting on our last competitor, but we have reached the cut-off. Lady Faiza Nabhas will be eliminated." He announced, causing the crowd to titter with excitement.

Zumra's satisfied smile had me narrowing my eyes in a glare at her until Amatista elbowed me, shaking her head. I sighed, turning my attention back to the king.

"Our next trial will be a bit different, and I'm sorry to say, done without an audience," Azurill smirked as the disappointed moans rang out. "For the ladies remaining, you will be assigned a time slot before you leave tonight. Make sure to see Lady Arianell before you retire to obtain it so you can plan appropriately."

He waved his arm to indicate the lady in question, and she waved from where she stood, her opal hair shining under the light of the moon and complemented by her teal gown.

"Your trial will be a date with yours truly." His wide smile seemed only the slightest bit forced as he glanced around at each of the ladies competing. "You will need to plan the date entirely, which Arianell, Emrys, and your guards can all help you with. I can't wait for the opportunity to spend some quality time with each of you, and see what you all come up with."

The crowd oohed and awed, but I rolled my eyes. A date? What kind of date could I come up with to impress the High King?

As everyone began to scatter, I stood up to find Lady Arianell, only to be accosted by Casaan. His black jacket was encrusted with red rubies, and a trail of diamonds connected the two buttons by his collar.

"Lady Jacinth," he greeted with that smarmy charm of his, "Lady Amatista." He bowed his head to her, and she greeted him politely in turn, with only the slightest downturn of her lips as she looked between us and eyed the tight hold he had taken of my arm.

"My father would like to see you, cousin dearest." His instruction was quite clear, and I nodded in acquiescence. It was easier to agree than argue in vain, after all.

"I just need to get my time slot from Lady Arianell, and then we can leave." I insisted, not wanting anything to mess this up.

My chance for vengeance hinged on this, and I wasn't about to lose it because of this waste of air.

"I'll join you," Casaan persisted, his expression flattening in a way that left chills trailing down my spine. I nodded in agreement, my eyes flicking to Amatista. She gave me a concerned look, but I shook my head slightly.

Casaan didn't bother with polite goodbyes and brought us straight over to Arianell. My hand remained tethered to him by the crook of his elbow, pulling me along in his wake as he strode quickly towards her.

"Lady Arianell, I believe you have something for my cousin?" he asked, and his voice was full of a pompous condescension that was grating. Her white eyebrow spiked high on her forehead as her eyes found mine. We shared a look as I rolled my eyes, and the slight smirk on her face in response was gratifying.

It was nice to find that not all nobles here were like I imagined. Carnelian and Casaan were perhaps not the only type of nobles at court, but they *were* the ones I've been forced to deal with.

"Yes, Lord Casaan, but I'm afraid it's for her eyes only. Competition rules, I'm afraid" she told him with a twinkling smile. "You wouldn't want to get her disqualified, would you?"

Casaan's ruby eyes narrowed, but he lacked the same force behind them that his father possessed. He huffed like the spoiled child he was and stomped off to wait for me at a water fountain nearby. I sighed miserably, dreading the conversation to come, before turning back to Arianell with a practiced smile.

"I apologize for my cousin, my lady." I dipped my head, but she waved me off.

"Don't worry yourself about it, Lady Jacinth." She smiled brightly, her shoulders straightening as she grabbed a potion and handed it to me.

"Swallow this, and your time slot will be revealed," she explained. "We've worked into the magic that each of the ladies will receive one of the available spots, and no one will accidentally be assigned the same one. This also prevents the others from knowing your time, thus preventing any potential sabotage."

I examined the potion; its emerald, sapphire, and amethyst coloring was a unique blend, and it had a dash of what could have been diamond, judging by its sparkle at least. I quickly swallowed it down and concentrated on the magic in my mind, waiting for the information I needed to reveal itself. It took a minute, but eventually the time became known to me.

I was lucky enough to get a night slot, meaning I had more options available. But now I needed to plan a several hour-long date tomorrow night, and I needed to figure it out fast.

Before I could get carried away, Casaan cleared his throat loudly, reminding me of his unwanted presence. I shut my eyes, counting to ten to reset my patience, and opened them to see Arianell watching me with an amused expression.

Thanking her quickly, I moved toward Casaan, but he grabbed my hand and pulled me along with him before I'd even made it two steps.

"Father expects updates, little urchin," he said harshly, despite the way his eyes followed the lines of my body.

"I've been a bit busy, you know," I defended myself tersely. It wasn't like I'd been purposely avoiding him. Not *entirely*, anyway.

Casaan scoffed, shaking his head as he practically manhandled me down the hall toward Lord Carnelian's rooms. My heart sank the closer we got, despite knowing I had no real reason to dread this meeting.

Our goals remained the same, nothing had changed there.

It was really only Carnelian using Ula's life as a bargaining chip that kept us from being on the same side completely. Okay, maybe I didn't *love* the thought of him being king, but we certainly both wanted Azurill gone.

The *High King*, I corrected myself, cursing mentally. This competition was seriously beginning to mess with my mind. Or maybe that was the much too pretty king.

We entered a ruby red door encrusted with gems that made me itch to pick them off and pocket them. Inside was the suite of rooms provided for the lord of Ruby Court, and we walked into the main living space that had dark black walls accented by scrolling red lines that looped and swirled, creating gorgeous patterns and keeping it from feeling gloomy. The furniture was a mixture of red and white, keeping any one color from becoming too overwhelming.

Lord Carnelian was seated on an elaborate red velvet chair that looked more like a throne, with rubies lining the sides of the arms and legs and tufted vertical lines in the padding that created a plush-looking seat.

Casaan brought me to stand before Carnelian and finally released my arm. I clenched my teeth to prevent myself from glaring at him as I eyed the indented fingerprints in my skin.

"Lady Jacinth," Carnelian mocked with a tip of his head.

"Lord Carnelian," I countered with an expectant brow raised.

His brief scowl was quickly hidden beneath a placid smile. Casaan dropped onto the white sofa beside his father and sprawled out, crossing his arms as he watched in amusement.

"I must admit you've done surprisingly well in the early trials," he began, his red brows quirking upward. "But from here on out, the competition will become fiercer, and the other ladies have a distinct advantage over you."

"I'm aware," I told him drolly, making his eyes narrow as Casaan smirked.

"Then I hope you have a good plan for your date?" he asked snidely, and I nodded firmly despite having no idea what I was going to do.

"Yes, and he's clearly interested in me," I told him, wanting this over with so I could get on with this madness. "I'll use that to my advantage and ensure I win this competition."

"Good." He hummed thoughtfully. "But you aren't the only one he's shown interest in."

My brows furrowed, since I figured that was obvious. He had eight women initially competing, and showing interest was a huge part of his role here.

"I have reports that he showed significant interest in Lady Sania of Pearl Court," he said, watching me carefully. I tried to hide my flinch at her name as best I could, but his sparkling eyes didn't miss a thing.

"You didn't think you were the only one, did you?" he asked, his lips turning up in a mocking smile. "Unless there's another issue?"

"Of course not, I just haven't seen the two of them together." I raised my chin, refusing to show any kind of doubt before the lord or his son.

"Perhaps you should secure his interest in another way." Casaan hinted, his eyes raking over my body in a way that left little doubt as to what he was referring to. I kept my face locked down, refusing to let my disgust at his suggestion show.

"After all, it's not fair for us to be doing all the work to ensure you win," he finished, taunting me with raised brows and a lascivious smirk. I ground my teeth, biting back the scathing remark that itched to leave my lips.

As if I wasn't out here doing everything I could, nearly dying by forest to secure my victory. What in Tartarus was *he* doing to ensure it?

"It's not a terrible idea," Carnelian said, but his head tilted to the side in thought before he shook it. "Perhaps something best left for later if necessary, however. We don't want him to lose interest too early and for her to have no tricks left."

My body was practically vibrating from holding back my anger as these two talked about me like a commodity to be traded away and used.

"Trust me, it's not necessary," I insisted, standing my ground. "I will win this competition, and you will keep your end of the agreement." I stared Carnelian down, knowing better than to voice aloud what that entailed in this palace.

Who knew which walls had ears.

CHAPTER 21

Jacinth

A ZURILL was flirting with Sania.

I don't know why that knowledge bothered me. Maybe because he was flirting with the lady of the court that should be ruled by my family? The very court he destroyed—as if he hadn't already done enough to it.

It bothered me *too much*. I shouldn't care. Not about what he does, nor who he does it with. Just because he flirted with me didn't mean he wasn't flirting with everyone.

Not to mention, I was flirting with him, and I hated him with a passion. Flirting with Sania didn't mean he actually *liked* her.

But everything was riding on my winning this competition. If I don't win, Ula could die, joining my family in the afterlife—utterly failed by me. All of them. My family *deserved* the vengeance that burned in my heart.

Anything else paled in comparison to that.

But to accomplish that, I needed the king's interest firmly set on me. Thinking of our upcoming date, I ran through a myriad of ideas.

We'd already been on a picnic.

Doing some noble, fancy event would bore me to tears.

He wanted to see authentic versions of us, behind the courtly masks.

He wanted to be more casual with us...

...because he was used to being in the formal situations court demanded of him.

That was it! The idea felt perfect the moment I thought of it. Putting him in an environment he wasn't used to would make him rely on me for the

147

night, while I showed him a side of both myself and of *life* that he rarely got to experience.

"Alfrikr," I turned my head to my guard as we made our way back to my rooms for the night. "I have an idea for my date. How do I go about getting this ready?"

He smirked back at me, raising a brow, "Already?"

"Well, we have limited time here." I huffed, making him laugh gruffly.

"Get me a list of what you need. I'll see to it." He promised with a nod.

"Thank you." I nodded in return, a small smile on my lips. He hummed, looking over me critically for a moment, making my nerves rise.

"The night after your date, we will begin training you with a sword," he suddenly announced, making my eyes go wide.

"What?" I shook my head in confusion before they narrowed at him. "Why, exactly?" I asked suspiciously.

He grunted in amusement, "In case you make it far enough to need it."

So one of the events would involve sword fighting, likely near the end. I looked at him, intensely curious, but I knew he wouldn't betray Azurill and reveal what it was. Instead, I smiled back at him.

"Don't worry, I can handle a sword," I told him confidently.

"Maybe so," he shook his head, his purple braids swinging with the movement, "But I doubt Carnelian or your father had you trained to the level you'll need. I'll pick up your training from wherever you left off."

I wanted to protest, but I was forced to admit that he was right. I'd learned on the street, so my fighting style reflected that. I didn't fight like a noble, and that could cause some issues. Another thought occurred to me then.

"What about the other girls?" I asked him.

"What about them?" He asked in return, surprised.

"Will they be trained too?" I pushed, needing to know more to shed light on what the trial might be.

He grunted, seeming unsure about answering, before he finally sighed. "Yes, they'll all be trained. Most will likely have the fundamentals down at least. No noble parent would leave their daughter wholly unprotected, but I have no idea what level of proficiency any of the ladies have with a blade."

Curious. It sounded like we would all need to be at a higher level of skill for the trial. Would we be fighting each other? Someone else? Some*thing* else?

It was clear that answers wouldn't be forthcoming right now, so when we reached my rooms, I wrote the list of what I needed for Alfrikr and saw him off for the night. Collapsing into my bed, my thoughts swirled with everything going on.

The thought of deep teal eyes going dull and lifeless haunted my sleep that night, but upon waking, the image was easy to chase away. Upon entering the breakfast hall, the other ladies, excluding Faiza, sat around the table. A seat thankfully remained next to Amatista, and I claimed it quickly.

"Good morning!" she chirped, and I returned her greeting with a smile, quickly digging into my food.

Azurill eyed me occasionally from the other end of the table, but my eyes narrowed upon realizing Sania was sitting beside him, laughing as her hand lightly swatted his arm. The smile on his face...

An elbow to my side made me grunt, turning to face Amatista incredulously.

"Stop glaring at them," she hissed quietly. "Act like you don't care who he's flirting with."

"I *don't* care," I argued mulishly.

Her raised eyebrows spelled out her disbelief quite clearly, but it wasn't what she thought at all. It was merely proof that I needed to do better. It had nothing to do with emotions of any kind.

"Showing you're unconcerned with the other competition will be attractive, trust me." She smirked slyly, "Men crave being desired, and it drives their own interest in a woman if they think they must chase it. They love nothing more than proving they can win your affection."

I didn't have much experience with men in a romantic capacity, since I didn't think having one-night-only romps with them counted, so I'd have to take her word for it.

"He clearly has a type, though," she muttered, observing Azurill like a science experiment. *Scholars*, I shook my head in amusement.

"What do you mean?" I asked her quietly.

"The two of you have many similarities." She observed, making me go completely still. "You have a similar color palette, your noses and mouths actually..."

She trailed off, her eyebrows creasing as my heart started to race and sweat began to bead along my temples.

"What are you planning for your date?" I asked her, desperately hoping to distract her. Dammit, *this* was what happened when you made friends—especially with a damn scholar.

She turned back to look at me, her eyes glinting, but she allowed the subject change for now. As we began to discuss our ideas, however, Zumra and Safira stood up to leave, and as they approached where we were sitting, Zumra slowed her steps with a nasty smile.

"Lady Jacinth, wonderful showing yesterday." Her fake graciousness made me grind my teeth in an effort not to throw my butter knife at her face.

"You as well, Lady Zumra." I cooed right back.

"I do hope you don't disappoint the High King with your date," she said, faux concern practically dripping from every word. "After all, a man like him deserves something with a bit more…class than some can offer."

I nearly laughed thinking of the date I'd planned for us. Zumra might actually faint when she finds out where I'm bringing him.

"Oh, don't worry about me, Lady Zumra," Azurill's voice called from down the table, making the lady twitch and turn to him with wide eyes. "I'm quite prepared for anything you ladies offer."

His twinkling eyes met mine, and I couldn't help the tiny, genuine smile that snuck out. His defense of me was surprising, but appreciated. Calling out Zumra as he just did, however, was what truly made my smile inch higher.

Watching her mouth fall open in shock was incredibly satisfying. As was her brisk, flustered nod in farewell before she took off, her embarrassment following after her like a bad perfume.

Safira's eyes met mine quickly, and I was surprised to find a conflicted look on her face. She ultimately followed her friend, but I couldn't help wondering what she'd been considering instead.

I looked back at Azurill, our matching smiles making my cheeks flush as I forced myself to look away. Only to land directly on Sania.

Her orange eyes were narrowed on me as she looked between me and the king.

There were too many people to watch out for in this snake pit. The more I got the king's attention, the more the other ladies paid it as well, and in a much less appealing manner.

WAITING FOR NIGHT to fall, I was twitchy as my maids helped get me ready. More than once, they had to chastise me to stay still before I ruined their work.

I'd allowed myself the vanity of having them do my hair and makeup, but I'd insisted on something casual. My hair would be half up, as I enjoyed wearing it when I didn't have to hide the braided locks beneath a hood, with the shorter pieces in front left down to frame my face.

My makeup emphasized my features, outlining my wide, pink eyes and pouty lips, but they didn't overdo it, keeping it light enough that I wouldn't look out of place where we'd be going.

My outfit was understated as well. My long white dress had a black corset over it, and matching leather cuffs around my wrists. In addition to the simpler dress, the gray cape I'd prepared to wear over it would help keep others from noticing us.

A smile graced my face at the thought of what Azurill would make of his own outfit. I hope he enjoyed it. I couldn't imagine him ever having worn anything like it before.

Once the maids had finished, I donned the cape and exited my rooms to find Alfrikr waiting for me with an amused smile. He looked me over, shaking his head, but the mirth on his face was too obvious to fool anyone into thinking that he disapproved.

I smiled widely back at him, "Let's go pick up my date."

His laugh rang out behind me, and I couldn't help the chuckle I let out in response.

"I can't wait to see his Majesty," Alfrikr admitted, his amethyst eyes lit up.

"Me either." The words slipped out without my notice, and Alfrikr's lips pulled into a smirk.

"Oh, I'm sure." His taunting tone was playful, but the wrenching in my gut wasn't.

I was merely excited to see him so off balance and out of his element, surely. I wasn't excited to see *him*.

Erodite, what was wrong with me?

I knew better than to fall under this spell. I wasn't a noble lady who could titter around court after this was over. This was a one-time indulgence, and that was all.

I couldn't get attached to *any* of it.

My resolution came as we neared Azurill's wing, and the sound of barking filled my ears. My head tilted, curious, as we made our way into his family's wing.

Alfrikr led us deep within it, making me vaguely uncomfortable. I'd assumed he'd meet us at the entrance, but apparently not. Instead, I was treated to the gorgeous blue and silver interior as we passed through.

The barking finally stopped, and I heard a voice before we rounded the corner and stumbled upon a woman kneeling before a multicolored dog, petting it lovingly as its tongue flopped out of its mouth happily.

The dog's fur was a sparkling blue and green, with bits of silver, which indicated a mixed breed from what little I knew. I was used to street dogs, after all. But I always relished any time I was able to get one to trust me enough to cuddle. This one looked like it might be a cross between a diamond-dust and an emerald-beryl breed.

Its long ears flopped adorably to the side, and its long fur shook as the woman petted it. Her sapphire blue hair was down to her waist, not done up at all for court, and her eyes looked…*weary*, was the only word I could use to describe it. The fabric of her silver dress wrinkled a bit as she stooped down to pet the excited animal.

Our entrance caused her to look up, her lips twitching as if she wanted to smile, but couldn't. The weariness in her eyes seemed to extend to her entire being.

"Queen Mother." Alfrikr bowed, and I quickly followed his action in surprise.

This was Azurill's mother?

I looked her over critically, seeing nothing of the queen before me, merely a worn woman who'd lost something vital to her spirit.

Her son, I realized in a rush. Azurill's grief over his brother had been clear, and watching the woman before me, I didn't doubt that she grieved fiercely for her lost child. One of her three boys, now gone forever.

I tried desperately not to think about how what I planned to do would affect her.

"Queen Mother." I reiterated, lagging slightly behind Alfrikr in my shock.

"Alfrikr, darling, you needn't be so formal here." She tried to smile again and failed.

"I do around this one." He winked at the queen mother, nudging me in the process. I rolled my eyes before I could stop myself, but the woman finally managed the slightest smile in response, so I considered that a victory at least.

"Ah, yes." She took a step toward us, the dog rolling back over to his feet now that his mistress had abandoned him. "This must be Lady Jacinth."

"That would be me." I smiled, nerves fluttering in my stomach for some reason.

"You were quite a surprise to many of us," she mused, inspecting me shamelessly.

"Well, that's me, surprising." I shrugged, not sure how to respond to Azurill's mother of all people.

My flippant words made her smile more prominent, however, and as the dog at her feet trotted over to us, ignoring Alfrikr and making its way straight to me, she watched curiously. The dog nudged my leg, so I leaned down to pet her, smiling to myself at the simple joy of not having to fake my pleased reaction to the friendly dog.

Its head butted against me again, but this time in pure pleasure as my fingers scratched along her head, making her pant in happiness.

"Well, I can't say I've ever seen Neasa so enthusiastic about a stranger before." Azurill's voice made my head snap up, my hand falling still on the dog's head as I looked up. The dog's—Neasa, apparently—petulant whine had my fingers digging back into her fur.

"She's beautiful," I told him quietly—honestly, which had to be a first between us. I loved mixed-breed dogs, seeing how the different gem combinations turned out in them. It was so much like the alchemy we used to make our potions, as if dogs were their own kind of magic.

"She's spoiled," he countered, raising a brow as he watched me relent to the dog's demands. I blushed lightly, but Azurill laughed quietly, patting his thigh softly. Neasa quickly abandoned me to rush to Azurill. He knelt down and let the dog headbutt him as he ran his hands up and down her body in quick, rough pats that the canine seemed to love.

"That's because you spoil her, dear." His mother interjected, a fond look on her face. "You always have."

"And who could blame me?" he asked, as the dog licked up his cheek. I laughed softly, and his mother turned to look at me once more. She examined me closely, making me nervous.

"Well, you two have a date to be on." She suddenly clapped her hands. The weary look was already beginning to reappear in her sapphire eyes. "I'm quite curious to hear where you're taking him, based on your outfits."

I bit my lip, embarrassed despite myself. I looked down, but was surprised to find a finger lifting my chin back up. Azurill's mother stood before me, smiling softly. "I was known to slip out from my father's manor from time to time when I was younger. I'd often wear such clothes to disappear among the commoners."

"You did?" Azurill asked, clearly bewildered, but she didn't turn to look at him. Instead, her attention remained fixed on me.

"It's good to get out of here every once in a while." She winked but then sighed deeply. "Perhaps I was remiss in keeping my sons so close. I thought if I kept them in the palace, there would be no real danger, but…"

She trailed off, her eyes watering, and I couldn't help myself from reaching out to grab her hand, squeezing lightly.

"I'm truly sorry for your loss," I told her honestly. It wasn't her fault I'd lost my family, even though she gave life to the man responsible. Even still, I couldn't imagine losing a child. The loss of everyone else had damaged me forever, but a child? I was lucky I was one myself at the time and didn't have to worry about that. But if I ever had one…I would burn the world before I let anyone hurt them.

"The loss of those we love will always leave a hole inside of us," I told her quietly. "But over time, the hole *can* be patched. Hold on to those around you, let them begin patching that hole."

Her wide sapphire eyes looked deep into my pearl-pink ones, and she let out a shuddering sigh. Earnestly, she said, "Thank you, Lady Jacinth. Truly."

She squeezed my hand as she continued, "You're right. I still have two wonderful sons to love and protect. I can't forget that."

I could almost *see* as the woman, who I'd heard from rumors had been hiding from court since her middle child's funeral, began to piece parts of herself back together. Enough to keep going. To remember who she was.

The sapphire in her eyes blazed.

I looked at her son, to see wide blue-green eyes watching us with a look I couldn't identify.

"Now, you two should get going. You have limited time to spend together, after all." The ghost of a smirk crossed her face, and she gathered Neasa up and kissed Azurill on the cheek, patting Alfrikr on the shoulder, before looking at me once more.

"It was wonderful meeting you, Lady Jacinth. I look forward to seeing you again," she told me, and I blinked in surprise at the confidence in her voice that she *would* be seeing me again.

"You as well, Queen Mother," I responded, eyeing Azurill in curiosity, but he quickly ushered me out, Alfrikr following along behind us.

"So, any hints as to where we're going?" The king asked, a forced levity in his voice that told me he wanted to move past the heavy conversation with his mother.

I obliged, smirking up at him, "Not a one."

"I should have known better." He chuckled, shaking his head before he turned to look back at my guard, "What about you? Any hints you can spill?"

"I'm not at liberty to say," Alfrikr smirked back at him. I laughed as Azurill's jaw dropped, and he jokingly put a hand over his heart.

"The absolute betrayal." He huffed, but his twinkling eyes betrayed his mirth. "You're supposed to work for me, you know."

"And you told me I had to assist Jacinth with this nonsense, so it's your own fault," he countered, raising an eyebrow at him.

I enjoyed their banter as we walked toward the palace gates, eager to see Azurill's reaction when we arrived. I was anxious, but for what, even I wasn't quite sure.

I had to secure Azurill's attention, or else I risked everything being in jeopardy. I haven't attempted to keep a man interested in me beyond one night before, so it was a novel experience. Especially when competing against some of the most beautiful women in the realm.

I didn't have a choice now, however. If I ever wanted to experience peace, I had to win this competition and claim my prize. The thought of that bubbling, smoking potion Carnelian had shown me was both a balm and a terror.

It would be my tool of vengeance, most assuredly, but...I'd also never killed a man before.

My eyes cut to the one walking beside me. Conflicting emotions rose within me, yet I refused to bend to them. Some small measure of regret for having to kill anyone was normal, I assured myself.

But this man deserved everything he'd wrought. He *did*. My mouth firmed into a straight line at the thought, closing my eyes momentarily to affix the vision of my parents' bodies in my head.

A firm reminder of why Azurill deserved to die at my hand.

Why he *had to*—no matter what.

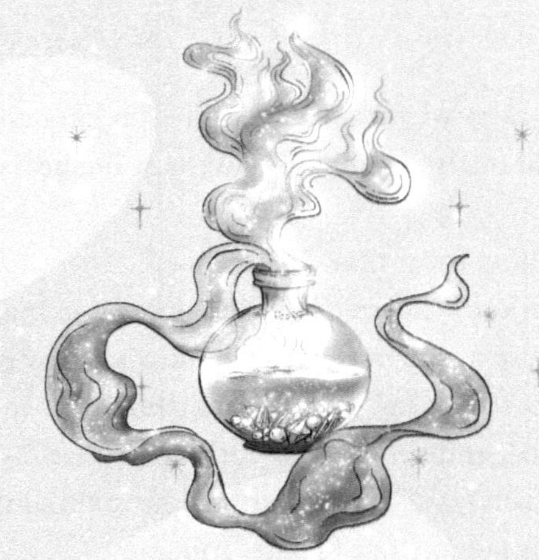

CHAPTER 22

Jacinth

WE left Alfrikr behind at the gates, prompting Azurill to raise a brow in question. I smiled charmingly at him, not saying a word, but reaching out to flip his cape's hood over his head. He huffed a laugh as I flipped my own up, following after me as I took off down the street.

"If my guards hadn't obviously approved of this, I might think you were bringing me out here to kill me," Azurill said jokingly as we descended into the poorer part of town.

I froze for a millisecond before forcing a laugh, winding my arm around his and bumping our shoulders together. "Oh no, too many witnesses saw us leave together."

"Of course," he nodded, all faux solemnity, "Probably best not to take me out when you were the last one to be seen with me." He couldn't hide his smirk, and I forced that veil of truth over myself once more, matching it.

"Exactly." I smiled brightly. "Don't worry, it's good to get out of your palace now and again."

We rounded the corner, and I saw the dirty, white brick building with the hanging sign in front reading '*The Bubbling Gem*', with a depiction of a bubbling potion being poured into a stein painted under it. I stepped up to the door, swinging it open and dragging Azurill with me.

I watched as he looked around and took a moment myself to take in the dingy tavern. A bar took up the back wall with stools lining it, all of them full. Worn, cracking wooden tables that looked hundreds of years old were placed close together throughout the rest of the space. I spotted a small table hidden in a corner that would serve perfectly for my needs and brought us directly to it.

"Leave your hood up," I instructed Azurill as we sat down. "Unless you want them to figure out who you are, of course."

"We certainly wouldn't want that." He nodded, his eyes glinting in the dim light of the tavern. "Not when tonight is supposed to be just us."

A barmaid quickly appeared to take our orders and asked with a smile, "What can I get you two?"

"How about a sparkling ale, since we're in the kingdom they originated from," I smirked at the king as I ordered the diamond-inspired drink, and he leaned back in his chair, smiling up at the older woman.

"I'll have the same." He flipped her a coin that had to be worth four times our order, and her wide eyes and open mouth showcased her shock quite clearly. I nearly sighed in defeat. The man knew nothing about how to blend in.

I suppose I shouldn't be surprised. He was meant to glitter and shine from his throne, not hide among the rabble.

"Sir, this is too much." The woman argued, but the sheen of tears in her eyes made me soften. It was obvious she needed it, but her morals were at least solid enough to argue.

"I insist," Azurill said plainly, a gentle smile on his face.

The woman took a deep breath, gathering herself, "Veritx bless you, sir."

She nodded before taking off to get our drinks, and Azurill turned his gaze back to me.

"I'd argue that was foolish, but it's nice to see you actually care about these people," I conceded begrudgingly.

"Did you think I didn't?" he asked, his brows shooting up in surprise.

"Many nobles don't." I sighed deeply. "But…you're truly not what I was expecting," I wrenched the words from deep in my soul, admitting the truth—to both of us.

"And what were you expecting, Mini-Dite?" He leaned forward, his elbows landing on the table in a way he'd never dare at the palace. My smile snuck out despite myself, but I was saved from having to answer right away when our drinks were quickly delivered. Obviously, the woman had rushed in an effort to earn her substantial tip.

I chugged back the sparkling, silver ale, watching as Azurill did the same. He almost fit in here, chugging ale in his peasant clothing, but something about him was just *too much* for a commoner.

He stared at me quietly, waiting patiently for an answer to his question.

"I expected you to be a pompous noble who didn't give a shit about the less fortunate." I finally told him, watching his brows furrow. "That you'd be eating up having the ladies in the competition fighting over you. That you'd be violent and cruel, capable of doing anything to secure your throne." I made myself shrug casually, like my heart wasn't beating out of my chest, like I wasn't hiding years' worth of contempt deep in my soul.

His teal eyes widened a bit, and he looked me over critically for a moment. "Well, I didn't expect such a scathing review."

His voice sounded uneven, and I knew he was trying to hide the hurt I saw brewing in his eyes. It shouldn't have caused the pang in my heart that it did.

"I said I was wrong, didn't I?" I replied, knowing that I had to fix this. For the sake of my vengeance, or perhaps…

He huffed a slight laugh, "Still, that isn't the impression I want to give to any of my subjects. I don't want them thinking I'm like Car—"

He cut himself off with a cringe, and I couldn't help the curl of my lips as I continued his thought, "Like Carnelian?"

He laughed quietly, taking a swing of his ale as he shook his head.

"You must know how he is." He raised his brows at me, but there was something deeper to his question, something searching.

"I have an idea." I shrugged as casually as I could. "We don't spend much time together, if you can believe it," I said dryly.

Azurill leaned forward, and I couldn't help leaning in as well, until we were close enough to whisper, and for other things I shouldn't be considering.

"I have my suspicions about him. I'll tell you that truthfully. But I'm less sure about you." He shook his head ruefully. "I shouldn't even be telling you this."

"Then why are you?" I murmured, our eyes locked on one another's, and it felt like the space between us was heavy with heat, like a flame could catch at any moment. Or perhaps it was more like a bubbling potion, about to combust and spew smoke into the air.

"I find that despite what my mind tells me is smart, the rest of me feels like being quite foolish when it comes to you." He admitted candidly, lifting a hand to push a curl behind my ear. My breath caught in my throat as my eyes fluttered.

"Something about you seems to make me quite foolish as well." The whisper was wrenched from my gut, and I couldn't stop it before it landed heavily between us. His intense stare burned through me as I licked my suddenly dry lips. "I shouldn't trust you."

"And why not?" He asked quietly, leaning a bit closer.

"As High King, you've done awful things," I tried to make the words land like the accusation they were, but my next ones came out too softly to make it land. "Haven't you?"

The uncertainty in my voice struck me like a blow. Knowing of the nebulous figure of a high king who had my family killed was one thing, but seeing the actual man before me, I couldn't quite reconcile him with that figure. My instincts screamed at me that something didn't fit, and I never ignored my instincts.

His eyes darkened, looking more kyanite than teal in the dim lightning of the tavern, and his face fell slightly before he took a swing of ale. I rushed to take one myself, anything to wet my parched throat.

"I have done terrible things," he finally said, a weight behind the words that made my heart race into my throat as my stomach fell to the floor. "But everything I've done has been in the interest of our kingdom. In protecting the people who live here."

His arm flung out to indicate the rest of the room, all of the people going about their nights as normal. "They're the lifeblood of our kingdom, whatever the other nobles may think, and I will always do everything I can to be the kind of king that deserves to wear the crown on my head."

His hand suddenly reached forward, grabbing mine. "What would you do to protect the people you love?"

Mother. Father. Juvela and her husband, Zav. Peony, and my aunt and uncle. Cor and our other guards and household members. Ula.wouldn'tMy eyes closed, but my fingers curled around his. There was a tragic irony to clasping his hand while the memory of reaching for my mother's and never making it stirred. And it was all because of him.

Right?

Confusion swam within me, and I opened my eyes, telling him nothing but the truth, "Anything."

"As would I." He smiled, matching my whisper and squeezing my hand, but that smile dimmed a moment later. "And there are some who think my brother's death has made the throne weak. Your lord among them."

He watched me quietly, and I dipped my head in agreement. He wasn't wrong; Carnelian was already taking advantage of this. To get *me* in. I was the one who would ultimately destroy this man, and for the first time, I questioned if it was the right thing to do.

Vengeance had been an unattainable goal for so long that it felt like a dream to get the opportunity for it. But was taking out this man, who apparently cared for the people he ruled over, and replacing him with someone like Carnelian, truly the best thing for Gemaria?

And since when did I care?

Street rats learn first and foremost that you must protect yourself because no one else will do it. But as a memory rose in my mind of sitting on my father's knee as he explained his duty to take care of the people of Pearl Court, of how, as nobles, it was our job to protect them, my entire worldview felt shaken to the core.

What was I? Street rat or noble?

Who was I? Jacinth or...*Lady Linnea Jacinth Marit?*

"The people deserve rulers who truly care. Who do their duty and serve them, not lord over them," I murmured, forgetting for a moment where I even was.

"These trials, they're all about making sure I'll have the right queen beside me to rule the realm for exactly that reason," Azurill said softly, something shining in his eyes that made my heart stutter in my chest. "One who can hopefully be more than an ornament to look pretty and give me heirs. I want a partnership like the ones my parents had."

"My parents had that too." The words came out of my mouth like spilled ink, my head too foggy to stop it as memories assailed me. "They worked together, ensuring the people were happy and safe. That they were thriving. Until..."

"Your parents live in Ruby Court, don't they?" he asked, his brows creasing as he considered my words.

"Oh, of course." I laughed, but the forced sound did little to cover my panic as I realized that I'd *massively* fucked up.

Thankfully, we were distracted, as at that moment the people in the tavern began pushing tables aside, and music filled the air. Couples stood up and began dancing to the tune, and I looked to Azurill, his brows creased as he clearly tried to make sense of my words, so I quickly stood, grabbing him by the hand.

"Come on, Veri." I smiled wickedly, "Time to dance like a normal person. If that ego of yours can take it, of course."

He chuckled, shaking his head as he gave up trying to figure out what my slip-up meant and instead gave in to being dragged to the floor. As promised, the dancing was *very* different from the kind done at court. Commoners didn't dance the way nobles did, structured and precise. No, they were wild and free, able to let loose with no constraints.

I loved all types of dancing, and had missed the regimented dancing of my youth that I now got to experience again at court, but I had thrived for years by dancing the way other peasants did. I threw myself into it now, and Azurill quickly caught on. His effortless grace was almost infuriating, but he made for a good enough dance partner that I couldn't be too upset.

He spun me around, my hood flying off and my pink hair tumbling around my shoulders as I twirled, before he pulled me sharply back into his body. Chest to chest, our eyes locked as his other hand found the small of my back. We danced in a circle as we followed the beat of the music, but our eyes never left one another.

I felt consumed by him as he surrounded me, leaving me thankful for the fresh breath of air when he spun me back out. As the song ended and moved into the next, I grabbed both of his hands with mine, pulling us toward one another again and back out, before we both spun with our hands crossing. As we came to face each other once more, the smile on his face only fed the one on my own like tinder to a fire.

I couldn't deny this was actually…*fun*. Dancing with him to the wild beat of the music allowed me to let go of all my reservations for a moment and just enjoy getting to dance with this charming, powerful, handsome-as-sin man.

As the next song began, with a slower, sultrier beat, Azurill pulled me into his body, enclosing me in his arms. His hard body was an illicit thrill against my softer one, and I suddenly ached to press more of me against him to see what reaction I could get. As I looked up into his eyes, I was surprised to find them lit up with an emotion I'd had yet to see from him.

He looked genuinely *happy*.

It was shocking enough that I was forced to realize I was feeling something similar. Which was *not* good. And even worse, as our eyes remained connected, he leaned in…

My heart beat like it was about to skip out of my chest entirely, and my soul felt torn in two, half of me desperate to experience what was coming, and the other disgusted with myself for it.

Teal consumed my vision entirely until my eyes fluttered shut and then… his lips sent sparks flying through my body, and I found my own responding without thought as I gave in to his kiss. My hands snaked up his tattoo-covered neck, over the shaved sides of his head, to grasp at the hair on top and *tug*, making him groan into my mouth.

He pressed me closer to him as his hand wound into my hair and returned the favor, making me moan and nip his lip in retaliation. His tongue danced with mine as his body did, and I eagerly met each motion with every part of me. His hand gripping my hair came to rest on my neck instead, curling around it, and his fingers trailed across my skin, leaving fire in his wake as he touched me. I could only think of ice and fire meeting, and the immediate spark precluding the melting of the ice.

For I was assuredly melting into him, and I didn't know where my head had gone, but it was a losing game trying to figure that out.

It was only when another patron bumped into us and we were jostled apart that I blinked dumbly up at him, satisfied to see he at least looked as wrecked as I was by the experience. I'd set out to seduce Azurill for my own ends but had somehow tripped myself up into forgetting the reason I was here, what I had to do, and mostly…that this had an expiration date.

CHAPTER 23

Azurill

WE'D decided on this particular trial so I could see how being in a relationship with each lady could potentially go. A date was theoretically a good way to see if romance could spark between us.

I certainly never expected a spark the size of a forest fire.

Starting the night out, I had already been enraptured. I could never explain to Jacinth how grateful, and flat-out amazed, I was at what she'd accomplished.

My mother had been listless and distraught since my brother's death, hiding from the court in a way she had *never* done.

Seeing her start to wake up at Jacinth's words made me incredibly thankful I'd insisted on her coming to my wing before our date. I'd merely intended on letting Neasa meet her, since my dog could usually take the measure of people quickly, and her instincts were never wrong.

Watching as she rushed up to Jacinth joyfully, demanding that she pet her, I was relieved. It told me that, whatever Carnelian's plans, whatever Jacinth's place in them, she was a good Elf at heart. That didn't mean she wasn't aware of or involved in any schemes, however.

She could be participating under protest. She could have been threatened. Or Carnelian could have fed her lies half her life for all I knew.

But that test told me that I may be able to trust her *just* enough.

Once we'd left the palace, I'd been honestly delighted to find out we were going to a tavern. I'd never had much chance to mingle among the common people as if I were one. Having a night where I could just be *me*, where I could drink, laugh, and not worry about my behavior, was a weight off my shoulders that I didn't even realize I was carrying.

Finding out that Jacinth had expected the worst of me coming into the competition left me even more conflicted, and a large part of me was unable to help feeling strangely hurt. She hadn't known me; it wasn't as if she could have guessed what type of person I was, especially when Carnelian was her example of a ruler. Still, I was relieved when she explained she'd been wrong.

But when she began talking of her parents…my alarm bells began ringing, because her parents *should* be alive and well if she was truly who Carnelian said she was, this mysterious cousin we'd never seen before. Yet she spoke of them as if they were dead. It was all incredibly suspicious, even if I found that I didn't *want* to doubt her. And that became even more true as the night progressed.

It was impossible to deny to myself that Jacinth was my favorite of the competitors. I would surely get to know the rest better, but she was far and away the most desirable, the easiest to talk to and laugh with. But that ringing alarm told me something was very wrong, and I'd learned to trust that instinct.

I'd wondered if perhaps Sania should be given more attention, as we'd been able to easily flirt and talk as well, but the spark between Jacinth and me was on another level. I couldn't even pretend that I didn't want to dive in and explore our connection, no matter if it blew up in my face.

Which it very well might.

Kissing her had been impulsive and stupid, but I couldn't seem to stop myself from doing it anyway. I'd never experienced a kiss like that in my entire life, and I'd kissed *a lot* of women. I'd done a lot more than that, too, and yet this single kiss had left me more affected than anything I had ever done before.

I licked my bottom lip, tasting the ghost of her own left behind. I was waiting for my brother and Balthazar to arrive, replaying the kiss on a loop in my head like the damned fool the woman seemed to make of me. I let my head fall forward into my hands, trying to think of explanations.

But the only one that made sense was that she was lying to me.

My heart ached at the thought, and I glared at the floor. I was not some schoolboy with a crush; I was the damned High King of Gemaria. One kiss was not going to be enough to make the rest of the world go away, no matter how much I might have wished it to.

So when my brother and best friend walked in and sat down, I explained exactly what happened.

"I told you!" Ruri exploded, standing up in a fury as his arms flailed around, "That woman is nothing but trouble. You should eliminate her now and kick her out of the palace as fast as possible."

"If he does that, we'll never discover what's going on," Balthazar explained to him calmly. "We need to investigate her further. I'll send someone to Ruby Court to do some digging there."

I nodded tiredly in agreement, and Balthazar's ice blue eyes took me in crucially. "You like her, don't you?"

"What?" Ruri snapped, making me sigh and throw my head back, tossing an arm over my eyes as he began to rant on all the reasons that it was a bad idea.

"I know!" I finally exploded, sitting up and glaring at him. "I'm well aware, Ruri. I'm doing my best here, okay? I'll meet all the other ladies for their dates soon. Surely, there will be another who gets my attention."

"How often have you actually been interested in a woman like this?" Balthazar countered, raising a brow at me. I glared back at him. Sometimes, having my best friend as the head of my guard was a complete pain in the ass.

"Never," Alwyn said smugly as he walked in the door. His short, sapphire hair looked so much like my mother's coloring. My distant cousin, Alwyn, was thankfully not related to the lord of Sapphire, the son of a minor Earl who happened to be blood to my mother's own house. Which meant there were no women in the competition related to any of my friends, thankfully. It made things much easier.

I directed my glare straight at him as he sat down beside Balthazar and asked, "What's this I hear? Are you actually enamored with one of the competitors?"

The amusement in his voice was clear, and he raised a blue brow at me as I ground my teeth.

"I don't know that I can trust her." I finally said, slumping slightly in my chair. "I can't be with someone I can't trust."

"Hmm." He hummed, tapping a finger on his chin. "Then maybe you need to show her she can trust you?"

"What do you mean?" Ruri asked him, offended on my behalf. "Who wouldn't trust Az? He's the High King, for Veritx's sake! Not to mention the Lord of Diamond, with the need for truth in his blood! There's no one she should trust more."

"You're young, Ruri," I sighed deeply, shaking my head slightly, "And perhaps too sheltered between the palace and the academy," I told him, thinking of my date with Jacinth among the people of Theiapolis. "No one trusts another just because of their position. In fact, it's often the opposite. She came here expecting me to be a monster who cared nothing for the people I rule."

Ruri looked even more outraged, but Alwyn spoke up before he could begin ranting once more.

"Exactly." Alwyn smirked in triumph as he leaned back in his seat, "You need to show her that you're trustworthy, and then she'll likely open up to you. Right now, you're still little more than strangers. You need to show her who you really are."

I thought over his advice, before thinking back to how she spoke of her parents, of what was implied by that. Maybe it wasn't just a slip, maybe...

"You know, Wyn," I said with a growing smile, "You might have a point."

I TRIED MY best to push Jacinth from my mind while attending the rest of my dates. My first date after Jacinth was going to be with Ophira. The Onyx competitor was often quiet, and I was hoping to learn more about her during this trial. Her date idea was a brunch, which I hated to think of as boring, but her conversational skills weren't really up to the task.

It was an agonizing affair, all told, and looking across the table at her, I forced myself to contemplate what it would be like to marry her. She was beautiful, of course, with her golden hair and dark skin creating a stunning combination. I could easily see myself taking her to bed had there been any spark of chemistry between us.

Instead, all I saw were years of strained, silent meals stretching out before me.

The next date was with the Amythest competitor, Amatista, whom I'd noticed had befriended Jacinth during the last trial. She took me to a museum in the city to explore the history of Gemaria, but she spent the entire time teasing me about Jacinth, with seemingly no interest in discussing herself at all.

I was starting to get desperate for a distraction.

Thankfully, Safira was next, and she had a surprisingly great date idea.

"I thought stargazing would make for a nice date," she said shyly, smiling up at me. I smiled back, and together we made our way to the blanket she'd prepared. There were snacks and wine available, and I actually found myself breathing a sigh of relief.

Safira giggled, looking down at her wine before looking back at me. "I'm sure this competition must be a lot for you."

I turned to face her with a smile, "It can be at times, but this is a nice break."

She blushed, giving her pale skin a rosy hue, "I'm happy to hear that."

We watched the stars for a bit, and I found myself enjoying this silence more than the last. I was starting to think maybe Safira wasn't as bad as I thought, but then she spoke up again. "Sapphire was very proud when your mother became queen during the last competition."

I looked over at her with my brows creased in confusion, "I'm sure they were."

"They would be even more honored if *your* queen also came from Sapphire." She swallowed hard, looking a bit nervous before she continued, "I'm sure your mother would appreciate it as well, especially with everything that's happened. I would be a good wife for you. You already have sapphire blood in your veins, and together, we could be a good match."

Her words were like a bucket of cold water. That calculation, that manipulation—I had to force my jaw shut as my fingernails gouged into the grass beside me. Despite any positive feelings curdling into nothing, I forced myself to consider what marrying her would be like just to be fair. I'd enjoyed tonight, but it was more for the opportunity to get a break and relax than as a real date. That could be okay; there didn't *need* to be a spark to marry. We could have a respectable relationship, give birth to several heirs, and continue just as we had tonight....

And I could die of boredom in the next decade. I truly wanted— *needed*—more.

Plus, I truly hated the attempt to manipulate me into choosing a lady from my mother's kingdom. Playing on her grief was a low blow, and I had to imagine the words came straight from her father's mouth, not hers.

Allirea was next, and the Opal lady had quite an inventive idea. She took me to a health center in the city to volunteer for a few hours. It was one I had visited before, but never to actually do the healing myself. Allirea worked her opal magic for the people there, and she was very skilled, but it didn't give us much time to actually speak.

I did enjoy watching the way her opal hair fell down her back in a shimmering white waterfall. Her dark skin shone with her own health, and those opal eyes could be mesmerizing to gaze into, but by the end of the date, the only thing I knew about her was that she was nice to look at, which is about what I went into it with.

Sania was my next date after that, and I found a smile tilting my lips in anticipation. She was one of my favorites so far, aside from Jacinth. She'd shown the most personality, and it was one I could see myself enjoying. So when she brought me to play croquet, with a sly smile on her face that told me she'd be real competition, I was actually excited.

"Do you play often, Your Majesty?" she asked as we began.

"It's been a while, but I've been known to play from time to time," I smirked, watching as she lined up her shot. I tried to enjoy the image of she bending over, but her orange hair turned pink in my mind, and I had to look away.

Whether I was imagining Jacinth or the Pearl Court daughter who should have been here instead, even I wasn't sure.

Sania made a yipping sound that was admittedly adorable as she hit the mallet and watched the ball sail through the wickets. I forced myself to focus on the lady before me and the game at hand before I could get too distracted.

"Well, you're certainly a talented player." I complimented, and she turned to me with a large smile, her orange eyes glinting in the sun.

"I think you'll find I can be a *talented* player in many things, Your Majesty." She flashed me a sultry smile before she waved me on to go next.

As I passed her to line up the mallet, I bent to whisper in her ear, "I'm sure you could be, Lady Sania."

The shiver that passed through her made me smile, and I quickly hit the mallet, watching the ball sail through the wickets before hitting her own ball in a brilliant roquet that made her pout.

"Would you rather I go easy on you, my Lady?" I continued our flirting, enjoying the chance to let my worries fade into the background. Sania's eyes narrowed at me, and for a moment, the flirty banter faded away, but she quickly shook her head, her smile returning.

"Never, Your Majesty." She lined up her shot before turning her head to shoot me a smirk, "I always play to win."

The rest of the game went much the same, and she did win in the end, with a lucky shot I pretended to be offended over. Her giggling was cute, but I forced myself to look past it as I did with the others and imagine what life would be like with her as my wife.

I could see the two of us having fun, but I needed to find out more. I needed to see if there could be a deeper connection between us, something beyond surface level. Hopefully, more time will also give me more insight into that.

This left me with only Zumra left to entertain, and I was already dreading it. Part of me wished I could just eliminate her, but the politics of the competition were just as important as the actual goal of it. I had to be careful and make sure I didn't upset the relationships with the other courts—Emrys was very firm on that point.

So I met Zumra for our date, and found out we were attending a play in the city. It was a popular spot for the upper class, who often liked to go to show off. Sure enough, Zumra was dressed to the nines in a stunning gown of black that shimmered with a possibly literal ton of diamonds. It made her emerald-green hair and eyes stand out even more against her bronze skin.

Thankfully, the play meant we didn't have to talk much. Zumra got to show off that she was on the arm of the high king, and I got to space out, wondering what I was going to do.

Time was ticking ever down, for all it felt like we'd just started. The idea that I would have a wife by the end of this was hard to swallow still, but it was a fact I had to face.

Along with the fact that I could only truly picture one of them in the role.

CHAPTER 24

Jacinth

MY nerves were completely fried after my date with Azurill. I wasn't sure what to do, not after my slip up, nor after that kiss. I felt like a worm at the end of a hook, struggling to move, and just waiting for the end to come.

Faiza and Amatista were goddess-sent in that respect. They kept me company and encouraged me, and while they didn't know the truth, I could share other aspects of what was going on with them.

"He kissed you?" Amatista nearly screeched, her purple eyes wide in excitement. She clapped her hands, a large smile on her face. "This is perfect! You're absolutely going to be queen when this is over."

I laughed slightly, shaking my head. "I wouldn't go that far; it was just a kiss."

"What do you think, Faiza?" Amatista turned to my other friend. "You're close with his Majesty; you can give us some insight."

"Well…" Faiza began, her turquoise brows rising. "Az *can* be a flirt. He certainly enjoys entertaining women, but I can't say I've ever seen him actually show interest in one beyond that. We've often teased him about how fast his interest fades."

"So the fact that he's been *entertaining* our girl here since day one should say something, no?" Amatista wiggled her amethyst brows, making me giggle at her ridiculousness.

I found myself thankful for the two as they debated back and forth. I'd never had friends before, or I hadn't since childhood at least. There was only Ula, who was more of a mentor than a friend. We certainly never sat together talking about boys or our feelings. Any other girls I met on the street were to be viewed as competition. For the best spot to sleep, for any food we could find, it was all too much of a battle for friendships to form.

Everyone knew you had to look out for yourself above all.

I had thought it would be the same here, especially as it was *literally* a competition, but Faiza and Amatista had both surprised me. Neither had any interest in being queen or Azurill's wife, and both seemed to want to be actual friends. They were even rooting for me to win!

It made me feel blessed and cursed all at once.

Warm friendship versus the idea of their reactions later. The betrayal might gut me just as much as them.

I no longer knew what the best path forward was, and the uncertainty was eating me alive.

I had to get vengeance for my family, but I wasn't quite as sure anymore that my parents would even *want* this. Or if I could even do it. Could I look at Azurill and watch him drink his end?

Would Carnelian kill me and Ula both if I didn't?

"What about you, Tista?" I asked her, countering her teasing and trying to distract myself from the heavy thoughts assailing me.

"What about me?" She blinked innocently, taking a sip of her wine.

I narrowed my eyes at her playfully, "Oh, don't play coy. Who's the lucky man at home that you'd give up being queen for?"

Her smile fell as her eyes shot to Faiza and then to her lap. She played with her fingers for a moment, a nervous tick I'd seen before.

"I won't say anything," Faiza promised, grabbing one of her hands. "I have my own prospect I'd do near anything to be with if I could."

I grabbed her other hand, creating a link between us all, "And I have no reason to judge."

'You can trust me' sat at the tip of my tongue, but the words felt like ashes in my mouth, gritty and course, and like they didn't belong. I could wish it was true, but I knew my lies and my mission meant it wasn't to be.

"It's not a man," she finally whispered, looking up with teary amethyst eyes.

"So? Who cares?" I asked, squeezing her hand for comfort.

"Everyone does," She laughed incredulously, "My father. My mother. The court." Her lips trembled, "I love her so much, and she loves me, but keeping to the shadows while my father sells me off will be the end of us before long, I know it. She deserves better than to be someone's dirty little secret."

Tears fell down her face, and I quickly pulled her into a hug, Faiza taking her other side cautiously. The two hadn't been friends until I brought them together, so I was happy to see her freely offer her support as well.

"There must be a way," I murmured to myself as I petted her purple hair and tried to soothe her. "Commoners are allowed to marry the same sex, and while I understand the nobility has heirs to consider, you're not even in line to inherit as a woman. There's no reason to deny you. Not beyond greed."

"Maybe when you're queen, you can make my father and the court allow it," she whispered back, though her hopeless tone said otherwise.

My heart clenched in my chest, and tears came to my own eyes. I wasn't sure if this was the reason she befriended me, perhaps thinking it the best shot for her future, or if that had only just occurred to her. After all, she hadn't wanted to admit what was going on at first.

But either way, she deserved better. A chance to be with the woman she loved. And I had no way to tell her that I would be the last person able to help after this was over.

WE WERE CALLED to the throne room several days later to find out who would be eliminated. My palms were clammy, and I couldn't seem to quiet my nerves. There was every chance my fuck up could spell doom for my chances.

Amatista grabbed my hand, squeezing it in support as we stood before the throne, waiting for Azurill to appear. Faiza caught my eye from the crowd, sending me a smile that I tried to reciprocate, but it quickly faded as I watched Carnelian force his way to the front. I immediately looked away, hoping he didn't notice.

I didn't have to ask to know how unhappy he'd be about me making connections among the court. His plans were firm and unwavering, while mine were crumbling. I had to be careful to maintain the veneer I always held with him and avoid facing his wrath.

When Azurill was finally announced and he made his way to the throne, his eyes locked with mine for a moment that felt like an eternity. I got lost in the swirling pools of teal that held layers I found myself desperate to unravel, *needing* to know the truth of him.

"Thank you, everyone," he began with a charming smile. "For joining us for this elimination round of the Diamond Queen Competition!" The crowd cheered for a moment before he continued.

"For this trial, the ladies had to arrange a date for us at an assigned time and come up with something for us to do that fit into that slot. The ladies did admirably, and I enjoyed getting to know you all a bit better," he said, turning his eyes to each lady in turn.

The fire in his eyes as he looked at me made me want to melt into the floor. Considering the glare Zumra shot me afterwards, I knew I wasn't imagining it either.

"Unfortunately, one must be eliminated today, while the other ladies continue to the next trial," Azurill said, while looking over the lords and ladies in the crowd. I was sure they would all be unhappy if their own candidates were eliminated, and with only one able to be chosen in the end, Azurill would likely have to do a lot of politicking to appease them afterwards.

At least since Diamond's candidate was eliminated first, they couldn't claim he was playing favorites.

"Lady Ophira Nephrite," Azurill looked to the woman in question, "While you've performed admirably, and I thank you for competing on behalf of Onyx Court, unfortunately, you won't be continuing to the next trial."

Ophira bowed her head sedately, "Thank you for the opportunity, Your Majesty. It's been an honor."

I couldn't make out any discernible emotion on her face, positive or negative. It was completely blank in a way I envied. Though that facade likely hadn't made her a thrilling date either.

Still, I breathed a slight sigh of relief, at least until my eyes caught Carnelian's across the floor. His hard gemstone eyes drilled into me, but he nodded slightly, and I returned the gesture. I was safe for another trial.

"Our next challenge will take place tomorrow," Azurill announced. "Ladies, your guards will lead you to the place where you need to be in the morning. This trial will take several days, and…" he smirked, looking among us. "I suggest wearing something you don't mind getting dirty."

That was suitably ominous, and we all looked among one another, curious as to what we'd be doing next.

When court adjourned, Carnelian was quick to find me, giving me a smug smile as he offered his arm.

"Cousin, come walk with me," he demanded, raising a ruby red eyebrow at me expectantly.

I dipped my head in agreement and took his arm, letting him lead us away from the crowd. He brought us outside to the gardens, where flowers and gems were tended into a beautiful symphony.

A deserted one, with everyone currently inside.

"You've done well so far, much better than I'd expected," Carnelian said, his voice was even, but the words put me on edge immediately.

"Isn't that a good thing?" I asked, adding a touch of confusion to my tone.

"Of course, of course." He nodded slowly, but I could practically see the gears spinning in his mind. "But it is curious. After all, you're not truly a noble."

I swore my heart came to a stop, or maybe the world did. Everything froze, and I nearly tripped before covering and making the step in time to keep up with him.

"But living on the streets clearly gave you the skills necessary to pull the deception off," he continued, and my heart resumed beating in my chest.

It was silly. I knew he was unaware, but the words had still left the ground falling out from beneath my feet.

"Yes," I agreed quickly, "I had to play many roles through the years."

"Hmm." Carnelian hummed with a slight nod of acknowledgment. "I suppose that explains the High King, then." He practically spat the title, and I nearly flinched at the venom in his voice before I caught myself.

I couldn't let myself slip up in front of him. Ula's life remained in his hands, and if I was going to save her, I had to make him think I was following his orders exactly.

Which I was, *wasn't I?*

"What do you mean?" I probed when he didn't continue.

"The flirting." His upper lip curled in distaste. "At least, it seems to be working on Azurill. He seems quite taken with you."

"That is the goal." I reminded him, trying to figure out what his issue was.

"It is." He grunted in recognition before humming slightly again, as he seemed to do when testing people. It was a tell he somehow hadn't curbed in all his years of ruling. "I'm merely concerned. I don't want you to lose sight of your purpose here. After all, you've never experienced such luxury. I'm sure pretending to be a noble and getting all the benefits of one would lead anyone to want to remain in that situation."

Ah. This wasn't about the flirting, not really. He thought a few fancy dresses might turn my head, making me want to remain here instead of fulfilling my mission.

The luxuries here were the least of the temptations I was experiencing, however.

"Well, don't fret," I told him solemnly. "I won't be losing sight of my goal, not when it comes to *him*." I made sure to infuse my voice with all the distaste I felt for Azurill before meeting him. It wasn't difficult, not when half of me still felt that way.

It was the other half that was the problem, and I buried it quite effectively the moment Carnelian had dragged me away.

"Good," Carnelian responded sharply, a slight smirk on his face, but his eyes remained hard. Looking into those red depths was always a chilling experience, but watching him now, I could see something complicated going on behind those eyes. Something I couldn't begin to suss out.

"You never did tell me what Azurill did to your family for you to hate him so much," Carnelian said casually as he resumed walking us around the garden.

I froze.

It took all my reflexes and talents at deception to make my body move in step with his again, ensuring the lord couldn't see the chaos he'd just caused within me.

I'd never said anything about my family to him.

He had no way to know that was why I hated Azurill.

He shouldn't even *know* that Azurill had done anything *at all*.

I'd only told him that my circumstances in poverty had prompted my hate of the high king.

Was he assuming something more personal happened, and landed on my family as a guess? Or was there something else going on here?

I shook my head, pushing aside my turmoil before Carnelian noticed it.

"No, I didn't," I answered, side-eyeing him so I could see his face. The upturn of his lips was subtle, but it told me everything I needed to know.

Carnelian *knew* something.

Panic flared within me, all-consuming. For him to know *anything* about my family…*he'd have to know who I really was.*

CHAPTER 25

Jacinth

My sleep that night was troubled with nightmares once again. After realizing that my identity might not be as secret as I thought, I escaped Carnelian as soon as possible to return to my rooms, where I could panic in private.

I'd forced myself to sleep, knowing that the next challenge would dawn bright and early, but my dreams of the night my world was ripped away chased me through until morning.

My thoughts were a whirlwind, and I had no way to make sense of any of it. I finally resolved to put the whole thing aside until after the next trial. No matter what was going on, I still had to get through this, and having my mind in chaos would only result in mistakes being made.

Compartmentalizing used to be easier.

I got dressed and ready, meeting up with Amatista before heading down to begin the next trial. We discussed our thoughts on what it could be along the way, and I even tried teasing Alfrikr into spilling it, but he was typically tight-lipped.

We stepped into the room where most of the other ladies had already assembled. All except Zumra and Safira. When they finally walked in, Zumra's eyes found mine immediately, narrowing in contempt.

I smiled back cheerfully at her, getting a sneer in return. Amatista laughed quietly from beside me, bumping me with her elbow. I shrugged in return, making her shake her head in amusement.

"Good morning, ladies," Azurill said as he walked in the door, a smirk lining his face that I knew spelled trouble.

"This morning will mark the beginning of your next challenge. There are many facets to being my wife and queen, and one of these will, of course, include having children," he continued, eyeing each of us in turn.

Something in my chest sank at the thought. I wanted a family beyond measure, to feel that sense of warmth and comfort that having one brought, and that I lost too soon. But I also knew that wasn't in my future; it was just too dangerous. And the idea that Azurill would go on to marry and have children with someone else...

I didn't know why I cared; I *shouldn't* care. He was the entire reason I didn't have any family left, why I could never have one myself. And if I got my vengeance, he wouldn't be around to marry anyone. All my doubts practically screamed at me, everything converging and leaving me standing on a precipice.

Where it led, I had no idea. I only knew that the thought of Azurill having children with any of the other ladies left a raging storm within my heart.

"To ensure you're up for the task of raising children, of raising the next *high king*, you'll all be responsible for taking care of a child for the next few days," Azurill revealed, his smirk widening as some of the ladies shifted uneasily.

It wasn't a secret that many noble ladies overly relied on their staff to raise their children. My own mother had been one of the good ones who remained fully involved, and from what I could tell of the Queen Mother, she must have been the same.

"These children belong to some of my own staff, and you are to treat them as you would your own child. You'll be watched and evaluated, so make sure you are taking the utmost care with them." He warned, and I watched his eyes flit to Zumra and Safira.

A soft huff from Sania drew my attention for a moment, but her narrow-eyed look of concentration wasn't enough for me to concern myself with. Zumra was the one who looked truly disturbed by our task. Something told me this might actually be worth watching.

The door opened, and a line of children walked in. A small smile I tried to bury appeared on my face, knowing this was probably as close as I'd ever get to raising a child.

The little boys and girls were swaying and bouncing, clearly fighting against their instructions to stay still. I remembered seeing kids on the street who drove their parents crazy with their inability to sit quietly; it seemed these weren't any different.

Lady Arianell stepped forward and offered her hand to the first child, walking them over to Lady Allirea. She introduced the two and then continued with the next child. I was the last in line, so I watched Amatista be paired with a squirmy little boy with silvery-blue hair named Eirian.

Finally, there was only a little girl left, and my throat clenched as Arianell brought her over to me with a smile.

"Lady Jacinth, this is Fiala." She introduced me, and I knelt before the shy little girl before me, hiding half behind Arianell's legs while the curtain of her violet hair obstructed her eyes.

"Hi Fiala, you can call me Jac." I smiled at her, spying a violet eye peeking at me. I offered her my hand, and she hesitantly put her own tiny one in it.

"Fia," she replied quietly, and my smile grew.

"Well, it's very nice to meet you, Fia." I told her, before adopting a secretive look, whispering, "How do you feel about ice cream?"

Her wide eyes rounded further, and she looked up at Arianell before stepping out from behind her legs.

"I *love* ice cream," she told me, with all the seriousness ice cream was due.

"Me too." I widened my own eyes at her. "What do you say we get out of here and go get some?"

Her head nodded fast and hard, and she grabbed my hand to begin pulling me along, making me chuckle as she dragged me through the door.

My eyes cut over to Azurill before he disappeared from view, catching him watching us with a slight smile on his face. I forced myself to think only in terms of the competition, because this was good for that reason alone, and any others were firmly pushed to the back of my mind.

"WHAT KIND OF ice cream do you like?" I asked Fiala as we exited the palace to head to one of the shops I spotted on our way back from the Forest of Discontent. That trudge had proved itself helpful in more ways than one.

"Cracked Diamond," she responded, swinging our clasped hands back and forth. Cracked Diamond was a shiny silvery-blue ice cream that tasted of berries and sugar and was Diamond Court's signature flavor.

"Oh, good choice!" I told her, smiling down at the little girl. "I like Pearlescent, myself." It was a taste of home I rarely got, but the bubbly candy flavor always brought back sweet memories.

"Hmm." Fiala wrinkled her nose in thought. "I've never tried it."

"What?" I gasped dramatically, putting my hand over my heart. "You must try some! It's *soooo* good."

She giggled in response, pulling me faster, and I laughed as I followed obediently. We got our ice creams, and I let her eat half of mine, stealing bites from her own that made her laugh each time. By the time we returned to the palace, she was clearly on a sugar high, bouncing around and talking a mile a minute, while I watched her with fondness.

I brought her back to my rooms and was surprised to see that a little bed had been put in the den. I knew with her current energy, she wouldn't settle down until she'd expunged some of it, so I instead knocked on Amatista's door, and she opened it with a frazzled look on her face.

"This is *not* for me," she whisper-shouted at me so the guards couldn't hear. I tried to hide my laugh, but it was impossible, earning a narrow-eyed look from her.

"Why don't we take the kids to run around in the playground out back?" I suggested, and she nodded quickly, looking like I'd handed her a life raft after being stranded at sea.

We brought the kids out to play, and we watched them run around and play games. We clearly weren't the only ones with the idea, as Sania, Safira, and Zumra all showed up with their own assigned children and sent them to play.

I bit my tongue, aching to scream at Zumra. The way she ignored the little girl she'd been given to care for to gossip with Safira, who at least kept her eye on her kid, was infuriating. Sania watched her little boy intently, with the same intense concentration she seemingly gave to everything.

"There you two are," Faiza said, and I turned my head to see her approaching us with a knowing smile.

"You caught us," I smiled, only to be interrupted when Fiala ran up to us.

"Faiza! You know Jac?" Her wide violet eyes bounced between the two of us incredulously. She was completely blown away that two people she knew happened to know one another. My lips twitched, but I managed to keep from laughing,

"I do!" Faiza confirmed with bright, sparkling turquoise eyes. She kneeled down to Fiala's level, whispering loudly like she was spilling a secret, "And you know what? She just *loves* to play."

Fiala gasped as I tilted my head at Faiza, wondering what she was doing. Fiala quickly grabbed my hand and looked up at me, "Come play! Come play!"

I laughed, letting myself be dragged to the playground. She took us to the slide first, and I followed her down at her instruction. I could feel the gazes of the other ladies, and I knew they would find this disgraceful, despite it being hardly any different from our obstacle course.

I ended up following Fiala through several playground attractions before she decided she wanted to play tag. She organized me and the children present to all play, so I ran back and forth, running from the kids and chasing them in turn. I purposely slowed myself down, letting them catch me, or feigning that I was just about to reach them before allowing them to dart away from the tips of my fingers.

I couldn't remember the last time I'd had so much fun, honestly. Children offered a simplicity and purity that adults just couldn't manage. It was all so uncomplicated for them. And these children had yet to experience tragedy, as I had at their age.

It was my turn to tag this time, and I chased a laughing Fiala, grabbing her up into my arms and swinging her in the air as she shrieked with the force of her giggles. I laughed as I finally set her back down, looking up and starting in shock when I found others had joined the crowd watching on. Brokk was standing and chatting with Faiza, but it wasn't that fact that grabbed my attention. It was that Azurill was standing next to them, watching me with a smile and a soft look in his eyes that had my own smile softening into something else.

Taking Fiala's hand, I brought her over with me, ignoring the emerald glare trying to burn me alive, along with the orange one critically dissecting the scene.

"Mister High King, sir." Fiala greeted Azurill, giving a sloppy curtsy that had Zumra scoffing. I whipped my head around to glare her into submission. I looked back to see Azurill watching intently, before he greeted Fiala in return.

"Lady Fiala," he bowed very low and kissed her hand, making her giggle. It was hard not to myself, watching a man who had to be over six feet tall bending to reach a tiny child's hand.

"Lady Jacinth." His teal eyes smoldered at me, twinkling with just as many facets as an actual diamond.

"Your Majesty." I bowed my head with a slight curtsy before looking curiously at the man beside him.

"Lady Jacinth, forgive me for not introducing myself earlier. I'm Alwyn, though I go by Wyn, if you please." The sapphire-haired man smiled winningly at me, kissing my hand.

"A pleasure to meet you, then." I returned his smile, nodding my head. Azurill gave an annoyed glare at his friend, and his mouth opened to say something when a shout interrupted.

"Watch it!" Someone snapped, and I turned to see Zumra's face screwed up with anger at one of the children. I narrowed my eyes, ready to intercede, when Faiza placed a hand on my arm. She shook her head, motioning to the king with a smug smile, and I turned to see that he was absolutely furious.

Oh.

That was when it all clicked. How quickly I'd forgotten that for all her differences, Faiza was still a creature of the court. She'd absolutely brought Azurill out here to see us all with the children and how we interacted with them. Even as Faiza returned to flirting subtly with Brokk, I watched her bring attention to different moments she wanted Azurill to see like a master.

I shook my head at her, but I had to admit that the help was appreciated.

"You're good with her," Azurill observed softly, watching as Fiala all but passed out with her head in my lap after running around for hours. I was smoothing back her hair as we watched the sun dip under the horizon.

"I've always liked kids," I responded quietly, looking up at the fading light, the sun setting on my first day getting to experience this. The day passed too quickly, and I feared the others would do the same.

"You'll make an amazing mother one day." His words could have come out flirty and suggestive, but instead, the sincerity in them blew me away.

How could this man be the same one who'd had *children* killed?

The image of my cousin Peony sped through my mind, and I tried to think of a way to bring it up without exposing myself.

"For all I desperately want that, sometimes it seems like bringing children into this world is more cruel than kind." I finally said, hoping this would go the way I wanted.

"What do you mean?" he asked, a lone teal brow rising, but his eyes became concerned.

"Just look at what happened to the children of Pearl Court." I looked up through my lowered lashes as Azurill sucked in a surprised breath.

His eyes went to his lap, and I watched as he shuddered for a moment.

"They say that it was a robbery, but why kill everyone, even the children?" I pressed, the feeling in my gut forcing my hand.

"They say that," he finally replied, his voice dull and flat to match his gaze.

"Was it not?" I asked him quietly, and his eyes shot to mine, before running over my hair and eyes with an intensity that took my breath away.

"What happened to Lady Linnea and her family was a tragedy." Talk about taking my breath away, I was fairly sure I was going to die from loss of air. Hearing my true name from his lips sent my heart soaring and falling all at once.

"One that can never happen again." Azurill's dark tone surprised me, but he looked at Fiala, running a hand over her hair with a gentleness so at odds with what I'd once imagined. "Never again."

CHAPTER 26

Azurill

Any mention of Pearl Court and what happened there was pretty much guaranteed to put me in a dark mood. When Jacinth, of all people, brought it up, with her hauntingly familiar hair and eyes, it was nearly too much.

The lady managed to invoke so many emotions in me that I had no idea what to do with.

Watching Alwyn subtly flirt with her had made me want to ring his neck, even if she didn't reciprocate. His sapphire eyes and boyish hair had managed to lure many a maiden to his bed and he wanted to put those skills to good use when it came to helping me find the right wife. It was his own way of testing their loyalty to me.

Watching him flirt with Amatista didn't bother me at all, but with he turned his charms on Jacinth, I found myself imagining different ways to kill him. Some part of me clearly viewed her as *mine*, and since I still didn't know what she was involved in, that was definitely concerning.

The only other competitor I really had as a backup if this blew up in my face was Sania, at least so far. Watching Alwyn flirting with her, I felt a twinge of annoyance, but nothing like when he aimed those deep-blue eyes of his at Jacinth.

And now here she sat, asking me about the biggest regret of my life. A dark mark on my reign that could never be erased.

I had no idea how to answer her, not when I refused to speak of that night ever again. So, I remained quiet, hoping she would turn the conversation in another direction.

"I should probably get this little one to bed," Jacinth eventually murmured, watching Fiala with a quirk of her lips.

She was so beautiful that it was sometimes difficult to look at her. Watching her with Fiala was like watching a future I ached for, even if I knew the likelihood of it happening was small. I was supposed to be finding out what she was hiding, but all I could think about was the kiss we'd shared.

That night was etched in my memory in vivid detail, and I found myself desiring nothing more than to repeat it.

"Let me help you," I told her, lifting Fiala so I could carry her back, her head resting on my shoulder as her messy, violet hair cascaded down her back.

I offered my free hand to help Jacinth up and then moved it to her lower back to guide her back to her rooms. It was too easy to imagine a future like this. Especially as we got to her rooms and laid Fiala down in her bed.

As my hand skated across Jacinth's back, moving to tuck Fiala in, I heard her breath catch. I turned around to face her, and the look on her face was haunted, as if she'd seen a ghost.

"Are you alright, Mini-Dite?" I asked softly, but with enough humor, that she could brush it off if she wanted, or feel free to explain.

She laughed through her nose, looking up at me with eyes made of liquid pearl. My hand found its way to her cheek, her eyelashes fluttering closed as my fingers sank into her cotton candy-pink curls. I leaned in, brushing my nose across her cheek, gratified when she leaned into it.

Our lips were so close, the breath escaping through her lips teased mine. It was a tantalizing torture as she moved her face the slightest bit to the side, leaving me to find the corner of her mouth instead.

"Veri," she panted, and my lips twitched. Very-Full-of-Himself, but she was the only one I wanted full of me. As she moved to escape me, I pulled her back sharply, her gasp of shock caught in my mouth as I crashed my lips to hers. The moan she let out was one of both pleasure and torment, and I couldn't agree more.

Whatever game lay between us, whatever untruths circulated, neither of us could deny the chemistry that pulled us together.

My tongue chased hers with a ferocity I'd never experienced before, desperate to taste and touch her in any way I could. My hands slid down her curves to her ass, grabbing her and lifting her up. I walked her out of the room, far away from little eyes and ears. Our mouths barely separated as she wrapped her legs around me, her hands clutching my head to keep me in place.

As if I wanted to be anywhere else.

I took us to the sofa, my body following hers down until I was pressing her into it. My cock was so hard it could cut the diamonds I was known for, and I couldn't help but thrust against the wet heat I knew was waiting beyond the underthings keeping her from me.

Her moan was music to my ears as she thrust back against me, and my hands flowed down her curves to where her dress was rucked up around her waist, finding her bare legs and running my palms down her thighs, then pushing them further apart so I would have no resistance to the paradise awaiting me.

"Azurill," Jacinth moaned, throwing her head back as I thrust against her hard, kissing my way down her neck, nipping at the perfect, pale skin on offer, wanting nothing more than to mark it up and leave some trace of myself on her.

"Fuck," she panted, and I looked up from her neck, smirking at her.

"Such language for a lady," I teased, before nipping at her cleavage, drawing a breathy gasp from her plump lips.

"You like it." She accused, fondly, if I wasn't mistaken. My smile widened, and I looked into those glowing pearls looking down at me.

"Guilty." I grabbed hold of her bodice with my teeth, dragging it down and exposing a gorgeous breast I needed to become intimately acquainted with. I sucked her nipple into my mouth, and she clutched my head as she moaned once more, squirming against me and rubbing against my cock until I groaned from the exquisite torture.

"We—" She began, before stopping to let out a sharp gasp as I nipped at her, leaving her nipple sharp and swollen and beautiful.

"We shouldn't." She whispered, but her face told another story, and her leg curled around mine, pulling me tighter against her.

"We shouldn't," I agreed, nodding slightly. "But I can't seem to help myself when it comes to you," I admitted in defeat.

I'd slept with enough women to know the difference between simple lust and something else, and the attraction I felt now was like nothing I'd ever experienced before. It was just...*more*. On all fronts.

I didn't just want to fuck her until she couldn't walk, though I certainly *did* want that. I wanted to talk to her for hours, until our voices grew hoarse and we knew everything there was to know about the other. I wanted to unravel her secrets until her loyalty was completely assured. I wanted to see another child in her arms, down the line. I wanted more than I could rightfully claim at the moment, but I burned for it with an untamable desire, nonetheless.

Her eyes told me many things, but chief among them was that her desire for me was just as aching and desperate as mine own for her. But they also revealed her conflict. I'd been playing these courtly games for years, and whatever game was afoot, I could tell she was starting to doubt her place in it.

Whatever Lord Carnelian had her doing, whatever lies she told—

"No matter what exists between us when it comes to truth and lies, Mini-Dite," I said slowly, keeping eye contact as I hovered above her, "Tell me *this* is true."

Her eyes clouded with worry, but she watched me with the seriousness my words demanded.

"You want this as badly as I do. For what exists between us to be real." I laid it out there, watching her eyes widen before they softened, growing wet with unshed tears.

"Goddess help me," she whispered, closing her eyes. When her lashes fluttered shut, a couple of rogue tears escaped, and I leaned down to kiss them off her cheeks. Her eyes opened once more, arresting me with their intensity. "*Truth.*"

My eyes flared in triumph at the confirmation, and I took her lips once more, running my tongue across her bottom lip until she let me back in, her tongue dancing with mine with the same grace she always danced with.

A loud knock sounded at the door, and I groaned into Jacinth's mouth as we rocked against one another. I didn't want to pull away, and hoped whoever it was would take the hint and leave.

Unfortunately, the knocking merely got louder until Alfrikr's muffled voice came through the door. "Your Majesty."

"What?" I snapped, glaring at the door and making Jacinth giggle beneath me. I narrowed my eyes at her playfully, thrusting against her and making her giggle rapidly dissolve into a moan. I smirked down at her, and she glared back at me, lifting her hips and circling them against my cock until I groaned, my head collapsing into her neck.

"Your Majesty, you have a meeting to attend." Alfrikr cleared his throat pointedly.

"Fuck." I swore at the reminder, panting against Jacinth's skin.

"Sounds like you have to go," she said lightly, but her frown was clear.

"You really think I'd just leave you like this?" I murmured, my fingers trailing across her thighs until they reached the apex, her breath catching as they slid under her panties and found the wet paradise awaiting them. I'm not sure who let out a louder noise of pleasure as my fingers circled her clit, two of them trailing up and down before circling her opening.

I thrust my fingers in quickly, even as Alfrikr knocked again.

"One minute!" I called back as my thumb circled her clit in time with the thrusting of my fingers, driving them into her hard and fast to ensure I got her off before I left. What kind of man would leave such a woman wet and wanting, after all?

"Az," she moaned, hips rotating against my fingers as I drove her to the brink. "Fuck," she grunted, her mouth pulling mine in for a rough, demanding kiss, the fire in it all-consuming, until I forgot about Alfrikr entirely and nothing mattered except her pleasure.

I could feel her walls fluttering, and crooked my fingers slightly, pressing against the wall inside her, and was rewarded with her tightening up before she released, her loud moans swallowed by my mouth as her orgasm crashed through her, coating my fingers.

I brought her down slowly, while her panting against my lips was rewarded with small kisses supped from her lips and light strokes of my fingers as she finished trembling around me. Her hand came up to my cheek, and she brushed a kiss so soft and beautiful across my lips that I had to close my eyes against the breadth of feeling in it.

Of course, Alfrikr had to destroy the peace of the moment, banging obnoxiously against the door. There was no way he was clueless about what had just happened here, so I was going to have to smash his face in during training tomorrow in retaliation.

After sucking her divine nectar from my fingers, refusing to waste a drop, I lifted Jacinth and brought her to the bedroom. I thought, not for the first time, that the red of Ruby Court didn't truly suit her. But with a last kiss, I finally dragged myself away from her and opened the door to the hall to glare Alfrikr down.

He glared right back, completely undaunted by my annoyance. "You have a meeting with the others to discuss plans for tomorrow. Get going."

"What a way to talk to your king." I joked, making him roll his eyes before pointing down the hall for me to leave.

I made my way down the corridor, only to stop short when I spied Sania walking towards me. The sway of her hips was exaggerated by the gown she wore, which sucked her waist in tightly and left her breasts heaving over the top. I found myself oddly unaffected by the sight, still wishing I could turn back around and spend the rest of the night between Jacinth's thighs.

"Your Majesty." She smiled brightly, but I could see the tension around her eyes. "I was hoping to see more of you today at the playground."

"I apologize, Lady Sania." I tried to smile charmingly, despite having the taste of Jacinth still on my lips. "I plan to spend a bit of time with each of you over the next couple of days while you're with the children."

The tension around her eyes softened, as did her smile. She sauntered closer to me, and I fought the urge to back away so she wouldn't smell another woman on me. It would just be tacky to rub her face in it, potentially literally if the way she was looking at me was any indication of her intentions.

"I'm happy to hear that." She placed a hand on my chest and looked up at me with twinkling orange eyes. "I feel like I can never get enough time with you."

"A tragedy I'll see about rectifying immediately, my Lady," I promised with a smirk. "Unfortunately, I do have a meeting I need to get to, but I'll be sure to stop by tomorrow."

"You better." She smiled saucily, running a finger from my chest up to my neck as she leaned in to whisper in my ear, "I'll be waiting for you."

She backed away slowly before slipping around me, leaving me with the odd feeling that she somehow knew what I'd been up to. She hadn't been so direct before, and it felt like she was purposefully upping her game. As if she were feeling threatened.

I shook my head at myself. There was no way she could've known. Still, the thought wouldn't leave me, even as I sat through our planning meeting and Arianell's lecture about showing favoritism.

She wasn't exactly wrong either. I needed to focus on giving equal attention to each lady in the competition. Even if I *was* dreading spending time with a few of them.

CHAPTER 27

Jacinth

IDIDN'T think I could feel more conflicted, but Azurill had managed to prove me wrong.

His answers about what happened to my family left me uncertain. While his guilt regarding it was clear, his words left me in doubt about the reason why. He acted like he thought it was terrible, which wasn't what I'd expected of him at all.

Or perhaps it *was* what I expected of the man I now knew, and not the idea of the High King who loomed large in my mind all these years—the villain who orchestrated the downfall of my entire world.

Since Lord Carnelian's slip-up, my mind was in constant turmoil. Thankfully, Fiala needed watching, giving me something to divert my attention. She was such a sweet girl, and taking care of her gave me a glimpse of what having a child might have been like. The way my heart ached as Azurill and I had put her to bed was wretched. It was too easy to imagine a future that would never exist.

And then, he'd surprised me all over again.

Despite all of my doubts and conflict, knowing he felt the same way was a beautiful torment. It could never be, but he left the taste of temptation on my tongue and my heart a desolate shell, hollowed out of my rage and pain, leaving only an aching desire and a longing that could never be sated.

I put a smile on my face and pretended like my entire world hadn't shifted, but Faiza and Amatista were too easily able to see the truth. More people that I'd let slip beneath my skin and into the heart of me. It was foolish. It was irresponsible. But it was the *truth*, nonetheless. Azurill might have been asking for himself alone, but I couldn't deny that my heart ached for everything I'd found here.

"Something happened," Amatista said, watching me with shrewd eyes. "You're trying too hard to keep that facade of yours up, even around us."

I sighed deeply, hanging my head as Faiza snickered, "Well, she and Az did disappear together yesterday."

"That's true." Amatista's eyes lit up. "Did something happen between you two?" She smiled teasingly, nudging my shoulder.

"Shh, little ears are listening." I narrowed my eyes at them, waving a hand to indicate the three children playing before us in the garden.

"Oh, come on, they aren't paying us any attention." Faiza laughed. "You can tell us."

"What's this?" Another voice interrupted, and I turned to face Zumra, who walked up to us with a sneer already on her lips. Her emerald-green hair was perfectly curled and shone brilliantly against her white dress. So pure and unstained, even though we were supposed to be taking care of messy little children.

"Does Jacinth have some gossip to share? Perhaps where she truly came from?" Zumra asked haughtily. I narrowed my eyes at her, but realized something very important was missing.

"Where's the child you're supposed to be taking care of, Zumra?" I demanded, standing to face her.

She scoffed, shaking her head, "I don't see how that's any business of yours."

"And yet, you keep trying to insert yourself into mine," I countered with a raised brow.

"That's because I know you have something to hide," she hissed, getting right in my face. I raised my hands and, using just the tips of my fingers, dug them into her shoulders to push her back out of my personal space.

She staggered backwards, gasping dramatically in shock. The area went deathly silent as she stared back at me with her mouth gaping open. "How dare you put your hands on me?"

"What is going on here?" I recognized the man with icy-blue-green hair who walked up to us as the head of the royal guard, Balthazar. Azurill's best friend. I nearly groaned, but managed to keep it contained.

"That filthy mongrel attacked me!" Zumra declared, pointing at me and making my eyebrows shoot up.

"You were in my face, I merely pushed you back out of it," I told her, rolling my eyes.

"Jac, what's going on?" Fiala's little voice rang out as she ran up to me, curling around my leg. I put a hand on her shoulder, smiling down at her.

"Nothing to worry about, darling. Right?" I looked up at Zumra and Balthazar, who looked between the two of us skeptically.

"I'd like to speak with each of you separately, just to be sure," Balthazar said, looking apologetic. "We need to be careful when it comes to our competitors."

"Of course." I forced a smile, knowing Zumra's position was infinitely better than mine. Would that be enough to influence his decision on this matter?

"If you'll both follow me, we can have the children watched over while we take care of this matter," he said, looking to Fiala with a small smile, before turning to Zumra. He was clearly looking for the little girl in her care, and upon realizing she was nowhere to be found, raised a brow.

"Where is your charge?" he asked slowly, his eyes slowly narrowing.

Zumra smiled widely, waving a hand breezily. "Oh, she's well taken care of."

"How so?" he questioned in return, crossing his large arms and making the muscles bulge as he watched her carefully.

"She was having a tantrum and would not stop screaming." She shivered, and her lip curled up in disgust. "I used an old family potion that my mother taught me. It puts a crying child down for hours." She looked so proud of herself, but my mouth dropped open in shock.

"You dosed her?" I gasped, feeling the horror in my voice down to my bones. Magic could be volatile and dangerous to give to children. They weren't fully grown and could react differently than a mature adult would. I thought it was standard practice to avoid giving potions to children unless it was absolutely necessary, but apparently, Emerald Court did things differently.

Zumra rolled her green eyes at me, "Don't be so dramatic, she's absolutely fine."

"You have no way of knowing that," I argued, the force of my fury making me tremble.

"She's right." I nearly jumped as Prince Ruri appeared from behind me. "It's too dangerous to give a child something like that."

His frost-blue hair fell in waves to his chin, framing his face and giving it a softer appearance, but the ice in his eyes was glacial as he stared Zumra down. I thought he'd looked at me coldly, but it was nothing compared to this.

"Prince Ruri," Zumra laughed, but it was forced now as her eyes darted between two of the closest people in the world to the High King she sought. "My mother used to give it to my siblings and me all the time. It's perfectly safe!"

"You have no way of knowing that for sure." He glared back at her. "Balthazar, send someone to confiscate the potion and materials in her rooms. Along with a healer to see to the child."

"Of course, my Prince." He nodded, then looked between Zumra and me. "Both of you will need to come with me."

"No, Jac did nothing wrong!" Fiala shouted, stomping her foot. "The green one was mean! She just made her move away."

I sighed heavily and kneeled down, taking her hands in mine. "Don't worry, Fia. I'll be okay. They just want to ensure everyone is safe, and I'm sure they'll see that nothing really happened here."

She pouted, her little violet eyes looking to the floor. "Okay, but you'll come back, right?" She peeked back up at me through the curtain of her hair.

I smiled softly, leaning in to kiss her forehead. "Let them try and stop me." I teased, getting a slight smile from the girl before I stood up and nodded to Balthazar.

Prince Ruri was watching me carefully, but something had softened in his bearing from the last time we'd spoken. He leaned down to Fiala's level, giving her a roguish wink. "Here, you can stick with me until Lady Jacinth is done."

"Thank you, Prince Ruri." I dipped my head deferentially, and he gave me a nod in return before I left to follow Balthazar, who met up with a few of his guards along the way to pass along Prince Ruri's orders. Two of them followed us as we were led to what must have been the guard's offices and barracks. We walked past a training ground surrounded by an observation deck and then into a hallway that led to several rooms.

The two guards brought Zumra and me each to different rooms, and I was then forced to wait for a while. As I sat there, I considered what Azurill's response might be to this before realizing that I should really be more concerned about Lord Carnelian's. I shivered at the thought, hoping against hope that he might not hear about this, but I knew in my heart that it was hopeless.

The man had eyes and ears everywhere. I was just lucky that my role here involved seducing Azurill, or else he might have caught on already that I wasn't exactly following orders.

The door finally opened to reveal Balthazar, who took a seat across from me. He placed a parchment down on the table along with one of the magic quills that always had ink.

"Forgive me for dragging you here, Lady Jacinth," Balthazar said, his face blank of any emotion, remaining purely professional.

"I can well understand the need for security," I told him, nodding slightly.

"Can you tell me about your confrontation with Lady Zumra in detail?" he asked, his eyes unblinking as he watched me.

I sighed, launching into a retelling of what had occurred. I watched as he took notes, nodding in parts, before he flipped to another piece of parchment, likely to compare my story to whatever Zumra reported.

When I was done, he nodded thoughtfully before smiling slightly at me. "It sounds like no harm was truly done. I can certainly understand your frustration with her antics, Lady Jacinth, and I apologize if you felt threatened while under High King Azurill's protection."

I couldn't help the slight smile that snuck out, "I truly don't blame the king for Lady Zumra's vendetta."

"I'm happy to hear it," he responded gruffly, nodding quickly. "I think we're all set here. You can return to Fiala, if Prince Ruri hasn't run off with her, of course." He chuckled.

I chuckled, unable to imagine the suspicious prince running around after a child. Then again, there was no reason for him to show *me* his softer side.

I made my way back to the gardens, entering them through the giant archway made of gems. The sun warmed my skin as I walked by the colorful plants and gems growing all around me. The winding paths split off into several different routes, and I went to turn right toward the playground when I spotted Sania heading my way, along with the child she was watching over.

"Lady Jacinth." She greeted coolly, looking me over.

"Lady Sania." I nearly stuttered, unsure how to handle the interaction. No matter how many times I'd thought about speaking to my cousin, I hadn't dared to. Now, I had little choice in the matter.

"I heard you had a bit of a scuffle with Lady Zumra." She raised her orange brow, brushing her long curls over her shoulder as she watched me steadily.

"Oh, nothing so dramatic." I forced a chuckle. "Just her being dramatic, in fact."

Sania smiled, but it looked forced, and there was certainly no humor in it. "I'm sure."

She moved to go around me, not even saying farewell, but stopped as she came level with me. She turned her head to the side to face me directly, and her orange gem-eyes glinted as they narrowed.

"You should be careful," she advised in a carefully neutral tone. "You never know what someone is willing to do to win."

With that, she walked away without another word, the child following obediently after her. The entire interaction left me feeling unsettled. Her cool demeanor could easily be attributed to several factors, but it was so at odds with her warning.

Unless she was talking about herself and trying to threaten me. But then why would she warn me at all? It didn't make any sense, and I hated not knowing what game she was playing.

Zumra and Safira's games were easy to figure out, but Sania was clearly smarter than them both. She was more subtle about whatever machinations she was up to, if she was indeed up to any.

I hadn't spent enough time around the other ladies in the competition to know their agendas either. Faiza and Amatista were friends enough for me. Except now I couldn't help but wonder if I did myself a disservice by not getting to know the others better.

Maybe it was time I found out more.

About *everything*.

CHAPTER 28

Jacinth

After a few days with Fiala, I was almost loath to give her back. We'd had fun together, making it feel less like a challenge and more like a break from the competition than anything else.

Now it was time to find out who would be eliminated and who would go on to the next round. I was anxious, hoping that what had happened between Azurill and me would outweigh whatever poison Zumra had certainly tried to spill. Perhaps literally, if the way she handled an upset child was any indication.

Amatista and I made our way to the throne room, our guards following us dutifully. Alfrikr hadn't stopped laughing about my "fight" with Zumra, though he'd initially seemed quite upset that the only time I'd needed assistance so far was when he'd been called away to speak with Azurill. Frankly, I thought it was probably for the better.

It prevented the situation from escalating any further, at least.

Aside from the fact that he was now practically glued to my side, ever watchful for any retaliation.

We lined up in front of Azurill's throne and waited for the High King to make his appearance. I hadn't seen him much since the night in my room. I knew he had to make time for the other competitors, but it left me with a sick feeling in my stomach I'd never experienced before.

When Azurill walked in, the eyes of the court followed him hungrily, several of my fellow competitors, most of all. My stomach sank as Sania watched him with the intensity of a woman who was willing to do whatever it took to win.

And maybe she would be the best choice for him, in the end. If he lived long enough…

I cut my thoughts off immediately. The confusion I've been living with since arriving here was always a steady presence in the background, but now was the time to don my veil of truth and pretend to be an insipid noble desperate to be queen.

"My Lords and Ladies, the Diamond Queen Competition is all about finding the best High Queen for Gemaria," Azurill began with a smirk firmly in place and a twinkle in his teal eyes, "As such, our competitors face trials that test them on different challenges they would face as queen. Our fourth trial was a test of child rearing. A queen is, after all, expected to produce children one day, and raise them to be the next kings, princes, and princesses of the realm."

A cheer rose from the crowd, all of them eager, or pretending to be, for the safety of a secured succession.

"Each of the ladies was assigned a child to take care of over the last few days, and each was measured according to how well they did," he continued, his smirk falling as he looked out among us.

"Each lady revealed much about what type of wife, mother, and queen they would be during this challenge, and I look forward to the next trials to learn even more about our competitors. But sadly, one must be eliminated today." Azurill said, and his eyes fell to my right.

"Lady Zumra Giada, I thank you for your participation in the Diamond Queen Competition. You've done Emerald Court proud, but it's unfortunately your time for elimination," he announced heavily, and the gasp that rang around the room at his words had me fighting a smirk.

Zumra's jaw had actually dropped as she stared at Azurill with wide, emerald eyes. Her emerald and teal gown studded with diamonds showed her confidence in an alliance that she was now realizing had slipped through her fingers.

"Me?" she stuttered, unable to believe what was happening. "But—"

Lord Emrys stepped forward then, his opal-white hair gleaming in the light of the throne room, and he grabbed Zumra lightly by the shoulders to lead her out of the room. His job handling inter-court relations had to be getting tested quite thoroughly during this competition. I didn't envy him in the least.

I breathed a sigh of relief, knowing I was safe for another trial, and as a bonus, I'd no longer have to deal with Zumra's cattiness. Azurill's eyes met mine briefly, and I knew the small smile that snuck onto his lips was all for me, making my heart pound within my chest, even as he hid it just as fast, turning to face the court at large.

"Our next challenge is one my own brother devised," Azurill told the crowd, smiling proudly as he nodded to Prince Ruri, who was standing to the right of the throne. He bowed theatrically, making the crowd go crazy.

"Our realm is one based upon magic, and every ruler needs to be adept at that magic. For this trial, each lady will be assigned a type of potion to create. She will have the flexibility to decide the details and what goes into it, as long as it creates a result within the parameters we've set," he explained, spreading his hands wide as he did so, his eyes focusing in on all of us who remained in the competition.

Our number was ever smaller, making me breathe a sigh of relief even as I straightened, realizing that the time to make a decision about how to move forward loomed ever closer.

"Each of you will need to acquire the right gems and carry out the alchemy to make the potion. You will then test the potion yourself, and the results will determine your competency with magic, as well as your place in this competition." Azurill told us, his voice kind but stern.

"Your guards will bring each of you to the gem markets tomorrow morning to get started." He instructed, before turning to the opal-haired lady standing off to the side. "Please see Lady Arianell to get your assigned task for this trial."

With that, he was quick to leave, and I could hardly blame him when I spied the lord and lady of Emerald Court, looking fit to be tied as they struggled to make their way over to him. I shook my head at their folly. Did they truly think they could change the result? Or were they hoping to at least get something else out of their daughter's failure?

I could easily see Azurill and his council offering discounted trade or more spots on said council as a way to shut them up.

I made my way to Lady Arianell when Amatista was done, looking quite pleased with whatever she'd been assigned. I tried not to let my nerves show. I knew *how* to do alchemy to create a potion, having done some on the streets on rare occasions, but nothing of the caliber I was sure they were going to expect.

I was going to have to create something way out of my magical league.

My palms were sweating by the time I'd reached Arianell.

"Lady Jacinth." She smiled kindly, her opal eyes swirling with color and looking like magic themselves. "You've been assigned the task of creating a potion related to the values of Diamond Court. Meaning it will need to relate to truth, power, or courage in some way," she explained, and I breathed a sigh of relief at how open-ended that was.

I thanked her briefly before letting my mind wander. There were so many ways to mix gems together that would create an infinite number of reactions, and I was going to have to narrow in on what I could make before tomorrow. Perhaps something easy that not even I could fuck up.

"What did you get?" Amatista appeared at my side, linking our arms together as we left the throne room.

"What did *you* get?" I countered, matching her smile as best I could. She laughed, throwing her head back.

"I was assigned Pearl Court," she explained, and my breath caught in my throat. My hands went to my neck, where my mother's necklace lay hidden beneath my dress. "I think a boring love potion should suffice, or perhaps one to increase lust? Either way, it'll be fine." She forced a smile now, making me curious about where her mind had gone.

"*Now* will you tell me what you got?" She nudged me, raising an amethyst brow. I explained what Arianell told me, and Amatista looked excited, her eyes and smile wide.

"You could create such wonderful magic for that!" she told me as we walked down the hall. "Perhaps a truth potion? Find out how Azurill really feels?" she teased, but I stilled, actually completely stilled, my feet not moving another step as it hit me in a dizzying rush.

A truth potion.

But for what I needed…if I wanted to know the truth…if I could find out what really happened to my family, *why* it happened…and how Azurill and Carnelian both played into it…

Diamond for truth. To reveal the unknown.

Pearl for love. For the family I'd lost. For the confusing feelings now consuming me for a key player in this tragedy.

Sapphire for prophecy. For seeing the unseen.

Emerald for the past. To direct the potion to the right time.

It would be a complex potion, layers upon layers woven together to spell out a story lost to history. But if it worked, each gem would play its part in revealing the truth to me.

I could know for sure what had happened. And while it would be traumatic as Tartarus to see it all play out, the sights my young eyes were spared once upon a time, it would set the path for my future—and I was beginning to think that was worth anything.

"Jacinth?" Amatista called, looking worried as she placed her hands on my shoulders. "What's wrong?"

"Nothing." I shook my head, though the hoarse tone of my voice didn't go very far in convincing her. I laid my hands upon hers, squeezing lightly. "Truly, I just had an idea. I know what I'm going to make."

"Oh," Her eyes brightened, lighting up her purple orbs until they shone. "What's your plan?"

"I'm going to see the past," I whispered in her ear. When I pulled back, her eyes were now wide, and she cut a glance at the guards before nodding firmly and dragging me back to our rooms. When we were finally away from the scrutiny of Azurill's men, she turned to face me.

"Okay, now explain," she demanded, crossing her arms and looking like a stern teacher. I nearly giggled at her expression, but managed to contain myself.

"There's something—" I bit my lip, suddenly realizing what I was doing. A heaviness settled in my chest, and I took a deep breath, bracing myself, and trying to find the right words that would offer truth without giving away a weapon that could turn around and stab me in turn.

"What is it?" Amatista asked, sobering, as her eyebrows creased in worry. She reached a hand out for mine, and I held onto her like a lifeline. I missed Ula so fiercely for a moment that I had to blink back tears.

"Something happened when I was young." I whispered carefully, "Something I thought Azurill had been involved in. But now..." I trailed off and looked up through a curtain of pink hair at the woman before me.

She could clearly tell that this was quite serious, and her face was appropriately somber, but her eyes revealed that her thoughts were already spinning away. She was *too* smart, and I knew it would be too easy to put the pieces together if I said much more.

"I need to know the truth." I finally said, feeling like the pressure on my chest had lifted some, allowing me to breathe. "This trial gives me the chance."

"What happens if this potion shows you Azurill was involved?" she asked, equally as quiet.

My shoulders hunched slightly as I curled into myself on the sofa, but I managed to shrug them lightly. "Then everything is as it was."

Her head cocked to the side curiously. "And if he wasn't?"

I sucked in a sharp breath, unable to truly consider what that would mean—but unable to bear the alternative.

"I can't really think of the outcome. Not yet." I admitted, shame lacing every word as my head dropped onto her shoulder. Ula would berate me for showing such weakness, but I was…*tired*. So tired of having to navigate all of this.

"Once I know the truth," I continued, barely a murmur at this point, "I'll decide from there."

Her fingers began running through my hair, letting me just *be* in a way I desperately needed. She shrugged her shoulders casually, and my head bobbed up and down with the movement.

"I'm with you, just let me know what you need," she promised, making me blink quickly as I tried desperately to prevent the moisture welling in my eyes from escaping.

"Thanks, Tista," I whispered, and let everything else slip away.

CHAPTER 29

Jacinth

THE morning dawned bright and clear, and I found my excitement for this challenge rising rapidly. The chance to play with gems and create a potion in a royal Gemlab was beyond my wildest dreams before I came here.

It certainly beat trying to do alchemy using subpar gems and cracked bottles, hoping against hope for the slightest bit of magic as I kneeled behind trash cans in a deserted alleyway.

And then there was the fact that all my hopes and future dreams rested on the potion I would create.

I was practically bouncing from excitement and anticipation by the time I finished dressing. With what I hoped to see today, I needed to feel like a piece of home was with me and had dared to dress in a way that could very well raise eyebrows.

I'd forgone the ruby-red that had dominated my attire since this scheme began. Instead, I'd gone for a mix of soft and bright pink shades. My off-the-shoulder underdress was a light pink, with sleeves that billowed out a bit before clinging tight to my arm right above where the brown leather cuffs that circled my wrists began. A marbled-pink and brown leather corset sat above a split skirt in the same marbled pink, which revealed the softer pink underdress in the center.

I wore a matching marbled-pink choker and topped it with my mother's pearl necklace, which was somehow gifted to me by the mysterious woman at the market. It matched perfectly with the pearl and diamond bracelet that never left my wrist.

All in all, I was certainly not dressed as the Ruby Court competitor should be, but I found I couldn't help myself.

I grabbed a few strands of my hair from the sides of my head and braided them back. I left the cotton candy-pink waves to tumble down my back, with a few pieces framing my face.

Today, I looked like a Pearl Court Lady.

The very thing I'd been prevented from being since that horrible night. The role that was ripped out from between my fingers as I was left tossed to the street like garbage.

I was fairly confident that no one would put together the truth now, at least…no one who didn't already potentially know.

But with the potion I'd be making, and the truth I'd learn, I decided it was time to reclaim this little piece of my identity, even if I was the only one who knew it.

I greeted Alfrikr with a bright smile, making his amethyst brows shoot up to his forehead.

"Good morning, Alfrikr." I practically chirped, not even aware I could make such sounds. "Ready to get to the market?"

He chuckled more warmly than I'd heard from him thus far. "Someone's eager this morning. Don't you want to get breakfast?"

I waved my hand in dismissal. "I'm not hungry, just eager to get started, like you said."

Said eagerness seemed to amuse him, and he shrugged, joining me to make our way out of the palace. I couldn't believe I would actually get to shop in Diamond's famous Gem Market. I'd dreamed of going for so many years, and the fact that it was finally happening caused my hands to shake with excitement.

I noticed the looks that I received as we walked the city streets toward the market. Everyone knew who I was now, and their excitement to see a competitor in the wild was obvious. I was just as interested in seeing them, however, as it reinforced that the people in Diamond Court were *happy* under Azurill's reign.

I'd seen most of the courts at one time or another in my years wandering from place to place and seeking new spots to stay safely. I'd been able to witness firsthand how many of the lords didn't bother caring for their people the way Azurill did, the way they were supposed to.

But the people here went about their days cheerfully, healthy and prosperous, as they spoke and laughed together, hurrying or meandering their way through the city. The clamor of their voices increased as we neared the market, and I took a deep breath as it came into view.

I'd gotten only a glimpse last time, but now I could make out the entrance entirely. The iron gates were wide open, with a blessing to Veritx across the top, which was currently split in half with the gates standing open.

Upon entering, I found a cobblestone path bordered on either side by permanent stalls, each with a little overhang to protect the goods laid out. Greenery grew off the tops of some, while others had fabric in all different colors draped from one roof to the one opposite, creating some lovely shade as you walked from stall to stall. Lanterns of all shapes and sizes dangled from the overhangs, lighting up the merchandise and enabling customers to browse no matter the time of day.

Sellers called out as we passed, but I knew from the smaller markets in other courts that those at the front rarely had the best goods—those lay deeper in.

I did keep my eye out while looking over the multitude of goods on offer, however. Despite being called Gem Markets, it was hardly *just* gems on offer. Oh, they were in abundance, of course, but there were also ready-made potions and alchemy equipment, along with unrelated goods, such as spices, weapons, and fabrics; anything you could think of.

I could hardly wipe the smile from my face as we came to a table full of sapphires. Alfrikr huffed with amusement as I leaned down and examined them, looking for the perfect one.

As much as Elvish gem magic was a science, there was a bit of instinct—or godly influence—that played into it. The type of sapphire I used would affect the outcome of the potion, so I opened myself up to the influence of the gods, something I so rarely did.

Immediately, my eyes caught sight of a sapphire toward the back of the table. It was cut jaggedly, which felt somehow fitting for a gem that would take me back to a past that left me full of jagged edges myself.

It was about the size of my palm, and the inside of the gem glinted more brightly while it seemed to almost dim around the edges, but despite its flaws, I knew it would work perfectly. I wouldn't need all of it, but the dust would keep, and I had no issue leaving it for the Gemsmiths to use for other potions. So, gem secured, we moved on to get the emerald, which took several different merchants to find the right one.

As we were making our way to find a diamond, I spotted something curious and paused mid-step. Leaning over the table directly in front of me was the same human man I saw sneaking into the market previously. He was speaking with one of the vendors, and they seemed to be working out a trade. His blue eyes were bright and sly as he looked up, catching me watching him.

His smirk as he looked me up and down might once have affected me, but now all I could do was compare it to Azurill's as he sauntered over.

"My Lady." He bowed theatrically, making me raise a brow, unimpressed with his flirting.

"Pirate," I responded dryly, making his smirk widen in delight.

"Ah, you know of me then?" he asked, reaching out a hand to one of the pink curls falling in my face, but Alfrikr stepped forward instantly, grabbing his hand and stopping it mid-motion.

"Touch her, and I'll put you in the ground, Riker." He spat, making the pirate, Riker, apparently, laugh loudly.

"Alfrikr!" His smile widened until I could see his tongue running along the back of his teeth, like a lion salivating over its prey. "I didn't even recognize you, with your new look."

He waved a hand at the armor he wore as a guard, but Alfrikr stared him down stoically.

"You two know each other?" I asked, mentally cheering that I'd pegged my guard correctly that first day.

"Oh yes," Riker responded, his dark hair rustling in the breeze as he leaned back slightly, his legs spread a bit as his hands hooked onto his belt buckle in a pose clearly meant to intimidate.

I found it intensely curious that *any* human thought they could intimidate an Elf, but the nerves I could barely distinguish in Alfrikr's eyes told me everything I needed to know. This pirate, human or not, was incredibly dangerous.

"Alfrikr here was part of Apsara's crew," he explained, as if that meant anything to me. His eyes were locked on Alfrikr's amethyst ones, and the fiery hate that rose in them surprised me. His entire bearing seemed to change, from loose and sultry to cunning and threatening in a moment.

His fingers moved from his buckle to the inside of his jacket, making Alfrikr grip his sword tightly and pull it partially out of its scabbard. Everything around us became tense, both men tightly wound and ready to spring at any moment.

"I'm not part of that world anymore," Alfrikr spat at him. "And you're not supposed to be here, Gunnlod. Take your crew and be out of port by sundown, or you're going to have problems."

"Going to run to your king and tattle on me?" Riker laughed, his fingers moving so fast I didn't even catch when he'd grabbed his dagger, only noticing it when he began to twirl it around nimble fingers.

Alfrikr smirked back at him, looking entirely unconcerned. "Maybe, or perhaps I'll send a message to an old friend about where The Anamnesis is docked. It's not often, after all, that one can find your ship so easily."

Riker's burning blue eyes stared back at him, his lip curling in a snarl. "I'll be done with my business and out of Gemaria by tonight, don't you worry your pretty little head about it. Perhaps I'll send a message to your old friend instead. Find Aletheia's Eyes and give *Captain* Nixie your regards."

His distaste as he snarled out the word '*Captain*' left me blinking in surprise at the heat he managed to pack into one word. Whatever dislike he felt for Alfrikr, his hate for this Captain made it seem inconsequential in comparison.

Alfrikr suddenly grabbed him by the lapels of his leather duster, pulling him in until their faces were close enough for my guard to speak directly into his ear, entirely ignoring the dagger aimed at his throat.

"Lay a finger on her, and I will hunt you to the ends of the earth, Gunnlod," Alfrikr's voice had deepened to a lethal rumble, making my eyes widen in surprise. I had never seen his temper flare like this. Purple fire raged in his eyes as his menacing words left his mouth. "You will never regret anything the way you'll regret touching her, that's a fucking promise."

With that, he pushed the pirate back, the man glaring as he straightened his coat dramatically. Before he could open his mouth to say a word, Alfrikr spoke once more.

"Now get the fuck out of here, Captain. And don't return."

With that, Alfrikr took my arm, gentle but insistent, and guided me past the seething pirate left in our wake.

"Is it smart to just leave him like that?" I asked him quietly once I knew we were out of range of human hearing.

Alfrikr scoffed, shaking his head. "He won't dare risk doing anything to bring Azurill's wrath down upon him. The pirates survive by staying as under the radar of the Fae as they can. Getting the attention of the High King, who is allied with one of the major Fae kingdoms, would leave them with a target on their back. Riker knows that, which is why he didn't stab me back there."

His wry smirk had me shaking my head at him. "It was a risk. He doesn't seem to like you very much." I teased him, and Alfrikr heaved a heavy sigh laced with a sadness I couldn't figure out.

"I used to be a part of the Apsara family's crew. The head of the family, Pike, gave each of his children their own ships to captain." He began to explain, and I perked up, curious to learn more about the pirates. "I was part of the crew of Aletheia's Eyes, captained by his daughter, Nixie."

As Alfrikr spoke, his amethyst eyes unfocused, as if he was seeing back into the past. "The Apsara family and the Gunnlod family are rivals, you see. Both families have their own lands they've claimed, and they've been in a deadlock power-wise for years, dating back to the rivalry between Pike and Tizoc, Riker's father. But Nixie and Riker…"

He shook his head, a haunted and unsettled look on his face. "Let's just say they took the rivalry to a different level and leave it at that."

"So why did you leave?" I couldn't help but ask curiously.

He looked down at me then, his eyes softening as he smiled at me. "I'd wanted to escape the pressures of my position and the expectations my parents had of me. So I left court to be a pirate, wanting to find adventure. It wasn't until I joined them that I realized how little my problems compared to the humans', and I resolved to help them where I could."

His face twisted then, a grimace lining it that seemed out of place, as he continued. "But when the rivalry between the two families escalated, I couldn't be part of it anymore. That's as much as I can say."

I tilted my head, watching the pained look on his face as he fought to get the words out, considering what I was seeing. "You truly *can't* say, can you?"

He shook his head, pointing to his mouth. I gasped, a hand coming up to cover my own. I knew the humans had figured out a way to use relics to wield magic themselves, but I had never seen the results of it.

Not until now.

Alfrikr had a magical gag. Meaning when he left, the family thought whatever he knew was too dangerous to let slip. They'd ensured he could never say a word.

I burned with curiosity, hating that I couldn't get to the bottom of what had happened.

Maybe one day that truth would finally come to light.

But it wouldn't be today.

CHAPTER 30

Jacinth

THE rest of our trip through the markets was considerably less eventful. I stopped by a diamond merchant who had a number of beautiful gems to choose from, and as I let the influence of the gods guide me, I zeroed in on a crystal-clear diamond that resembled a heart in shape. The shining jewel had a teal color, the same as Azurill's eyes, in the center, and I knew immediately that it would be perfect for my potion.

All that was left was to find the right pearl, and I clutched at my mother's necklace as I walked the path through the markets, keeping an eye out for just the right vendor. It was as I rounded a bend in the path that I spotted it. The dark-skinned merchant gave me a knowing smile as I approached, their hair and eyes the lightest shade of pink I'd ever seen. It seemed vaguely familiar, but I couldn't place from where.

"As I prayed to the gods this morning, the knowledge came to me that a very special customer would come by my table today. I didn't believe it, *couldn't* really, but it's true," she whispered as I walked up, soft enough that even Alfrikr, leaning against a post across the path and watching closely, wouldn't hear her. She looked me over closely, her eyes shining with unshed tears.

I shifted on my feet, uncomfortable. Maybe I shouldn't have worn the pink after all. If she knew…

"You don't remember me, do you?" She chuckled, sniffing slightly as she blinked her tears away.

"Should I?" I asked her warily, narrowing my gaze as I looked her over more critically. Something about her nagged at my memory, but it was just out of reach.

"My parents worked in your household," she said, keeping her voice low as my heart about stopped. "We played together sometimes as children, Lady Linnea."

I hadn't heard my true name directed to *me* from another's lips outside of dreams and visions since that night my parents died. My breath caught in my throat as my heart raced, and a ragged gasp tore from my mouth. I had to wave Alfrikr back to his post as he swiftly stood to attention.

My memory clarified as I looked at her, remembering playing from time to time when her parents brought her along. It was usually only when they couldn't find childcare, but I'd always looked forward to those days.

"Dalia?" I asked in a strangled whisper, and she nodded, smiled brightly.

"Oh, my Lady." She laughed wetly. "Knowing you live, that House Marit's blood lives on…" She shook her head, wiping a stray tear away.

"No one can know," I told her urgently, grabbing her hand and squeezing. "It's too dangerous."

She nodded smartly. "Of course, my Lady. I would never betray you, you have my oath to Erodite on that." Her words relaxed me slightly; an oath to our goddess was absolute.

"Thank you, old friend." I smiled sadly, and her own matched it. "Things are coming to a head now, and I need a pearl to help me see the truth of things. About what happened that night…and who was truly responsible for the deaths of my family."

Her eyes nearly glowed as she realized the part she had to play today. "I'm honored my pearls will go to such a worthy cause. I can only hope this will lead you to your rightful place, my Lady."

"I have no rightful place, Dalia. Not truly." I shook my head, my defeat and the raw pain I felt surely all over my face.

"Nonsense." Dalia insisted sternly, "The gods answered my prayers today with knowledge, sure enough, and they don't do that unless a great destiny is at play."

I opened my mouth to argue, for surely whatever role the gods saw fit for me was not one I cared for, not if the rest of my life thus far was anything to go by. Dalia, however, refused to hear it.

"When my prayers were done, I knew just the pearl to bring with me today. A special one, that I hope you'll find fits your needs." She smiled, pale pink eyes shining brightly, contrasted against her lovely dark skin.

Dalia leaned down behind her table and brought out a tray that held a pearl like I'd never seen before. It was huge, for one, and the hue so closely resembled my own coloring that it was uncanny. It looked like it had been crafted in my image.

The shining pearl was perfectly round, with not a blemish to be seen, and as I picked it up, nearly entranced by its appearance, I felt the tell-tale tingle of the gods' presence. My hair stood on end as a strong gust of wind blew through the market, extinguishing the torches and leaving the vendors scrambling to relight them.

Dalia smiled truly, nodding to me. "You see, the gods know what they're about."

"Apparently." I couldn't argue with her after that and smiled slightly. "How much for it?"

She scoffed, shaking her head. "As if I would ever ask my Lady to pay for such a gift. Please, take it. House Marit lives through you now. Thus, my loyalty is as it ever was, *yours*, Lady Linnea."

I was pleased to know there were still those out there whose loyalty to my family was so great that their allegiance was unquestionably mine at my mere appearance. Perhaps I was wrong to think no one cared about House Marit anymore. Or perhaps she was an outlier.

There was only one way to truly know, but it was unfortunately a risk that I couldn't afford to take.

After thanking Dalia and promising that I would find her when this was done to let her know the outcome, Alfrikr and I made our way back to the palace, my mind no less troubled than before.

But I had a challenge to win, and maybe in doing so, some of those troubles would be resolved as well.

Entering the palace, Alfrikr instructed me to wait while he spoke to Lady Arianell to find out when I could use the Gemlab that Prince Ruri apparently frequented for my trial. Each lady still in the competition would be overseen while creating their potion, and I couldn't help but wonder who exactly would be present.

I hadn't thought much about how they would test the effectiveness of the potions. Surely, some of them would have obvious results, but mine would be quite difficult to judge. If all went well, I would learn the truth, but the judges would not see what it showed me.

Alfrikr returned with the news that I would be next up after Lady Safira finished, and I let out a slow breath at the news. I didn't know whether to be elated that I would soon know the absolute truth or terrified to experience that night once more, let alone the ramifications once I knew.

I didn't allow myself to dwell on what those might be. It was a moot point. Either way, I would have big decisions to make once it was done, but nothing could be decided before then.

When my turn finally came, I took a steadying breath, stilling my shaking hands as I gathered my gems and made my way to the Gemlab, ready to brew my potion. Walking in, I stopped short as I found Azurill waiting, leaning casually back against a table.

"My King." I curtseyed, raising a brow at him.

His smirk quickly turned into a smile as he saw me, but his own eyebrow spiked up as he took in my pink dress. "My Lady." He nearly purred.

I bit my lower lip, trying to contain all the words desperate to spill out, but his eyes locked onto the motion, and he licked his lip in turn. I shook my head, breaking our stare and moving forward to the table to deposit my materials.

I took a look around the room, taking in the arched, wooden bookshelves stuffed full of books, potion bottles, and more. The room had been lined with what I knew to be spelled rock, as many Gemlabs were, to keep magic contained within the room. Unlike Carnelian's Gemlab, which was very cold in appearance, this had an old-world charm that I loved. Fern leaves fell from the tops of the bookshelves, and warm diamond-shaped teardrop-style lanterns hung from the ceiling.

"I had our original Gemlab repurposed for solely our alchemists' use, and built this one for my brother," Azurill said softly as he stepped up to the other side of the table, running his hands across the wooden surface. "He goes to Ceridwen Academy in Amethyst and has found that he loves nothing more than experimenting with magic."

I couldn't help returning his smile, even as my eyes refused to meet his, skittering down to the table to unpack my gems. "You're a good brother. Many wouldn't make them a lab for their own personal use."

I looked up at him then, unable to help raising a brow, a twinkle in my eye, "Though I can't help but wonder why you've commandeered your brother's lab for this competition instead of having us use the other."

Azurill chuckled deeply, making a shiver run down my spine. "I'm afraid Ruri's got the alchemists working around the clock on potions for our protection, just in case. This was the only way we'd get you all in. And he was very insistent that the competition includes a challenge such as this."

My hands stilled briefly as I reached for a large potion bottle, but I forced myself to keep moving. It shouldn't be a surprise; Prince Ruri was clearly all too aware of the daggers at their back.

"So, how does this work then?" I asked, my hands flourishing over the table. "I was given Diamond Court and decided on a truth potion, but I will be the only one to see it when I drink it, so how will you judge its effectiveness?"

"What truth are you aiming to see?" Azurill hummed, looking me over carefully.

"The only one that matters," I responded quietly, pain shuddering through my words despite my best efforts to suppress it. "The one that will tell me how to move forward."

I met his eyes carefully, and the intrigue and caution in his gaze were mixed with a soft affection and fierce lust, creating a look as complex as the potion I was about to brew. How was it possible for this man to feel so much at once?

Azurill rounded the table and moved to stand before me, slowly raising his hand until he was cupping my cheek. My eyes closed as I leaned into it, unable to help myself. The desire to lose myself in the present was too much, especially when the past awaited.

I opened my eyes, meeting Azurill's teal orbs, to find him watching me intensely.

"It will show you something of the past?" he asked, raising a brow, eyes briefly flitting to the combination of gems now sitting on the table. I nodded into his palm, and his lips tilted up into a smirk. "Then I'll be able to tell if it worked. Your eyes will give it away."

"How so?" I asked as he stepped back, my brows furrowing.

His head cocked to the side curiously. "Have you never seen a potion like this in action?"

I dipped my head down briefly, but made myself lift it back up to meet his eyes. The shame I felt for not receiving the education I should have was present, but I was also proud of all that I had managed to teach myself while living on the streets. I took the foundation my parents and teachers had instilled in me and let it grow like an out-of-control weed. I sucked up any knowledge I could everywhere we went. But still, I knew there were things I was lacking in.

That was never more apparent than now, as my entire house of cards threatened to crumble before the High King. Any noble daughter would have been taught this, making it glaringly obvious that something about my story was off.

"Well," Azurill continued, allowing my silence to be his answer. "Your eyes will cloud over as you see the truth you are seeking. The colors of the potion will swirl through your eyes, and that will be all the indication I need to know it worked."

I nodded sharply as he smiled softly, and wanting to prevent any further slips in my armor, I quickly got to work.

CHAPTER 31

Jacinth

I GOT to work, grabbing the diamond, pearl, sapphire, and emerald gems I'd purchased, and began crushing them down into dust. Azurill's eyes watched me intently as he leaned nonchalantly against the edge of the table. I was glad my hands were already busy, preventing me from fidgeting under his stare.

"Tell me, High King Azurill," I said playfully, a grin peeking out, "Is the king attending each trial himself today?"

Azurill's smirk turned slightly predatory, and he leaned further over the table and into my space. "Why, is my Lady Jacinth jealous I may be paying others the same attention?"

I scoffed, shaking my head. "Hardly. I merely find it curious that you alone are observing, *Veri*."

"Ah." He leaned back with a knowing smile, making my fingers itch to be buried in his hair, wanting to harshly tug on it in rebuke as I attacked his lips once more. "Well, my Lady, let me assure you that we have divided the trials among my council. My brother is attending Lady Amatista, Arianell is with Lady Sania, Emrys oversaw Lady Safira, and Wyn will be with Lady Allirea."

"Ah, so you were lucky enough to get me then," I replied innocently.

The deep rumble from his chest as he laughed warmed me from the tips of my toes to the top of my head. We were in dangerous territory, and I had to move quickly to determine what would happen from here. The future of the king before me rested on the result of this potion, as did the kingdom he ruled.

Whether anyone knew it or not, the fate of everyone in Gemaria rested on this one potion, and I felt the responsibility lay heavily on my shoulders.

"Did you think I'd let any other see to you?" Azurill asked, the heat in his voice making my hands shake slightly as I poured in the sparkling white water from the crystal lakes, the solution used to bind the potion together and liquify it, into the large bottle I'd selected.

"I suppose I should count myself lucky then." I teased him lightly despite the gravity of the moment.

I let the magic guide me as I grabbed the first batch of gem dust. I slowly dropped half of the diamond dust in before adding one-third of the pearl dust. I used a long wooden stirring spoon to combine the first layer of the potion, letting it mix fully before continuing.

Azurill watched everything carefully, and I did my best to forget about him as I worked. I added three-fourths of the emerald, then another one-third of the pearl again, before stirring once more. The magic was heavily reliant on following your instincts as they came, telling you which action was next, and I felt that surety and wholeness only the gods' magic could offer filling me up. It was a feeling unlike anything else in this world, and I fully understood why professional alchemists chose to dedicate themselves to performing this magic as their life's work.

I added the sapphire before letting the remaining pearl filter in, stirring them together with the rest of the potion, and then added the rest of the diamond. As I stirred in the final ingredient, I could *feel* the potion as it began to bubble. The colors of each gem swirled together; the silver, blue, green, and pink layering in amongst one another, turning mostly pink and silver as the potion began to smoke.

I stepped back as the final sign rose to the ceiling, the smoke tinged with the colors of the potion itself. I allowed myself a small smile of pride. I may not have been taught magic and its alchemy formally, but I'd picked up a lot over the years, and being able to create such a complex potion was all the proof I needed to know I'd done well.

"Why such a complex potion if you've never made one like it before?" Azurill suddenly asked, making me jump slightly as I was torn from my thoughts.

He stood and walked over until he was right next to me, both of us leaning over the table to observe the potion as it settled.

"Because I have to see. There's no other way to find out the truth, and this offered an opportunity for it that I may never get again." I told him, perhaps too honestly.

His eyebrows furrowed in confusion, and his head tilted to the side. Our eyes met, and I knew mine surely begged him to ask no questions. He sighed in defeat after a moment, turning to look away, but I grabbed his hand and brought his focus back to me. This time, I reached for his cheek, my fingers trailing down the sharp cheekbones and strong jawline on display, before going to his neck, my hand clasping over the diamond tattoo that I knew only started the giant piece that continued down his shoulder.

My hand on his neck kept him in place, and I briefly looked up at his crown, the gem of every court represented, with the diamond that stood for truth and power being the most prominent of all in the dead center. I knew that the truth of him could make or break me now, and I wasn't sure when I'd lost myself to his power.

Looking down, I took in his too-handsome features, the teal hair shaved back on the sides but flopping playfully on top, the sparkling blue-green eyes that saw straight through me, and the long, dark teal jacket with silver detailing matching the vest underneath, hiding a body I knew would fit perfectly against my own.

I looked down, seeing my pink skirts brushing against the teal of his pants. It all came down to this, in the end. The interactions of Diamond and Pearl, and what hid within their history. Knowing he'd all but killed my family himself, I'd wanted so much to continue hating him, wanted nothing more than vengeance for their deaths.

And yet, my traitor heart would throw away my family's vengeance for the chance of a future with the man before me.

But there *was* a chance—a chance my heart knew something my mind did not. And I had to trust in that now. As I spied the potion's last wisps of smoke dissipating in the air, signaling its readiness, I met Azurill's eyes with a fierce look.

My other hand came up until both hands cupped his neck, and his own came to rest on my hips automatically.

"Trust me, Veri," I whispered, a smile flitting across my face at the name. Things were so different now from when I'd dubbed him that. "Just for a little longer. Let me find out the truth. Find out if indeed the truth will set me free, or if it will damn us all."

His forehead fell to mine, and I closed my eyes, knowing this could potentially be the last time I could allow this. If my doubts were wrong, I couldn't live with knowing these feelings lived in me for such a monster.

I'd slay him, as any monster should be, and live out the rest of my life in heartbroken shame.

I quickly reached up and tugged his head down, going to my tiptoes to claim his mouth with mine. His groan was lost in my mouth, as our tongues met with all the desperation I could feel pounding inside my heart. I let myself enjoy this, enjoy what I could, for as long as I could.

When we finally pulled back, panting for air, I smiled shakily before reaching for the potion. I clasped it in my hands, looking down at it with trepidation. As the potion began to shake in my hands at the thought of what I was about to experience, Azurill's hand reached out and grabbed the bottom, steadying it, while his other came around my back, steadying me.

"What's wrong?" he asked, concern all over his face.

"I don't want to do this," I admitted pitifully, hating the whimper in my voice. "I don't want to see."

"See what?" he asked, brows furrowed as he tried to make sense of what could have happened in the past that could be so integral to our future. "What has you so scared?"

I laughed wetly, shaking my head. "I'll tell you once I'm done."

"Mini-Dite, please." His voice sounded desperate, and I hated that I put that feeling there even as I welcomed the knowledge that whatever this was between us, it was clearly mutual.

I braced myself to return to the worst day of my life. To the source of all my nightmares. To the end of everything for the girl I was once. I braced myself to see the bodies and blood, to see the ones I loved cut down. Braced myself to find out whether the man my heart yearned for had that blood on his hands, or if the man who held my strings and my friend's life in his hands had more of a handle on this realm than we all thought.

"I'll see you on the other side," I whispered to Azurill, and brought the bottle to my lips, swallowing mouthfuls of the glittering potion.

And then the world disappeared in a swirl of silver.

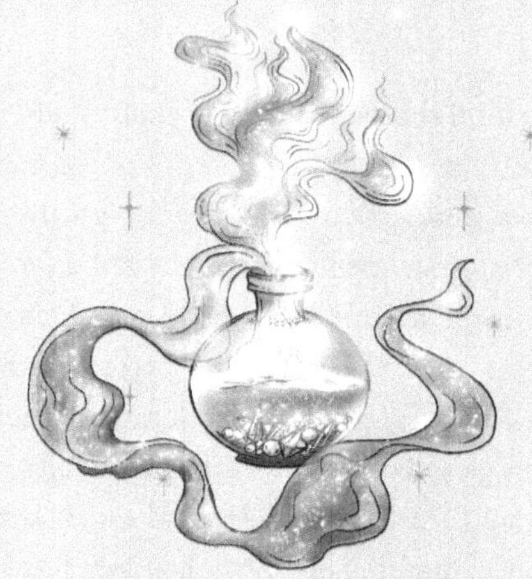

CHAPTER 32

Jacinth

I SAW nothing but a cloud of silver until the smoke slowly cleared, leaving me standing in a familiar room. My eyes immediately locked onto the people sitting around it—my mother, my father, my aunt, and my uncle. Servants also filled the room, coming and going as they served my family.

I stepped forward, my entire body shaking as I forced my feet toward them. A tear slid down my cheek as I watched my parents laugh, my mother leaning into my father as he wrapped an arm around her. I couldn't help a small smile at the familiar sight. Unlike many nobles, they were so truly in love, and they never failed to show one another how deeply that love went.

I heard a crash from the front of the room, and my eyes fell closed automatically as more tears streaked down my face, but I couldn't remain blind; I had to see.

The men swarmed into the room, some of them wearing masks while others didn't bother, and they instantly began cutting down members of our household as our guards tried fruitlessly to defend against the unexpected attack. My father jumped to his feet, slipping a potion from a pocket and throwing it at the attackers. I sucked in a breath as I watched a handful of them be consumed by the resulting smoke, screaming as their flesh boiled off their bones, leaving me wide-eyed in shock.

My father didn't hesitate, taking the distraction the potion afforded to wrestle one of the men to the ground and take his sword. But it was all in vain. There were too many of them, and they quickly overpowered him, the sword falling to the ground as another blade slid deep into his stomach.

My gasp was so loud that I covered my mouth with my hands like someone might have heard me. But I was merely a ghost here—or perhaps, I was surrounded by ghosts, and I remained the only real thing here.

Watching as my mother tried to get to my father, my heart broke entirely, ripping straight down the middle. One of the attackers grabbed her, dragging her across the room as one of the men propped my father up so he could see her. Two other men got their hands on my aunt and uncle, and I couldn't stop the sob that left my lips as both their throats were slit.

Their bodies were thrown to the ground like trash, their blood leaking out and pooling on the marble floors. My hands fisted as I struggled with my inability to act. I wanted to kill these men more than anything, but I knew it was useless. None of this was real, not anymore.

My eyes turned back to my parents, where the men were taunting my father with what they would do to my mother.

"I've never had a lady before." One of them licked his lips, his hands trailing up my mother's side. My mother's eyes narrowed as she snarled, and I watched in shock as my very ladylike mother snapped her head back, breaking the nose of the man threatening her. A surprised smile lit my face as I watched her turn quickly and knee him between the legs.

The man crashed to the ground, but a couple of the others moved in, and I grit my teeth as they slapped her so hard she fell to the ground. They manhandled her back up, each man holding an arm and keeping her in place.

"You bitch," the man she fought stumbled back up, "We could have made this painless for you, but now, it's going to hurt."

"Rue, we have our orders, and they don't include playing." Another man stepped forward, chastising the snarling man, who was clearing fuming. I squinted in contemplation, his voice sounding eerily familiar, but I shook off the thought as I watched his eyes cut to my father, who was struggling against his bonds, and then back to my mother. Suddenly, he surged forward, and my parents cried out in tandem, my own voice adding to the chorus, as a dagger went through my mother's chest.

She slumped forward, with only the two men holding her arms keeping her upright, while the clear leader snarled at this Rue. "If you can't behave yourself, then go elsewhere."

The man fell back, his eyes going to the ground as he mumbled angrily to himself.

"What do you want?" My father asked desperately, his eyes glued to my mother. When he finally pulled them away, they went to the doorway on the left, leading back to where our bedrooms were located. He gulped audibly, sucking in panicked breaths. I could see how terrified he was already, but now most of that terror was for *me*. He forcibly looked away from the path to where I lay sleeping, not knowing that it was too late and other attackers were already on their way there.

"We are merely getting rid of the opposition. Ensuring that when the time comes, the path to the throne will be clear," the man said, confusing me as he walked up to my father. He removed his mask then, and I staggered backwards in shock.

"Casaan," my father spat angrily, "I should have known. Your father has always desired more than he's owed."

"Oh, Elros," Casaan stepped forward, slithering toward him. "My father *will* be High King. As long as the blood of House Marit is extinguished from Adamah, of course."

My father stilled completely. "What?"

Casaan laughed, a cruel sound that echoed around the room as my father's eyes slid past the heir of Ruby to lock on my mother's. Both looked horrified, and I knew at that moment that, even despite their wounds, their only concern was *me*. Tears flowed ever faster from my eyes as pain consumed me, but my anger kept me standing, kept me watching, and prevented me from falling into a pit of despair.

"Oh yes, a little prophecy gifted to my father." Casaan smiled widely. "If a single member of House Marit lives, my father will fail to take the throne. Should your house fall, however." He shrugged casually, "Then his path is assured."

"All Hail High King Carnelian." One of the men in the background cheered, prompting whoops and cheers from the other men.

My blood turned to ice in my veins.

"All hail the High King." I'd heard one of these men say that night as I hid within the closet. I thought it was straightforward. Simple. The High King was to blame for this tragedy that had befallen my family.

Azurill was innocent.

My mind spun in so many directions, and I didn't know how to process any of them. Watching as my parents were killed, as Casaan left and gave the others an order to clean up and leave no witnesses, didn't help with my clarity of mind either.

It was a horror show. All of it.

What I didn't understand was why Azurill had seemed so guilty when speaking of my family, but as my vision turned silver again, I wondered if perhaps I was about to find out.

When the fog cleared, I was greeted by the sight of Azurill standing over a field of bodies. I recognized a few of them, men who had participated in the murder of our household. So many lay dead before me, and I couldn't help my mouth from falling open at the grisly sight.

Azurill himself was shirtless for some reason and completely *covered* in blood. It was so wrong to feel myself grow wet at the sight. He looked like a wild animal, bloody from head to toe, and with a crazed light in his eyes…but he'd killed the men who helped kill my family. He'd brought the vengeance I had been aiming for all this time, years before I had ever met him.

"Azurill. It's time to go." Balthazar walked up to him, wiping blood from his forehead.

"These men were pawns," Azurill spat angrily, shaking his head. "They can claim what they like, but I know this was no robbery, *I know it*, Zar. No one kills an entire household just to rob a lord."

"We'll figure it out," Balthazar reassured him carefully, putting a hand on his shoulder. "But this is not the way. Not for the king. I doubt anyone will shed a tear over an entire crime ring being wiped out, but this isn't who you are."

Azurill's eyes seemed to clear, and I only noticed as they returned to their regular hue that they hadn't been teal at all, and I wished I'd paid more attention to see what in Tartarus they'd looked like. He looked down at the bodies arrayed around him with clear despair as he staggered back, hanging his head. "Fuck, what have I done?"

"Nothing we ever have to speak about again," Balthazar promised, gulping as he looked over the carnage Azurill had somehow wreaked singlehandedly.

It didn't make sense. It looked more like a Fae had done this. While Elves were strong, we weren't as strong as they were. This looked like someone had ripped through these men. Azurill carried no sword in his hand, no weapon that could explain their state. What in the Otherworld had he done to them?

The silver smoke returned, and I swore to myself, wanting to know more. But the potion, the magic, the gods, they were running the show here, and I was helpless to do anything but be taken along in its wake.

Azurill was right about one thing, though. *He didn't get everyone.*

Vengeance was still possible.

I knew it would be difficult. With Ula's life in Carnelian's hands, I would have to play this very carefully. But a smile came to my face as I thought of what Casaan had said.

With a member of House Marit alive, Carnelian would fail to take the throne. Which meant one thing…

I was the threat hanging over Carnelian's head.

And whether he'd figured out I lived and sought to manipulate me to ensure his rise, or if he planned to kill me at the end of this, his plans didn't matter, because I would see the end of House Rousseau the way he sought to end House Marit.

I would avenge my parents and everyone who died thanks to one man's greed for more than he was given. I would be the knife in the dark coming for the lord's neck. Or perhaps I would stick it through his chest to return the favor his thugs paid my mother.

The silver smoke cleared, and I found myself sagging into Azurill's arms. I was panting, and my entire body was shaking uncontrollably as he staggered and then brought us carefully down to the floor.

"Jac, what's wrong?" Azurill asked frantically, concern and panic fighting one another for dominance in his voice.

All I could do was whisper, my shaking hand coming up to clasp his, "I was wrong. Everything's changed now."

"What's changed? What did you see?" He asked quietly, forcing his anxiety back to be there for me, and it made me appreciate him even more. I smiled up at him, stroking his tan cheek.

"I saw the truth. I know now I was wrong, and that everything must change." I said quietly. "I know…" I struggled with my next words, the admission taking much from me. "I owe you the truth as well."

His eyebrows flew up in surprise, and he opened his mouth to speak, but my fingers fell softly across his lips, silencing him.

"I do. You deserve the truth. But I can't—" I cut off, my words choked in my throat as I struggled not to cry. Seeing my visible struggle, Azurill pulled me into him, hugging me to his body. As his hand began to stroke my hair, so gently, so at odds with the blood-soaked warrior I'd witnessed, I let my head fall to his shoulder.

For once in my life, in the arms of a man my heart couldn't help but yearn for, I let everything go. In great heaving sobs, ones I'd never allowed myself after that day, I let the grief explode from my soul, pouring out in tears and tremors.

And Azurill held me through it all. Stroking my hair and back, murmuring gentle words of comfort. I'd never experienced anything like this before. I hadn't allowed myself to get close to anyone outside of Ula until I came here. And now my heart was so tangled up over this man, it was ridiculous.

I would have to tell him the truth. Tell this man comforting me so sweetly that I'd planned to kill him. I would be lucky if he listened, if he didn't order me imprisoned or executed. The fact that this could go very badly wrecked me all over again.

He didn't need me. He had plenty of options. Noble ladies of the realm were literally fighting to become his queen, and I was nothing but the lost little girl who'd planned to assassinate him. But…something about the way he held me gave me hope.

If I'd learned one thing living on the streets, however, it was that hope was the most dangerous thing of all.

CHAPTER 33

Azurill

To say I was unsettled was an understatement.

In the time since we've met, Jacinth has proven herself to be a strong lady who could go toe to toe with any courtier in the building and come away the winner.

To see her fall apart so completely…

I couldn't help but be worried about what she saw. Her vague promises beforehand led me to believe that her thoughts and feelings about me, her lord, and her past, were all somehow mixed up together, but I couldn't quite put my finger on the full picture of this particular puzzle.

I knew her story didn't quite make sense, but I didn't know the extent of it. We both wanted to trust the other, but there was something in the way, holding her back from taking that step.

My concerns rested on who she came here with and what his plans were—and what plans he may have involved *her* in.

I could only hope that whatever she saw would help to cross that final barrier. The longer this competition went on, the more I could see a real future take shape. I could see Jacinth beside me, as my partner. I knew it was reckless to put my hopes on one lady at this point in the competition, but I found myself helpless against the pull I felt toward her.

My heart decided for me, and whatever reservations my mind held, it cared not a bit for them.

Still, my advisors did what they did best: advise me.

"Please tell me you at least have backups in mind," Ruri begged, and I nodded once in confirmation.

I hated that, as king, I couldn't just lay all my hopes on Jacinth as I wished. I knew it may not work out, or she may fail a trial, and I'd be forced to eliminate her. Or perhaps I'd find out what Carnelian's plan was and be forced to imprison her.

I shuddered at the thought, my entire being rebelling against the idea.

"Sania seems a good choice," Ruri hinted, though Arianell scoffed, shaking her head. "What?" Ruri asked, a perplexed expression on his face.

"That girl is more than she appears," Arianell swore. "She hides too much within her eyes for me to be comfortable with her."

"She's probably the one I get along with best after Jacinth," I admitted to her, and she shook her head.

"What about Allirea?" She countered, her head tilting to the side curiously.

"She's as beautiful as the next, but even on our supposed date, there was just no connection between us." I sighed miserably.

"How about Amatista?" Emrys asked, his brow cocked in query.

Ruri laughed, shaking his head as he raked back his frosty-blue wavy hair. "She completely bombed this trial."

"What?" I asked, confused. She was from Amethyst, and she'd already proven how smart she was.

"Yeah, her potion was a disaster and nearly exploded. The other ladies, I believe, all at least managed to make a working potion. Even at varying skill levels," Ruri explained, looking amused.

"She's friends with Jacinth, right?" Wyn asked as his sapphire eyes met mine knowingly.

"You think she did it deliberately, don't you?" I asked him, a smirk rising against my will.

"I do," he confirmed with a nod. "The two are very close, I have no doubt she's well aware of whatever has gone on between you and your *Mini-Dite*." He snickered teasingly, and I glared back with no real heat.

"In that case, we'd best hope the rest of this competition goes as you wish," Balthazar stated, making Ruri roll his eyes.

"The girl is here under Carnelian's thrall—" Ruri began to argue, but I interrupted.

"I'm not so sure about that," I told them, and they all looked at me in surprise. "Something happened today, and she's promised to tell me everything when she's ready. I'll keep you all updated on what happens, but don't discount her on his behalf."

Ruri agreed mulishly, but the rest were more accommodating. We moved into reviewing the results of the trial, each of them explaining how the ladies fared. It was clear Amatista would be eliminated, but we still had to assign points to each of those remaining. If it got to the point that no one failed a trial as we got further on, then those would be the deciding factor.

After our meeting, I felt at a loss and found myself going to see my mother. Especially since she was watching Neasa. My troubles wouldn't be soothed until Jacinth could tell me everything, but I'd found my dog could usually at least dull the sting.

"What brings you here, Az?" My mother asked happily as I walked into her living area. Neasa made straight for me, and I knelt down, letting her rub her head against mine as I ran my hands through her fur.

"Would you believe me if I said girl trouble?" I smirked, making her roll her eyes.

"It's been a long time since you needed me for such things," she said wistfully, and I brought Neasa with me to sit beside her on the sofa. She jumped up between us, curling into me as I pet her.

"I can't remember ever feeling so mixed up about a woman in my life," I told her honestly, chuckling despite myself.

"What troubles you, son?" Mother asked softly, her entire demeanor brighter since her talk with Jacinth. Her long sapphire hair fell past her shoulders in gentle waves, brushed out as normal once again instead of being ignored. While her mourning dress remained, in a deep teal so dark it was nearly black, she had begun wearing her diamonds once again, which sparkled against her pale skin.

While my bronze skin had assuredly come from my father, the rest was a solid split between my parents. It had always felt right, the mixture of my parents, when they were always equals, partners in everything. Something I desperately wanted for myself.

"I'm drawn to Jacinth beyond all others," I admitted to her, keeping my eyes averted from hers and firmly on Neasa. "But she's been troubled herself, unsure of what, or who, to trust." I sighed deeply, my head falling back and eyes fluttering closed as I explained the rest to her. When I was done, she hummed, making me open my eyes and lift my head to look at her.

"What?" I asked, waiting for her response.

"It sounds like you both came into this with expectations that didn't match reality." She smiled softly, reaching out to brush my hair back. The hair I had down the middle of my head was usually firmly brushed to the right, with the front pieces flopping over the side of my forehead. My mother, as always, was determined to ruffle it back, but the motion made me smile regardless.

"I think once she's ready, you need to hear her out, and then give her your own truth in turn." She sighed sadly, her sapphire eyes glassy, and I could only imagine that she was remembering my father. "Relationships only work if you meet one another on equal footing. You both need to put that work in."

She tilted her head, appearing to be thinking something over. "You'll both have pasts to contend with, but the past is just that, the past. You only need to be concerned with the present and future. And what the two of you can make of that future, together. If she's truly the one, then the past should remain where it lies, and the two of you can come together as equals in the present, setting yourselves up for an extraordinary future."

I nodded as I thought over her words, even as I was unsure of my own ability to let the past go, but I leaned over and kissed her cheek. "Thank you, Mother."

"Oh, my boy." She smiled, grabbing my hand and squeezing it. "I hope for your sake that you can resolve this." She paused for a moment, a smirk sneaking out as a teasing twinkle appeared in her eyes. "And not for nothing, but I like her." She winked, laughing as Neasa barked in agreement.

I thought it over until it was time to call the ladies together for the elimination and to inform them about their next trial. I walked into the throne room, searching Jacinth out immediately. Her eyes were red and slightly puffy, and I had to work hard to keep my face neutral.

Scanning the rest of the ladies, Safira and Sania looked the most eager, while Allirea seemed unconcerned, and Amatista was focused on Jacinth just as much as I was. Leading me to be sure we were right, and she'd thrown the trial on purpose. Whether for her friend's sake or her own, I couldn't be sure.

"Ladies, the time has come once again to see someone eliminated from the competition," I told them after I was announced. "You all have done a wonderful job, of course." I heard a faint snort, and the smirk on Amatista's face nearly made me laugh out loud.

My words were all prepared in advance to ensure we didn't alienate any courts during the trials. It was important for political reasons, but we knew every court that didn't win would inevitably have issues they would raise.

Related to the competition or not, the loss of a queen would have them finding *something* to complain to me about.

"Lady Amatista Iolanthe, you have proven yourself a fierce competitor of Amethyst Court; however, your time in the competition has unfortunately come to an end," I told her, feigning sadness that she returned just as authentically as she curtsied her thanks.

I saw her father watching on from the crowd, and bit my lip as I saw his eyes go wide and his face turn red, his wife frantically patting his arm and whispering in his ear to calm him down. So most likely, Amatista was only here because her father had insisted. I knew the number of ladies who actually wanted to marry me and become queen was equal to the number who were forced into it by their fathers for politics.

Unluckily for them, I had no desire for a political marriage. My eyes sought Jacinth once again, hoping against hope that I'd found a way to avoid such a marriage.

Jacinth carried my future in her delicate hands, whether she knew it or not.

The future of Gemaria itself.

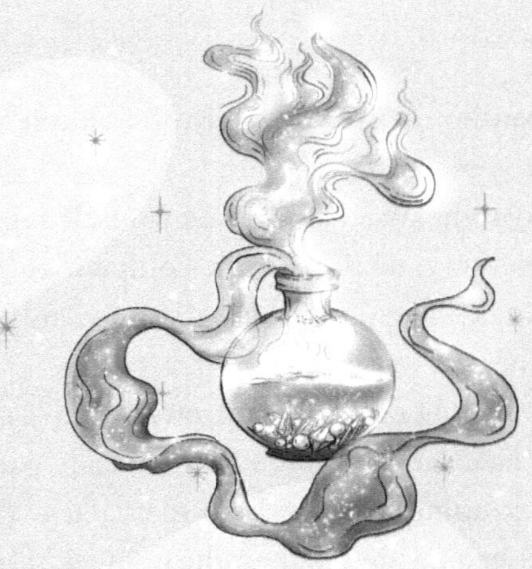

CHAPTER 34

Jacinth

I GRABBED Amatista's hand after her elimination, looking over at her and getting a nod in return. I knew she had purposely blown the trial, not wanting to get any further into the competition as we approached the final few rounds.

But I would really miss having her here for this. At least she and Faiza would remain at court, thank Erodite.

"For you ladies remaining in the Diamond Queen Competition," Azurill continued, as I forced myself to continue avoiding his searching eyes. "Your next trial will only be revealed to the public after it's concluded, so please go see Lady Arianell after this for your instructions. For everyone else, since we have a spare night tomorrow, we will be holding a ball. I'm looking forward to seeing you all there."

I quickly ran to find Arianell after we adjourned, and she smiled as she handed me the potion that would impart my instructions. I gave a soul-deep sigh. After the last potion, I was hesitant, but I downed it anyway.

The knowledge came quickly. Our challenge was to be of a political nature, and the ball was no coincidence. We were each assigned to find out a piece of information by the end of the ball. A test of our competence when it came to court intrigue and political acumen. An important skill for a queen.

I was given the task of figuring out the marriage plans of Opal Court's heir, Laxus Beryl. Opal Court had remained very quiet about the issue thus far, and no one had been able to figure out who he had his eye on, if anyone.

228

I figured that was an easy enough task. I was sure this trial must have been Emrys's idea, as the man in charge of the most intrigues of them all. He surely didn't want to deal with a queen who was inept at politics and navigating the court—and we all knew gossip and intrigue were the name of that game.

I knew the best way to get to Laxus was going to be his sister. I had hardly spoken to her during the entire time I'd been here, but with both of my friends now out of the competition, perhaps she wouldn't find it too strange for me to reach out.

Or it might be incredibly obvious.

Either way, I had to try. And I had just the opportunity as I spotted her walking just ahead of me on the way to dinner that night.

"Lady Allirea," I called to her, and she paused, turning around to face me with surprise.

"Lady Jacinth." Her voice was soft, and her opal eyes swirled with color while her bright white hair shimmered with the odd trace of blue, green, and pink. The white created a beautiful contrast against the ebony of her skin, and I found myself wondering why Azurill would be interested in someone like me when Allirea was here.

"We haven't had much of a chance to speak yet, and I find all my regular dinner companions now gone." I smiled slightly and was rewarded when she laughed quietly.

"Indeed." She agreed with a nod. "Lady Ophira was the only one I really knew."

"Would you like to sit with me tonight?" I asked her and was happy when she agreed. As she began to tell me about herself, the fact that she was a healer stood out to me.

Plans circulated in my mind and I couldn't help saying, "I had a friend come down suddenly with a sickness. She began to just waste away, and regular treatments did nothing for her. Another has taken over her care for now, but I have to admit that healing has never been my specialty, and I wasn't able to identify what the illness was."

Her opal brows scrunched together as concern flickered in her eyes. "Wasting away?"

"Yes," I nodded, sighing sadly. "She got worse and worse as time went on, until she could barely get out of bed, and then, not at all."

"I would need to see her to be sure," Allirea said carefully, but her eyes darted around, and her voice lowered. "There are two things it could be. One of them is indeed natural, but the other…" she paused, meeting my eyes, "The other is a silent killer. A poison that sucks the life from the victim. I can't know for sure, like I said, but if she suffers from this still, I promise you now, on my honor as a healer, I will do everything I can to help."

She reached out to clasp my hand, and I found myself squeezing it back. Was it possible? Could Ula have been poisoned? Why? By who? Who would have anything to gain from a street rat falling sick—

The thought lodged in my gut. Only one man had benefited from it thus far. My eyes found Carnelian across the large hall, thankful he was otherwise engaged. He was speaking with Lord Darcel, Sania's father, as they were seated next to one another tonight.

If he had poisoned Ula…it meant that he had to have found me before I ever broke in, which didn't make any sense at all. He would have just killed me. He wanted any who possessed Marit blood dead, and he could have taken me out then with none the wiser.

I sighed silently, not sure whether to be relieved or not that it was likely natural. That wasn't even the only issue now, as Carnelian held the keys to her freedom. I certainly couldn't get her help while she was locked up in his castle. I had no idea how to overcome that obstacle, and it was becoming ever clearer I was going to need help in that respect.

I looked at Azurill, who was sitting beside his family tonight. I watched him laugh with his brother and mother, smiling softly at the sight of his joy. I would have to shatter that happiness soon, but for now, he could live in the illusion.

I turned back to Allirea, continuing our conversation even as I tried to work out how to get Ula to her. I found, to my surprise, that she was very kind, which maybe I should have expected of a dedicated healer, but as a noble… well, one glance across to where Zumra sat glaring at me set the expectation.

"So your brother is the heir, right?" I asked, leaning my chin on my hand as I looked at her.

"Yes, he's to be the next lord of Opal," she answered, with a gentle smile. "Laxus will be a good lord, just like my father." Her smile dimmed slightly, "Though, I do hope he'll not force his daughters into such spectacles as this."

My eyebrows flew upwards, "Your father forced you?"

She nodded hesitantly, "It's my duty as a daughter of Opal Court, of course. But I wish to heal, not marry. A husband will expect me to stay home with children, and would that not be a waste of the good I can do in the world?"

She looked so despairing, her eyes falling to her lap where her fingers tightened on each other. I sighed, sick of this same story. Lord after lord forcing their daughters into marriages they didn't want. Faiza. Amatista. Allirea.

"I'm sorry, Allirea," I told her honestly. "I hope that, whoever wins, they are able to change things for future generations."

Her eyes shone with her agreement, nodding silently. I wanted to steer the conversation back to her brother, so close to getting what I needed early, but it wasn't to be. Ophira came over to see Allirea, and I wasn't able to turn the discussion back to where I needed it.

As I readied for bed, I thought of perhaps going to see Azurill now, but my confidence was lacking. I wasn't sure I could find the right words yet, so I decided to put it off. I settled into bed and decided I would glue myself to Allirea at the ball tomorrow.

I awoke in the middle of the night, something having disturbed my sleep. A blurry shadow crept across the room, and for a moment, I was sure I was having a nightmare of the past. The one I'd had last night had been more intense than normal after taking that potion, so maybe I was still caught in one.

But the shadow crept to my bed, and my heart began to race wildly. Through slitted eyes, I saw their arm rise, the distinctive gleam of a dagger in their hand. My eyes went wide, and I rolled quickly as the dagger plunged down, hitting the mattress instead of flesh. I let myself roll off the other side of the bed and jumped up, fully awake now.

I'd spent years sleeping lightly, having to wake quickly to avoid being robbed or killed, and a few weeks in a palace didn't erase those instincts. My assailant came around the bed, chasing after me with a growl, but I kicked out as they approached, surprising them and making them fall back.

"Alfrikr!" I yelled, even as I moved forward, punching out as the man stood back up. As the commotion of my guard breaking in reached us, the man tried to run, heading to a tapestry hanging on the wall. I grabbed him by the back of his jacket and threw him backward before delivering another punch that sent him down hard right as Alfrikr burst in with his sword drawn.

His purple eyes alighted on me first, frantically taking in my ruffled appearance, before falling on the masked man lying out on the floor, groaning in pain.

"I woke up to this man trying to kill me. He had a dagger drawn and was going straight for me," I explained, still panting. "I managed to roll away, thank all the gods."

Alfrikr glared at the man, moving quickly to disarm him and take him into custody. More guards poured in, the others on duty having alerted them at my scream for help, and we all watched as Alfrikr ripped the mask off my attacker's face.

He revealed a man with light green hair and eyes, clearly from Emerald Court, which had me raising a brow. Could Zumra really be so stupid as to send an assassin after me that would implicate her? Then again, I'm sure she didn't expect him to be caught.

"Jacinth!" I turned my head to the door, finding the High King himself running frantically through the doors. Balthazar and Ruri were right behind him, both grave-faced. Azurill immediately began checking me over like he might find me bleeding out from a wound I was unaware of, so I grabbed his hands in mine, squeezing them comfortingly.

"Azurill, I'm fine," I assured him softly. "I woke up before he could accomplish his goal."

"He tried to kill you?" he asked, his voice a low growl that had me pressing my thighs together. The look on his face so reminiscent of the one he'd worn when he'd killed those responsible for my family's deaths.

"Yes," I confirmed with a nod. "But I fought him off." Azurill shook his head, his hand coming up to cup my cheek before sliding into my hair. His eyes were intense, like he was on the verge of lashing out and was trying to use the image of me before him, fine and well, to calm down. I was clearly not the only one to think so either.

"Your Majesty," Balthazar interjected, his voice purposely calm. "Lady Jacinth managed the assassin well, but we can have her checked out by the healers just in case. We should deal with the assassin and figure out how he got in."

Azurill nodded, but I spoke up then, "He tried running away when I called for Alfrikr. He went towards the tapestry."

I pointed them to the wall, and Balthazar nodded, walking over with a curious look on his face. He pulled it back, but it seemed like an ordinary wall.

"Wait, let me try." Ruri stepped forward, pulling a potion from his pocket. He threw it at the wall, and the seam in the corner where the walls met lit up with a glowing blue light. Not all the way up to the ceiling, but up to the height of a normal door.

Azurill stepped forward, his eyes narrowing. "What is that?"

"A potion that reveals hidden things," Ruri smiled in satisfaction. "I had a feeling we might need it at some point, so I've been carrying it since the competition began." Azurill nodded to Balthazar, who ran his hand up the glowing seam, finding a latch that opened a hidden door.

"Where in the Otherworld did this come from?" The king growled, "These rooms are supposed to be free of any hidden passageways or doors."

"Unless they used magic to make one," Balthazar countered, raising his brows. Azurill looked to him before turning back to where Alfrikr now had the assassin in onyx chains.

He walked over, grabbing the assassin by the chin and forcing him to meet his eyes. The assassin glared at him, his jaw moving back and forth like he was grinding his teeth.

"If you value your life, you'll tell me everything I want to know," Azurill said, his voice deadly calm in a way that sent shivers racing down my back. I would hate to be on the other side of that. Couldn't have happened to a nicer guy.

The assassin, proving he wasn't very smart, or didn't value his life at all, merely laughed. "My life is forfeit either way. Why would I tell you anything?"

Azurill smiled, but it wasn't a smile I'd seen from him before. It was almost frightening to witness. "Because I could let you die quickly, or I could draw it out. I could keep you alive for *years*, if I wished."

"Or we could use a truth potion on him?" Ruri suggested, looking slightly conflicted, exposing the uncertain youth he really was behind his title.

"I thought they weren't reliable?" I asked, making everyone look over at me. I almost shrank under all their gazes, but I firmed my spine. "Since everyone perceives things differently, wouldn't the truth potion just pull out *their* truth, and not necessarily the actual truth?"

"That's true," Ruri admitted grudgingly. "But because we're asking after orders he was given, it should be fairly straightforward. And then you can play with him after, brother." He told Azurill with a catlike smirk.

The assassin's eyes went wide with fright, looking between everyone present, but shrinking under the king's gaze. "No! Please, I'll tell you!"

"Will you now?" Azurill purred, a smirk rising and making the assassin's panic rise in tandem at how delighted he appeared to have someone to torture.

"Yes! I swear to Soteria I'll tell you everything, just don't drag it out," he begged, sweat beginning to bead on his forehead. "She promised this would be quick and easy, and I'd be set for life after."

"Who?" Azurill demanded, his teal eyes lit with a fire that promised retribution.

"Lady Zumra," he said heavily, his eyes closing in defeat. "She said she was unfairly eliminated and it was Lady Jacinth's fault. She thought that if she took her out, then you'd need to bring another competitor back in to have the numbers work out for the final trial. She said there was precedent for it."

"The last time a lady was killed in the Diamond Queen Competition, they did have to bring back an already eliminated competitor to fill the ranks properly," Balthazar added, nodding slightly as understanding crossed his face.

"Guards," Azurill called sternly, "arrest Lady Zumra Giada of Emerald Court, by order of the High King." The guards nodded, and Balthazar told several to go, while the others remained here.

"Ruri, go get Emrys." Azurill turned to his brother. "We'll need him to do damage control with Lord Khader and Lady Umina. They won't be happy to have their daughter arrested. We'll need to explain everything to them."

Ruri nodded, taking off to find the only man who might be able to manage this mess. Balthazar and Alfrikr grabbed the assassin, taking him away to extract any more information they needed. But Azurill stayed, making me raise a brow at him.

"I'm not leaving you here alone after that, Mini-Dite." He smiled slightly, though the stress was clear on his face.

"And what are you going to do?" I asked him, amused. "Sleep at the end of my bed like a watch-dog?"

He flushed, looking slightly embarrassed, before glancing around the room. Spotting the chaise lounge, he shrugged and waved an arm towards it. "That'll work well enough."

I couldn't help but sigh, shaking my head at him. "The bed is big enough for two if you truly insist on this."

"That would be most improper, my lady." Azurill teased, but his tongue played across his teeth, making him look like a predator about to lunge for their prey.

"Would it?" I asked innocently. "I would hate to impinge on your virtue, so if you're not up to the task, Veri, just say so."

His low growl filled the room, and chills broke out across my skin, a shiver of anticipation wracking through me.

Just waiting for the predator to make his move.

CHAPTER 35

Jacinth

In a blink, I found myself tossed down on the bed, Azurill looming above me. His teal eyes were like silver fire, a shade I'd never seen in them before, but as his lips found mine, all thoughts flew from my head.

"Tell me," Azurill murmured between kisses, "Mini-Dite," his lips found my neck, "Does what you need to tell me," teeth bit down hard on the column on my throat, making me moan and arch into him, "Mean this needs to end?"

I gasped, struggling to form a sentence, only able to get one word out, "No."

"Perfect," he purred, before he ripped my sleep dress straight down the middle, leaving me bare to his gaze.

"Az," I panted, my head swimming with everything that had happened tonight.

"They could have killed you," he hissed, his hands landing on my chest, feeling my heartbeat, before slowly tracing the length of my body.

"They failed," I assured him, watching the path of his hands closely as he seemed to reassure himself that my skin remained unblemished.

"I need to block out everything but you," he said, his voice lower and deeper than I'd ever heard it. His head cricked to the side suddenly, almost violently, making my face crease in concern as the veins on his neck bulged, his tattoo seeming to almost come alive with the movement.

Before I could ask any questions, he moved down the bed, his hand resting on my hip as he spread my legs apart with his shoulders. His eyes were burning bright as he looked into mine, the silver color so vivid it was just begging me to ask questions, but his next words banished them entirely.

"So if it's okay with you," he smirked slowly, raising a brow despite whatever difficulties he was having managing his own emotions, "I'm going to bury my face in your cunt and not come up for breath until morning."

"Oh," I breathed out, surprised. My heart picked up pace as anticipation swept through my entire body. I didn't let myself think about any of the things we needed to talk about, letting my desire take the lead for a change.

"Please." I nodded, gasping as he dove his head down and licked a long line up my cunt. My legs bent completely over his shoulders as he settled in, his hand moving up and grasping my breast as his tongue circled my clit, forcing me to let out a chorus of moans I'd never heard myself make before.

Every other sexual experience I'd had paled in comparison to just having this man between my legs.

I'd never allowed myself to truly let go during sex. Not when I had a thousand other considerations to worry about. Not when half the time it was to butter someone up to get a better place to stay or a warm meal. Or they were just a tool to get off with quickly before going about my day.

It was never like this. I'd never burned for them the way I did for Azurill.

And burn I did. My skin felt like fire as I bucked up into his mouth. His fingers plucked my nipple to a hard peak as his tongue found its way inside me, his other hand holding me open while his thumb found its place on my clit. It was nearly too much.

His tongue thrust into me with single-minded dedication, the undulations creating a cascade of pleasure that had my body nearly vibrating. I actually whined as he pulled his tongue back, but his fingers replaced it, sliding down my cunt and bathing them in my arousal before he thrust them inside me.

I gasped loudly at the sudden motion, making Azurill snicker quietly into my skin. He pressed biting kisses up and down my thigh, starting with the right, until he reached the apex of my thighs, before moving to the left and starting again. He seemed incapable of words, losing himself in his task the way he'd needed.

Whatever it was that drove him, he seemed earnest in his promise to go all night, dragging it out and slowing down anytime I felt any buildup, not letting me approach climax at all.

What felt like hours later, I couldn't help whining, "Azurill, please. I need to cum."

He looked up at me, his usual teal beginning to show through the silver now. He didn't say a word, merely adding another finger and sucking my clit into his mouth, his tongue swirling around it until I felt the telltale rush as my orgasm spiraled rapidly closer.

My moans increased in volume, and I felt momentarily worried that they'd carry to the other competitor's rooms, but it flew out of my head as Azurill's fingers began thrusting faster. My walls started fluttering around them as I felt a powerful climax begin.

He'd been edging me for too long, and I couldn't help screaming his name as my orgasm finally crashed over me. I could feel my arousal rush from me in a torrent as my head thrashed back and forth, my hips rising from the bed uncontrollably. Azurill's arm came up and forced my hips back down, making me squirm as the aftershocks shuddered through me.

"Az," I panted, reaching down to run my hand through his hair, appreciating the teal locks left on top that enabled me to do so.

"Jac," he murmured as he finally pulled his face from between my legs, kissing my hip.

"I know I'm certainly doing much better," I said impishly, if not a bit tiredly, "But how about you?"

"Getting there." He smirked, but it slowly faded as he watched me. "I suppose when we have our talk, there are some things I should tell you too."

"Like what just happened?" I asked, raising a brow.

"Like that, yeah." He chuckled, shaking his head as he lifted himself up and crawled further up the bed. He lifted his arm and pulled me into his side. I'd never been a cuddler before, circumstances had never allowed it, but I couldn't deny the pleasure I felt as I draped myself over his body. My leg wrapped around his as my arm fell across his torso.

"Don't get too comfortable, I'm not nearly done." I looked up at him incredulously at his words, only to see him smirking with his eyes closed. My head crashed back down to his chest in exhaustion.

"In that case, I'd better get whatever rest I can." I chuckled, letting my eyes fall shut. My head rose and fell with his breaths, his fingers brushing softly through my hair and lulling me into a temporary sleep.

I knew he meant what he said, and I was more than willing to indulge whatever madness had overcome him tonight.

But first, sleep was definitely needed.

CHAPTER 36

Jacinth

I WOKE briefly to the feeling of Azurill kissing my hair, the sky still dark so he could sneak away before dawn broke, and anyone saw him leaving my rooms. I fell back to sleep immediately, still worn out from Azurill's marathon. He'd let me sleep for maybe an hour before he'd woken me the first time, repeating that pattern repeatedly through the night until I physically couldn't go on anymore and he'd exorcised whatever demons had driven him.

When I woke up later that morning, I was still exhausted, overstimulated, and somewhat sore. I knew I needed to be at the top of my game for the ball tonight and my trial, so I forced myself to get ready and made my way down to the alchemists for a potion to heal and reinvigorate myself.

Entering the main Gemlab, I was surprised by the sheer size of it. It was about ten times the size of the one built for Prince Ruri, with a bunch of stations set up for multiple alchemists to work at once.

One of the specialist healers I recognized made their way over to me, smiling pleasantly.

"My Lady." She curtseyed, and I took a moment to take her in. She had slate-grey hair and eyes paired with dark black skin, the grey hue marking her out as being from Onyx Court. While the onyx black color they were known for had mostly been lost in its lords and ladies and replaced by gold, its people still often had black, grey, or other similarly dark shades.

"How can I help you today?" she asked, a smile firmly in place. As I explained what I came for, she nodded knowingly. "Of course, I have just the thing."

While she went to grab the potion, I examined the large wall of finished potions she was rifling through. There were bottles of all shapes and sizes, filled with potions of every color imaginable.

"Here you are, my Lady," the alchemist said, handing over a potion that was a shimmery dark purple, likely a combination of amethyst for increased clarity, opal for healing, and onyx for relaxing certain parts of the body.

"Thank you." I gave her a tired smile and quickly drank the potion, feeling its effects immediately and sighing in relief. The alchemist tried to hide her smirk as I gave the empty bottle back, making me grin.

I saw myself out afterward and spent the rest of the morning relaxing. By the time lunch came, Amatista and Faiza were both waiting for me, with concerned looks on both their faces as I approached them. When I got close enough, they pulled me in for hugs, babbling a mile a minute as they tried to ask a million questions about what had happened.

Apparently, everyone had already heard about the attack and Zumra's arrest. I'd nearly forgotten the entire ordeal after how I'd spent the rest of my night.

"I'm fine," I promised them both. "I woke in time to prevent them from succeeding, thank the gods."

"You could have been killed!" Faiza fretted, her fingers digging into the arms of her chair.

"I can't believe Zumra went to such lengths." Amatista tutted, shaking her head. "I knew she was awful, but I had no idea she was that stupid."

I chuckled at Amatista's comment. "I had the same thought myself. I have to assume she trusted that there wouldn't be anyone to rat her out."

"That's an awfully big risk to take," Faiza said, her face scrunched in thought. "Especially with all the security for the competition."

"She was clearly desperate," Amatista pondered. "Perhaps she felt that any risk was worth it?"

"She did seem to come here thinking she was going to sweep this competition and end up queen of Gemaria," I added, making them both nod.

"That's true. And you two didn't get along from the start," Faiza said, shaking her head. "Her elimination happened in the same round that the two of you had that little scuffle in the gardens as well. She must have blamed you."

"That woman has no sense of personal responsibility." Amatista sniffed in disdain, making Faiza and me chuckle, nodding in agreement.

"Lady Jacinth." I froze at the sound of that voice, turning to see Lord Carnelian looking down at me.

"Lord Carnelian." I forced out the words, pulling the veil of truth tight over myself, not letting the slightest hint of my real feelings escape. Knowing what had truly happened now, what he'd done, I wanted nothing more than to take my silverware and ram it through his eyeballs.

"I was hoping to check in and see how you were doing after last night," He explained, putting on a front of care and concern, while dismissing my friends without saying a word. I ground my teeth behind my smile, nodding as pleasantly as I could manage.

"Of course, my Lord, that's very kind of you." I turned to Faiza and Amatista, "If you'll excuse me, my ladies, I'll return shortly," I told them, hoping it would mean Carnelian would keep this short.

I stood up and joined him, taking his arm when he offered it. He walked us out of the main room and down the halls toward where his rooms were.

"Don't worry, I won't keep you long," he promised, amusement crossing his face. "I have a meeting to keep, but I felt it necessary to ensure you were well enough to still carry out your mission," he said as he closed the door behind us.

"Of course, my Lord," I told him, nearly biting my tongue as I held myself back from attacking him now that we were alone.

"Zumra has always been overly emotional." Carnelian hummed, taking a seat. "But as long as you can continue then no true harm was done. I'll be able to pacify her father later."

My nails cut into my palm at the reminder of the future he had planned. Of course, he'd surely free Zumra the moment I killed Azurill to get her father on his side. I wasn't dumb enough to believe he had any plans to let me live now. Not when he'd likely figured out *exactly* who I was. And more importantly, what that meant for his plans.

If they were going to succeed, I would have to die.

I didn't know how he'd figured me out, but maybe my coloring and vague statements alone had been enough to get him thinking. Either way, it spelled doom for me unless I was able to act first.

"I'll be just fine." I smiled placidly, sitting back into the sofa across from him as I prepared to lie my ass off. "Azurill believes me to have real feelings for him, so he won't see it coming."

"Good." Carnelian nodded in satisfaction. "As we approach the end, it's more important than ever that you give your all to the competition. Do not let yourself get distracted."

"Distracted?" I asked him, a lone pink brow rising in question.

"Yes." His red eyes flared, making me swallow. "Whether that be with the women you've surrounded yourself with or the man you've come to kill."

The words were more honest than I'd expected of him, and I could only imagine he hoped to test me for some reaction. I kept my face blank, thankful I'd practiced taking on my acts as if they were authentic, that veil of truth never failing me.

"Never." I swore—*lied*. "These relationships are merely tools to help me with my mission."

"How so?" he questioned, cocking his head and making a waterfall of ruby-red locks fall over his shoulder. He leaned forward, his elbows braced on his knees as he faced me, red eyes staring a burning hole into my pink ones. Like if he looked hard enough, the truth of my soul would be revealed to him.

"Having the ladies around me not only helps to sell the lie that I'm a noble lady, but they've helped me in the trials," I explained, working hard to keep my fingers and feet from twitching as my nerves rose.

"And Azurill?" Carnelian asked, a snake-like whisper that invited only damnation.

My eyes narrowed back at him, "If I want to win, so that I can pull *your plan* off—I need to make him want me. And he'll only want me enough to pick me over all the other ladies, if I show him that I desire him too. Regardless of my real feelings."

"Hmm." The lord hummed, but whatever he was about to say was cut off, as the door opened and my heart dropped.

Casaan.

The image of him sliding his dagger into my father, laughing in his face as he all but promised to kill me, flashed across my vision, making me see nothing but *red*.

The red of my parents' blood.

The red of his eyes.

The red of his hair, his coat, his entire *being*.

The red I promised myself I would spill from him before this was over.

Both of them.

"Ah, Jacinth," he purred, making me want to puke as he collapsed onto the sofa beside me, putting his arm around my shoulder. "I didn't know you were visiting."

"We were just discussing her strategy for winning the competition," Carnelian told his son sternly, making Casaan sigh and shake his head.

"Never any fun," he muttered, rolling his eyes toward me as if I'd commiserate with him.

"You can be assured that I will do everything I can to win," I swore, looking deep into Carnelian's eyes, making myself a promise in that moment as I spoke nothing but the truth. "I will not stop until I have taken vengeance. No matter the cost."

Carnelian's lip curled up, "Good."

I'd ensure he ate that godsdamned word before this was through.

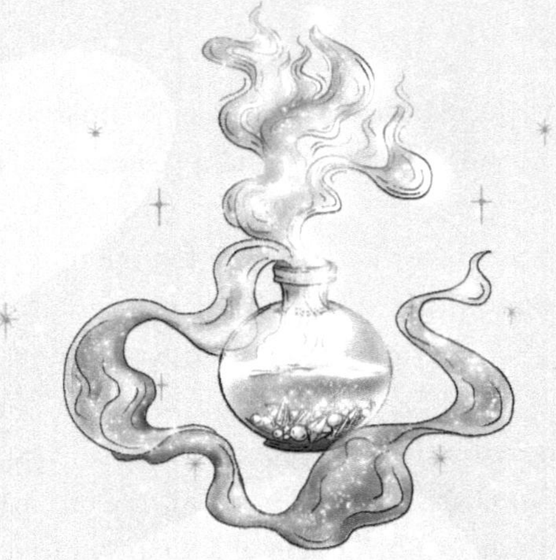

CHAPTER 37

Jacinth

MAKING my way to the ball that night, I felt conflicted. My dress was designed to incorporate as much of Pearl Court into it as I thought I could get away with, the color shifting from red to pink to white. The red bodice looked like it had been dipped in pink, and was decorated in rubies and pearls that created stunning swirling motifs. Diamonds crafted similar patterns along the bottom of the pink and white skirt, bringing together bits of all three of the courts that dominated my mind.

Walking into the ballroom, I felt the heavy blanket of stares as every eye fell on me. As one of only four competitors left, I knew that those eyes would follow me all night.

Another part of the test.

After all, queens always had eyes on them as well, and they had to work around it to discover all the gossip and intrigues swirling around the court.

I knew my mission for the night, so I took note of where Opal Court's members were standing. The lord and lady were off to the left, speaking with Safira's parents. While Allirea was next to her brother, *my target*, Laxus. My eyes slid right over where Carnelian stood nearby, zeroing in on the man he was speaking with, Lord Darcel Helmi of Pearl Court.

I'd barely seen my cousins, outside of Sania, since arriving, and seeing Darcel's face caught me so by surprise that I had to pause and collect myself. His chin. His nose. Those were my father's, and it felt like a dagger straight through the chest to see it.

I couldn't deny that I'd seen similarities between Sania and myself, but nothing on this scale. Seeing parts of my father's face on the stranger who replaced him made something burn inside me. Darcel and my father may not have been close, but seeing him laughing with the man responsible for his own blood's death was disgusting.

I quickly grabbed a drink to wash the heavy thoughts away and began moving again. Faiza and Amatista were across the room, but I'd made them aware of my goal for the night already. I spoke to courtiers as they came up to me, either congratulating me on my performance so far, trying to find out more about me, or wanting gossip about the attack. I took the time to speak to them all, since it helped play into my own game.

Allirea was a bit of a loner here, so I knew she would stick close to her brother. When I'd finally wandered close enough to where they were standing, I headed to a nearby sofa and sat down, sipping my green champagne.

Another tactic. Showing people that Zumra and Emerald Court had failed where I succeeded.

But the most important tactic: isolating myself.

Left all alone, near Allirea, within her eyeline even, I watched the crowd as I waited. Sure enough, her eyes caught on my form, and her lips twitched down.

I had to hope my overtures of friendship so far would see me through this plan. Her promise made me think that it would, and I found myself feeling a bit bad that I was using her here. But it was necessary, and it wasn't like I wouldn't want to befriend her. She was kind, and I hadn't met many genuinely kind people in my life before now.

I watched her elbow her brother, his opal eyebrows shooting up as his head swung toward me. Allirea whispered in his ear before he sighed, dipping his head in a nod.

I hid my smirk in my drink as they made their way over. My eyes shot up, only to catch on teal ones across the ballroom. *Watching.* My slow smile was even more important to hide now, but knowing Azurill couldn't take his eyes off me left me feeling many things.

Cherished, in a way I'd never felt before. That he would seek to protect me even in so public a space.

Hot, like my skin could catch fire at any time from the heat in his gaze.

Excited, knowing the possibility of a real future was before me.

Terrified, knowing how easily it could slip through my fingers once I told him the truth.

Instead of dealing with all of that, I focused on my mission, looking up at Allirea and Laxus as they approached.

"Lady Jacinth, do you mind if we join you?" She asked, and I smiled up at her.

"Of course, Lady Allirea," I told her. "Please, sit."

"This is my brother, Lord Laxus Beryl, heir of Opal Court." She introduced us, looking at him fondly.

"My Lady." He kissed my offered hand, and I returned his greeting as they both sat down. Laxus took the chair beside the sofa while Allirea sat next to me, putting me in the middle.

We spoke for a while about trivial matters, getting to know one another a bit, while I waited patiently for the right moment.

"Do you mind if I ask, my Lady," Laxus began, looking curious. "What do you plan to do if you don't win the competition?"

I laughed lightly, shaking my head. "I haven't thought that far. Why? Interested in adding yourself to my dance card?" I teased him, making it clear I wasn't serious as my eyebrows danced up and down. Allirea giggled into her hand as her brother huffed a laugh.

"No, I'm afraid my dance card is already full," Laxus responded, his dark skin blushing slightly. "I just find myself curious what all of the ladies plans are. Only one can win, and I know some of them have other plans already."

He looked knowingly at his sister, who smiled back at him. It seemed he at least accepted his sister's wish to be a healer instead of a wife, even if their father didn't.

"Oh? What are your plans then?" I asked him, resting my elbow on the sofa's edge to lean toward him slightly. "Maybe you'll inspire me into a solution."

"Well…" he drew the word out, glancing again to his sister, who nodded back at him. My brows rose, wondering if my assignment wasn't some arbitrary task to prove my effectiveness, and there was a reason that the crown was interested in this knowledge.

"I have my eye on Lady Safira's younger sister, Celestine," he admitted, but his opal orbs glimmered brightly. "I hope to speak to her father about it, but I need to wait to see if Lady Safira wins or not."

"Ah, because it'll be easier to convince them if they already have a loss under them?" I asked him, smiling lightly to take any sting out of the words.

"Exactly." His lips curled ruefully.

"Well, I think you have a good chance either way," I told him truthfully. "I know Sapphire Court is ambitious, holding dreams of a high queen in their future. Especially since their cousins managed to marry into the royal line last time. But for a second daughter? Opal Court is a great place for her."

"That's what I've told him," Allirea interjected, rolling her eyes. "But he's a stubborn one." She teased her brother, and I could see the love between them so clearly, making me ache for my family. While I'd never had a brother, I knew my parents had been trying for one, they'd just never had the chance.

And then there was Peony, my cousin who had been like a sister to me, whose loss had left a gaping wound inside me.

"I just don't want to risk them saying no," Laxus admitted, looking slightly abashed. "Celestine is wonderful, and I promised her I would do everything I could to make her my wife."

"You love her," I said, slightly surprised.

"I do." He smiled, that love shining through as obvious as his love for his sister. I found myself strangely jealous of this Celestine, who had a man who loved her so truly.

I had never experienced such a thing, nor had I ever really cared to, not after my life was ripped away from me and my entire future went with it. I lived my life like it had already ended, like I was a ghost haunting this world until my desire for revenge was sated.

Yet now…I found myself *wishing, hoping, wanting.*

And the dead didn't wish for anything.

CHAPTER 38

Jacinth

AFTER speaking to Allirea and Laxus for a while, Allirea whispered that she had her task to complete, and I nearly smiled as I told her I did as well. I decided to mingle for a while to make that lie seem plausible, working the room until I'd exhausted my patience.

I found Lady Arianell on my way out, her opal eyes shining as she smiled slyly at me. I whispered what I found out in her ear, watching her eyes widen in surprise. She gave me a nod, and I went on my way, eagerly anticipating the results of this trial.

The thoughts sparked by my conversation with Laxus didn't go away, however. They lingered, and I knew I had to tell Azurill the truth. I gave myself a thousand excuses of why I couldn't do it right away, when the truth was that I couldn't bring myself to do it, and went back to my rooms to hide like the coward I'd suddenly become.

When we were called for the elimination the next morning, I waited nervously for Azurill to appear. I couldn't seem to stop fidgeting with my dress, plucking at the gems and embroidery. I'd never been so unsettled in my life as I was now just thinking about what I had to do.

He could kill me for planning to assassinate him. Or he could send me to some prison, never to see the light of day again. The endless possibilities weighed on my mind. A new voice inside me whispered that there was hope, but I had never known hope to be anything worth listening to. Not when it betrayed me every time.

And yet, my heart beat furiously against my chest, like it was reaching out toward where Azurill sat on his diamond throne.

That hope remained, fighting to get out amidst the ruins of my past.

I wanted it. I wanted *him*. There was no use pretending otherwise, not anymore. I wanted the life I had lost back. I wanted to be a noble, I wanted to marry the High King. I desired nothing more than to keep Azurill forever, despite every negative experience from the past telling me it could never be.

If I was going to move forward, I had to beat those voices down and be who I always should have been.

Lady Linnea Jacinth Marit.

A noble woman unafraid to tell the king the ugly truth, with hope that he would see the real *her* through the mess, and want to keep her anyway.

"Thank you all for your efforts in this last trial." Azurill smiled out at the crowd. "Unbeknownst to everyone except the competitors, they were each given a task to find out a specific piece of information about a noble at court."

The crowd began to murmur, and Azurill put a hand up, silencing them. My lip twitched up, impressed at his control over his court.

"We gave them innocuous facts to discover, nothing that would be too invasive," he explained, making the crowd relax further. I wanted to roll my eyes at their idiocy, but it worked out in our favor this time.

"Only one competitor was unable to obtain the information." My shoulders sank in relief, knowing that I would be safe from elimination. "Lady Safira Mazarine, I thank you for your participation in the Diamond Queen Competition, but here is where it ends."

Lady Safira bowed her head, her cobalt hair creating a curtain around her ghostly pale face. When she looked up, her defeated expression showed that she clearly knew this was coming.

"I thank you, my King, for letting me compete in the trials." She curtseyed before glancing back to her father, who looked beyond pissed, his nose scrunched up as his lips formed a pale line to try to keep his outburst contained. Safira winced, and I found myself actually feeling sorry for her.

At least Laxus would likely get his bride now.

"The next trial will take place in three days," Azurill told us. "Allowing the remaining ladies time to get some last-minute training in. Each competitor will have to fight the other, and then me. They will gain points during each fight, and the lady with the fewest points will be eliminated. This will be swords only, with no magic permitted."

We all looked at one another, surprised that we would have to fight Azurill himself. At least we weren't expected to win, merely gain enough points to outpace each other.

When court dispersed, I made my way back to my rooms, but paused as I heard a ruckus coming from next door. Thanks to the circular hall with its tall ceilings, the acoustics echoed the cries and screams coming from within like they were being amplified.

The rooms for Sapphire Court competitor were to my right of my own, and maybe because I was trying to find another excuse to put off going to Azurill, or perhaps because I'd felt bad for Safira, but either way, I knocked on the door.

"What?" Came the muffled reply, voice hoarse from overuse.

"Safira? Can I come in?" I asked, hesitantly, my hand on the doorknob.

"Fine," She replied, low and monotone.

I opened the door to see the room had been trashed. Things had been thrown every which way, with paintings ripped and thrown on the floor, cushions punctured and scattered. It was an absolute disaster.

I'd certainly done this myself once or twice. When everything had gotten to be too much, I let it out on some shitty space we'd managed to find. Since Safira was sitting on the floor with her back to the now cushion-less sofa, I slid down next to her.

"Are you okay?" I asked quietly, getting a rough chuckle in return.

"Why do you care? I know my friend tried to kill you, and we've been competing against one another." She threw her hands up in the air slightly. "Congratulations, you've beaten me."

"I'm not sure Zumra was ever anyone's friend, to be honest," I said, watching her eyes close in pain, telling me everything I needed to know. Their dynamic was a forced one based on proximity, and Zumra had to have taken her nastiness out on Safira more than once.

"And it seemed like your father was pretty mad. I thought maybe you could use someone to talk to," I admitted with a shrug.

Cobalt blue eyes found mine, and I swore I could see the mask crumple and fall off her face as she burst into tears.

"No one's ever offered to talk to me before." She sniffled, and my heart about broke for her. For all my struggles, at least I'd had Ula to talk to when I needed it. I debated what to do for a moment, but this whole experience had ripped away my armor, leaving bare the bleeding soul beneath who knew what having support meant to those of us who'd lived without it for so long.

"Well, you can have me now," I offered sheepishly, watching her tears fall faster as she threw her arms around my shoulders in a tight hug.

"I'm sorry I let Zumra talk to you that way," she said softly. "I've always just followed her lead. My father said if we wanted to keep our place in society, we had to make connections, so I didn't know what else to do. If I walked away, he'd be so mad. Our parents are good friends, after all. But now he's embarrassed because of what she did, and even if she was awful," Safira nearly choked on her tears, and I ran a hand down her back comfortingly. "She was the only friend I had."

"You can definitely do better than that," I promised her. "I may not be much, but Amatista is a lord's daughter too, and Faiza, while the daughter of an earl, is friends with the High King himself. Plus, both of them are so kind and just…*good*. It's a rare thing to find."

Safira chuckled, pulling back slightly and wiping the tears from her eyes. "You think you're not much? You might be the daughter of the lord's cousin or whoever, but you've been the talk of the court."

"Really?" I asked, surprised. I thought I'd had a fairly good handle on the gossip raging across the court, but perhaps everything about me personally was kept well out of my hearing.

"Of course!" She smiled, but it was tinged with a delicate sadness. "It's clear the king favors you, and everyone wants to know everything about you." She giggled, shaking her head. "Even the peasants love you. They cheer for you in the streets. I've gone out and seen signs around the city. People who are following the competition have all made them for their favorite competitors. There's more supporting you to win than anyone else."

I blinked in surprise, not realizing that I was such a favorite. Or that others had realized that Azurill favored me himself.

That bit of hope stretched and grew within me, taking up yet more space.

"I can see it, you know," Safira whispered, alarming me when I looked over to see her sapphire eyes were swirling, the blue forming layers that seemed to continue into infinity. "You're on a precipice right now. One from which you could fall or fly. Your next steps will determine the course of the rest of your life. Your *ruin* or your *rise*—and you'll bring all of Gemaria with you."

I shivered, knowing a prophecy when I heard one. I had known that Safira was adept at them, but I'd yet to truly see it in action. It meant one thing for sure: the time for delay was over.

It was time for me to confess everything.

And hope that Azurill didn't kill the hope struggling to break free.

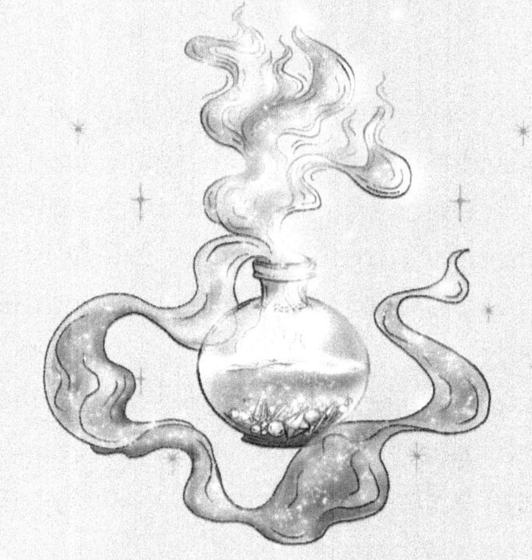

CHAPTER 39

Jacinth

I ENDED up spending most of the rest of the afternoon with Safira, much to my surprise. But stripped away of Zumra and the competition, I'd found a very sad, lonely lady in desperate need of friends, and *Erodite*, could I relate.

It also had the added benefit of wiling away the hours until night fell around us, which meant that fewer people would be populating the hallways now that I'd finally got up my nerve to speak to Azurill. The last thing I needed was witnesses seeing me going to his rooms.

Safira's prophecy had given me the last push I needed. If my next steps were to determine everything, they needed to be the right ones.

Alfrikr led me there, looking curious all the while, but he dutifully announced me. After Azurill called for me to enter, I took a deep breath, my shoulders rising and falling as I contemplated the mess I was in. Alfrikr's hand fell on my shoulder, and I looked up, catching his amethyst gaze. He nodded once, calming me slightly, before opening the door.

I walked in, feeling like I was marching to the hangman's noose. Azurill was standing before a long kyanite blue sofa, its circular shape seeming to surround him from where he stood before its center. He looked momentarily surprised, but his eyes turned considering when he took me in. I was sure my nervous expression had clued him in to why I was here.

"Here to finally tell me what's going on, Mini-Dite?" he asked, shrugging off his stiff court jacket and leaving him in a teal button-up shirt with silver embroidery running along the edges.

I tried to smile, but it just wouldn't come.

"Yes, Veri," I said morosely. "I am."

He frowned in concern and took the few steps needed to reach me, grabbing my hand. I looked down at where he held it, tears rising to my eyes as I wondered if this would be the last time he'd touch me in such a way.

He led me to the sofa, each of us taking a seat. With the round shape, we were facing directly across from each other, and the closeness was setting my nerves further on edge.

"I'm going to ask you to let me tell the full story before you say anything," I requested, my eyes closing as I gathered myself. He hadn't let go of my hand, and the soft press of his fingers and palm against my own sent all the blood there racing straight to my heart.

"Jacinth," he called softly, his tone achingly sweet, and I wanted to bottle the sound to remember it forever. The knowledge that someone cared for me in such a way was so strange and yet so beautiful. And all it could take is a few words to have it all torn away.

I opened my eyes, meeting the beautiful teal ones staring back at me. His elbows went to his knees, enabling him to lean further toward me. The hand not holding mine went to my cheek, stroking the skin there as I tried to imprint everything about this moment into my memory.

"I want you to know that this story does turn around, so I beg of you, Azurill, let me get this out," I begged Azurill, who looked more disconcerted by the second, but he nodded his confirmation.

"My name is—" My voice caught. I hadn't spoken it aloud since I was a child, and the truth trembled on the tip of my tongue. "My name is Linnea Jacinth Marit."

Azurill pulled back immediately, his eyes blown wide as he opened his mouth to speak, but I held up a hand, a plea for him to remain silent. He closed his mouth, his lips twisting, and I fisted my hands in my skirts, trying to keep myself together even as I wanted to rattle apart.

"My father was Lord Elros of Pearl Court, and I was the noble daughter of Pearl, until that night." I shivered, trying to repress the memory so recently awakened. "I was a little girl at the time, but my guard woke me from my sleep, and he immediately shushed me, telling me that I was in danger and needed to remain quiet. I nearly screamed as he dragged the already dead body of my cousin, Peony, to my bed, tucking her in as if she were me."

Azurill appeared as if he'd seen a ghost, but I forced myself to continue.

"He tried to run with me, to get me to safety, but the attackers were closing in. We entered the living room, and I saw the bodies of my entire family laid out before me. If I thought seeing Peony's body was bad, seeing the bloody remains of my parents' bodies, their hands reaching out for each other from across the room…"

My words caught, and I bit my lip to prevent tears from leaking out. Azurill's eyes were wide as he digested this part of my story, and recognition shone in them as I spoke about the placement of their bodies.

"I tried to scream, to cry, to fight my way to them," I smiled sadly, "but my guard was too loyal for his own good, and he was determined to save me. When he heard the men coming back, he hid me in a closet and told me to run the second I had the chance. To not stop running until I was safe." I couldn't stop the tears from trailing down my cheeks, and I didn't even bother to wipe them away.

"I watched through a crack in the door as they killed him, his body falling to the floor to join everyone else I loved. Once the attackers finally left, I followed his directions. I ran—and I haven't stopped running since that night." I admitted that truth to both of us at the same time. I hadn't ever stopped, had never thought it safe enough to. I thought I'd found a life I could live with on the streets, but I'd been fooling myself for years. Grasping onto whatever lies I had to so I could convince myself everything was fine.

It was never fine; it was a forest fire.

"I had nowhere to go, no money to buy food. I was slowly starving, scared, and alone. My resentment grew and *grew*. I finally found someone to help me, a woman named Ula who'd lived on the streets all her life, who taught me how to survive. How to steal, how to lie, how to keep myself alive and one step ahead of everyone else. I believed that if anyone ever found out who I was…"

I trailed off, meeting his eyes for a moment before continuing. "That you would have me killed."

He reared back in shock, his mouth gaping open, and I looked away, unable to take the sight right now.

"You see, the men who attacked my family, they hailed the High King," I turned my eyes back to him, letting him see the sad truth within them. "They said he didn't want a drop of Marit blood left alive."

Azurill's eyebrows furrowed as he cocked his head, trying to work it out.

"I spent years wanting to get vengeance for my family, a chance to finally sleep peacefully and not see their broken bodies in my dreams," I cried, my head falling forward and my hair curtaining my face. "And I finally got the chance. Ula fell sick, and we didn't have the gems to help her. I went to Ruby Court since we were close by, and I figured the banking capital of Gemaria would be the best place to find some dumb man I could steal coins or gems from."

"One man in a tavern mentioned to his friend that they'd found a fault in Lord Carnelian's vault security. They were fixing it soon, but it was now possible to break into. I traded with him for a map and stole into the castle. But I was caught and brought before Lord Carnelian. He offered me a way to get out alive, and a way to save Ula—but more importantly, he offered me a chance at vengeance."

I thought back, recognizing now the clues I'd missed before about Carnelian. He'd played me the entire time, and I'd missed it. Azurill's face had gone hard, and I could tell he was working to keep any discernible emotions locked down. He didn't want to give a thing away. I sighed miserably, but continued my explanation.

"He said he was working on a way to take you out and become High King himself," I told him, gravely serious, worry lacing my words. "I agreed to join the competition and win, where I'd poison you the night of and then disappear. Carnelian would take over, he'd heal Ula for me, and I'd have vengeance for my family." My lips pursed as I thought about how stupid I had been, letting that horrid lord lead me down this path.

"But I realized quickly that who you were didn't match the image I'd always had of you." I admitted softly, "That you were hardly the boogie man who'd invaded my dreams for so long." His lips twitched down into a frown at that, but I kept going.

"I began to doubt more and more, especially when you spoke of what happened to my family, and then Carnelian slipped up. He mentioned me getting vengeance for my family, but I'd never told him about my family at all." I frowned, furious anger racing through my body. I took a deep breath, looking up at Azurill through watery eyes.

"I was so torn, Azurill." Tears choked my words, and I cleared my throat to continue. "I thought you were responsible for ripping my entire life away from me, but I found myself so drawn to you despite it all. You were charming and caring, fiercely protective and generous. And I felt myself tearing apart by inches as I fell for a man I thought had committed such an absolute *atrocity* against my family."

My tears fell steadily, and I watched Azurill's hands twitch as if to reach for me, but he forced them still. I could feel my heart tearing further, cracking along the fault line created by falling for a man I believed to be the blackest of villains.

"I used the trial to take a potion that would show me what really happened that night, and it did." I laughed wetly. "Oh, I saw alright. I saw Cassan had been there that night."

Azurill sat up straight at that news, and I nodded grimly.

"He stabbed my father himself," I spat, my hands fisting as I tried to contain my rage. "Carnelian apparently heard a prophecy that said as long as any person with the blood of House Marit lived, his plans to become the high king would be ruined. But if every member of House Marit was gone, then he would succeed at taking the throne."

Azurill's eyes narrowed, his lips curling into a snarl at the news. I watched his eyes shift from teal to silver, the transition mesmerizing.

"I believe he knows exactly who I am, Azurill," I told him, looking away in shame. "I don't know whether he knew as soon as he saw me, or if he figured it out later. All this time, I was working for the man who was actually responsible, while planning to take vengeance on the only man who did anything to get justice for my family."

His eyes widened in surprise, and I nodded. "I saw you, covered in blood and surrounded by the bodies of the men who were there that night. And I can't thank you enough for doing…whatever it was you did. You got some of the vengeance I'd always longed for. But two remain: Carnelian and Casaan. All of House Rousseau, truly. I'm positive they're all in on this."

I wanted to scream my frustration to the world, but that time would have to come later.

"I believe he still thinks I'm with him. That I'll kill you for him." My voice cracked around the words, tears falling over my cheeks in steady handfuls. "I would *never*. Not now. And I'm sure he also plans to kill me when I'm done. After all, if he knows who I am, he knows he won't get the throne with me alive," I said shakily.

I'd survived so much, endured tragedy and starvation, all because some arrogant little man wanted more than the gods had given him.

"I want you to know, that every single thing I felt, everything I said," I told him desperately, shifting forward quickly and grabbing his hand now. Squeezing even as his fingers stayed stiff. "All of it was true, Az. All of it. I promised you '*truth*' that night, and I meant it. I've felt more true, more *real*, with you, than I have in my entire life."

Azurill stood, leaving me sitting with my hand grasping air and my mouth still open to spill my heart out on the floor some more, but he simply walked away. I slid from the sofa, crashing to my knees as heaving sobs ripped from my chest. Azurill ran as fast as his legs could take him, slamming the door behind himself.

Leaving me, *alone*, as I had always been.

CHAPTER 40

Azurill

I RAMMED my fist into the closest wall, feeling my knuckles crack under the pressure.

I *had* known she was up to something. I couldn't truly hold it against her when I'd suspected she was doing *something* for Carnelian.

But the confirmation was…

I had never been more conflicted, and as high king, that was saying something. The truth of her identity was both a shocking discovery and somehow completely unsurprising.

Lady Linnea Marit *lived*.

I had beaten myself up over the loss of House Marit for years. A critical failure of our spy networks, of the protection we offered our lords, of justice itself. Elros and Lulit were amazing, loyal Elves who deserved better. Everyone in the household that was slaughtered that night did. But I'd agonized over the loss of little Linnea most of all.

She was so *young*, and to die so brutally was an injustice that I could never reconcile. It had lived like a shadow in my heart, one that had only begun to lift when I met *her*. Not even knowing who she was, seeing the vision of what I'd expected the daughter of Pearl to be was enough to begin healing the long bleeding wound.

It filled me with joy to know that she lived, even as I despaired and raged at what she'd been forced into. From having to see her family executed, twice over now, to living on the streets and having to turn to a life of crime, all the way to being manipulated by Carnelian into becoming his assassin.

And then there was the fact that I struggled with most now—knowing she'd planned to kill me the entire time. She'd flirted and teased while behind her smile, she plotted my destruction.

It stung badly. *No*, that was hardly descriptive enough to encompass what felt like a dagger to the heart. Our connection had been built over the length of the competition, but for half of that, she'd not just been playing a game; she'd actually planned to joyfully assassinate me.

It was enough to make my head spin. The two extreme revelations on such opposite ends of the spectrum that I swung from one to the other like someone had flicked an arrow to spin quickly around them.

I suppose the real question was, what did I do now?

I had to speak with everyone, but I first needed to get a handle on what *I* wanted before they tried to decide for me. I didn't want them throwing her in the dungeon. So that was one thing I knew for sure. She had to continue in the competition, which was another.

I also knew we had to deal with Carnelian and his son. If Jacin—*Linnea*, had desired vengeance for this long, and been willing to kill the fucking High King for it, then she deserved to take their lives herself. But we needed to plan how to handle the downfall of House Rousseau, a nice bit of turnabout for what they did to House Marit.

I knew she had to be involved in all of it, but I wasn't ready to see her yet, to speak with her…it was just too much.

And yet, when I thought of who I wanted to talk all this over with, my mind landed on her immediately. My heart ached for her still, despite all the lies revealed.

I'd known she was lying, I just hadn't known the extent. And who could truly blame her? She'd heard as a child that the High King was responsible for what happened to her family. After seeing such gruesome tragedy in action and having a perfect target for that rage, it only made sense for her to protect herself.

Why would she have trusted me when she expected me to kill her the moment her truth was revealed?

It explained why she needed the potion, and I suppose I was grateful that our connection was enough to make her doubt what she thought she knew. That she couldn't reconcile the truth of me with the image in her mind. It explained why the potion had affected her so powerfully.

Veritx, she relived her the night her entire family was murdered just to find out the truth. That took extreme courage, the kind of courage a queen needed. The kind that would put the good of others above their own pre-conceptions and search to find the truth, no matter the negative effects for themselves.

If I hadn't wanted her to win this competition already then that might have cinched it alone. Though the last trial would be the one that truly determined the outcome. Or at least, that had been the plan.

Before her.

I had never expected to find someone like her here.

It was almost funny. She was pretending to be a lesser lady, when she was in fact a lady of a great house. She deserved to be Pearl Court's competitor.

I nearly winced at the thought. Sania had been trying to up her game, but the more I fell for Jacinth, the harder it was to entertain her, or the others.

Frustration rolled through me like thunder. I didn't know what to feel. I didn't know what to do.

And that was before I even considered that she'd seen what I'd done to those men who'd attacked her house. Shame still lived within me to this day for what I'd done. For failing House Marit and for the monstrous actions I took following it.

She'd seen me covered in blood and surrounded by the bodies of the men I'd just destroyed. She didn't seem too disturbed by it, but she must have been. Balthazar was my best friend, a seasoned guard and warrior, and yet he'd been fucking terrified of me.

If—*if* I decided to move forward, *well*, she'd given me the truth of her, terrified as she'd clearly been to do it, so perhaps I owed her the truth of me in return.

If she knew the truth of me, the way I now knew hers, and we both somehow managed to accept one another...we could build a foundation stronger than the diamonds my throne was carved from. We could see Gemaria prosper for hundreds of years—together.

But could I trust her?

After all her lies?

When she had been planning to *assassinate* me?

I honestly didn't know if we could move forward from that.

Maybe fighting her in the upcoming challenge would help illuminate the issue. Fighting her did hold a certain appeal; just the thought of her moving gracefully around the ring as our weapons clashed sent a thrill through me.

We'd already tested the ladies' skill with magic; now we needed to test their martial prowess. For a queen needed to be able to protect herself, her king, her heirs, and her kingdom. And potions weren't always available, nor the the raw gems we could use for broader, more wild magic.

That could be just the thing I needed to work all of this frustration out.

CHAPTER 41

~~Jacinth~~ ~~Linnea~~ Jacinth

I HADN'T seen Azurill at all over the past three days. I buried myself in training with Alfrikr, hoping to take the edge off. I couldn't help feeling like I was standing on a cliff, waiting to fall over the edge.

After leaving Azurill's rooms, I went to my own and called for Faiza and Amatista. Thankfully, they were able to navigate my breakdown with ease. I didn't tell them the truth; I couldn't handle seeing their heartbroken faces after dealing with Azurill's. But they let me cry it out, keeping me sane when I was ready to spiral.

The trial offered an escape, and I grabbed hold of it with both hands. Everything else I was dealing with was just too much, so focusing on the sword in my hand as I fought Alfrikr was a welcome respite.

And now, the last three competitors stood once more in the arena, armored up with weapons in hand, as the cheering crowd called our names and held up banners with our names and likenesses embroidered on them.

I blinked in surprise at the sight of them. Safira had told me the people loved me, but to see the sea of people holding up signs and cheering me on, was touching in a way that I couldn't explain. For a girl who had to hide her whole life, this level of acknowledgment was overwhelming.

I had already been surprised when Faiza, Amatista, and even Safira came to wish me luck before the trial. Allirea had also wished me luck, as had Ophira, who I'd never spoken to before, but was there to support Allirea. Sania was alone, and I almost felt bad about that, wishing I could speak to my cousin, but her haughty expression was enough to keep me at bay.

She didn't know who I was, other than a lady competing with her for the prize she wanted. One she may win if Azurill wanted nothing more to do with me.

Speaking of, the man himself finally walked into the royal booth, while the crowd cheered at his appearance.

"Citizens of Gemaria, it warms my heart to see you all here for the penultimate trial of the Diamond Queen Competition!" he yelled, a charming smile firmly in place as he worked the crowd. "This will sadly be the last trial you'll be able to witness, for the most part anyway." He teased, making the crowd "*ooh*" and "*aww*".

"The fighting order today was chosen at random. Each lady will receive points based on the fights between each competitor and then the final fight with me. We will begin with a bout between Allirea and Jacinth, followed by Allirea and Sania, and then Jacinth and Sania." Azurill announced, looking firmly out at the crowd and not down at us, avoiding my eyes and making my stomach sink.

The guards stepped forward and directed Sania to the side to await her turn. Her eyes caught mine and she raised an orange brow. "See you soon," she whispered, winking at me. It was innocuous really, but still, chills went down my spine. I knew she truly wanted to win. She'd clearly kept from making friends, focusing only on winning Azurill.

The thought made me sick, but it also made determination surge through me. My hand clasped my sword's hilt, squeezing tightly. I started off needing to win so I could poison Azurill, but now…now I needed to win because I could finally see a future, and it belonged to him.

"The fights are to a yield," Balthazar instructed, looking between us. "If one opponent does not yield, you're allowed to knock them out, but no killing blows. Understood?"

We both agreed, Allirea and I smiling at each other, and I knew this fight wasn't the one I had to worry about.

"Begin!" Balthazar called, and I began circling around Allirea, but she matched me step for step. I'd never seen her fight before, so I didn't know what she was capable of, but she hadn't seen me either. On the other hand, Sania and I would both get to see the other fight before we faced off against one another.

Allirea surged forward, and I brought my blade up to block her, quickly forcing hers down to the ground before I looked up and softly whispered, "Sorry about this."

With my other hand, I punched out, sending her staggering backward, barely keeping hold of her sword in the process. It was obvious that she wasn't very experienced, and as I advanced, I noticed that her hold on the sword's hilt was shaky at best.

I swung down, and her block couldn't hold up to the power of the blow, sending her sword skittering to the sand. I brought my blade to her neck, and she smiled slightly at me. "I yield."

I smiled back at her before stepping away, swinging my sword down with a swoosh of air. The crowd cheered, and I bowed dramatically, amplifying their applause. I could hear my name being shouted enthusiastically, bringing a tear to my eye as I smiled up at them, blowing a kiss. They seemed to love it, but I forced my attention back down to where Balthazar was stepping forward.

"Good job, ladies." He nodded gruffly. "Next up is Sania and Allirea. Jacinth, if you'll step over here." His arm swung out to indicate the area Sania was now stepping out from. Her strut as she confidently headed to the field made me raise an eyebrow, but I settled in to see what she could do.

The fight lasted longer than my own did, but I could tell Sania had the advantage over Allirea. It figured that a healer didn't spend much time fighting, while Sania had clearly been trained. The result was expected, and Sania ate up the crowd's response even more than I had.

When it came time for my turn against Sania, I stepped out into the arena, preparing myself for a much harder battle. As soon as it began, she narrowed her eyes at me and lunged quickly. As much as I didn't want to be fighting my own blood, there was nothing I could do, and I refused to sacrifice this competition for her. So I spun quickly away, bringing my sword up to hit her in the back and sending her falling forward.

She glared as she caught herself and turned around, but I kept my own features perfectly neutral. When she swung again, I brought my sword up to block her. She parried, and I gave a riposte that left her off balance as she jumped back. I advanced my attack, landing blows on her shoulder and thigh. She swiped my own leg, but I managed to spin away before it did could do any damage.

Her anger at getting hit, while not managing to land a solid blow in return, was clearly rising. Anger could make you sloppy in a fight, and as she furiously tried to get a hit on me, she also began making more mistakes. Her footwork was off, her posture was suffering, and she wasn't paying nearly enough attention. I took advantage of it, landing another blow to her stomach that sent her falling back and landing on her ass.

I quickly brought my sword to her neck before she could get up, "Yield?"

She huffed, glaring at me as she ground her teeth. She tried to move up, but the blade at her throat stopped her in her tracks. Finally, she huffed, "Fine, I yield."

The crowd went wild as I offered her a hand up. She ignored it, rolling away and getting up by herself. I shrugged, leaving her to stew in her righteous anger. I was just happy to have succeeded in beating them both. I would have been embarrassed if I hadn't been able to defeat two noble ladies after years of fighting for scraps on the street.

I looked at the royal booth, only to find that Azurill's seat was empty. I blinked in surprise, turning to look around, only to find him stepping through the side door we had all entered through earlier. He stepped out onto the sand, his eyes briefly meeting my own before going to each lady in turn.

He walked out to the middle of the arena, raising a hand to silence the crowd. They responded instantly, and a hush seemed to move through the entire city.

"Next up, each of the ladies shall fight me to a yield," Azurill called out, his blue-green hair glinting brightly in the sun. I briefly mourned that he shaved the sides, leaving less hair visible, but the look definitely worked for him. It was hard to imagine him otherwise.

"A queen must be able to fight for her people," Azurill shouted, a smirk rising on his lips. "She must be able to protect those who cannot protect themselves, while ensuring the stability of this kingdom. Today, we see which of these ladies has what it takes!"

The crowd roared in response, and I couldn't help but smile at the way he was able to work them. But my smile fell as Azurill turned, his eyes meeting mine as they flared with an emotion I couldn't identify. His face was locked down otherwise, and I swallowed hard as I fought not to flinch back from his gaze.

Having to fight him right now may prove more dangerous than any of the other trials. He'd been avoiding me since I'd told him the truth, and I had no idea what he was feeling about any of it.

Was he upset? Angry? I couldn't begin to guess, and as I stood back to watch him fight, I could only hope he didn't feel the need for revenge himself.

Since Allirea had the least number of points from the fights thus far, she was first up to fight Azurill, meaning I would be the last.

Azurill didn't press his attack, letting Allirea showcase what training she'd had. Her form was good, but her swings were lacking power. It was only because Azurill held himself back and didn't actively try to take her down that she was able to get a few more points in before he finally ended it with one swift strike that sent her sword tumbling into the dirt.

When Sania cockily stepped up, I wanted to groan. She smirked at him, her eyebrows rising as she made a blatant show of checking him out. I couldn't entirely blame her. He was fitted out in silver armor with kyanite detailing worked into it. The armor looked like it was molded to his body, showing off his considerable assets. I rarely saw this type of expensive, magically reinforced kind of armor, but I would definitely say that it was worth whatever it cost.

Still, she didn't have to be so fucking classless about it. Wasn't she a noble lady?

The urge to gouge out my cousin's eyeballs came the moment Azurill smiled back at her, saying, "Lady Sania, are you ready?"

"To get sweaty with you? Absolutely," She replied with a giggle that grated on my ears.

His laugh was rough and deep, and she didn't deserve it.

I was forced to watch them flirt back and forth as they fought, while I glared at them both from the sidelines. Maybe he decided I wasn't worth it after all. Maybe someone like Lady Sania *was* a better choice to be his queen.

Azurill didn't hold back as much with Sania, meeting her on more equal footing, which only made me more pissed off. When he finally ended the fight by knocking her on her back, she actually said, "I doubt it'll be the last time, Your Majesty."

I was going to kill her. Maybe him too. My hands curled into fists, my nails biting into my palms, and my teeth ground back and forth. It was only Allirea's interference that pulled me out of my bloodlust.

"Don't worry," She whispered, smiling softly as her opal hair shone in the light, "We all know Lady Sania isn't the one for him." She winked before pushing me forward as my name was called.

I passed Sania as she made her way to the sidelines, and her raised brow and smirking lips had me narrowing my eyes back at her. She clearly thought she was winning.

Maybe she was right.

I didn't have to wait long to find out. As I neared the center of the arena, Azurill was there waiting, and his eyes were steady on me for the first time since I spilled my heart out.

We stood there, facing one another, our faces both completely blank, yet a wealth of emotions were hidden behind our eyes.

A muscle in his jaw jumped, and before I knew it, his sword was flying at me.

CHAPTER 42

Jacinth

INSTINCTIVELY parried his blow, meeting him with a riposte that had him twirling his blade in his hand so he could come right back at me from above.

He wasn't playing around. Unlike the other ladies, I was getting his full skill, if not his full power. I could tell he wasn't aiming to kill, thank Erodite, but he was obviously still aggrieved by my lies.

I couldn't even blame him for it. I would be too.

I swung my sword from below to meet his strike, and our blades clashed with a deep reverberation. His eyes glinted silver for a moment before returning to teal, piquing my curiosity even more. Our faces were close as we both struggled to overcome the other, and I could see every twitch of his jaw as his emotions got the better of him.

Unable to stand being so close, I pushed off him, pulling my sword free and standing back. He began to circle me, looking as much like a predator as he had in my vision, and I warily turned in time with his steps.

"What would you have done?" He finally spoke, a deep thread of pain echoing in his voice that I wished I could wash away.

"Had I found out you'd been responsible?" I asked quietly.

"Yes." That was all he said as he watched me closely. I sighed deeply, shaking my head and making my braid swing back and forth with the motion.

"You would never have done it." I countered him, but he only laughed wryly.

"You know that's not true. What if your parents had been one of those I'd killed that night? Left in a bloody pile," he asked, cold and aloof as he raised a brow expectedly.

I spun towards him, feigning left before slashing my blade quickly to the right and hitting his torso, leaving him blinking in shock. I nearly got another hit to his shoulder while he was distracted before he seemed to wake up and blocked me.

"If that was the case, then my parents would have been guilty." I snarled, trying to make him see sense. "Everyone you killed that night deserved their fate. But my parents? They were innocent. And you avenged them."

"That doesn't answer my question," he nearly roared, only to remember our audience and lower his voice as he rushed in, hitting my upper back as I tried to duck away from a side thrust.

I glared back at him, spinning my blade before going high, aiming for his thick head. He jumped back, meeting my blade as we began to go blow for blow.

"You want to know if I would have killed you?" I asked harshly, "If I would have gone through with it despite what I feel for you?"

My plain words caused him to halt for a moment, letting me get a hit onto his thigh as his block failed to hold. He recovered, forcing me backward as his sword rained down on me.

"Yes, that's what I want to know." He insisted, making me scoff.

"I can't give you an answer, because I don't know!" I snapped, frustrated at the position the world had put me in. "That's why I doubted the story I thought I knew. That's why I used the potion! I was hoping, praying desperately to Erodite and Veritx and all the damn gods that you weren't the one behind it. Because I couldn't stand the thought of killing you."

I panted, trying to keep the power behind my strikes, but my strength was failing as we went ever harder, the emotion between us driving us to a fever pitch. When he suddenly let go of his sword and let it tumble to the ground, mine kept going, and I barely managed to stop my blade before it reached his neck. I blinked in shock, my hand trembling as I realized how close the blade was to his skin.

"Then I yield," he whispered, his eyes alight as he stepped back, bowing towards me. The noise of the crowd cheering sounded as if it were far away. My eyes were stuck on Azurill as he walked away, completely bewildered by what had just happened.

"I told you!" Allirea laughed as I made my way back to the sidelines, making me shake my head fondly at her.

"I have no idea what just happened," I admitted to her, making her scoff.

"Of course you do." She laughed, her opal eyes bright, "He *yielded* to you. Only you. If that doesn't say something, I don't know what does."

That was exactly the thing that left me confused. Why would he have yielded to me? One minute he was pissed off, and the next…

It didn't make any sense.

I wanted to go to him so badly, but it was then announced that the elimination would be happening this afternoon. Everything seemed to be moving too fast, and I was left adrift.

It wasn't a surprise when Allirea was eliminated. Azurill thanked her kindly for her participation, but we'd all seen it coming, and she didn't seem at all unhappy at the result.

"We now have our two final contestants!" Azurill exclaimed. "Lady Jacinth Tawny of Ruby Court and Lady Sania Helmi of Pearl Court!" The court clapped briefly before letting the king continue.

"The final trial will be the day after tomorrow, giving the ladies time to rest today. We will of course have a celebration tonight, honoring the remaining two competitors before the final trial begins," he explained, smiling slightly from his diamond throne.

"This final trial will be different," he said heavily, looking between Sania and me. "You will be dropped into the city, where you will be assigned a specific object to obtain. This object is of vital importance, as it will be a tribute to the gods to ensure the winner's reign is blessed. That is all I can tell you as the rest is for you to determine, but I wish you both luck in your trial."

That was suitably ominous.

At least we had some time before then. I still didn't know what to do about Carnelian and Casaan, and I could only hope that Azurill had an idea. We were getting close to when a move would have to be made.

Time was rapidly running out.

Considering we had a celebration tonight, that was true on multiple levels. I raced back to my room to take a bath and prepare for the night to come. I was pleasantly surprised when Amatista and Faiza came by, joined by Allirea.

"We noticed you two forming a friendship and decided to invite her along," Faiza explained cheerfully, her turquoise locks already done up and her makeup pristine, while I looked like something Azurill's dog had drug in.

"In that case, you should have invited Safira," I teased, laughing at the shocked looks I received.

"What?!" Amatista demanded, her hands on her hips. "You'd better explain that."

As I got ready, I told them all the story, seeing the expected sympathy shining on Faiza's face, the calculation on Amatista's, and the reservation on Allirea's. My new friends couldn't be more different from one another, but as we all chatted and they helped the maids readying me, I found myself more grateful than I could say for their presence.

"What about this one?" Allirea pulled a dress from the pile on the bed, the color a pinkish-red, with a line of long, rectangular rubies that circled the hips. The sweetheart neckline was enhanced by the points at the tops of the cups and the rubies that dotted across it. The fabric had a subtle pattern to it, almost like a damask, and it came with sheer gloves that ended high on my bicep.

"That's perfect!" Faiza cried, clapping her hands excitedly, "What do you think, Jac?"

I smiled at their excitement, looking to Amatista, "What do you think, Tista?"

"I think it has just enough pink for you, without scandalizing the lords." She winked, making me chuckle as I nodded my approval.

I found myself hoping Azurill liked it as well. I was getting increasingly anxious about his response, especially since I had no idea what to make of him yielding today.

"Azurill won't be able to take his eyes off you," Faiza reassured me softly, once the other two were caught up in a debate over the best methods of healing something or other. I should have known those two would get along as soon as they got past any initial standoffishness.

"You think?" I asked, wincing at how pathetic I sounded. Her hand clasped my shoulder, her turquoise eyes luminous as she smiled knowingly.

"I've known Az for a long time." She raised her brows, a smirk forming on her lips. "I have never seen him so mixed up over a woman before."

"I think I've left him more mixed up than he cares for," I muttered darkly, and watched in shock as Faiza threw back her head in laughter.

"Oh, Jacinth." She shook her head, "That's what love is. Trust me, you've enchanted the High King, but even more importantly, you've enraptured *Azurill*."

CHAPTER 43

THE ball was made more bearable by having my friends with me, but watching Azurill work the room was a study in frustration.

At least so far, he'd avoided both me and Sania, thank Erodite. I wasn't sure I could take it if he'd gone to her and ignored me.

Prince Ruri kept close to him, with Balthazar shadowing his other side. I couldn't help wondering if he'd confided in them about what was going on. Their protectiveness was heartwarming, but I had a feeling I would soon be on the receiving end of their wrath once they knew the truth.

Prince Ruri had been suspicious of me from day one, thanks to his low, albeit well deserved, opinion of Carnelian. He'd probably be pissed when I demanded to be the one to kill him, but I wasn't walking out of here without vengeance for my family. Even if the target had changed.

"Lady Jacinth." I fought back a cringe as Casaan's voice reached me, turning reluctantly to face him. I exchanged looks of commiseration with the ladies around me as he asked, "May I have this dance?"

"Of course, Lord Casaan." I nodded demurely, taking his hand, and he swept me onto the dance floor.

"You've done very well so far, especially for one of your station." His back-handed compliment was delivered haughtily, and I fought to keep my eyes from rolling.

"Thank you, my Lord. I've done everything I can to ensure our plans succeed," I told him, but my eyes caught on the orange-haired figure Azurill was approaching. I narrowed my eyes, watching as she smiled and took his hand. I looked away, my heart throbbing in my chest, refusing to watch them together.

"And you've done so admirably," Casaan smirked, his ruby-red eyes meeting mine. "You could quite easily fit into court, you know."

I wanted to scream, especially as Casaan's hands began moving south, caressing my hips. All the while, Azurill redirected his position on the dance floor, leading him and Sania directly into my eyeline. As Casaan babbled, I tried to keep from reacting, but Azurill's glare was impossible to ignore.

We may have been dancing with other people, but the pull we felt to one another was inescapable, our feet and our eyes seemed to drift right back to each other each time we moved them away.

I jumped as Cassan's hands began moving from my lower back down to my ass, making the bastard laugh. My rage was palpable, but I calmed myself by imagining him with a knife sticking out of his ruby-red eyes. Azurill's glare, on the other hand, was arctic, shining with a silver gleam as he ground his teeth. I shook my head at him subtly and stepped back, turning my gaze back to the cocky heir.

"My offer is still open." Casaan licked his lips, running his eyes over my body, and I shivered in disgust as I practically *felt* the slimy caress skate over me. "You're welcome to join me in my rooms tonight."

"That would be a bad idea during the competition, my Lord," I refused politely, giving him a plausible excuse. The egos of men like him were so fragile. I wasn't even sure if he knew who I really was and he wanted to bed me before killing me, getting to claim he fucked the last of House Marit after murdering her family, or if his father had left him out of that aspect of his plan.

"We wouldn't want to jeopardize my win so close to the end, would we?" I pressed when his lips turned down and a sneer of offense crossed his face. My words made him relax, and he chuckled, so confident in himself that he surely believed every woman here would kill for the chance to fuck him.

"Your dedication is something else, Jacinth," He whispered in my ear. "Most ladies would have found a way into my bed no matter the obstacles once I issued an invitation."

I rolled my eyes, looking to Azurill, who appeared to have had enough. He ended his dance with Sania, bowing to her and following the proper protocol, but her frown of confusion made it clear that he was rushing through it, his countenance tense and obviously on edge.

He walked up to where I was stuck in Casaan's arms, and cleared his throat. "Mind if I cut in, Lord Casaan?"

The heir in question wrestled with his expression, trying to hide his distaste and only barely managing it. "Of course, Your Majesty."

He bowed to us both, leaving me to take the king's hand as Casaan rushed over to the table filled with alcohol where he downed a glass of champagne. I was happy to put him out of my mind however, giving Azurill my full attention instead.

He twirled me into his arms, holding me close to his body, the heat sinking in where he was pressed against me. My back was to his front, with our arms crossed and resting over my waist. It gave Azurill the ability to put his head on my shoulder, leaning in to whisper in my ear.

"Mini-Dite," he purred, making me relax slightly, my eyes closing in relief at hearing the ridiculous nickname.

"Veri," I returned breathily, leaning my head back onto him as we swayed together.

"Watching you dance with him was a torture I can't describe," he murmured, making my breath catch in my throat.

"As it was to be forced to dance with him." I replied, making him chuckle. He spun me out, only to bring me back in, pressing my chest against his as his hands quickly found my hips. He made an effort to map every spot Casaan had touched, banishing the feeling of his revolting caresses and overwriting him completely from my body.

"I find myself both jealously coveting you and yet frustrated beyond belief with the circumstances we find ourselves in," he said quietly, even as his fingers burned into my skin through layers of cloth.

"I wish I'd led a different life," I told him sadly. "When I was a child, I told my father I wished to marry you, you know?"

He pulled back to look at me, his eyebrows raised in surprise, but I could see the pleasure brimming in his eyes as he chuckled. "I wasn't sure you'd even remember that. Your father had mentioned it to me, but I didn't think…"

He trailed off, before meeting my eyes once more, the light in them dimming and swirling with confusion. "Does that wish still live on? Even all these years later?"

"It does," I breathed, tears pricking my eyes as I nodded with a trembling smile. "I can't erase the past, but I can promise you a future. As long as I can finally get the vengeance my family deserves and put them to rest at last."

"Yes, about that." He grew seriously very quickly. "Meet me in my rooms after the ball. We need to plan quickly and quietly. We don't have much time."

"No, we don't." I agreed darkly, shadows forming in my eyes at the thought of what was to come.

Azurill's expression softened slightly, and his hand left my hip to clasp my cheek, "I promise you, I will ensure they get what they deserve."

"No, Az." I shook my head adamantly. "*I will.*"

His heated look in response stayed with me through the rest of the ball. Since he couldn't play favorites in public, we spent the rest of the night on opposite sides of the hall, only our eyes meeting again through the remaining hours. When it was finally over, I paced my rooms until a quiet knock sounded, and I opened it to find Alfrikr waiting.

He took me to Azurill's rooms and let me inside, and I stopped short in surprise when I realized that no one else was present. I thought that he'd surely have his council present to discuss what to do about Ruby Court. But instead, I found only Azurill, his jacket stripped off, leaving him in a silver button-down and a teal vest that matched his pants.

"Jacinth," he greeted, smiling slightly. It was a highly encouraging sign.

"Azurill," I returned, sauntering over to the drink tray by the sofa that had two glasses and a bottle of champagne set on it. I poured myself a glass as I continued, "So, does this mean you forgive me?"

Silence followed my question, and I set my drink down, about to turn to look at him, when a rush of air blew past me and my back suddenly hit the wall. He grabbed my wrists, holding them in one of his large, slender hands and pinning them to the wall above my head.

His other hand came around my waist, pressing our lower bodies together even as my upper body remained flat against the wall. I looked up into his eyes, his blue-green orbs refracting over and over like the most brilliant diamond. My breath caught as he leaned in, until all it would take was the slightest movement to take his lips with mine.

"Forgive you?" He gave an amused rumble, the vibration echoing through my body. "Not quite yet."

"And what will," I began breathily, undulating my body pointedly against his, "Push you over the edge?"

I bit my lip, wishing my dress wasn't in the way so I could press myself to him more fully, when I gasped in shock—the gods or Azurill or *whoever* having apparently my prayer. Azurill ripped my surely very expensive but definitely very beautiful dress straight down the middle, the two pieces falling to the floor and sending rubies flying in all direction. I felt myself growing wet at the show of strength, and pressed my now bare thighs together to try to relieve the ache.

I was left in nothing but my measly underthings and my long, pinkish-red gloves. Azurill licked his lips as he watched me panting in anticipation against the wall. There was nothing to hold me back now. I could give into him with zero guilt, and the freedom I felt in that was a *revelation*.

Azurill stepped back toward me, his hands finding the bare skin of my shoulders as he began to run his hands slowly down my body. His palms encompassed so much of me at once, and the feel of his hands cupping my breasts, running over my stomach, pinching my hips… I was sure I'd never been this worked up just from someone touching me above the waist before. My lower half wasn't even involved yet and I was about to turn into a puddle.

"You're so fucking beautiful," Azurill whispered in a rough voice, "*Linnea.*"

A ragged gasp tore from my throat, my heart surely about to rip out of my chest and fly away. My watering eyes met his, liquid pools of teal that shone with a light I had never seen before—a light that shone straight through to the *real* me.

"Az." I struggled to voice my words, the emotion choking me. "Please."

His lips caught mine, and as his tongue caressed my own, his fingers were busy ripping away my panties, a rush of cool air hitting my now exposed and overheated flesh. When he pulled his mouth away, I whined in protest until he began kissing down my body. Nipping and licking along the column of my throat and making me groan in delight, biting and sucking at my nipples in turn, and making me moan as the feeling shot straight to my clit.

He hit his knees, grabbing my thighs and hoisting me up until both legs rested over his shoulders, the wall doing the rest of the work to keep me upright. My gasp was lost in the moan that followed as Azurill dove into me with all the enthusiasm he'd been keeping leashed.

His tongue was *too* talented, licking up, around, and then down before swirling along my clit in repeated tight circles. My hand reached down to clutch at his hair, yanking on it and screaming out as he suddenly sucked my clit into his mouth, his teeth lightly scraping over it and making my voice hit a pitch I didn't even know was possible.

His other hand remained busy, teasing along my entrance before thrusting two fingers inside me. The sound was obscene in the very best way, my arousal having been built up after all the teasing. It allowed him to easily slide another finger in, those long, slender digits reaching up within me and hitting a spot that had twinkling diamonds flashing in my vision.

My hips bucked up into his mouth, his rumbling laugh adding an exquisite vibration just as his lips closed around my clit and his fingers thrust in deep and hard, forcing my orgasm from me without warning.

"Azurill!" I couldn't help screaming as my climax wracked through me, my entire body shaking as my nails gouged into the wall while the other hand used my grip on his hair to ride out my orgasm, forcing his face deeper as I undulated against him.

Not that he complained. He seemed quite happy to be buried between my thighs, lapping at me as he brought me down, until I sagged completely against the wall. Before I could begin to move my legs off his shoulders, he looked up with a pleased smirk and maneuvered my legs from their current position to his waist, hiking me further up the wall.

His hands went to his belt, unbuckling it quickly, before undoing his pants and shifting them down until his cock finally sprang free. My mouth about watered, and I reached out a hand to wrap around the hard shaft, pumping it once from the bottom to the top of his weeping head.

"Linnea," Azurill groaned, his head falling forward to rest against mine as I explored the delicious specimen before me. Enjoying the long descent each time I moved my hand, getting more excited by the second at the thought of it inside of me.

It had been way too long since I'd enjoyed a long, thick cock such as this, and Azurill promised to be a ride I'd enjoy for a *very* long time.

"I need you, *now*," he growled, brushing my hand away as I smirked delightedly.

My breath hitched as he notched himself at my entrance, pushing in slowly as my cunt stretched around his girth. My hands found his shoulders, digging my nails in and bracing myself as he filled me completely, bottoming out after an endless eternity of a minute.

We both watched the tantalizing image of his cock being engulfed, but once he was in, our eyes met. The spark between us ignited into a flame, and our lips met in a crash that I felt reverberate through my bones...though that could have also been the thrust of his hips as he hammered his cock back into me.

I was deliciously full, my tongue dueling with Azurill's as my limbs wrapped around him, and it was almost too much—this perfect moment I thought I could never have.

My hips thrust back against him, meeting his rhythm as he drove inside me with all the passion we'd had to hold back until now. When our lips parted to breathe, he instantly found my neck, leaving biting, sucking kisses that inflamed me and would surely leave marks tomorrow.

My hands clawed at his remaining clothing, throwing his vest to the floor before ripping his shirt straight down the middle and knocking it away. It provided me with a gorgeous view, his chiseled chest colored in the gems of every court. My hand found the pearl over his heart, making me swallow hard for a moment, before I distracted myself with the lines of his muscles instead, and I raked my nails down them. The hiss Azurill gave had a smirk rising on my lips.

"Fuck," Azurill groaned into my skin, "Never felt anything this good before. You're a dream I never thought I'd get, Linnea. A ghost that haunted me all my life, brought to life before my eyes in the form of the most perfect woman I could imagine. It feels like it can't be real."

"It's real, Az," I replied, my voice throaty and low from our exertions. "It's more real than anything I've experienced in fifteen years. My life ended the day my house fell. I've felt nothing but grief and anger since that day…until you." My voice caught, and he looked up to meet my eyes, slowing his thrusts slightly, the moment between us so intense, it felt like it could snap at any second. "I came here for vengeance, for an end to it all, but instead, you've made me feel like my life has begun again."

I slid my hand up to cup his cheek, our hips meeting and grinding together, my mouth opening on a silent moan, before I was able to whisper the words. "You're right, I *was* a ghost. But you've brought me back to life, Az."

Azurill moaned desperately, grabbing my face and bringing me back for a kiss that left my toes curling. He thrust his hips up into me in a hard, frantic rhythm. We clutched and clawed and bit at each other as if we could crack each other open and reach what laid inside, but as I felt my orgasm approaching, I didn't want it to end.

It was inevitable, however, and I let loose a bellowing scream as my orgasm exploded, my legs tightening around his hips as I bit down on his bottom lip. My walls clenched around Azurill's cock, making his hips stutter before he followed right behind me, releasing deep into me with a tortured groan.

"In this life, Mini-Dite," Azurill began, his teal eyes twinkling with promise, "I will ensure you have everything you were ever kept from. The rest of your long life will make your years outside court seem like a blip in comparison. I will give you everything you've been missing. I will ensure the rest of your life makes up for every year you lost."

My breath hitched at his heated words, his eyes captivating me as if I was under a spell as he concluded, "I will give you a life that shines brighter than any diamond."

I couldn't begin to form words, grabbing his face and bringing him in for a hard kiss, hoping to make him as breathless as he made me.

We were panting, sweaty, and yet not nearly done, our eyes met with a knowing gleam, and before I knew it, I was bent over the sofa, with Azurill sliding back inside me. The connection between us drove us on, the sofa, the bed, the wall again. It never felt like enough.

But we were determined to keep going until our bodies could no longer take it.

CHAPTER 44

Jacinth Linnea

WAKING up in an unfamiliar bed was normal for me. I did it constantly before coming to court, so it shouldn't have seemed strange at all.

And in many ways, it wasn't. It wasn't the bed at all, really. It was waking up in the arms of a man that my heart had somehow grown attached to, despite everything within me rebelling against it at first.

But now my head rested on his chest while my legs tangled with his. Yet more importantly, I was here as *myself*.

"Good morning, Mini Dite." Azurill's low rumble made chills break out over my skin, only for his hand to sweep down my side, soothing them over.

I sighed contentedly. "Good morning, Veri."

"We have today to plan before the last trial begins tomorrow," he murmured into my hair, "Before I call my council in to discuss everything, however, I still owe you my own truth."

In all the amazement of him accepting *my* truth, I'd forgotten that he had his own that needed to be brought to light.

"Before we call your council in, we should probably put on clothes." I teased, just to hear his morning-rough laugh in return. I traced my fingers over his tattoo once again, something I did often last night, still marveling that the pink pearl rested directly over his heart.

It took a while, with shared kisses and touches seeming much preferable to covering up, but we eventually managed to get dressed and sat on the chaise in his room, our hands entwined.

"You said you saw me that night." Azurill began uncomfortably, his eyes averted to the floor. "That it looked like the men had been ripped apart."

281

I squeezed his hand, nodding even if he couldn't see it. "They deserved it."

Azurill laughed sadly, shaking his head. "They did, but the way I did it…" He sighed miserably, "Every king since my ancestors forged these kingdoms into one, has had this same tattoo I do."

I looked curiously at him, and he lifted his face to meet my eyes head-on.

"It's spelled to pass from high king to high king, as long as they share my family's blood." He explained quietly, sorrow looming in those beautiful teal orbs. "Each gem," he pointed to the diamond on his neck, "This isn't just a tattoo; the real, actual gems are worked into the skin with magic."

My eyes went wide at the explanation, reaching out for his neck. He flinched slightly, as if expecting admonishment or disgust, and I softened, rolling my eyes fondly at him as I ran my fingers along the shape of the diamond. It felt just like a normal tattoo. Whatever magic had changed its properties to slip beneath the skin must have been powerful beyond measure.

"Because of this, I can call the power of the gems at any time," he continued, watching me closely for a reaction. "The nature of the tattoo means I can also combine all of the gems, and their properties seem to be amped up by the tributes to each god that surround them." He pointed to swirling designs surrounding each gem, and I realized they were highly detailed, yet so small that it was hard to notice unless pointed out.

"It allows you to do things with them that others can't." I realized, remembering the vision I saw. "You can do unbelievable things with them, can't you?"

"That's one way to put it," he said ruefully, squeezing my hand like I might leave if he didn't hold on. "Sometimes, the power is…too much. It can warp my reactions, make me more vengeful or violent." He hung his head, and I couldn't stand seeing him so upset over this.

"Azurill," I cupped his cheek with my free hand, "You are not a monster, okay? You're one of the best men I've ever met. We are all susceptible to those urges; you just have extra power behind them. Taking out a group of murderers who deserved it is the very last thing you should feel shame over. And who knows?" I shrugged casually. "Maybe it'll come in handy with Carnelian."

He stared at me blankly for a moment before barking out a laugh, shaking his head with a growing smile. "I should have known you, of all people, wouldn't mind. Not when you were out for blood and vengeance."

"Of course." I smiled impishly, shrugging. "Plus, it's very sexy when your eyes go silver and you get all growly."

His lips swept mine up once more, and I laughed into his mouth, wondering if this is what happiness felt like.

It sadly couldn't last all day, however. We had a job to do, after all. So, Azurill called his council into the room, and I watched anxiously as they all took in the fact that I was present. Ruri was the only one who seemed to really mind, rolling his eyes and collapsing on the sofa.

Arianell came forward and pulled me into a hug, much to my surprise.

"It's going to be so nice to have another woman around!" She groused good-naturedly. I laughed slightly, shaking my head.

"I still have to actually win," I reminded her, but before she could respond, Ruri spoke up.

"Why is she here?" He demanded, and Azurill reached over and slapped the back of his head. "Be nice. That's my future wife you're talking about."

My cheeks went red, a flush working its way down my body, which seemed to have gone strangely numb, even as I felt my blood rushing to my heart, pumping away twice as fast as normal.

Future wife.

I swallowed hard, trying to hold my emotional reaction in. Azurill came over and directed me to sit with him, keeping our hands together all the while. I had never loved him more. *Appreciated him more,* I corrected myself in a panic.

But I thankfully didn't have long to dwell on that mental slip, as Azurill launched into an explanation of everything that had happened since he'd last spoken with them about me. The reactions around the room varied, as we knew they would. I had prepared myself for it, but it was still overwhelming.

"You cannot be serious!" Ruri raged, throwing his hands up in the air. "You can't trust her!"

"She told him the truth, Ruri." Balthazar defended us, and I found myself completely shocked. I thought he'd be the wariest of them all. "She was manipulated by Carnelian, and when she realized the truth, she immediately confessed."

"She can't be held responsible for thinking it was Azurill." Wyn spoke up next, "She was a *child* when she heard Az was responsible for destroying everything she knew. I'd be pissed off too."

"Are you sure you can trust her?" Emrys asked, looking between us. "No offense, Lady Jac—uh, Lady Linnea." I smiled slightly at him, letting him know none was taken. It was reasonable for them to be worried.

"Trust me, I want nothing more than to get vengeance for my family," I told him, before looking over to Azurill. "Well, almost, anyway," I admitted.

Azurill smiled softly down at me, and I heard Arianell sigh happily. She reached up to dab at her shimmering opal eyes.

"I'm just glad you've found someone you actually want to marry," she teased with a shrug. "I thought that might have been an impossible task, to be honest."

Ruri continued to grumble a bit, but I knew the only way to convince him would be proving myself, which I set about trying to do.

"Carnelian wanted me to kill Az using a potion, but only after I won for some reason," I told them. "I'm not sure why, but there has to be a reason for that."

"Maybe to ensure he can have a cleaner sweep when he comes in to take over," Emrys suggested, striking his chin thoughtfully.

"He likely planned to kill Linnea after she completed her task," Azurill explained, his voice hard as he tightened his fingers around mine. "Which would leave him to come in and take over once he either proved Ruri incapable or killed him."

"So we need to time this perfectly." I jumped back in. "If I can hopefully win this last trial, then that night I'll make it seem like I'm going to kill Azurill." My voice dropped to a low growl at the thought, but I shook myself out of it. "Carnelian will likely only tell me the next steps then, but I imagine he'll want me to go to see him after. We need to make him come to Azurill's rooms instead, far away from his guards and allies, so that we can kill him. And Casaan."

"That will be difficult, Carnelian's always been a paranoid bastard," Wyn added, raising a sapphire brow.

"Maybe if you tell him that you don't feel comfortable staying in the palace once it's done, then you could convince him to go to Azurill's rooms to meet you." Emrys suggested, his opal eyes far away as he thought through the plan. "If you can get him and Casaan to show up, maybe with the excuse to the staff that they want to check on you or something of the like, then they'll be let in. You can also tell them they can raise the alarm then."

"Or we avoid them going to Azurill's rooms and just arrest them in their rooms?" Ruri asked, rolling his eyes. Emrys shook his head firmly in disagreement.

"Not only do we not want them to have support, but we can't just arrest them without proof of a crime either," he insisted. "We have Jacinth's, sorry *Linnea's*, word, yes, but most of the court only just met her and is more likely to take the word of a great lord. It would be a 'he said-she said' mess."

"We can use a truth potion," Ruri countered, leaning forward on his elbows. Emrys smirked, looking almost excited at being challenged.

"Truth spells can only be applied during court cases with the participant's agreement. Which Carnelian would never give," Emrys told him, and Ruri slouched back into his seat, running a hand over his face. He looked suddenly exhausted, and my heart ached for him.

"I know how you feel, Prince Ruri," I said softly, and his snarl as he looked up and opened his mouth to say something likely nasty did not slow me down at all. "If I had known about the threat to my family before they were killed, I would have done anything to save them. Especially after losing family, you're even more desperate for it. I didn't have that chance, but I know the horrible, aching emptiness left behind in its wake."

His eyes looked so young at that moment, *so scared*, that I smiled slightly at him. "I will do everything in my power to make sure that this family isn't further fractured. You have my word as the true-blooded Lady of Pearl Court."

He blinked in surprise, shifting his gaze to his elder brother. Azurill nodded at him, looking down at me with something warm in his eyes that I wanted to hoard for myself.

A warmth I hadn't felt in fifteen years. The warmth of a *family*. Of a *home*.

Perhaps I was closer than ever to recovering some sense of that.

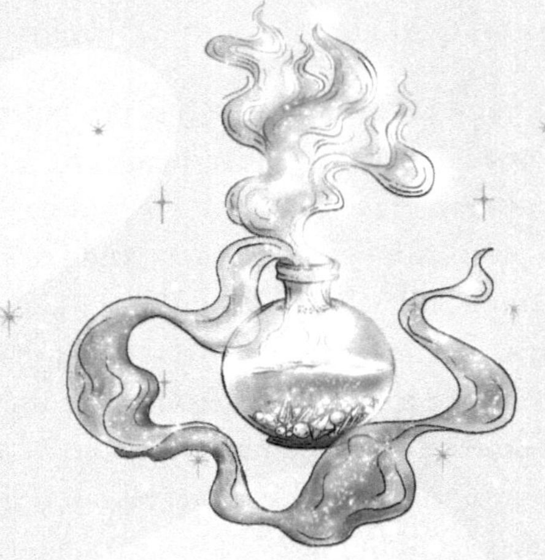

CHAPTER 45

Linnea

"Be careful," Azurill said quietly, biting his lip as he struggled to contain everything he wanted to say, but couldn't. "Be smart, but most of all, use your heart. I've seen you since you've arrived here, the way you are with people. You have a natural warmth and compassion that draws them to you. You had to bury that for so long to protect yourself, but you don't have to do that anymore."

He reached up to brush away the tear I felt slipping from my eye. I nodded silently, struggling to form words. I reached up and kissed him, a part of me terrified that I would fail this trial and have to watch as Sania walked away with everything I've ever wanted.

With the man who owned my heart entirely. I knew I could never get it back, and my entire future now rested on the results of this one trial.

"I promise," I whispered as we pulled back. I took a moment to caress his face, mesmerizing this moment, just in case. But then it was time to sneak away, Azurill watching me worriedly as I rushed back to my rooms to change for the competition.

I'd definitely stayed too long. I should have returned to my rooms last night, but I couldn't seem to help myself when it came to him.

I brought out the outfit I'd worn for the obstacle course, still not sure what we'd be doing in the city, but the fact that they'd requested we wear these made me suspicious. When the knock came, Alfrikr walked in with a smile on his face, a blindfold hanging from his fingers.

I sighed deeply, "Really?"

"Sorry," he snickered, not sounding the least bit sorry. "You're not supposed to know exactly where we drop you."

"And what am I supposed to do when I get there?" I asked, as he began tying the damn thing around my head.

"You need to find the Takara family," Alfrikr told me quietly. "There is a golden ring in their possession, studded with diamonds all the way around. That's your target."

"And I supposed to figure out how to find this family on my own?" I asked testily, making him chuckle.

"I've seen you handle worse odds before." His hands came to my shoulders, keeping me upright. "You can do this. I believe in you." His voice lowered, "Az believes in you. Just follow your heart."

Follow your heart. I had only just begun to learn how to do that, but so far, the results had definitely been worth it.

Now it was time to put it to the test.

Alfrikr walked me through the palace and out into the city streets. I could tell we were getting quite deep into a city I already wasn't overly familiar with, as we went up hills, down them, and seemed to be walking to fucking Pearl Court at this rate. By the time we came to a stop, I was exasperated and ready to get going.

Alfrikr removed my blindfold, smirking at me as I huffed, rubbing my eyes against the blinding sunlight. It seemed like the sun dragon must have had a few extra flames along their scales today, and I found myself wishing night would fall so the moon dragon could take over instead.

"Good luck on your quest, Lady Jacinth," Alfrikr told me solemnly, before disappearing into the city as if he'd never been there.

Leaving me to look around and take in my surroundings. The area had businesses and residential buildings mixed together as far as I could tell. Buildings several stories high lined either side of the cobblestone roads. Some were made of stone, and others were brightly painted wood, creating a beautiful mishmash of colors and textures.

And somewhere within was the Takara family, and the object I needed to win this competition. A fierce resolve rose within me. I may have started this competition with the goal of killing the high king, but I was now determined to marry him against all odds.

I began walking up and down the street I'd been left on, thinking through the few clues I'd been given. If I was going to win this then I had to consider all angles. I decided to start with the most simplistic route. A couple and their two children were passing by; a man with blue hair so light it looked almost white and a woman with dark sapphire-colored hair.

"Excuse me?" I called to them, making them both stop to look at me. "I was hoping you could point me in the direction of the Takara family?"

The couple looked at one another before smiling secretively, looking almost excited, oddly enough.

"Oh, my Lady," the woman began, "I'm afraid we aren't allowed to tell you, but I'm sure you'll find the right path."

I blinked in surprise, a soft "Oh" leaving my lips without my permission. The woman gave me a wink before huddling the children further along down the street.

Okay, so they'd clearly gotten all the citizens in on this, then. I was as impressed as I was surprised. How did they manage to get the message out to everyone?

While they didn't help lead me to the family I needed, the woman did mention finding the right path. Which meant I needed to find the right people to point me in the right direction. I tried asking several more people up and down the road, all with similar answers.

My frustration began to rise, and I took a deep breath as I considered what else to try. It was then I saw a young woman holding a baby on her lap, struggling as she begged for coins on the corner.

Follow your heart, they said, and my heart ached at the sight. It was so similar to my own experience, only I'd been the child myself, and without a mother to protect me. All thoughts of the competition left my head, and I walked up to her, slipping a few coins out of my pocket to hand her. Her eyes went wide, and her hand shook as she reached out to let them fall into her palm.

"Thank you, my Lady, you don't know what this means to me," she said tearfully, looking over the amount I'd given her. It may have been overly generous, but I knew what it felt like to survive the night with no food in your belly or a roof over your head.

"I do, actually." I smiled sadly, enclosing her palm around them. She smiled shakily, but held onto my hand, making me look at her curiously.

"Head further south, my Lady," she said in a low murmur. "Toward the residential section, where a pink house sits within a sea of blue. If you see the city gates, you'll have gone too far."

A surprised gasp slipped from my lips. I had completely forgotten about my goal in the face of her struggle, but I was indeed meant to be finding someone to give me the right clue. They'd told me to follow my heart, so perhaps they meant for us to find people needing help?

I thanked the woman profusely, taking off south and keeping my eyes peeled for the residential section. I spied it in the distance and ran the rest of the way, until I began seeing townhouses and apartment buildings surrounding me. I wandered aimlessly, keeping my eyes peeled for a pink house in a sea of blue.

As I passed through the streets, I finally spied several blue houses clumped together ahead. I sped off, my heart pumping as I indeed discovered a neighborhood full of different shades of blue. The long, winding street continued, slightly uphill, and as I crested the hill, I saw it.

A small, lone pink house sat at the bottom of the hill, surrounded on all sides by blue. I made my way to it and knocked on the wooden door, waiting until it was answered by what had to be the oldest Elven man I'd ever seen, with deep wrinkles lining his face and his hair having gone completely pale, who smiled at me kindly.

"Lady Jacinth, please come in," he said, much to my shock.

"Oh, of course," I said, my nerves rising as I looked around, unsure of my purpose here. "I'm honestly not quite sure why I'm here."

He chuckled warmly, "I know. High King Azurill was clear about that. You have two options before you, my Lady. I can give you a clue to someone who will get you to the family quicker, or if you help me, I can take part of the way in return."

Follow your heart.

My mind said getting there quicker was imperative if I wanted to win, but…if this man needed help, then I knew what the right choice was.

"I'll help you, of course." I smiled back at him. "What do you need?"

The man's smile widened, and he waved me through to a back room, which was filled with boxes from floor to ceiling. My eyes widened as I turned to him, and he looked around the room with a sigh.

"These items belonged to my beloved wife," he said quietly, grief echoing in his voice. "I can't bring myself to go through them. My daughter packed everything up before she returned to Onyx Court, but I need the papers she packed away. There's important information in them. If you can help me locate them, I'll help you in return."

"Right," I sighed, putting my hands on my hips as I observed my task. "Okay, nothing to it but to get started."

I began opening boxes, rifling through their contents as I watched the sun sink lower in the sky, biting my lip. But I kept on, and finally hit what I was sure I was looking for in the sixth stack of boxes. I checked the papers to be sure, and stopped in my tracks upon realizing they were instructions for his daughter for use upon his death.

A deep sigh left me, my body nearly shuddering with it, as I considered why he needed these now. I left the room, papers in hand, and found him drinking tea as he looked out on his little garden.

"Are you sick?" I asked quietly, making him turn his head to look at me. He sighed lightly, putting down his tea and coming closer.

"I'm dying, my Lady. The gods call me home, and I'll be able to see my wife again in the Otherworld." He looked at peace, and I found myself envying him for that surety. He had clearly lived a full life that he was happy with, and he seemed just as pleased to face what came next.

I swallowed hard, nodding at him. He chuckled raspily, taking the papers and laying them out neatly on the kitchen table, adding a note on top that had to be for his daughter.

"Well, we'd best get you where you need to be, hm?" he said after setting everything as he wanted it.

"How long do you have?" I couldn't help but ask.

"Not much longer, maybe tomorrow, maybe the next day," he replied, easily as anything.

"You shouldn't be alone," I argued, making him laugh and shake his head.

"High King Azurill said you were a feisty one! But I promise you, I won't be alone. My community will be here for me, and your desire to help an old man shows the kingdom will have a good queen in you, should you win, my Lady. Now, come along," he insisted, leading the way to a horse tied up beside his house.

"This is for you," he explained, while handing me a piece of paper. My eyes widened when I realized it was a map. Not just any map either, but one that had a star dotting the end point, with the name Takara right above it.

"Good luck, my Lady." He winked, making his way back inside as I shook my head in confusion. Azurill and his tests. The man lied to me about what the outcome of helping him would be, but in the very best way. This was much better than going through even more people to get clues. A direct map to the family meant my win was on the horizon.

I jumped up on the horse, eyeing the setting sun with a racing heart, and took off down the road, following the map to my future.

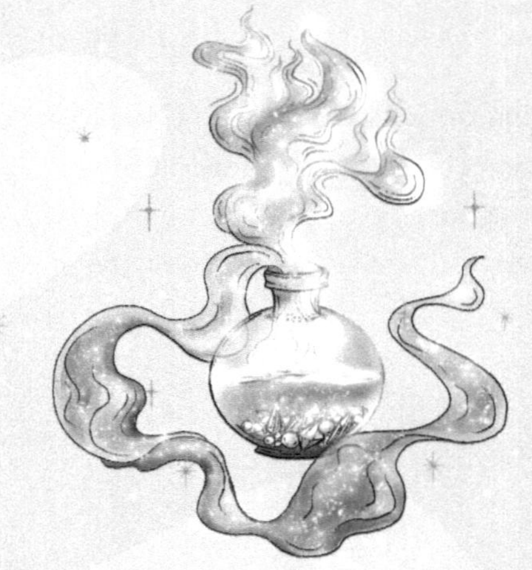

CHAPTER 46

Linnea

THE Takara family was quite a way across the city, and I rode as fast as I safely could without hitting any pedestrians, following the directions written out for me.

They lived in the poorer area of the city, near where the Forest of Discontent had spat us out. I slowed the horse as I neared my destination, and coming to a stop as I hit the street the star indicated. Dismounting, I tied the horse to the nearest tree, and made my way further down the road.

I was keeping my eyes peeled, examining every house for any indication of which one they lived in, when a little girl ran up the street with tears streaking down her face. The sun had already set completely, and I could only hope Sania had been similarly delayed. If we both succeed in getting the items, who arrives first may be what makes or breaks this for me.

"Are you alright?" I asked the girl softly, not wanting to scare her.

She hiccupped, looking up at me with luminous green eyes, tears over-flowing in buckets from them. She shook her head, whimpering, "I miss my daddy."

My heart clenched, and I kneeled down to her level. "Can I tell you a secret?"

She nodded slightly, and I leaned in to whisper, "I miss mine too."

"What happened to yours?" she asked quietly, lisping the tiniest bit. She grabbed at her long green hair, twirling it around her fingers in a nervous action I'd seen many children do. Myself included.

"He was killed," I told her, keeping my tone as light as I could. "What about yours?"

"He was too." She sniffled, rubbing her nose with the back of her hand. "He was a solider. Mama says he was very brave, and he served the realm, but I just want him back."

She broke down in tears again, and I hugged her to me, stroking her hair as I murmured to her. "I know, I would do anything to see mine again. But you know what?"

"What?" She hiccupped through her tears.

"My mother was killed along with my father, and I'd do anything to see her again, too. But it sounds like you still have yours, yes?" My voice was quiet, tinged with the pain of that loss and the vengeance I sought still incomplete.

I couldn't help wondering if it would ever lessen.

The little girl pulled back, looking at me with wide eyes. "Really? You lost her too?"

"I did." I nodded sadly. "Now, I bet your mother is really worried about you. Why don't we go see her?"

She nodded hurriedly, looking guilty, and I knew her poor mother was probably dealing with enough already without her child taking off. I had the little girl lead me back to her house, and she brought me to an apartment building where several adults, including one distraught-looking woman, were talking outside.

"Annika!" the woman cried as she spotted us, running immediately in our direction. The little girl took off, launching at her mother like a cannonball and making me smile softly. Pain wracked through me at the sight, right alongside my happiness at seeing them reunite.

"You were not supposed to take off on me like that," her mother cried, clutching her tightly. "I told you that we had an important job to do—"

"I missed daddy." The little girl interjected fiercely, making the woman's face crumple. "But it's okay, I found Lady Jacinth! And she told me she lost both her parents, not just one, and she'd do anything to see her mother again, and then I felt really bad."

The woman looked equally exasperated and fond as she listened to the child's babble, stroking the girl's hair as she calmed down from her fright.

"Ah, I see you did indeed find her." The woman's opal eyes locked on mine, and I realized then with a start that they must be the Takara family. The little girl didn't exactly do as she was supposed to, but she *did* find me.

"Lady Jacinth, thank you so much for returning Annika." The woman rose and came to take my hand, squeezing gratefully. I assured her it was nothing, but she smiled knowingly. "Come in, I believe there's something you need."

I followed them inside, Annika grabbing my hand and leading me along. Her excited bouncing was so at odds with the tears she couldn't stop earlier. I noticed the tea set out and realized they must have been expecting me. Azurill had certainly crafted quite the operation here.

"Please, have a seat." She smiled, pouring me a cup. "I'm Mica Takara, by the way. High King Azurill mentioned you needed something from me in order to win, but he didn't elaborate on what it was," she said as she sat down across from me.

She took a sip of her tea, fiddling with her cup nervously. I took a sip of the tea myself, gulping down more than was polite, only now realizing how thirsty I was. Let alone how hungry. I'd been at this trial all day, after all, with nary a minute to slow down and eat or drink.

"For our trial, we were told we each needed to bring back an item that will be given as tribute to the gods," I explained, taking a deep breath. "I was told I needed to get a ring from you. A golden ring with diamonds studded around it."

The woman gasped, lifting her left hand as her fingers went to twist her wedding ring around. A golden band…with diamonds surrounding it. *Fuck.* My heart fell into my stomach as my eyes widened.

"Your wedding ring…" I whispered, trying to come to terms with the idea, but it wasn't happening. The woman's eyes watered as she looked down at it.

"Celadon and I met when we were young." She said quietly, her eyes stuck on the ring. "Our parents both worked at the market, and their stalls were next to one another. We fell in love so slowly over the years, that I never even noticed it happening. But Celadon, he saved up for years for a ring. He told me he knew I was it for him the day we met, but I never believed him, not until he asked me to marry him, and showed me this beautiful ring that he'd only been able to get because he spent all those years saving for it. All because he thought that I deserved the best."

Tears fell down her face as she spoke, and moisture formed in my own eyes in sympathy as I grabbed at my chest over my heart, unable to believe that Azurill could ask me to do this.

"It's the same reason he joined the army." She sniffed, trying to stem her tears, looking so much like her daughter despite their different coloring. "He wanted to provide the best for me, *for us*, and the army paid more than any other job he could get. But there was an attack on the city. One of the lesser-known pirate families are apparently trying to make a name for themselves."

Mica's eyes closed in pain, and I bit my lips, trying to stop myself from making a sound and intruding on her pain.

"He went to help. To protect the city. To protect us. But he never came home. Leaving me and Annika on our own." She gasped for breath lightly. "If it weren't for the High King's support afterward, we would never have managed."

She went silent for a moment before opening her eyes. I could see the struggle in them, looking between me and the ring from the man she loved since childhood.

"Celadon hoped the ring could be passed down to Annika, but if the king needs it, I have to imagine there's a reason of some sort, even if I can't see it yet." Her face crumpled as she moved to take the ring off her finger, but before I knew what I was doing, I was reaching out and grasping her hand, stopping her.

Mica looked up at me with wide, surprised eyes, "Lady Jacinth?"

My hand was shaking as it held hers still. My whole body might have been. My entire future rested on taking this ring. The ring would be the tribute to ensure my reign as queen was blessed. It was the only way to win and even *become* queen.

The only way to marry Azurill.

My heart felt like it was splitting in two. I wanted nothing more than to win and marry him. I could admit now, even if only to myself, that I had somehow fallen in love with him. Despite everything, I yearned for Azurill with a ferocity that I'd never felt for anything besides vengeance in my entire life.

But I looked at the trembling hand covering Mica's, where the bracelet my own parents had passed down still circled my wrist. I needed that ring, but how could I take it from Mica? From Annika? Only a monster could take such a precious item from a grieving family.

"I—" My breath stuttered, "I can't take it."

"But Lady Jacinth," Mica shook her head in confusion, "You need it to win."

"Do you see this?" I asked her, lifting my hand and adjusting my pearl and diamond bracelet. When she nodded, I continued. "My parents gave this to me right before they died. It's been the only thing I had to connect me to them since. I wouldn't dream of taking an item like that away from you or your daughter."

Tears filled her eyes, along with a look of such intense thankfulness that I had to look away from it. "What about the competition?"

I looked back at her, taking a deep breath, even as my heart broke into pieces at the thought of Sania winning. Knowing Azurill would be out of reach forever. This was the problem with hope. The second you let it gain a foothold, it has the power to break you. And I could feel all the hope I'd built up now crumbling to dust.

I should have known better. I *did* know better, but I'd let myself forget. Let myself get swept up in Azurill and everything he represented.

"Any competition that asks for such a thing isn't one that I want any part of," I told her, and whether she was able to tell that was only half true or not, she reached out and hugged me. I let myself fall apart for a moment, kissing goodbye the future I'd envisioned.

But I buried it beneath the veneer I'd used for years to hide my emotions, rebuilding it brick by brick until I could make my way back to the palace. Knowing that I'd have to stand before Azurill and watch his beautiful face be swept by devastation as I announced my failure.

When I approached the palace, I found Alfrikr waiting for me. Sania had not returned to the palace yet, so I was led to my rooms to wait until she arrived for the final elimination. It was absolute torture. It took an entire extra day for her to arrive back, somehow taking twice as long as I had, leaving me to pace my rooms as my anxiety ate away at me.

I'd spent the entire day cut off from everyone, forced to wait until Sania made it back, abiding by the rules of the competition. Everyone had to find out the results at once, and I wasn't allowed to speak to anyone, even Azurill, in order to keep to those rules.

When the time finally came, Alfrikr led me back to the throne room, where Sania was already waiting. She looked worn and filthy, but triumphant, and my heart sank further. When Azurill walked into the room, I avoided looking up at him, keeping my eyes on the floor to avoid seeing his crushing disappointment when he realized the truth.

"Ladies and Gentlemen!" Azurill called out as he sat on his diamond throne. "I thank you all for coming to the final elimination of the Diamond Queen Competition. The round you've all been waiting for, where we'll find the next Diamond Queen of Gemaria."

The crowd cheered, and I spared a glance at Sania, who looked quite pleased, a smile on her face and her chin tilted haughtily in the air.

"Lady Sania, please step forward," Azurill commanded, and I watched her bounce forward in her excitement. "Do you have the item you were assigned?"

"Of course, Your Majesty." She curtseyed before him and pulled a dangling necklace from her pocket, holding it up for inspection. Azurill stepped forward and took it, nodding at her to step back. She did so happily, shooting me a look full of condescension as she did so.

"Lady Jacinth, please step forward," Azurill called, making me sigh deeply as my shoulders shrank under the view of the court.

I stepped forward, curtseying to Azurill and finally looking up at him. Our eyes met in a clash of pink and teal that still sent a shiver down my spine, even as I prepared to announce my failure and destroy everything.

"Do you have the item you were assigned?" he asked, a strange look in his eyes, looking almost frightened for a moment as I opened my mouth.

"I do not, Your Majesty," I answered quietly, and a lone gasp was heard around the court, as the rest of the crowd had gone deathly quiet.

"And why not?" Azurill asked, leaning forward, a smile twitching on his lips, confusing me thoroughly.

"The ring you sent me for belonged to a grieving widow, whose husband died protecting this very city. The ring is meant to go to their daughter, and while she was willing to hand it over just because you asked, I refused to take it from them," I admitted, closing my eyes briefly, before gathering my courage and opening them to see his expression.

I was completely taken aback to see the pride burning in his eyes.

"You refused to take it from them. Was this because you didn't want to win?" he asked, a large smile growing on his lips that didn't make any sense.

"No," I shook my head, now wholly confused at his reaction. "I didn't think it right to take such a precious item from them, just for the sake of my own future. It would have been cruel."

Azurill looked down for a minute, and when he looked back up, his smile was nearly beaming as he looked at me. "I must admit, this trial was the one I was the most set on, but also the most concerned about."

I blinked at him, trying to figure out what was going on here. A look at Sania proved her glee at my failure had already turned to bewilderment.

"This trial was all about testing one of the most important aspects for a queen: the ability to put our people first," he announced, a gleam dancing in his eyes. "You consistently chose to help people when the choice was presented, which is why you finished in half the time. Refusing to help people and choosing yourself instead made this particular trial much more difficult. You chose to help people. You followed your heart and refused to take something precious from them just to help yourself. You've more than proven throughout this competition that you have what it takes to be the Diamond Queen, and have thus proven yourself the champion!"

My heart raced, feeling like it might soar out of my chest as his words penetrated my dazed brain. Azurill stepped off his throne, offering me his hand, and I took it, blinking owlishly.

The idea that an entire future with this man was still possible had rattled my mind, but in the best of ways. Tears sprang to my eyes, disbelief and relief battling for dominance within me, and I gasped as the realization that I'd actually *won* settled within me.

"Ladies and Gentlemen, I give you the next Diamond Queen!" Azurill announced, his eyes twinkling at me as he smiled broadly. My own smile grew to meet it, and I couldn't help throwing my arms around his shoulders. Even though I told myself not to seem too enthusiastic, so that Carnelian wouldn't catch on, I reminded myself that this would be expected.

I allowed myself the moment to bask in this. I'd go back to pretending in a minute, but for now, I just wanted to bury my face in Azurill's neck and breathe in his scent, leather and mint and spice. His own arms came up to hug me to him, his broad hand covering my back as he whispered in my ear.

"I knew you could do it, Mini-Dite."

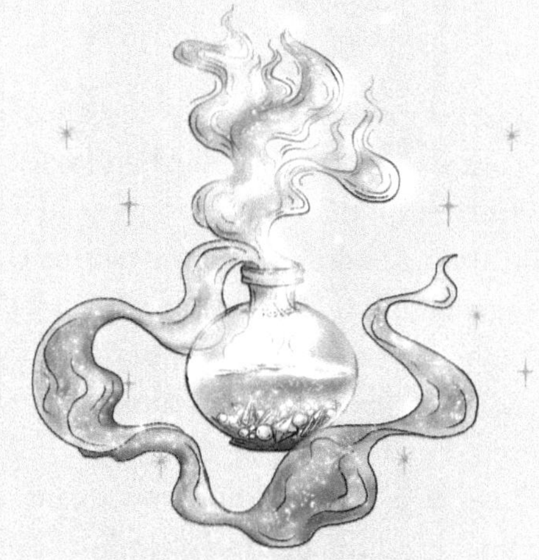

CHAPTER 47

Linnea

A CELEBRATORY ball was to be held that night, so I was whisked away from Azurill before I could even fully appreciate what had happened.

I had won.

I had actually won the Diamond Queen Competition. It felt entirely surreal, a childhood dream long lost and somehow resurrected.

I was definitely still in a daze, my mind unable to wrap around the idea that I would actually marry Azurill and become queen of Gemaria. It seemed like I would wake up at any moment and find myself sleeping on a lumpy mattress in an abandoned apartment, finding out the entire experience had been a dream.

I pinched myself on the arm to be sure, but it twinged in pain, and I remained wholly awake.

As the maids came in to help get me ready, they left my curls down, and braided some of my hair as I liked, creating a band across the top of my head that resembled a headband—or a crown. They dotted it with diamonds that twinkled in the light of my room. My makeup was done to match my features, giving me a dusting of pink across my lids, and outlining my eyes in black to make them pop.

When they pulled out the dress, I nearly gasped in shock. It was a lighter shade of blue than the kyanite shade they used for the royal family, and in fact matched the diamond tattoo on Azurill's neck perfectly. It also matched the diamonds strewn across the dress itself. Some of the diamonds were pure silvery white, and they were used to surround the light blue diamonds. The off-the-shoulder gown had gems across the neckline, continuing down to where the sleeves gripped my arms, with another set done like a belt around my waist, circling both my wrists where the draping sleeves narrowed in.

I hid my bracelet beneath the sleeve, but my pearl and diamond necklace was given all the attention as it draped down above my cleavage. I touched the large pink pearl dangling from it, overflowing with gratefulness that this piece of my family had found its way back to me. But there would be time later to focus on its miraculous recovery, for now, I turned my eyes downward to take in the rest of my dress.

The skirt itself had large slits in it up to my thighs, the blue fabric shimmering as I pushed my leg through to take it all in. The bottom of the dress flared dramatically around me, but the jewels on it were the real showstopper. Extra-large gems, representing every court, were all around the bottom, with some even sneaking a bit higher than the double row of gems. They were so large that the highest ones came to my calf.

It was a dress fit for the queen of Gemaria.

When the time came, Alfrikr arrived to escort me to the ball. I was led through a hall that circled around the back of the ballroom from its regular entrance, and Alfrikr explained that I would be announced before entering. I waited for my cue, knowing I would be introduced under my false name, but I could hardly wait for the confrontation with Carnelian to be over so that I could be my real self again.

I would finally be able to stop running.

"Now introducing, your future queen, Lady Jacinth Tawny!" the herald announced, and I swept into the room to the cheers of the court and its assembled guests. Azurill was waiting by the Sacred Gems, looking surreally small in comparison. He stepped forward to meet me, kissing my hand as I curtseyed before him.

He smirked up at me as his lips lingered on my skin, causing my skin to flush, remembering the last time his lips graced my skin. I was already anxious for a repeat of that night, but it would have to wait for this final task to be completed.

Azurill swept me into his arms as the music swelled, and I clasped his hand as he began to lead us.

"How are you feeling, Mini-Dite?" he asked quietly, ensuring our words were kept just between us.

"Overwhelmed, I think," I admitted, laughing slightly. "I never thought I'd get something like this."

"Like what?" he asked curiously, his head tilted to the side.

I lifted my hand from his shoulder to his cheek, running my thumb across it. "A future. I thought it was long lost, and my life would be nothing but surviving until it ended. But now…"

I trailed off, watching his face soften as he raised a brow, "Now?"

"Now, there's so much at my fingertips. I never thought I'd have the chance to live a real life again. Now, there's you, and that's more than I could have ever expected in any life," I told him earnestly, watching the heat spark in his eyes.

"Fuck, I really want to kiss you, but that would probably blow our entire operation," he murmured huskily, his hand knotting into my hair and tilting my face up toward his.

"Oh, Veri." I laughed, my voice rougher than I intended, "Maybe I was just that good at seducing you."

"That must be it," he whispered, before his lips met mine. We had to keep it light before we scandalized the entire court, but it was absolutely worth it. When his lips parted from mine, he pulled back to look at me, his eyes twinkling like thousands of diamonds.

"You must know I never expected anyone like you, Linnea," he whispered so very softly, so no one would hear my true name. Just hearing it from his lips sent my heart pounding in my chest while tears formed in my eyes that I had to blink away.

"I expected to be stuck with some vapid noble who wanted a crown. I always wanted a partner, like my parents had in each other, but I thought it was a lost cause when I started this competition. And then you walked in and turned everything I expected on its head. With that haunted look in your eyes and coloring that reminded me of my greatest regret…" He shook his head, a soft smile forming on his face. "And yet, you could make me laugh. You challenged me. You enchanted me like I'd never experienced before. I can't wait to have you ruling beside me, but even more than that, I can't wait to spend the rest of my life with you."

I couldn't help but kiss him again, my chest bursting with the feelings he inspired in me. I could only thank Erodite for leading me to this. I thought I'd been abandoned long ago, but perhaps this was always where I was meant to be. I may have had to go the long way around, but looking at Azurill now, I couldn't help but think it was worth it. Every night that was spent cold and hungry. Every day that I worried about being found. If it all led to him…then it was worth it.

When the song came to an end, we had to separate to work the room and mingle. I spent some time with my friends before making my way through the other nobles. When I spied Carnelian nearby, I excused myself from Lady Zariza Nephrite of Onyx, Ophira's mother, to head over to him.

"Lord Carnelian." I greeted him with a nod.

"Ah, Lady Jacinth." Carnelian's ruby eyes narrowed as they glinted down at me. "I was beginning to think you'd forgotten why you were here."

"Never, Lord Carnelian," I swore, taking a calm sip of my champagne as I imagined stabbing him repeatedly in the heart. "In fact, I'm here because it's time to follow through. Do you have the potion?"

"I do." He raised his brows expectantly.

"Azurill invited me to his rooms tonight," I told him, forcing myself to keep that veil over my features and only show him what he expected to see. "It's the perfect opportunity. I'll stop by and get the potion after the ball. Meet me at Azurill's rooms at midnight, and then I can slip out after it's done, while you handle the rest."

"Why don't you come to my rooms after it's done?" he asked, not looking impressed with my idea.

"Because I want to slip out right after it's done. But it's too risky for me to stick around with all his staff and family around." I told him, looking around as if I was nervous. "You can raise the alarm or just take over as you please. I'll head directly to Ruby Court to collect Ula."

"Hmm." Carnelian hummed, watching me carefully. "Very well. I can see your point. If you head to my castle, I'll send word that Ula is to be healed, and you can make your way from there."

Liar.

Was he planning to send word for them to kill me? Or was he planning to have them capture me so he can kill me himself? I didn't know, but I couldn't wait to end him myself before he could carry out any of his nefarious plans.

I spent the rest of the ball anxiously awaiting that chance, and as Lord Carnelian escorted me back to his rooms after, I felt like I might vibrate out of my skin. The idea that my vengeance was so close was as tantalizing as the idea that once it was done, I would have a whole new life with Azurill to live.

"Make sure you don't get this potion on you. Mix some in his drink when he's not looking, and you should have no issue," Carnelian explained, as he handed over the bottle with the swirling black, white, green, and pink potion inside it. "It will be completely undetectable once mixed with any liquid."

My hand closed around the bottle, nodding as I met his expectant gaze. "Not quite as bloody as I hoped, but it'll have to do."

Carnelian smirked, shaking his head. "It's best if no one knows exactly what happened, trust me on that."

"Very well." I sighed loudly, "I'll see you at midnight then."

"Yes, Casaan and I will come check on you, and everything will then be as it should be." He smiled smugly, and I had to clench my free hand into a fist to keep from punching him.

I made my way back to my rooms for appearances' sake before swiftly taking off for Azurill's rooms. By the time I made it there, I stopped short when I realized he was only wearing a pair of grey sleep pants, his tan upper body completely exposed, and his tattoo standing out in sharp relief. My eyes couldn't help tracking over his body, from the lines of his collarbone down his muscled abdomen to the V of his hips that led to where his pants hung low off them, teasing me with a trail of blue-green hair leading straight down.

"Look at you." I looked up at his gravelly voice, surprised out of my admiration, and found him staring at me in turn. "In my colors, like a true Diamond Queen."

I couldn't help the flush that took over my skin, pleased that he enjoyed the dress as much as I did. I'd barely blinked before he was suddenly in front of me.

"When will he be here?" Azurill growled, his eyes glinting like silver fire.

"Not until midnight," I told him, breathless as I found myself lifted off the ground. In a blur of movement, we were suddenly standing before his bed. The wide window allowed in the moonlight, which spilled over his bed, but I barely got a glimpse of a plush-looking kyanite-blue blanket and silver pillows before Azurill grabbed me by my arms to pull me into him, his mouth crashing into mine.

My hand found his chest, bracing against him as I surrendered completely to his plundering of my mouth. My tongue danced with his until I grew truly desperate for breath, and nipped his lip as I pulled back. Our eyes met, and I took a step backward; a predatory gleam sparked in his eyes and he pulled my hand, keeping me from escaping. I smirked playfully at him before I turned around, eyeing him as I gestured to my laced-up back pointedly.

A slow smirk appeared on his face to match mine, and he stepped forward, his fingers finding the laces and beginning to slowly untie them. He pulled my hair to the side, giving him space to work, but he took full advantage of the situation to kiss my neck. I moaned as he nipped the sensitive skin, kissing a path down my back as he exposed every new inch of skin to his lips.

When he reached the bottom of my laces, I let go of the hold I'd kept on the dress, letting it pool to the floor around me before turning to face Azurill. His eyes dipped down to take me in, licking his lips as he reached to grab me by the hips. I took the opportunity first, however, grabbing the edge of the pants he wore and thumbing them down over his hips, exposing him inch by inch until he was fully released.

His heavy cock jumped before me, making me smile slyly, but it was quickly wiped from my face as he pulled me into him. He kissed me hard as his hands found my breasts, squeezing and pinching and pulling moans and groans from me. Not to be outdone, I reached down to grasp his cock, letting my fingers wrap around his girth and pumping up and down. I reached down to slide my fingers through my rapidly pooling arousal before returning to his cock, using it to ease the glide of my hand around him.

He let out a tortured groan as he realized what I was doing.

"Do you object, Veri?" I teased lightly, even as his fingers chased after mine and took a swipe through my drenched folds for himself.

"Only that I didn't get to have a taste first, Mini-Dite," he grumbled, nipping my neck in retaliation. He brought his fingers to his mouth and sucked my arousal from them, making more pool between my thighs as his cock pulsed in my hand. "Fuck, I need you. Now."

His kiss was wild as he grabbed me by the waist and hoisted me onto the bed. He fell between my thighs, his cock sliding through the wetness gathered there for him. I thrust my hips up against him, chasing the feeling. I hadn't been able to stop thinking about how it had felt last time. It was so different from any other experience I'd had, and I was just as desperate as he seemed to repeat it.

His hands raked through my long hair, guiding my head to his to kiss me once more, as if his lips were drawn to mine beyond his control. It was frantic and hungry, the air around us feeling electric as we came together. His cock finally notched at my entrance and pushed in slowly, my back arching as he filled me completely.

The stretch was deliciously painful, the pleasure overwhelming, the slight pinch as he sank into me. More than that, it gave me that feeling of belonging that I'd lost. I'd hadn't had a home in years, but here, with Azurill inside me, I finally felt like I found a home again.

As he pulled his hips back, he pulled away to look down at me, our eyes meeting as he thrust back in. My lips parted on a gasp, and his eyes refused to leave mine as his hand slid up my body to grasp my breast, flicking my nipple before finally sacrificing eye contact to suck it into his mouth. My back bowed off the bed as I chased his lips, his teeth biting lightly around it as the feeling went straight to my clit.

His hands slid up my arms to hold my wrists above my head, his hips speeding up as he thrust into me with increasing speed, hitting harder and deeper, making me all but sing for him as my moans pitched higher with each thrust. I ached to wrap my arms around him but settled for my legs, crossing them behind his ass as I used the leverage to meet his thrusts. The sound was obscene with how wet I was for him, but the slap of skin on skin echoed through the room regardless.

When he finally released my breasts, he looked down at me with eyes shifting from varying shades of teal to silver and back again, the magic inside him was charged, and I swore I could feel it sparking between us. I arched my neck up to attack his lips, pulling him back to me the best way I knew how.

"Azurill…" I panted into his mouth.

"Linnea," he growled back, making me shiver against him.

I strained against his hold on my wrists until he smirked, finally releasing them before I used my new freedom to force him over, rolling us so I was on top. He groaned as he slid even deeper inside me, and I matched him with a scream of pleasure as I bottomed out on his cock. I quickly began to move, riding him hard as his hands found my bouncing breasts before falling to my hips and helping me. His hips thrust up every time I moved down, and I could feel my walls quaking around him as he spun me up further and further.

He leaned up and caught my mouth, releasing one of my hips so his fingers could find my clit, circling it and making me moan loudly even as our tongues dueled. My body trembled as the pleasure overtook me, and I couldn't do anything as Azurill pushed me backward, caging me in as my back hit the end of the bed. He grabbed my thighs and wrenched my legs apart as he pounded in with single-minded determination, so I reached down to rub my clit myself, making him groan, his eyes glued to the sight.

I could feel my orgasm rapidly descending, the tide inside me rising like a wave as I screamed out his name, a rush of arousal coating his cock as it crashed over me. His hips stuttered as he watched me cum, biting his lip as he watched the show. My back arched with pleasure as I rode it out, my nails digging into his thighs, the only part of him I could reach to ground myself. As my orgasm began to ebb, Azurill flipped me over and had me grab onto the headboard before he began to thrust into me hard and fast. My sensitive walls fluttered around his cock and his hands gripped my hips in just the right spot, making my eyes widen when I realized that I was going to cum again.

"Fuck," I yelped, "Azurill!"

As the second wave overtook me, Azurill's hips sped up slightly before he thrust once, twice, and came with a shout of my name, filling me completely as he fell on top of me. Letting go of the headboard, we both crashed down onto the pillows. Sticky and sweaty, but wholly satisfied.

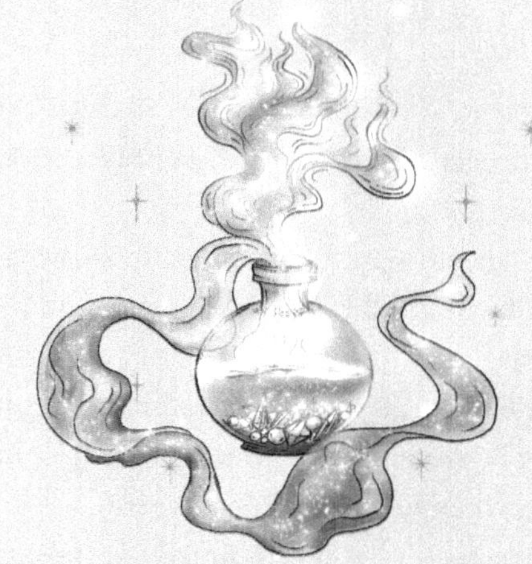

CHAPTER 48

Linnea

As the time ticked ever closer to midnight, we were forced to get out of bed, bathe, and redress. We knew the scent of sex wouldn't help sell our lie, but there was also no way Azurill was about to let me bathe alone. He certainly attempted it, of course, but he was quickly drawn into the water with me.

I limited us to one round there, knowing he would go all night if I let him.

"Once we're done with Carnelian, we can spend as much time in bed as you want, Az, I promise." I rolled my eyes at him, but he pulled me back into his chest, wrapping his arms around me from behind as his chin rested on my shoulder.

"I don't care if we just sleep, I just don't want to let you out of arms," he murmured in my ear, making me practically melt back against him. I wrapped my arms around his, closing my eyes for a moment as we swayed back and forth, enjoying a moment where we could just be. I hoped that once Carnelian was gone, this could be how it always was.

A knock at the door had us both sighing and pulling apart. He dropped a quick kiss on my head before we walked out into the main living area, opening the door to let Balthazar, Alwyn, and Ruri in. I wrapped my arms around myself, the nerves hitting me suddenly as I realized this was it; it was finally time to carry out the vengeance my family was due.

I had always thought that when the time came, I would avenge them with bloody glee, but now, I had something to lose.

"Don't worry, my Queen," Alwyn smiled charmingly with a bow, "We'll make sure this all goes swimmingly."

"She's not queen yet, Wyn, it's not proper to call her such until she's taken the vows," Ruri grumbled slightly, but there was a teasing note to his voice that warred with it.

"She's queen in all but name, now shut up so we can go over the plan, little brother." Azurill chastised him, making Ruri roll his eyes, but he sighed and nodded in defeat.

"Carnelian will be here at midnight," Balthazar began as we all sat down. "So we'll be waiting in Azurill's bedroom for you to lead him in there. Then we can ambush him when he's least expecting it."

"Unless he is expecting it." Alwyn pointed out, raising a sapphire eyebrow.

They argued back and forth, but there was no indication that Carnelian knew anything, so we could only follow the plan and hope for the best. Alwyn, Balthazar, and Ruri stood and went to determine where they'd position themselves in Azurill's room, and Azurill shut the door on them with a smile before turning to face me.

He opened his mouth to say something, but the door flew open before he could, and our heads turned to face the intruder. My heartbeat tripped over itself in my chest, fearing Carnelian had realized what we were up to, when it slowed in confusion at the sight of Lady Sania. Her orange hair was up in a high ponytail, and she wore leather trousers with a peasant blouse, looking very unlike I'd ever seen her, more like I dressed when I was up to no good.

I stood up in alarm, her orange eyes glowing with hate as she stared at me, a sneer on her lips. But as Azurill stood, everything moved too fast for me to react—Sania had already thrown a potion on the floor before us that exploded when it hit, black and pink liquid going everywhere before it turned to smoke, rising from the floor and assaulting my lungs.

I tried to move, only to find that I couldn't. I was completely paralyzed. My eyes frantically tried to find Azurill's, but they were frozen as well. All I could see was the triumphant look on Sania's face.

"Sorry to ruin your plans," Sania smiled, a nasty thing that I wanted to claw off her face. "Actually, no, I'm not." She laughed, sauntering forward toward where we stood like statues. I listened for the others, but no noise came from Azurill's room. I could only hope they were at least hearing this, even if the potion had reached them, too.

"Watching the two of you was honestly sickening, I must admit." She rolled her eyes, "But it did help with the plan, even I will never understand what you saw in her over me, Your Majesty." She bowed mockingly as she spat his title.

"Nothing to say, my dear King?" she taunted as she stepped in front of him. I could barely make out his profile, just enough to see that she was running her finger along his face. I could only imagine how much he wanted to rip it away from his skin.

"Well, I suppose that's for the best. Anything you have to say will only hasten your demise." She laughed cruelly. "Your precious Jacinth, oh, I'm sorry, your precious *Lady Linnea,* that should be, shouldn't it?" She gasped dramatically, putting her hand over her mouth as if shocked.

If my body wasn't already stuck, I absolutely would have frozen then. As it was, it felt like my heart was going to explode as the implications crashed around my mind. Each one was like a dagger to all of my hopes and dreams.

"Oh, did you think no one knew who you were?" Sania laughed cruelly as she stepped in front of me. "Did you think it happened by chance that you were caught that day?" She smiled widely, seeing something she was pleased by in my eyes. Likely, the panic was bubbling away like a nearly finished potion in there. "Oh yes, we knew long before you stepped foot in Ruby Court. He went to great pains to find you, you know. One little Marit rat still skittering around in the gutter. Just where you belonged."

She looked at Azurill then, smiling widely, and I could only imagine how he must be straining to move, his eyes likely gone fully silver, if the way her smile dropped was anything to go by. It was satisfying to at least some true nerves rise to the surface of her haughty exterior; looking distinctly unsettled as her eyes skittered away.

"Unfortunately for you, neither House Rousseau nor Helmi can allow you to live," she said with a faux frown on her face. "Fortunately for you, however, you still have a purpose to serve."

She walked forward, until we were directly face-to-face, no more than mere inches separating us. "Your family was smarter than they appeared, and placed a damn blood lock on the vaults. You must be wondering why Carnelian hasn't killed you?" she asked, cruel satisfaction practically dripping from her words. "With our loyalty to the future king, he will help us unlock the vaults using Marit blood, letting us finally access all the wealth of Pearl Court that should have long been ours."

She reached out and gripped my hair, pulling my face to hers with a sneer. "*Years*, we've had to rely on Carnelian for support as we withered due to your insipid family locking away everything! But now, not only will we finally have everything we're owed, but with the deal done, and Carnelian king, I will marry Casaan, and become the next High Queen after Sienna."

"All it'll take is getting rid of the king, and then you." She stepped back, letting me go with a shove hard enough that I tipped back and fell to the floor. Unable to catch myself with my frozen limbs, my head hit the floor hard, leaving me blearily blinking as she walked over to Azurill, pulling a potion from her pocket. She cut her eyes to me with a wicked smirk.

"Might want to say your goodbyes to your precious High King. This is where it ends for him." With that, she poured the black, opal, pink, and green potion down his throat, reaching out to block his nose and force him to swallow.

My soul seemed to cry out from inside me, even as my heart broke into pieces. I should have known this was all too good to be true, but I'd finally believed something better was in store for me. The loss of Azurill meant there was no future. It all would end with his death. I'd lost too many already, and I didn't even want to continue on without him. There would be nothing left worth living for.

Not that I'd have long, presumably. At least I would be joining him soon.

That didn't stop my fingers from trying to move, grappling for purchase so I could claw my way over to him. It didn't stop my heart from disintegrating into dust, or my soul from screaming even as I tried to use my voice to join it. I was a storm of despair and rage, wrapped in a block of ice that couldn't even weep. All of my tears, screams, and desperate begging were locked behind frozen lips, even as my teeth tore into them in helpless panic.

The world seemed to pause as I watched Azurill fall to the ground, his skin turning an alarming shade of blue, before Sania grabbed me by the hair, beginning to pull me away.

"It's time for you to serve your purpose." She spat, dragging me behind her. Leaving my eyes locked on Azurill, fighting for any last look I could get.

One I would wrap around my heart and keep with me until I could join him in the Otherworld.

CHAPTER 49

Linnea

Having dragged me back to Carnelian's rooms, Sania smiled happily when he opened the door. His eyes widened as she presented me like a prize, before he yanked her into the room by the arm.

"Casaan, grab her!" Carnelian demanded, pointing at my prone body. He turned rapidly to Sania, his eyes narrowing on her and making her smile fall from her doll-like face, withering under his intense gaze. "What have you done?"

"I thought you'd be pleased! I killed Azurill and got the Marit bitch so we can carry out our plans," she said, crossing her arms petulantly, looking like she was torn between pouting and crying.

"We had a plan!" he snapped, smoke practically coming out of his ears; he was fuming so hard, his face turning an unnatural shade of red to match the rest of him. "What did you use to supposedly kill him?"

"A potion!" she cried, holding her hands up in defense as he closed in on her, grabbing her arms and shaking her hard. "I made it myself, using onyx, pearl, and emerald."

"You absolute fool!" he yelled, spittle flying from his mouth and hitting her cheek, making her flinch back. "That won't kill him!"

"What?" she said, confused, mirroring my own thoughts.

"Azurill is the High King, you silly little girl! You have no idea of the magics you're dealing with." He harshly rebuked her, but she stood her ground, squaring her shoulders back as she met his red eyes.

"I saw him turn blue!" she argued, putting her hands on her hips. It made Carnelian pause, and he turned to his son.

311

"Go check," he commanded, and Casaan nodded before taking off without a word, clearly knowing when not to push his father. "The rest of you, prepare to leave."

He turned then to face me, a slow smile growing on his face. "At the very least, we have a way to lure him out should he have survived."

"You really think he did?" Sania asked meekly.

"Yes," he said, his voice clipped and harsh. I didn't know what to think; hope and hopelessness warred within me. If Azurill lived…

When Casaan came running back into the room, wide-eyed and breathless, we all knew the king lived. My heart soared as my fire, once ready to be extinguished, now seemed to reignite in my chest, until it was screaming for vengeance once more. Against every single one of them: *Carnelian. Casaan. Sania.*

Traitorous, back-stabbing, cowards. All of them.

Azurill lived, which meant there was hope for a future. If my love truly lived, I would fight with everything in me for that future together. All I had to do was wait for this potion to wear off and then… I would find my moment. I would show them *why* you never mess with the followers of Erodite. The goddess of love and hate was the most passionate of goddesses, and her followers had a capacity for both that was seriously intense.

Azurill had my love, and I would do anything to be reunited with him, and these traitors had my hate. I couldn't wait to show them how dangerous a thing that was for each of them. It fueled my need for vengeance in ways they didn't yet understand. *But they would.*

I already knew Sania was no true follower of Erodite. She would never have turned against her blood if she had been, for there was no greater sin to Erodite than to turn on the love of partner or family. She and her treacherous family chose wealth and power over blood ties. I wanted to laugh at the knowledge that they'd done all of that, only to be locked out of the vaults.

As it was, I sent a prayer in thanks to my father for thinking ahead.

"We'll return to Ruby Court immediately," Carnelian declared, but as he ran a hand through his long ruby-red hair, I could see the frazzled look in his eyes as his plan fell apart. "You'll be a useful hostage, and with your blood, we can finally open Pearl Court's vault. But don't worry, at least you'll be reunited with your dearest friend."

Ula.

Fuck, I'd tried not to think of her during all of this, tried to push thoughts of her to the deepest recesses of my heart so I could stay on task, but worry for her rose swift and hard. He could have been doing anything to her during all this time, especially since he never planned to let me live. And I'd all but handed her over to him.

I'd have to find a way to free us both. There was no other option. Ula had done so much for me; getting her out of this mess was the least I owed her.

Carnelian smirked at me as he instructed others to carry me out, and I could feel whatever potion Sania used pulling at me, my eyes slowly falling shut even as I tried to fight it and stay awake.

I desperately looked around to see where we were, for anyone I knew, even one last glance at the palace, but it was no use.

Blackness rushed in, and the next thing I knew, I opened my eyes to a wood-paneled room and smoothed rock under my feet. I blinked drowsily, finding myself in the middle of a room, surrounded by guards on all sides, with a ring of people a bit closer, comprised of Carnelian, Sienna, Casaan, Sania, and her parents, and…*Ula.*

My eyes widened, looking between them all, but lingering on the mint-green hair and eyes I hadn't seen in what felt like an entire lifetime. I tried to move, only to find myself unable to. I feared I was still frozen, but upon looking down, I found that I was merely tied to a chair. Onyx chains were crisscrossed around me, keeping me pliant.

"Good of you to finally join us, Lady Linnea," Lord Darcel drawled, raising his orange brow at me. I narrowed my eyes at him, sneering back.

"You don't get to speak my name you traitorous bastard," I growled, straining my chains and fighting against the drowsiness induced by the onyx.

He laughed lightly, turning his head to Carnelian, "You did say she was spirited."

"Yes." Carnelian stepped forward, his arms crossed against his chest. "But we don't have time for her foolishness. Word from the capital has already spread; we must work quickly."

"What do we need?" Darcel asked, an excited gleam in his eyes.

"Blood," Carnelian answered, and I scoffed, knowing they meant mine. *Of course.* He stepped forward, knife in hand, and grabbed my arm. I braced myself, readying for the pain, but when he brought the knife down, he fell backward, crying out in pain.

I blinked in surprise, and everyone looked at him and me in varying states of shock. Carnelian got up, brushing Sienna off with a glare when she tried to help him. He dusted himself off, and motioned to Darcel, who stepped forward and took the knife. I glared up at him, unable to believe I was related to this piece of shit.

I felt a bit of satisfaction watching him get similarly hurt trying to cut me, but I couldn't understand what was happening. Carnelian stepped forward again, grabbing my chin.

"What is happening?" Sania demanded, her petulant tone grating on my nerves.

"Where is it?" Carnelian asked me, making me shake my head.

"Where is what?" I truly had no idea what was going on, but he somehow had an idea.

"You're protected," he ground his teeth back and forth as Casaan scoffed in the background.

"By what?" he asked his father, who turned his glare on him, making him shrink back like the child he was.

"By something powerful." He ran his eyes over every inch of me before narrowing in on my necklace. My mother's pearl and diamond necklace. He reached out for it, and I wanted to slap his hand away, but the onyx chains kept me still. Thankfully, when he tried to grab the pearl hanging at the end, his hand stopped an inch away.

He ran his hand through the air above the pearl, seemingly feeling it out, before he growled, a sound I was surprised to hear from him. "A goddess. I would guess Erodite since the power lies in the pearl."

A gasp left my lips in tandem with Sania's.

"*My goddess?*" she asked, with a wailing note of panic in her voice. I laughed raggedly, lifting my head to look at her.

"Did you really think she would favor you after your wretched family betrayed mine?" I taunted her, leaving her wide eyes to find her father, frantically seeking reassurance. There had been something distinctly strange about that old Elven woman who'd given me the clam, and I realized now she must have been a messenger of some kind. Erodite had ensured that I had that necklace, and I could only send my thanks to my goddess for her protection.

"Regardless." Carnelian cut through the racket. "We need her blood. It will just have to be given willingly instead." I glared at him incredulously.

He glared right back at me, "You will cooperate."

"Really? Will I?" I scoffed, shaking my head, my eyes finding Ula's once more. A sinking feeling grew in my chest when she wouldn't meet my eyes, so I moved back to the ruby-red ones staring at me patiently.

"Oh yes." He gave me a smug smile, "Unless, of course, you don't care for your dear friend, Ula, here?"

I looked between the two of them as Carnelian walked over to her, placing his hand around her neck and squeezing slightly. Ula stiffened, looking back at him with wild eyes.

"You wouldn't!" she cried, and I had to fight back the nausea as I realized that she actually trusted him to some extent. "I did my part!"

My eyes closed in defeat. I didn't want to believe it. Ula had been there for me since I was a *child*. She'd all but raised me since the day she found me. Been there for me every day since. Taught me everything she knew. Kept me safe…

But she also taught me to survive.

Which is why I *did* believe it.

"What did he offer you?" I asked her softly, my eyes locking onto hers. Her face crumpled, her eyes closing as she shook her head.

Carnelian merely laughed, "Oh, don't play at guilt, my dear. You played your part fabulously! As soon as I located you, Lady Linnea," he spat my title like a curse, "I realized there was one sure way to get you here. Ula had to be convinced, don't get me wrong, but she soon saw the benefit of helping me. Small bits of poison, just enough to make Ula sick, but not *too* sick, to get you to just the right place where you'd walk into my castle willingly. A few false leads, and it was all too easy to draw you right in. As if I'd ever let a worker who knew of such a hole in my security live."

He shook his head at me like I was the biggest idiot he'd ever seen, and I couldn't even disagree with him. I'd been played from the beginning. From long before it, even. How long had Ula been planning this?

"What'd you get for selling me out?" I asked her dryly, even though I was swallowing back the tears I wanted to shed over her betrayal. For so long, she was the only person I trusted. But I had other people now, and Ula had always made it clear that she was out for herself first and foremost.

"Enough wealth to get herself out of the gutter." Sania laughed from the sidelines. "*Some people* don't want to live like rats, you know. Even if filth like you seems to prefer it, no matter how much you play at being a lady." She taunted, a proud look crossing her face as she lifted her nose haughtily.

"I'm sorry, Jac," Ula cried out, even as Carnelian's fingers clasped around her neck and squeezed. "He already knew who you were! I wouldn't have ever told him, but it was already too late."

"So you got what you could out of it," I answered back, raising a brow at her as I grit my teeth.

"Like I always taught you." She raised a brow back, a pleading look on her face. I closed my eyes to it, not wanting to see the earnestness on her face after what she did. She didn't deserve it. Even if I could understand it.

She didn't come from the same world I did. One where betrayal, like the kind perpetuated by the Helmi's, was seen as the worst action one could take against their blood. One where loyalty was expected among the nobility, even when they tried plotting to advance their station, it was assumed that they did so within the confines of that loyalty.

She came from the world I had grown to know. One where you did anything you could to survive. It was cut-throat, and Ula had taught me long ago not to trust a soul on the streets. She was right, and it was more proof that I never really belonged there. I tried to fool myself into being…if not happy, at least accepting of my circumstances. But after returning to my world, after being reawakened by Azurill, after finding friends I could rely on, I knew I could never go back.

"If you don't freely give your blood, your little friend here will die," Carnelian said with a bored tone that showed how little he cared about this. His only stake in this side of their plan was obviously just to get his loyal minions to stop mooching off him and finally be self-sufficient.

"Why should I care?" I asked him, keeping my face totally blank. "She literally just admitted to betraying me."

"Because I've learned a bit about you, watching you all this time," Carnelian said, a knowing gleam in his eye. "You may not want to care, but you do. You'll never forgive yourself if you let her die now."

I stared him down, watching Ula begin to choke as he tightened his fingers, a cruel gleam in his eyes. I wanted to call his bluff, believe that he wouldn't actually go through with it. She was his only leverage, after all. But as her eyes began to bulge and her skin tinted blue, I realized he seemed excited by the prospect of getting to kill her…

"Fine!" I finally cracked, along with my voice, "Fine. I'll give you the damn blood. But I don't give you permission to hurt me otherwise or in any way kill me. If you try, consider my permission revoked."

Azurill lived. I repeated the thought in my mind. There was still a chance I could get out of this before they could do anything, and money wasn't worth Ula's life, betrayal or not. Hopefully my words would cover my own ass in the process. Magic had an intelligence to it, based on intent and feeling, so I had to believe Erodite had my back here.

Carnelian released his hold on her neck with a disappointed sigh, and she fell to the ground, coughing and spluttering as she rubbed her neck. Our gazes met, and she shut her eyes to avoid the pity I knew was brimming in my stare. She'd made a deal with a demon, and she knew as well as I did that she was now reaping what she sowed.

Casaan stepped forward, blade in one hand and a potion bottle in the other, an amused smirk on his face. He brought the knife to my cheek as he knelt down beside me, digging the point in just enough to pierce the skin and make me bleed, but not a true cut. "Bet you wish you'd taken me up on my offer now, huh?"

I turned my head to look the lascivious bastard right in the eye, smiling sweetly at him, "I'd rather have died in the competition than ever lower myself to fuck the likes of you."

Watching his face fall into a furious little pout that I'm sure he thought was more of a glower, he ripped the sleeve of my dress down, nearly exposing my breast in the process. He ran the gleaming blade of his knife across my upper arm harshly, the blood spilling into the bottle he quickly raised to it.

"Maybe they'll let me take you before we kill you," he whispered into my ear, reaching up to push a curl of hair behind my ear, while I tried to twitch away from him. He laughed low in his throat, "I can make you scream in all kinds of ways before your final death."

"Or maybe *I'll* kill *you*," I responded as calmly as I could, knowing that I was basically provoking a deranged toddler. He proved me right by growling before backhanding me, sending the chair toppling over. I grunted as I hit the floor, the shock running up the right side of my body.

"Stuck up bitch," he snarled, reaching to grab me by the shoulders. "I'll show you—"

"Casaan!" his mother snapped, and I looked up, bewildered to find that Lady Sienna was my unexpected savior. "That's quite enough. You'll soon be a prince; you need to start acting like it."

Their blood acquired, the nobles were seemingly done with me for now. They left me surrounded by guards as Casaan whined to his mother about them ruining his fun and Sania whined to her father about her betrothed now wanting me, too, on top of Azurill and Erodite already favoring me over her. It was all just too much for her delicate ego to handle, apparently.

Carnelian watched me the entire time as the others made their way out. I tried not to show any reaction, but their ridiculousness made it difficult. His eyes narrowed on me before he spoke, "You might have a bit of protection for now, but we'll find a way around it. These things always have their loopholes, and you'll work just as well alive or dead when it comes to baiting Azurill. Don't get too comfortable."

"Gee, how difficult that will be in these chains," I replied sarcastically, before he shut the door with a glower.

If I had to die before leaving this room, I swore I'd find a way to take him and his pig of a son with me first.

CHAPTER 50

Azurill

A RAGGED gasp tore through my throat, and I blinked my eyes open to find Balthazar, Alwyn, and Ruri hovering above me.

"Brother, are you okay?" Ruri asked frantically, his hands fluttering around like he wanted to touch me to be sure, but was afraid of hurting me.

"What—" A cough forced its way out before I could finish, and I reached up to rub my sore throat. "The fuck?" I finally croaked out.

"We heard Lady Sania enter, but we were frozen before we could get out of the room," Balthazar answered, helping me sit up, with Alwyn taking the other side.

"Probably for the best, all things considered," Alwyn added, sapphire brows rising sardonically. "Something tells me she didn't want witnesses."

"Linnea?" I asked, looking around frantically as the memory of what had happened crystalized.

"Slow down, Az." Ruri grabbed my shoulder, but I brushed him off.

"Slow down?" I scoffed, shaking my head. "Where is she?" I demanded.

"They're gone," Emrys announced as he entered the room, Arianell following behind him and wringing her hands nervously. "Not one Ruby or Pearl courtier is left in the palace. All their carriages and horses are gone, too."

"How did they get out so fast?" Balthazar growled, a severe frown marring his face.

"They were clearly planning this," Arianell spoke up, shaking her head. "They were prepared."

"They have Linnea?" I demanded, looking between them all. They went quiet, refusing to meet my eyes, which was answer enough. I nodded, moving to grab my armor and weapons.

"Woah, woah!" Balthazar grabbed my hand as I reached for my sword, and I raised a brow at him. "We need a plan before we run off half-cocked, Az."

"Zar, I am not letting them have her one second longer than necessary, do you understand?" I met his eyes, letting him see the resolve pulsing through me. She'd been through enough in her life thanks to that asshole, I refused to let him take any more from her, especially not on my watch.

"They took her for a reason, don't you think this may be a trap?" he asked quietly, frosty-blue eyes watching intensely.

"I don't care," I snapped, looking at each of them in turn. "If you want to stay here, then fine, but I'm going after her. *Now*. She's been on her own for years because I failed to protect her family from the same fuckers who just took her! But now she has me." I panted, the pure rage coursing through me making it hard to breathe. "And I'm not leaving her alone ever again."

I turned and grabbed my sword, hefting its weight up and watching as the light made the blade shine. I couldn't wait to dull that shine with the ruby-red blood of the traitors who dared to take the woman I love from me.

"Now, which of you will help rescue your High Queen?" My brow lifted, and each of them bowed their heads in turn.

"Good." I nodded firmly. "Then let's go."

"Brother…" Ruri said slowly, walking up to me as I grabbed everything I needed. I sighed heavily, closing my eyes briefly and wishing, for just a moment, that he'd just go get ready and leave this for later.

"Ruri—" I started, but he held up a hand, and I fell silent.

"Do you love her?" he asked quietly, the suspicion that had been in his eyes from the beginning was gone, and all that was left was concern and a sort of bewildered confusion. "Truly?"

"I do." I nodded, my voice low as my thoughts went to wherever she may be right now. "More than I knew it was possible to love anyone. I didn't understand before. Not really. But loving her? It's changed everything, Brother. It's changed *me*. In a way I can hardly explain, but that feels more momentous than any act I've ever taken as High King."

Ruri nodded slowly and then smiled slightly. "Alright then, I'm with you."

I let out a slow breath, clasping his shoulder in thanks. He returned the motion, and our foreheads thunked together. Something we'd done for years, but the gesture was more reassuring than I could express.

"I'll go get ready," he said as he took his leave, and I was left in my empty bedroom with only my weapons for company. I had lived alone for decades, but one night with her in my bed had left the place feeling hollow without her, much like myself.

THE ROUTE TO Ruby Court was fairly direct, but we wanted to stay on backroads as much as possible. Both our horses and we ourselves were too recognizable. While Carnelian surely knew I was coming, he didn't need to know precisely when. Alfrikr and Brokk had joined Alwyn, Arianell, Balthazar, Emrys, Ruri, and me, along with some of our other guards and members of our army.

I was prepared to destroy Ruby Court if that's what it took. If stealth didn't work then I had the backup necessary to ram our way inside with brute force.

We came across several Ruby Court guards that we had to silence as we made our way across the court. I felt bad that we had to kill them, but they'd chosen their side, and they knew the cost going in. Treason wasn't something we could take lightly, and death was always the punishment.

But worse than even that, they'd taken Linnea. That earned them a fate worse than death. They were lucky I was in such a rush to get to her, or I would have taken my time with each and every one of them.

We left the main bulk of our force in the woods surrounding Carnelian's castle. The gray rocks shimmered with ruby-red flecks, looking ancient and foreboding from where it loomed in the distance. We had to take a few guards patrolling in the woods out, but that was just as easily accomplished as the others. We inched closer to the tree line; the guards around the perimeter were clearly tripled, but that wouldn't prove an issue as I nodded to the group of archers I'd brought along.

They pulled back their bowstrings, and a volley of arrows rained out of the forest and straight into each guard before they realized what had happened. With that, those of us heading inside ran forward, splitting up and making for each of the entrances. As I headed to the main door, I felt the haze of magic growing stronger around me. I raised my hand, letting it funnel through me, and the door blew open, letting us rush inside.

The clearly surprised guards raised their blades to keep us back, but with a few quick slices of our swords, they were each left in a pool of their own blood. Every door we went through seemed to have people waiting, and as more guards descended, I looked to Balthazar, who faithfully followed behind me. I nodded, and he nodded back with a deep sigh.

I remembered Linnea's reaction to finding out about the powers I possessed, the understanding she showed, and with that thought powering me, I ripped off my armor and exposed my chest—shocking the men before me into stillness for a moment. A moment they'd regret, as it gave me enough time to summon the magic from my tattoo, the different magics of each court rising out of my skin and swirling together into a ball before me. Their eyes widened, and they turned to run, but it was too late.

I sent the magic flying forward, and it blasted through them, blood and guts splattering everywhere. I called it back to me and gathered it like a gauntlet around each hand, watching as it swirled and surrounded my forearms. The colors of each gem sparked around them, lines of pink and blue, green and red, white and black, amethyst and silver, all dancing and ready for what was to come.

When the next room was full of guards, I punched straight through the first one to attack me, creating a crater in his chest. I ripped my arm from the bloody mess left behind, ignoring the red splatter now staining my hand. The guards looked at me in horror, the truth of my power finally revealed, showcasing the magic their lord coveted even when he didn't understand the depths of it. I gladly used the opportunity their shock presented to annihilate their numbers.

I blew the next door off and came to a room filled with yet more guards, but these ones were more prepared. They had potions in hand that they all immediately threw at me. I waved my hand in front of myself, putting up a barrier and watching as their potions rebounded. The result was just as catastrophic as if I'd used my magic on them. The potions were clearly deadly, and that death found them all quickly.

The next couple of rooms were empty, but when I entered the next, I found a smirking Casaan waiting for me. He clearly found my blood-soaked appearance unsettling, but it wasn't until he saw the magic around my arms that his smirk fell entirely, his entire confident gait loosening.

"Casaan," I rumbled, my voice deeper than normal from the magic coursing through me, and I was positive my eyes were pure molten silver death by now. "My betrothed has a particular bone to pick with you, and considering I owe her for being incapacitated while she was kidnapped, I think you're just the apology gift I need."

Casaan scoffed, but his eyes betrayed him, skittering to the door as he looked for escape. "If you speak of that little street rat whore who won your little games, there's little point in that; she's long dead."

My eyes narrowed in rage, but my magic was shimmering in the air, and I could *feel* the lie. The power of diamond lay in truth, and in this state, it was no problem to see right through him.

"Is that so?" I nearly purred, my magic flashing around me, likely pulsing in time with my eyes. Casaan gulped, staggering backward slightly as I advanced. When he tried to turn and run, I lashed out with onyx and dragged him right back.

"I can *feel* your lie, but just for attempting it…" his scream was music to my ears, and as I removed the dagger made of pure magic from his stomach, I turned him to face me. "Of course, after calling the future High Queen such names, you deserve—" another scream brought a wide smile to my face.

"Now, where is she?" I asked him and a sob left his mouth, making me roll my eyes at his pathetic response. I shook him, barking at him, "Where?"

"If I tell you, it's all over for me anyway," he hissed, before clamping his mouth shut. I sighed heavily before shrugging casually.

"Very well, we'll just do this the hard way." I smiled at him, making his eyes widen in fear. "Oh, don't worry, I still need you in one piece for Linnea. I won't damage you. Too badly, anyway."

He tried to fight, but it was little use, and I held him to the wall before sending my magic into his head, his thrashing not impeding me at all as the magic sought the location of my beloved from his mind. When I found it, I pulled it out as painfully as possible, not blunting the edges at all as I could have. His cries soothed the raging beast inside that was not yet sated. The magic was a force all its own, and when I gave myself up to it, I never knew how lost I would get within it.

And yet, my mind remained focused on one thing today. My mission still crystal clear, no matter how much power I called.

Linnea was like a beacon in my heart, calling me ever forward.

I grabbed the idiot sobbing on his knees. I did promise her she'd get her vengeance, after all. And what kind of king would I be if I didn't keep my word to my queen?

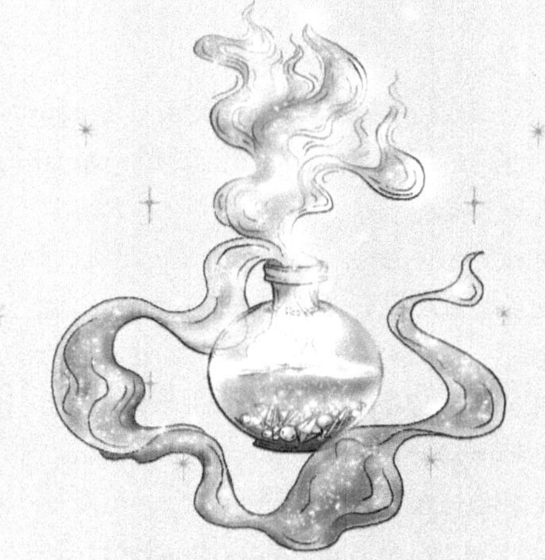

CHAPTER 51

Linnea

BEING shackled to a chair was boring beyond measure.

I couldn't relax, or the chair would tip over when my weight went too far to one side. The guards surrounding me were twitchy enough already, and the bang as the chair fell was likely to make them accidentally attack me in their fear.

They were right to be afraid.

The noises started a while ago, and as the roar of battle got closer, a smile began to tilt my lips. Carnelian had no idea who he was dealing with. Azurill played his truth close to the vest, letting Carnelian assume whatever he wanted, and filling in the gaps with wrong ideas that led him to this incredibly foolish scheme.

He'd been planning this for so long, seeding dissent among the lords and taking out my family to make way for the bootlickers who'd trot along faithfully in his wake.

And I was determined to show him what a mistake that truly was.

They'd left me much as I was, not realizing the gems on my dress were sharp enough to cut onyx. I began slowly running the chain along the sharp diamond encrusted around my wrist the moment Carnelian left the room. The guards were too concerned about who was coming to worry about who was in the room with them.

Another mistake.

The sound of a man flying into the wall made my head whip up from my task. The scream that followed made my smile broaden.

Azurill.

He was in the room next to me now, and I could practically feel his presence pulsing from it. The magic was rabid, thrashing at the walls and tearing apart any in its way.

The guards seemed to sense this too, however, and they immediately panicked. One of them looked back at me, considering, before looking to the back wall. He nodded to himself before stalking over to me, and I began to struggle in my chains as he dragged the chair backward.

"What are you doing?" Another guard asked him, confused.

The sound of a door opening filled my ears, as if the air had been sucked out of the room, and the guard picked up the chair with me in it, shoving me into what I knew right away was a closet. I stopped struggling immediately, my breath caught in my throat as panic overtook me.

"What does it look like?" The guard snapped, sweat beading at his temples, betraying his nerves. "I'm making sure she's out of sight."

With that, he shut the door, leaving me in pitch-black darkness. I closed my eyes against the tears filling them, memories assaulting me that were fresh once more since the magic trial. My heart was beating faster than I knew was possible, my limbs all shaking under the onyx chains. Panic was all I knew for a moment. Except…I also knew I wouldn't get anywhere like this. I slowly opened my eyes, spotting a small crack in the doorframe that let me see out to the room beyond.

So much like another closet, another fight.

But this time would be different. I wasn't a child anymore, and the enemy wasn't coming for me, I'd already been taken by that very same enemy. This time, it was my savior breaking into the house, coming to *free* me.

I wasn't a damsel in distress any longer, not like I was then. I was a grown woman who had spent her life learning how to survive. I wasn't going to let his small, dark space entrap me forever. In my youth. In my dreams. In these chains.

I was done hiding and running.

As I spied the guards preparing to attack through the small peephole, I began working again on the chain holding me. I was going to get out of this, and meet Azurill on equal footing. I refused to be trapped in the past anymore. I had a future waiting for me just beyond this door.

I bit my lip in excitement as the chain finally began to give way. I ran my wrist back and forth more quickly over it, and as a body crashed through the wall, flying back and hitting the opposite one, leaving an Elven-sized hole in it, the onyx chain finally gave, slinking to the floor with a loud clink.

The guards stood ready, but they were basically trembling like children at this point. The sound of loud, slow footsteps made one of them actually drop his sword before he skittered quickly to pick it up. When silver eyes appeared through the brand-new, giant hole in the wall, my smile broadened into a full grin.

"Azurill!" I called, throwing open the closet door fully, and those silver orbs found me immediately. The rage in them made me shiver in delight, and I let the remaining chains fall to the rocky floor as I stood and kicked the chair back, making it hit the closet wall. It made some of the guards turn back to look, and the split focus enabled us to work in tandem.

Azurill attacked the guards looking at me, and I threw myself at the guards watching him. The surprise was likely the only reason I was able to wrestle the guard's sword away, weakened as I still was by the onyx. My strength was coming back, but I definitely wasn't at my best quite yet.

I ran my new sword through the guard who chose the wrong lord to serve, catching sight in my peripheral of the massacre Azurill was making of the others. While I'd barely made it two steps from the closet I'd been trapped in, Azurill had already taken out half the room. Blood and limbs were splattered all over the once pristine space.

Watching as he used his magic to rip a man in half shouldn't be so arousing, but I couldn't help but bite my lip and press my thighs together before turning to the next guard who got brave. He clearly realized that I was the easier target and tried to grab me.

Azurill was there before he could, and I watched in awe as the man's hands disappeared before they could touch me. As the last guard fell into a pool of his own guts and blood, Azurill stood mere steps away from me. His blood-streaked chest was heaving, and his tattoos were glowing, with power seeping out and running in lines to form gauntlets around his forearms.

I'd never been so turned on in my *life*.

"Linnea," he breathed, the sound like a whisper but deeper, the thrum of power in his voice giving it a rumble that had me snapping out of my fog of arousal so I could throw myself at him.

"Azurill," I cried as I threw my arms around him, uncaring of the mess that was surely ruining my dress. I only cared that he was alive and before me now. His arms came around and held me tightly to him, his lips finding my neck and pressing urgent kisses to it, as if he was trying to assure himself that I was real.

"I'm so sorry, Nea," he murmured, the soft words and the new nickname making my heart trip in my chest. It was even better than Jac, because it was *true*. I hadn't minded going by my middle name, but I'd missed being my true self more than I knew. I hadn't heard anyone call me Nea or Lin or Linny, let alone Linnea, in so many years that every time I heard it now I felt breathless.

"You have nothing to be sorry for, Az." I buried my nose in the crook of his shoulder, inhaling his scent and letting it calm my racing heart.

"Still, I brought you a gift to make up for letting this happen," he said, an undertone of *something* to his voice that had me pulling back to look at him.

"A gift?" I raised an eyebrow at him, unable to help my smile.

"Oh yes, only the best for you, my love." He pressed a kiss to my cheek before stepping away, leaving me blinking away tears. *My love.* I definitely never expected to hear those words directed at me in my lifetime, and my heart did this weird melty thing in my chest that made it feel as if it grew in size in the process. All to encompass the love I held for this man. This Elven king who didn't care that I'd spent years out of court and living on the streets, who didn't care that his brother was suspicious of me, who didn't care that he'd been *right* to be—he loved me despite every reason he shouldn't.

And I was determined to spend the rest of my life proving myself worthy of that love, and ensuring he felt how encompassing my own love for him was. A scale I'd never known was even possible before meeting him.

Because no one else had ever seen all my lies and faults laid bare—and loved me anyway.

Azurill reached back through the hole in the wall and pulled a weeping man through it roughly, throwing him at my feet. A smirk graced my lips the moment I saw the short red hair. *Casaan.*

"Oh, love, you give the best gifts." I smiled widely at him, reaching to give him a lingering kiss above the beaten heir. When I pulled back, I couldn't help asking, "Please tell me you have a knife?"

Azurill smirked and pulled one out of his waistband, handing it over with a flourish. Taking it from him, I twirled it through my fingers as I admired the blade. Perfectly sharp and deadly, and encrusted with the diamonds of the court I'd spent years blaming for *his* crimes.

I leaned down to Casaan, balancing on the balls of my toes, and brought the knife to his cheek.

"You know," I began conversationally, "I was merely going to stab you, the way you stabbed my father. The way your men stabbed my mother. A knife sliding deep in your chest to take vengeance for what you did that night."

Casaan looked up at me with wide ruby eyes, trembling already as he shook his head desperately.

"But then you threatened to kill me in the vilest way I could imagine." My face, my voice, everything hardened in an instant, and I could feel Azurill snap to attention as the growl escaped his chest. But I kept my eyes locked on Casaan's.

"Please, I'm sorry!" he begged, tears beginning to fall from his eyes.

I scoffed at him, shaking my head, "Pathetic. Just a pathetic little man, riding daddy's coattails and taking advantage of those weaker than you. I could think of all sorts of creative ways to use this knife you know—"

"That's enough." The hard voice of the lord I most wanted to see sounded through the room, and I immediately jumped to my feet, Azurill and I both instinctively stepping together in front of Cassan and blocking his father from getting to him.

I heard the rustle of others stepping around us, and spared a quick glance to confirm Balthazar, Ruri, Emrys, Alwyn, and to my surprise, Arianell had joined us. All in battle armor with bloody swords and knives in hand. I was particularly curious about the double-bladed dagger Arianell was wielding, but kept my attention focused on the asshole in front of us for now.

"Enough?" I laughed wryly, "I haven't even gotten started yet."

"Nor will you." The bastard glared, his ruby eyes flaring with rage as he looked at us.

"Sorry, *Lord* Carnelian." Watching his eye twitch in annoyance was more satisfying than it should be. "But you made the mistake of leaving this Marit alive, and I'm going to ensure you're much too dead to ever take the throne that rightfully belongs to Azurill. I'm going to take the vengeance you've owed me for *far* too long."

Carnelian laughed, and I twitched forward, Azurill laying a hand on my lower back and calming me for the moment. When Carnelian pulled out a familiar-looking potion, however, my eyes widened, and I barely got to scream, "No!" before it was flying through the air.

Years of being a thief had given me instincts I trusted beyond anything else, and years of dance before that gave me the grace to move and twist through the air with reckless abandon. Both served me well through the years, but never as well as now.

I threw myself into a flip, sending me flying through the room in a dizzying spin. Before the potion got halfway, my hand snatched it midair, and I landed with panting breath. I turned my glare on Carnelian, backing up and placing the potion hurriedly into Ruri's hands as Azurill engaged the lord with blades. Azurill laughed in his face as he easily batted each blow away with the power running through him.

But he owed me blood, and blood I would take.

I rushed behind Carnelian while he was distracted with fighting Azurill, jumping on his back and placing my blade to his throat. He came to a standstill as my knife cut into the skin, his red blood dripping like rubies, matching the rest of him.

"You had my parents killed. My entire godsdamned household!" I screamed in his ear, "You forced me to live in hiding on the streets while you feasted and slept in feather beds. While I slept on lumpy mattresses in the cold, my stomach rumbling from hunger, and the nightmares of the night you destroyed my life ran on a loop in my head." I finished with a hiss.

"True power is only gained from bold moves." Carnelian sneered, even as he kept his head and neck completely still. "Your family was weak, and they lost everything because of it."

"They were strong," I argued, passionately. "Stronger than you'll *ever* be. Because they knew the value of love and loyalty, two things you will never understand."

"And you do?" He laughed wryly. "I've seen how you were raised, and I know you were taught to look out for yourself, to ensure your own position and survival. Just as I do. Don't be a hypocrite."

It was my turn to laugh, "A hypocrite? I was forced into survival mode because of you, but I was *not* raised that way. My *parents* raised me; Ula just picked up the slack once your monsters took them from me. And now, you're going to pay for every drop of blood spilled from *my* blood."

I swung myself around him and pushed him into the wall in one move, wanting to look him in the eyes, and then…I sank the knife deep into his chest. Not close enough to his heart to kill him, but close enough to watch his eyes widen in panic. When I pulled the knife out and stuck it in his abdomen, followed by his thigh, I watched happily as he sank back into the wall, his strength leaving him in ruby-red drops gushing from the wounds.

"Bring me Casaan," I said, waiting until Azurill and Balthazar brought the now sobbing would-be-prince before me. I looked into Carnelian's eyes, "You tried to exterminate House Marit, and for that crime, I will succeed where you failed and destroy every drop of Rousseau blood in this despicable court. Your line, your lands, your imagined dynasty, all *gone*. All thanks to the one little girl you couldn't kill."

If looks could kill, the hate and impotent rage in Carnelian's eyes as Ruri and Alwyn held him still would have left me dead on the floor, the way he'd once *thought* he'd left me. I looked down at Casaan consideringly, grabbing him by the chin and forcing him to meet my eyes.

"It seems only right to start with the one who started it all himself. The man who killed my parents directly." I smiled, a chilling thing, devoid of all warmth. I buried the new life and emotions I felt now for a moment to live in that wrath I'd spent so many years drowning in.

And then I stabbed Casaan straight through the heart.

The scream from his father echoed, and I looked to see Sienna racing into the room towards her son. A part of me almost felt bad for a moment before I remembered who these people were. They had brought this reckoning on themselves.

Emrys grabbed her, wrapping his arms around her flailing body as she tried to escape his grip, before manhandling her out of the room altogether. I looked at Azurill as I pulled the blade from the chest of my parents' murderer. There was no disgust, not from him, only understanding and vindication.

Erodite, how I loved that man.

"Once we're done with this one, we need to deal with the rest of them," I told him, and he smirked slowly at me.

"Does that mean the rest of us can play with the other members of House Rousseau? Or are you going to be greedy with them too?" he teased, making me bite my lip to stop the laugh from bubbling up.

I turned to Carnelian, considering. The shocked devastation in his eyes was everything I wanted, but I could tell he hadn't given up. Not yet. Maybe never. I hated to admit that I saw pieces of myself in him, but it gave me enough insight to know the truth.

People like us, we didn't bend. We could only break.

So I slipped my knife to the center of his throat and rammed it straight through. Watching with a smile as the great lord *broke*, his blood gushing out in ruby-red waves as he choked on it. His great noble blood turned against him in the end, destroying everything he was.

It was beautiful.

As I watched the light leave his eyes, my shoulders sank in shuddering relief. A type of peace I had never known overtaking me as I looked at the two dead lords before me. My family was finally avenged, and now, as I looked back to Azurill, my king, my love—I knew the future was finally looking brighter than any diamond.

CHAPTER 52

Linnea

"LOOK who we found, trying to scurry away like the rats they are," Emrys announced dramatically as he and Balthazar returned with several guards, each holding the arms of Lord Darcel, his wife, Grethyn, and finally, his daughter, Sania.

"Anyone want to explain why Lord Darcel here is carrying a vile of blood in his pocket?" Emrys asked, quirking a brow in my direction.

I was too busy glaring at the family in question to answer for a moment, lost in thoughts of how different things could have been if they hadn't betrayed us.

"My father was smart enough to lock Pearl's vaults with a blood lock," I finally explained, "As long as a member of the main line of House Marit lived, no others could open it."

"Damn," he whistled, "I knew Lord Elros was a crafty one."

I ignored his commentary, still staring at the members of House Helmi, and jumped when Azurill appeared beside me. He put a steadying hand on my back, and I turned my head to meet his eyes. I could see the question in them, and I wanted to reassure him I was alright, but my thoughts were so consumed, it would have to wait.

Instead, I stepped forward, grabbing Azurill's hand for strength as I opened my mouth to ask the only question left that mattered, "Was it worth it? Betraying your blood?"

"It would have been," Lord Darcel declared, looking down his nose at me. Those orange eyes, just like his daughter's, were full of unearned haughtiness. The features he shared with my father hurt too much to look at. Luckily, his

333

shoulder-length orange hair was completely different from the shorter pink locks my father had.

"Had Carnelian succeeded, I'm sure you would have quickly found out how little power you'd have had as one of his subordinates," Azurill spoke up, glaring at my cousin. "Count yourself lucky you'll never have to experience such."

He turned to face me then, running a thumb down my cheek, "What do you want done with them, my queen?"

I couldn't help smiling at him, squeezing his hand. "I want to spill their blood over where they had my parents' spilled."

Azurill smirked, nodding, "As you wish."

WE LEFT EMRYS and Arianell behind to manage Ruby Court. They would organize the task of stripping the castle's wealth and magic to bring back to Diamond, before Azurill figured out who would take over as lord of the court. I had my own ideas about that. Brokk's father may not be worthy, but we knew his son was. And if we secured the match with Faiza, it would not only help my friend, but would tie Diamond to Ruby.

Azurill's smile when I brought the idea up was enough to banish the darkness consuming my thoughts over what had to happen next.

We took a carriage to Pearl Court, and crossing the border, I closed my eyes and let the feel of the magic overcome me. When the carriage stopped, and Azurill jumped out, offering me a hand down, I stepped out and nearly fell to my knees.

Tears filled my eyes immediately, and Azurill wrapped his arms around me as a sob ripped from my throat. I collapsed into his arms, my hand coming up to cover my mouth in a vain attempt to prevent the sounds from escaping. But seeing it for the first time since that night brought everything back in startling focus.

The palace was crafted from white and pink marble and was crafted into several domed sections that were connected by long corridors. The largest and tallest dome made up the main section, where the great hall and all the main rooms resided. The giant pink door studded with pearls welcomed me home as one of the guards on the property opened it. Azurill had sent men ahead to clear out any who may have been loyal to the usurpers who'd taken over, leaving any who'd expressed dislike of them. We'd have to figure out restaffing in the future, but that was a problem for another day.

When I'd finally cried myself out, Azurill wiped my tears away, whispering in my ear, "You've overcome so much, you deserve this palace and court more than anyone. But I selfishly wish to keep you with me. Say the word, however, and we'll keep you as Lady of Pearl Court."

I laughed lightly, leaning up to kiss him. My hand came around to hold the back of his head, keeping our foreheads together as I whispered back, "As happy as I am to return home, I'm not sure I could live here again after all that's happened. Perhaps one of our children could take over one day?"

A wide smile broke out on his face, "An excellent idea, my love."

He led me to the door, and I gasped in shock as we walked through.

"Welcome home, my Lady," The woman said, tears already running down her face.

"Juvela?" I whimpered, running and throwing my arms around her. She laughed wetly, hugging me tightly and petting my hair as she used to do when I was young. She'd been my nanny for many years, like a second mother, and I had thought her to be lost with all the others.

"Oh, my darling girl," She murmured, kissing the side of my head. "I'm so sorry for everything that's happened. But your parents would be so happy to see you home again. As am I."

"I thought everyone was gone," I choked out, squeezing her again.

She pulled back to look at me, marveling as much at my appearance as I was at hers. "We were out of town that night. When I returned home the next morning, I found out what had happened. I was devastated, but I did try to work for House Helmi at first. When it became clear they were not like your parents, however, I left. I haven't been back until now. When I heard the news that you were alive and coming home; I returned immediately. You deserved to have a friendly face here to greet you."

"Thank Erodite." I closed my eyes momentarily, amazed to have even one precious person returned to me. "Any chance you'd want to come to Diamond? I'm to be married, and as High Queen, I'll need a nanny once we have children."

She laughed merrily, "Oh, my girl, you'd have to bat me away with a stick. I've missed you too much, and we have so much to catch up on!"

"We appreciate you returning to meet with Linnea, my lady," Azurill stepped forward, sliding an arm around me, "More than I can say."

"Your Majesty." She curtseyed, her pink eyes glowing as she smiled imp-ishly, "You must tell me how you charmed our Linnea here, then."

I laughed, shaking my head at her, "Where is Zav? He's got to be around here to rein you in, right?"

She faux glared at me as her husband came in from the next room, "I'm never far, you know that, little Lady."

I smiled widely, taking a running jump as I threw my arms around him. He laughed loudly, the sound filling the air as he spun me around like he did when I was a child. I looked over to Azurill, noticing the bright smile on his face that matched my own.

I could feel the magic of Pearl Court filling me up, finally standing in my home after so many years away, and with Juvela and Zav both returned to me, I felt light enough to fly.

I had once thought my life had ended right here in these halls, but now, it felt as if my life had finally begun. With Azurill beside me, I knew whatever was going to come next would be even better than I could imagine.

Once we got rid of the usurpers, all would be right with the world. Every single person responsible for my family's end would be gone, and I could finally live free of the need for vengeance that had been rotting in my heart for years. Instead, I could now live with nothing but love in there.

The way it had always been meant to be.

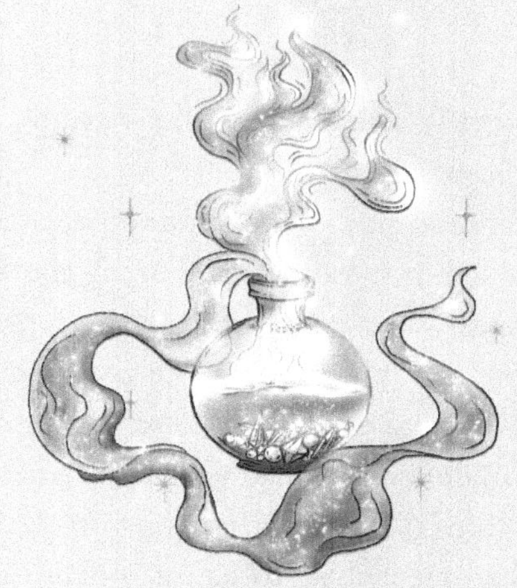

EPILOGUE 1

Linnea

"I MERELY mean to state that, as her role in the competition was not undertaken with her real identity, and her true one means that she could only participate as Pearl Court's competitor, that—"

"Lord Neel," Azurill snapped, the ice in his eyes shutting the rambling lord's lips at once. "If you mean to say that your future Queen was ineligible, I can assure you that's not the case."

"In fact, since Sania was not the true Pearl Court contestant, with Lady Linnea still alive, and with Sania working for Carnelian and all, we can actually consider her the Ruby Court competitor. In that case, Lady Linnea would be Pearl Court's," Emrys interjected, before Azurill could rip the lord of Sapphire Court apart.

His bitterness over the situation could be understood, since his daughter hadn't won, but at least his second daughter had secured herself a great marriage to the future lord of Opal Court. Still, I was determined to help Safira get out from under this prick in the future.

We'd been round and round this discussion for over an hour after Azurill laid out everything that had happened to the lords. With Ruby and Pearl both needing new heads, and Emerald in a precarious position thanks to Zumra, the lords were all understandably shaken and all seeking to reassure their own positions.

"Now, the marriage and crowning will be taking place within the week, and at that time, we'll announce our decisions on the fates of the courts in question," Azurill announced, and with that, court was clearly adjourned. He stood, taking my hand, and leading me out of the room.

"Do you think they'll fight against what we're planning?" I asked him quietly, getting a small snort in return.

"I'm sure they'll argue, but they won't put up any real fight. Don't worry, Mini-Dite," he teased lightly, pressing a kiss to my cheek.

The rest of the week was taken up with so much planning, my head was about ready to spin off my neck. Thank the gods for Faiza, Amatista, and Allirea, who helped me more than I could ever express. But more than even them, the Queen-Mother, Elestren, had wasted no time in taking me on as an adopted daughter, thrilled that I was marrying into the family.

She and Juvela had teamed up to help me plan the wedding, and they took so much pressure off my shoulders. I was able to eagerly look forward to marrying the man of my dreams instead of wanting to tear my hair out.

When the day finally dawned, however, I was a bundle of nerves. As much as I was anticipating this, it was still a huge step, becoming not just Azurill's wife, but High Queen of Gemaria. I was still adjusting to people even referring to me as Lady Linnea. And my friends made certain to chastise me for not telling them, lovingly expressing that they wouldn't have said a word to betray my confidence, but with the teasing I loved from them. Amatista insisted every time that she had figured it out, and I always expressed my doubt with a laugh, despite fully believing her. She was too smart for her own good, and the look on her face was priceless.

If this was what my life was going to be like from now on, I couldn't wait. And today would cement that, along with my marriage.

My ladies surrounded me as I was helped into my dress. It was beyond anything I ever imagined. The gown was silver at the top, with a sweetheart neckline, then shifted to blue at the top of the skirt, and faded into pink at the bottom. The sleeves were off-the-shoulder, ringed by large diamonds at the top, with sheer pink fabric that draped to the floor, split down the middle so my arms were free to move. The entire dress was encrusted with diamonds, kyanites, and pearls, matching the colors of the dress, and combining both of our home courts with the family I'd be marrying into.

In addition to my mother's necklace and bracelet, Azurill had asked to take care of the rest of my jewelry, so I was waiting to see what he'd selected for me as Elestren, or El, as she insisted I call her, brought the boxes over.

"Azurill asked me to give you this before you opened them." She smiled softly as she handed me a letter, and I took it with a shaking hand.

To the Love of My Life,

I am more excited than I can express to marry you today. More than any other man in history has been, I'm sure. You amaze me in so many ways. Your strength and resilience, along with your kindness and beauty, are unmatched and unequaled by all others. I know you will be a High Queen who shines through the years like the brightest of diamonds.

I wanted something that would represent everything you mean to me, how deeply my heart beats for you, but found everything lacking. How can I possibly give you any jewels that could compare to yourself, my perfect Pearl?

The best I can do is offer you this piece of myself. These items have been passed down in my family for generations, and I had them altered slightly to represent you as well. A piece of me and a piece of you, forever intertwined, as we will be after today.

You were the greatest surprise of my life, Mini-Dite, and I can't wait for you to continue surprising me each and every day.

With all my love,

Azurill

Aka Veri Full of Himself

I laughed wetly at the end, knuckling away tears so I'd wouldn't destroy my makeup. The artists had worked hard to make me up just so, and they would absolutely kill me if they had to redo it now.

But that sweet, sweet man had a way with words. My fingers itched to open the boxes, and as his mother handed me the first one, I snatched it eagerly. Opening the top, I gasped, finding a stunning necklace that would layer perfectly with my mother's. It had diamonds and sapphires worked all the way around it, but a few pink pearls had been added in, including one that was directly in the center when it was clasped around my neck.

The next box was larger and contained a diadem that would soon be replaced by a full tiara. This one was all diamond, with sapphires creating looping designs on the sides, and the center design had been replaced with pink pearls. It was absolutely gorgeous, and I immediately handed it over to be put in my hair. Most of it was left down and my curls were now high-lighted by small diamonds that twinkled as I moved my head. The top of my hair was gathered up and pinned to create a pink waterfall that flowed down the back. The diadem fit perfectly right at the top, looking as if it was made specifically for me.

"Oh, Nea, you look absolutely breathtaking," Faiza gasped, leaning over to hug me tightly. I squeezed her back, thanking her with a kiss on the cheek.

Amatista was next, hugging me tightly and whispering, "You will be the best queen this kingdom has ever seen."

"And I'll make sure you live your happily ever after as well, Tista," I whispered back, closing my eyes as I made my promise. I wouldn't let her father sell her off for an alliance. I would ensure she lived the life she wanted with the woman she loved.

Allirea leaned in to hug me next, and Safira even made an appearance. The others were still on edge around her, but I knew with time we could break those barriers down. When the time finally came, Zav appeared to walk me down the aisle. Elestren and Juvela, along with Allirea, Amatista, and Faiza, all left to join the crowd.

"Stop trembling, little pearl, this is a happy day," Zav whispered, winking at me when I looked up.

I couldn't help my smile, leaning into him as we walked out. "Thank you for doing this."

"It's my greatest honor, Linnea," he said, growing serious. "Your father was one of the greatest men I knew, and I owed everything to him. I'm so sorry that we were separated for so long. We spent so many years mourning you, little pearl, but Juvela and I will always be here for you. Never question that."

I fought back the tears, pressing a kiss to the side of his jaw where I could reach, and he gave me a quick side hug before we appeared at the end of the aisle.

My breath caught as I looked up, finding Azurill waiting for me at the other end. Everyone else might as well have not existed at that moment. Everything I'd ever wanted was staring back at me, and I could have run to the end of the aisle with the anticipation buzzing in my chest. It felt like his soul was pulling at mine, like a magnet forcing me forward.

He took my hands when we reached him, his teal eyes luminous as he stared back at me with an expression full of love and awe. I squeezed his hands, barely paying any attention to the vows, just wanting to be married to the man before me.

"By the grace of the gods, Veritx, god of Diamond, and Erodite, goddess of Pearl, we join these two in sacred love and marriage for eternity." Ikelos, the Sacred Gemholder, concluded, and with that, it was finally done. Azurill leaned down to kiss me and the crowd cheered as I lost myself in his lips.

Before I knew it, we had to part, and we smiled at one another foolishly as Ikelos came over with the diamond scepter in hand, handing it to Azurill.

"My dearest wife, please kneel," he said with a wide smile, and I knelt before him with a racing heart.

"Today, you have become the wife to the High King of Gemaria, and now you must be sworn in as its High Queen," he stated, a gravitas to his voice that pulsed with power.

"Do you, Lady Linnea Alankar, swear by the Sacred Gems and all the gods, to rule well and wisely, for the good of all, from the highest to lowest, with fairness and grace?" he asked, holding the scepter above my right shoulder.

"I do," I swore with a nod, and the scepter, with its large diamond on top, surrounded by the smaller gems of each court, pulsed with light at my answer.

"Do you swear to abide by the laws of the lands and the gods, to ensure the kingdom continues to rise and flourish?" he asked, the scepter above my left shoulder this time.

"I swear." I nodded, the light pulsing once more. I understood more was happening than I could see. With each oath, the gods would delve deep inside my very soul, searching out my worthiness for the task set before me. The light was their acceptance, and a breath of relief left me at each one. I had worried I wouldn't be found worthy, but Azurill had declared that ridiculous to even consider.

"Then by the grace of Veritx, and all the gods, I now pronounce you, Lady Linnea Alankar, High Queen of Gemaria." He held the scepter over my head, and light exploded out of it, bathing the room in an otherworldly glow.

The crowd hushed at the display before exploding in cheers as Azurill helped me stand. He waved a hand, and several men came to remove the expansive backdrop decorated with flowers and gems, along with the gorgeous marriage arch, which was blocking where his throne stood. I gasped when I realized that another throne had been added to the dais, and turned to look at my new husband with wide eyes. He smiled slyly, offering a hand to help me up the steps.

I took it, looking back with watering eyes to the new throne stationed beside his. Where his was carved from a diamond with a blue center, mine had been carved from an ultra-rare diamond with a pink center. The gems of every court were displayed across the arched backrest and pink pearls had been added along the arms and legs. It was truly made just for me, and I stared at him in shock as I turned around to sit in it.

"You deserve it, my love," he whispered, pressing a quick kiss to the side of my mouth.

I sat down, feeling the enormity of the moment as the crowd hushed, the entire room seeming to resonate with power for a moment before a gust of wind rushed through the room. Azurill smiled broadly before he gestured to Ikelos, who handed him what I guessed to be a crown covered with a silver cloth.

He faked tugging the cloth off, teasing me for a moment, before he finally smirked and removed it, making my mouth drop open. The tiara was similar to his crown, but more feminine and delicate. A large diamond sat in the middle, the silver sparkling metal flaring out from it, and two large pink pearls were anchored on either side. The other gems of every court were worked in around them in beautiful swirling patterns.

I reached up and removed the diadem, handing it off to Ikelos, before Azurill placed the crown on my head.

"All hail High Queen Linnea!" Azurill called, the rest of the room echoing him, before he sat down on his throne beside mine, reaching over to clasp my hand. I squeezed his, our arms reaching across and connecting us from our joint thrones, staring out as the court kneeled before us both.

This was the future. *My future.* One I never expected to have, but one full of love and happiness, replacing the vengeance and wrath that once consumed me.

I couldn't wait to see what it brought next.

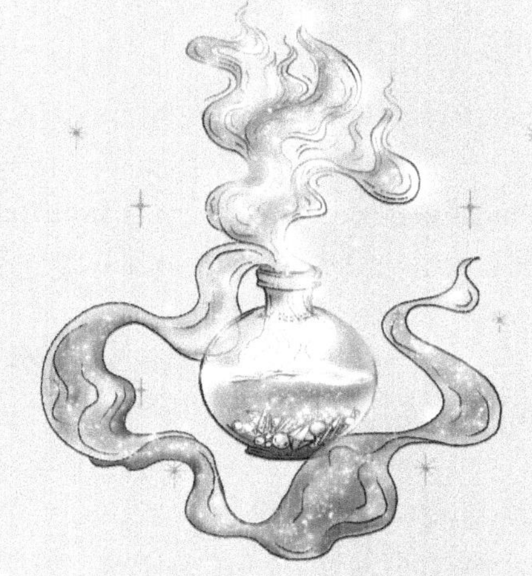

EPILOGUE 2

Linnea

"I MIGHT actually kill him," I said, rolling my eyes as Faiza let out a bark of laughter, shaking her head and making her turquoise waves fall over her shoulder.

"He's undeniably stubborn, but I think you're breaking him down." Her smile was brighter than the stars, and I prayed to Erodite that smile wouldn't dim because of her ridiculous father.

I'd been working on getting his agreement for her to marry Brokk for months, but even with the knowledge that she would be the Lady of Ruby Court, a significant step up in the hierarchy, he wasn't fully convinced. He claimed it was due to Ruby Court's reputation, but we'd made it very clear that this would be a new court, one with a completely fresh slate.

I was convinced that his hesitation was just because he didn't want his daughter to outrank him. *Ridiculous*, as I said.

We walked into the office I shared with Azurill, preparing to go over the contract again. The spacious room had a wall made entirely of windows that looked out onto the garden, and the city beyond, a constant reminder of all we were working for—*who* we were working for. We made several trips through the city every month, making sure we mingled with the common people. I never wanted to be the type of queen who sequestered herself away in her palace, ignoring those I was responsible for.

Our office always felt like such a warm space, with our opal-wood desks shimmering brilliantly under the many lanterns, and an abundance of flowers arranged throughout. Today, however, I was surprised to find the room already occupied. Azurill wasn't supposed to be done with training for another hour, but there he sat, and worryingly, he didn't even look up when we entered.

I shared a concerned look with Faiza, who dipped her head meaningfully before quietly exiting, leaving me to slowly approach my distracted husband.

"Azurill?" I asked, my brows furrowed as I took in his stiff posture. He was bent over a piece of parchment, his fingers holding tightly to the edges, but his eyes...

They were flashing silver.

"Nea," he whispered, looking up at me in surprise. "When did you get here?"

My brows flew upward. Azurill was one of the most attentive and observant people I knew, so the fact that he didn't even notice me was shocking.

"Never mind that." I waved my hand, brushing off his question. I was much more concerned about whatever was happening on that page to make him so tense. "What's going on?"

He sighed deeply, slouching back in his chair, something that I knew he rarely ever allowed himself. His father's lessons regarding a king's behavior had been deeply embedded.

"I received a letter from one of our allies. A friend of mine." He looked up at me apologetically, handing me the letter.

I took the letter from his outstretched fingers, watching carefully as he ran a nervous hand through his teal hair. I took a quick look at the signature on the bottom before reading. My head tilted to the side in contemplation. I'd had a lot of lessons on the political hierarchies of all the other continents, but admittedly, there had been a lot of names and places to remember that usually didn't affect my everyday life.

I looked up into the blue-green pools I loved to get lost in, finding a swirling mix of emotions awaiting me there. His concern clashed with his anticipation, completely torn on how he was feeling about whatever message was contained within. A quick skim of the contents itself left my breath catching in my throat.

This certainly changed things. I was suddenly very glad I'd been taking magic lessons, too. We were going to need a lot of potions for what was coming. I swallowed hard, trying again to remember who exactly this friend of his was.

"Who is King Calix?" I asked, biting my lip as I sank into Azurill's lap, his arms surrounding my waist automatically, while mine went over his shoulders. I contented myself with brushing my fingers through the soft hair at the nape of his neck, the familiar movement calming.

"He's the King of Night Kingdom, in Celesterra," he answered, watching for my reaction. His lips curled into a smirk when my eyes widened.

"We're going to Night Kingdom, then?" I double-checked, and my anxiety about the potential consequences of what the letter claimed was happening mixed with excitement at the idea of getting to visit a new continent.

"Yes, Mini-Dite, we are." He looked like he was trying to memorize my features, just in case, his throat bobbing on a hard swallow. "And you're going to need new armor immediately."

"To war we go then," I said, an ominous feeling rising within me. He nodded, cupping my cheek and running his thumb gently across my skin. He leaned in, placing the softest kiss on my lips, and I wanted nothing more than to chase him and demand more. But if what King Calix claimed was true, we didn't have time to delay.

"To war we go."

WANT MORE?

Get Exclusive Bonus Content!

Scan the QR code below to sign up for my newsletter and you'll receive a welcome email with a password granting you access to the exclusive bonus section on my website that contains some awesome content! You'll have access to NSFW art and bonus scenes!

You can also sign up via my website at

www.rachelfallonauthor.com!

GET CAUGHT UP ON THE SERIES NOW:

THE STAR QUEEN CHRONICLES

Book 1: *Of Darkness and Ruination*

Book 2: *Of Light and Freedom*

Book 3: Title to be Announced – Coming 2026

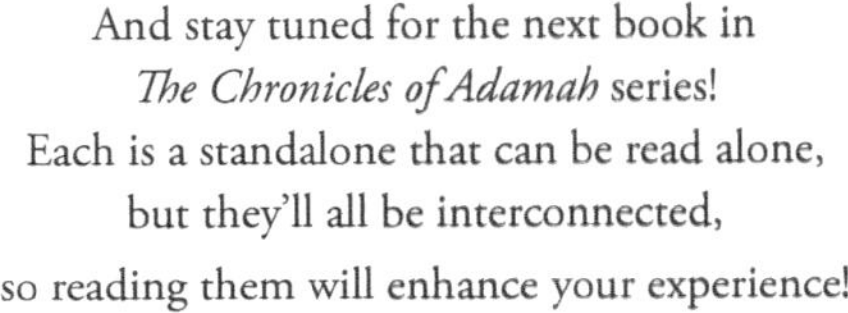

And stay tuned for the next book in
The Chronicles of Adamah series!
Each is a standalone that can be read alone,
but they'll all be interconnected,
so reading them will enhance your experience!

THE CHRONICLES OF ADAMAH

Book 1: *Of Diamonds and Vengeance*

Book 2: Title to be Announced – *Coming Soon!*

Book 3: Title to be Announced

Book 4: Title to be Announced

Book 5: Title to be Announced

Book 6: Title to be Announced

About the Author

Rachel Fallon is a writer and cat mom from Massachusetts who's been obsessed with making up stories all her life. Always one to day-dream, and with an incredibly active imagination, she's spent her life making up stories in her head and watching them play out like movies. She had always wanted to write a book, but after being left with brain damage from being in a coma, she was unable to write creatively for a decade. The ability switched off like a light.

As a huge lover of fantasy and romance, she's always read stories and watched movies and TV shows where the two are intertwined, even dating back to childhood. She craved the chance to tell her own story full of fantasy and romance, and the rise of romantasy opened the door to her dreams. Right after finding the genre, her brain damage finally healed, like a light being switched back on. The timing felt like fate, and she began writing stories online to flex the unused muscle, retraining it to write creatively once more.

The encouragement she received and requests from people to write her own book inspired her to actually give it a shot, despite still finding her footing. While working full time, she made room where she could to map out her world and start writing. She was surprised by how quickly the story began to come to her, with the expansive world of *The Star Queen Chronicles* begging to be told!

Acknowledgments

The hugest thank you to my mom, without whom none of this would be possible because I'd be totally lost. I can't even put into words what your support means to me, because it's broader than I think words exist for. For so much of my life, your own life was my idea of what success was. I looked to you in everything, even when I pretended I didn't. And when I realized my dreams were slightly different, the fact that you were there, supporting me still, meant everything to me. Though I never stopped looking to your example and finding myself lost for how to match it. I still strive for the kind of easy stability you seem to inhabit, even while throwing myself into an industry as uncertain as this one. You've been larger than life in a lot of ways to me, but equally as grounded, like the only port in the constant storm that is my general bipolar upheaval. I can't thank you enough for all of the support you give me, but I will keep trying to remind you with an excess of gifts that you insist I don't need to spend money on.

To my daddy, who shaped so much of who I am, including my filthy mouth and my obsessive love for fandoms. Who let me play with his sword collection even when the swords were bigger than I was. Who dragged me to every Renaissance fair in full costume. Who introduced me to Buffy the Vampire Slayer and The Lord of the Rings. You singlehandedly instilled within me this lifelong love of fantasy. If I had never found Buffy and fell in love with Spike, I wouldn't be writing Romantasy today. If you hadn't given me this obsession with swords, letting me watch with stars in my eyes as amazing women demolished the men around them with their sword-work, I wouldn't be writing badass females who can wield better than most men. If you hadn't made me dress up every year, I wouldn't throw myself into every ball I attend or every dress I describe in painstaking detail on page. I can never thank you enough for all of these facets of me that now directly inspire every book I write.

To my stepdad, Steve, who has been the most amazing and supportive person on the planet. Who helps without complaint, despite already giving me more support than I probably deserve. Who had already taken me in and made me family without blinking. Becoming my one-man shipping department and carrying so much of that load that constantly overwhelms me and leaves me manic and depressive in swings, not knowing how to handle it. Ensuring I can make it to all of my events, whether it's checking my car is good to go or dropping me off at the airport. Feeding me when I realize I haven't come up for air and eaten properly in days. Helping take care of my aging cat. The list is so long, but I notice and log every single thing, and try to find my own ways to pay that back where I can. Thank you so much for everything you do. I truly can never express how much I appreciate it, but I hope you never forget how much it means to me.

To my PA's, Sarah & Kristen, who have joined my team and taken over with the kind of force usually reserved for hurricanes. I was absolutely drowning under everything I needed to get done, and you guys came in and started turning everything around. You guys have been on board for every idea, listening to me talk through all of my anxieties and wild swings, cheering me on the entire time. I have no idea how I didn't completely fall apart before you guys came on, and I can only thank you a million times for becoming these load-bearing pillars in my life. You're incredible, and I love you both so much!

To all of my author friends, who help shape this amazing community online that lifts one another up and cheers everyone's successes. Who are there when bad days hit, and I spiral, needing a hand to lift myself out of the gloom. Who help me feel less alone in this very isolating career. Those who have been at events I've attended and made those experiences some of the best of my life. You guys all astound me with your incredible kindness and your insane talent, and I find myself feeling so privileged to have you in my life.